THE RED EFFECT

Harvey Black

ISBN-13: 978-1-9832-0214-8

About the Author

A qualified parachutist, Harvey Black served with British Army Intelligence for over ten years. His experience ranges from covert surveillance in Northern Ireland to operating in Communist East Berlin during the Cold War where he feared for his life after being dragged from his car by KGB soldiers. Since then, he has lived a more sedate life in the private sector as a director for an international company and now enjoys the pleasures of writing. Harvey is married with four children. For more from Harvey, visit his website at www.harveyblackauthor.org.

Also by Harvey Black:

Devils with Wings
Devils with Wings Book 1
Devils with Wings Silk Drop Book 2
Devils with Wings Frozen Sun Book 3

The Cold War
The Red Effect
The Black Effect
The Blue Effect

Force Majeure
Purgatory
Paralysis

Cold War Redux
Duplicity
Deception

Praise for Harvey Black - Amazon book reviews

"I loved it, I read this great book from cover to cover and whole-heartedly recommend this book. A great debut book, a talented author." – DG Torrens

"Harvey Black is on to a winner here. A well researched first book with a gradual build up of confidence in the prose which bodes well for the future." – Paul C

"The story is well paced and very well researched. The authors own military background comes though in his writing." – Nick Britten

"An excellent first book, full of historical facts and clearly written by someone who has a passion and deep knowledge for his subject. An author to watch out for in my opinion." – Melanie Tollis

"The amazing writing ability of Harvey would be missed, the atmosphere, the daring the drama, all are brought out on a tale well woven and well paced and so well written." – Parmenion Books

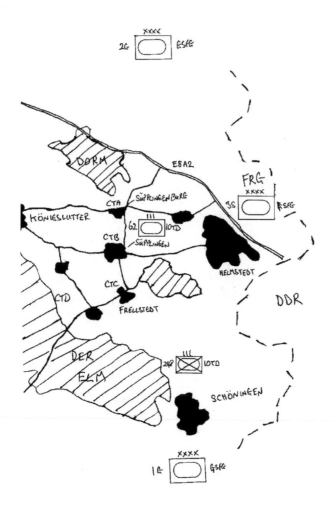

Helmstedt – the inner German border, 1984.

Introduction

'Today, West German imperialism is United States' chief ally in Europe in aggravating world tension. West Germany is increasingly becoming the seat of the war danger, where revenge-seeking passions are running high...The policy pursued by the Federal Republic of Germany is being increasingly determined by the same monopolies that brought Hitler to power.

'The Rhineland politicians fancy that, once they get the atomic bomb, frontier posts will topple, and they will be able to achieve their cherished desire of carving up the map of Europe again and taking revenge for defeat in the Second World War.

'One of the most ominous factors endangering peace is the bilateral military alliance that is taking shape between the ruling circles of the United States and the Federal Republic of Germany. This factor remains an objective of unflagging attention.'

Leonid Brezhnev
23rd Party Congress
March 1966

Chapter 1

'I repeat again and again: we do not seek military superiority. We have never intended and do not now intend to threaten any state, or group of states. Our strategic doctrine is a purely defensive one. Allegations that the Soviet Union is building up its military might on the European Continent on a scale not called for by its defence requirements have nothing to do with reality. This is a deliberate deception to the public at large.'

Leonid Baskov, October 1979

Baskov's Kremlin office. May 1981. The Red Effect – 38 Months

He sat behind his large, over two metres wide, heavy, leather-topped, teak desk leafing through some papers brought in by his secretary earlier that morning. Directly in front of him stood an extension to his desk, like a large 'T'; a meeting table of the same style extending away from him. Capable of accommodating up to sixteen visitors sat around it. On his desk, to the right, sat two telephones, a multi-compartmented container for pens and pencils, and, to his left, his elaborate intercom system: thirty buttons linking him to various offices and members of his Politburo within the Kremlin.

Immediately in front on his desk was his favoured, elegant, calf brown briefcase, its gold combination lock glinting. He shifted in his low-backed leather armchair, a bit like a captain's chair but without the swivel. As he leant back to read a memo, the contents of which made him smile, the chair creaked under his weight. He placed the memo back down on the desk and checked his metal bracelet wristwatch: five minutes until he was joined by his Head of KGB. He knew the man would arrive at exactly ten; he was always on time.

Born into a Russian working family, Baskov started his career as an engineer in the iron and steel industry before being conscripted into the army. During the Great Patriotic War, World War Two, he served with distinction, leaving as a major-general. He then soon played a key role in Russian politics, becoming a member of the Central Committee in 1952. By 1964, he had succeeded Nikita Khrushchev as first secretary, finally inheriting the mantle of General Secretary of the Communist Party of the Soviet Union. At seventy-four years old, he was the most powerful man in one of the most powerful countries in the world. There was a knock at the door and his secretary stepped through into the office.

"Comrade Aleksandrov is here, Comrade General Secretary. Shall I show him in?"

Baskov checked his watch and smiled. It was ten o'clock exactly. "Yes please, and some drinks."

"Right away, Comrade General Secretary."

The secretary left the room and was immediately replaced by the Chairman of the KGB, Yuri Aleksandrov, who strode across the room towards the desk where Baskov had risen from his seat and come round to greet his fellow Politburo comrade. They hugged, kissed cheeks and shook hands.

"Take a seat, Comrade Yuri."

The Head of the KGB, (the *Komitet Gosudarstvennoy Bezopasnosti)*, or the Committee for State Security, was probably the second most powerful man in the Soviet Union, controlling over twelve directorates. From the First Chief Directorate responsible for Foreign Operations (Espionage) to the Operations and Technology Directorate, the research laboratories, covering such items as recording and surveillance devices, and the fearsome Laboratory 12, dealing in poisons and drugs.

Aleksandrov pulled out a seat from the meeting table and sat down as Baskov went round the other side, picking up a model of an artillery piece as he did so. He sat opposite his Chief of the KGB.

Baskov inserted a shell into the gun and pulled the lanyard, but it didn't fire. "I must get some spares for this from the Egyptians," he said, looking up at Aleksandrov from beneath his bushy eyebrows. "Well, Comrade Yuri, you have some concerns about our American foes?"

The sixty-six-year-old politician, with his heart-shaped face and his heavily receding, steel-grey hair, looked back and nodded slowly. Aleksandrov was the son of a railway official Vladimir Aleksandrov, and his mother Lilya Brashmakov, the daughter of a wealthy Muscovite businessman. Initially educated at the Water Transport Technological College in Rybinsk, he too ended up being conscripted into the army. A Russian World War Two war hero, he took part in partisan guerrilla activities in Finland. After the war, he was elected as Second Secretary of the Central Committee of the Communist Party of the Karelo-Finnish SSR, Soviet Socialist Republic. He later held the position of Ambassador to Hungary during the Hungarian Revolution in 1956 where he played a key role in crushing the revolt by convincing Khrushchev to use military intervention. The Hungarian leaders were later arrested and executed. As Khrushchev's protégé, he quickly rose through the Communist Party ranks. After serving in the Communist Party of the Soviet Union Central Committee, he was appointed Head of the KGB in 1967. Six years later, he became a full member of the Politburo.

Yuri and Leonid looked at each other across the table. Both dressed in plain suits. Aleksandrov's was grey with a metal pin in the shape of a Soviet flag in his left lapel, whereas his leader wore a black flannel suit with a white shirt and polka-dot tie, and a display of medals pinned across his broad chest.

"Yes, Comrade General Secretary. I recommend that we increase our intelligence efforts if we are to establish any contingency plans President McKinley's Administration may have to launch a nuclear strike against our motherland."

Baskov continued to pull at the lanyard, but the artillery piece still wouldn't fire. "You are suspicious of everyone, Yuri." The squarish, jowly face continued to smile as he persisted with tugging in frustration at the lanyard. Before Aleksandrov could answer, Baskov held his hand up as his secretary knocked on the door and proceeded to bring in a tray with china cups and saucers, a decorated, slender coffee pot and a small plate of biscuits. They sat silently as she poured their drinks, adding milk and sugar in the quantities she knew they liked, and placed the cups and saucers in front of them. Baskov thanked her as she left the room, and he indicated that Aleksandrov should help himself to the biscuits.

"Is there something particular that has you so concerned, Yuri?"

"There are a few things, Comrade Secretary. We know they are sneaking around the Greenland-Iceland-United-Kingdom-Gap. We are also aware of their incessant clandestine activity around the Norwegian, Black, Barents and Baltic Seas."

Baskov crunched on a biscuit and took a sip from his cup, pulling at the lanyard yet again. This time it went off with a loud bang, making them both jump. Baskov laughed. "It was originally designed to fire paper caps, like you find in children's toy guns. But they wouldn't work, so they developed these blank shells for me. Anything else?"

"They're getting too close to some of our key military bases. Their forces are obviously testing our detection systems and seeing how quickly we react, and, more importantly, if we react."

"Do we respond well?"

There was a pause before Aleksandrov replied. "They respond as best they are able, Comrade General Secretary."

"Is there more?" Baskov got up and grabbed some more shells from his desk then returned to his seat.

"They have started to fly squadrons of bomber aircraft directly towards our airspace, peeling off at the last minute. It's a very provocative act, Comrade Secretary."

"Ah, I see how this works now. You have to pull this lever."

Aleksandrov smiled. "It won't help us stop a US nuclear strike, Comrade Secretary."

"Very true, Yuri, very true." Baskov pushed the artillery piece aside and started to fiddle with his signet ring. He pointed to it. "It says on the inside 'To Leonid Baskov from Novorissisk'. It is a memento of a full year spent there: three hundred days of battle with no retreat. We were allies with the West then. It does sound ominous, Yuri, but surely they are just testing our systems and reactions yet again?"

Aleksandrov put his coffee cup down and leant forward. "But are they covering for something else, Comrade General Secretary?"

"What are you proposing?"

"Operation RYAN." RYAN, or RYan, was an acronym for Raketno-Yadernoe Napadenie, or Nuclear-Missile Attack.

"What will this involve, my old friend?"

"The First Directorate will take control. Every one of our agents, our residents abroad, will be tasked with monitoring all American personnel who are associated with the launch of a nuclear weapon, and any facility that is associated with nuclear launch sites."

Baskov frowned for the first time. "That will require a huge number of resources."

"If they are preparing for a nuclear war, Comrade General Secretary, we must know when they plan to launch. RYAN will be the most comprehensive intelligence-gathering operation in our history."

"Go on."

"If we can establish when they plan to launch, we can initiate a pre-emptive strike of our own."

"I agree with you, Yuri. The McKinley puppet would like nothing better than to push the nuclear button and obliterate our motherland. You must initiate your plans immediately. Don't forget to use the army's GRU assets."

"I will, Comrade General Secretary. I won't rest until I know what they're up to."

"Now to other matters, Yuri. I want to talk to you about Poland."

Chapter 2

Checkpoint Charlie, American Sector, West Berlin. June 1983. The Red Effect −13 Months

The black Range Rover came to a halt on the eastern side of the barrier, which quickly lowered behind them. The barrier had the new vertical struts intermittently spaced along its length, which had been introduced after an escapee had accelerated their car, a low, open-top sports car, beneath it, escaping from the German Democratic Republic to the American Sector of Berlin in the Federal Republic of Germany.

A *Grenztruppen* officer, as usual, stood opposite the passenger door and looked at the two occupants inside. After waiting a few moments, he did a circuit of the vehicle, going through the pretence that he could make the decision to prevent the representatives of the British Government from passing into East Berlin. He came back to the passenger's side window and looked in again. He stood proud in his grey uniform, green piping on his jacket and cap, along with a band around his lower left sleeve declaring him to be *Grenztruppen der DDR*.

"He's new, Jacko," the mission commander said to his driver, a member of the Royal Corps of Transport. He was an experienced driver who knew how to handle the 2,000-kilogram heavyweight vehicle at speed, particularly when the Soviet or East German Army attempted to prevent them carrying out their tasks by ramming them or attempting to block them in with various vehicles.

"His uniform looks pretty new," responded the driver. "Straight out of officer training school, I reckon."

"He's certainly making a meal of it," chided Bradley who was in command of the operation they were going to conduct today. He too was badged as Royal Corps of Transport, RCT, but was in fact from the 'Section', the specialist unit tasked with intelligence gathering and acquisition in the Eastern Sector of Berlin.

"Here we go," informed Jacko. He put the vehicle into gear, as the border guard raised the barrier and indicated with a flick of his wrist that they were free to pass through.

Jacko manoeuvred the black, four-wheel drive Range Rover around the chicane of concrete blocks, wire fencing and barbed wire. Once free, he went through the gears as they increased speed leaving Checkpoint Charlie, situated on the junction of Friedrich Strasse, Zimmer Strasse and Mauer Strasse, behind them. "Where are we going?"

"Karlshorst."

"Sneak around their railway sidings, eh?" Jacko changed down and swung right onto Leipziger Strasse, slotting in with the small blue and white Trabants and the occasional Skoda or Moskovich car that were going about their day-to-day business. The occasional Trabant rattled past, its 500cc, air-cooled, two-stroke engine sounding like a demented sewing machine, their occupants peering up at the black vehicle that towered above them; some putting a hand up in a desecrete wave.

"Let's hope the bloody dogs aren't out today," responded Bradley.

"I think even the transport police are afraid of them. Just a poke around?"

"Yeah, we've not been for a couple of weeks. Just a quick in and out visit; then I want to try Pankow sidings."

Jacko pulled out and overtook a few cars before slotting back in again, heading east along Spittlemarkt, Gertrauden Strasse, crossing the River Spree, a long barge passing beneath them.

"I'm just going to check in. *Phoo, phoo.*" Bradley blew into the black handset, initiating a signal. "Hello, Three-Zero-Alpha, this is Three-Zero-Bravo, over. Hello, Three-Zero-Alpha, this is Three-Zero-Bravo, over."

"Three-Zero-Bravo, this is Three-Zero-Alpha. Go ahead, over."

"En route. Delta, Hotel, Zulu, Echo; then Papa, Yankee, Kilo, Lima. Roger that, over?"

"Roger that. Go easy. Three-Zero-Alpha, out."

Bradley placed the handset back in its cradle.

"The big cheese, eh?" Asked Jacko.

"Yes. He thinks there's something up."

"He's always had a good nose for the Russkies' tricks. We've got company."

"Where, Jacko?"

"About four cars back. One's a black Skoda and the other a cream Lada. Two-up in each."

Bradley peered in the additional mirror he had fixed by the side of his sun visor, giving him a better view of what was behind them. "Got them. They wouldn't happen to be wearing black leather jackets, would they?" He laughed.

"How did you guess?" Jacko grinned. "What do you want to do?"

"Leave them for a while. Let them get a bit slack then we'll make our move."

"Karl Marx?"

"Yes."

Bradley didn't need to look at the map. He had been operating in East Berlin for over a year now. However, he could always find their position on the map, just in case they had problems and needed assistance from the West. Jacko changed down, passing the 'House of Teachers', or the 'Congress Hall', on their right, the aluminium-coloured dome distinctive, and shortly after turning right into Karl-Marx-Allee. The dual carriageway was a little busier; East Berlin was starting to wake up.

"Still with us?"

"Yep, still two cars, but they've swapped the cream Lada for a white one."

"Looks like they may have a full team on us today then."

They shot round a roundabout and past the fountain in Strausberger Platz.

"Keep your speed steady, Jacko."

Jacko looked to his right with a grin. "Are we taking them up the slope then?"

Bradley returned the smile. "Why not? It's about time we introduced them to this one. They never learn."

They continued east, passing ugly, grey concrete blocks of flats. The Section referred to them as Lego. The components for the blocks were brought into the city by train, on flatcars. The prefabricated sections appeared to be of three types: one blank, one with a window, and one with a doorway. They were then assembled into ugly concrete towers where eventually some fortunate East German would make one of the flats their home.

Karl-Marx turned into Frankfurter Allee as they drove past the Frankfurter Tor. They crossed the bridge taking them over the S-Bahn railway line that ran north-east to south-west beneath them. They would normally have turned right down Am Tierpark to get to Karlshorst, but they needed to shake off their tail first.

So, Jacko turned left into Rhin Strasse, passed the Friedrichsfelde-Ost S-Bahn station, right onto Allee der Kosmonauts, through two long S-bends, forking right down a narrow, hard-packed, dusty road, Elisabeth Strasse, until they came out opposite the Kienberg. The pine mountain, as it was known locally, was in the district of Marzahn-Hellersdorf. Families often went there at weekends or during the school holidays. It was a mere sixty metres high, but it would serve their purpose.

"See them?"

"Just make them out through the dust." Jacko laughed.

The Range Rover ground to a halt as Jacko expertly applied the dif-lock, locking the front and rear drive shafts together, which would give them better grip for what they were about to do. Foot on the accelerator, the four-litre V8 engine growled and pulled the vehicle forwards, rapidly gaining speed. They crossed the dirt road in front of them, headed straight through the treeline ahead and proceeded to climb at a forty-degree angle up the side of the hill. The jacked-up

7

suspension bounced the cab violently, but gave them better clearance, Jacko gripping the steering wheel tightly for fear of losing control of his charge. The armoured plate beneath, fixed to the underside of the vehicle, ground against the earth and rocks as they passed over them, but it protected the vulnerable chassis from any impact.

"Whose...bloody idea...was...this?"

"If I remember...rightly, Jacko...i...t...was yours."

Jacko maintained a steady speed, instinct wanting him to slow down, but his training kicking in, and the momentum upwards was maintained. *Crunch*. Both hit their heads on the roof as the Range Rover hit a rut and faltered, but the powerful engine pulled it forward again.

"Shit."

"Geronimo," yelled Jacko, enjoying every minute of it.

Bradley clutched the grab handle above him as they weaved around one of the pine trees, crossing tracks that helter-skeltered down from the top. They reached the summit but didn't hesitate as they sped across the crown then careered down the other side. Their bodies shook and their teeth rattled as the vehicle, almost out of control, ran and occasionally surfed down the side of the hill, branches from the trees whipping the sides of the car making both men inside flinch.

Once at the bottom, they clawed their way to a metalled road. The dif-lock was disengaged, and, within minutes, they were heading towards their original target.

"That's sorted the buggers." Jacko laughed as he weaved in and out of the traffic.

"Well done, mate." Bradley joined in the laughter. "But I wish I hadn't had such a big breakfast."

They drove through various residential areas, Jacko weaving in and out of traffic, turning down different roads, completing circuits, constantly checking in his rear-view mirror to confirm they had truly lost their tail.

Bradley looked over his shoulder and scanned the cars behind them. "All clear by the looks of it, Jacko."

"For now, at least." Jacko heaved a sigh of relief.

They drove past more of the concrete tower blocks that were trying to pass themselves off as flats, and, after about fifteen minutes, found themselves on Langer Weg. Now they were amongst row upon row of garden plots and summer houses, some simple one-room structures, others grander with maybe two or three rooms: places where families could escape the hustle and bustle of the city at the weekend, or those retired staying there for a proportion of the summer months.

They were close now, and Jacko slowed down as he turned right onto Balzer Weg, a partially metalled road, but he was glad they were in a four-wheel drive vehicle all the same. It was still quite early so the road and surrounding area were relatively quiet.

"Take the next left, Jacko."

"Roger." He turned the wheel and the vehicle leant over slightly as he turned into Bahn Weg, the area quite leafy, most of the plants and trees in full bloom. So, the homes were partly hidden but, more importantly, the two operators were partly hidden from the occupants. They were now travelling south, running parallel with a railway line on their left that ran from north to south. Their target a spur on the far side where the local Russian tank battalion loaded or unloaded their tanks and other equipment if they were going on exercise somewhere outside of the city, or on returning from an exercise.

"Here will do." Bradley pointed to a gap in the copse that ran alongside hiding the railway line from view, except for the occasional glimpse of the upper embankment. He wound down his passenger window so that he could listen and smell the air as well as look.

Jacko steered off the hard-packed road, and the vehicle disappeared in amongst the trees. The Range Rover snaked through the undergrowth, the occasional low branch of a conifer screeching along the bodywork as they edged closer and closer to the railway line.

"That's my paintwork buggered," exclaimed Jacko, proud of the condition he kept his vehicle in.

"Stop moaning. You've had worse," responded Bradley, tapping the dashboard. "This'll do."

"Engine on or off?"

"Turn it round so we can make a quick exit; then off."

Jacko manoeuvred the four-wheel drive until they were facing the way they had entered the copse while Bradley pulled the kit he would need from his bag. He grabbed a pair of binoculars, a pocket tape recorder, Nikon camera and handheld radio, a Teleport 9. Jacko switched the engine off and ensured his driver's door was locked.

"I'll do a radio check as soon as I'm out."

"OK."

Bradley eased the passenger door open and slung the binos and camera over his shoulder, put the recorder in his parka pocket, and eased the door shut with a click. Jacko leant over and closed the window, locking the door after him. Bradley moved away from the vehicle and spoke into his handset in a hushed voice.

"Juliet, Bravo, radio check, over."

"*Bravo, Juliet, five and five, over.*"

"Roger, out."

His driver had informed him that the signal was strong and the clarity perfect. He shivered. Although June, the morning was quite fresh and he was glad of his Bundeswehr, green German Army parka.

Bradley stopped and listened. He could hear a rhythmic clang of metal against metal coming from the direction of the railway line. He knew it was a good sign. He gave the thumbs up, the excited response from Jacko indicating he knew his tour commander had heard something, which could only mean they might get a meaty target today. It also told him to be on his guard as the Soviets would be more alert than usual.

Bradley moved west, making his way through the trees in a half crouch, instinctively keeping his profile as low as possible. He arrived at the edge of the copse, the trees giving way to the railway embankment, some twenty-five metres away, that sloped down towards him. He looked left and right; all was clear, and he jogged over to the embankment scrambling up its shallow sides until he could peer over the top. In front of him were two parallel rail lines and, down in the dip on the other side of the embankment, a thin line of trees. Slowly, he moved across the tracks until he was able to see more and more, conscious that he was also becoming more and more exposed himself the closer he got to the other side. He crouched down, pulled his binos off his shoulder and scanned the area through the trees. Apart from some of the larger trees filling the lens of his binos, he was finally rewarded with a view through the gaps that brought a smile to his face. Tanks!

He quickly ran across the lines, shuffled down the slope on the other side and made his way to the treeline that was only a few paces away. Creeping through the pines, no more than a couple of trees deep, he soon reached the edge on the far side, finding a good-sized trunk to hide behind, next to a small mound covered with a sprinkling of grass and scrub. It was enough to conceal him, he thought.

He leant against the tree. In front of him was a line of heavy-duty flatcars, some with T-64 tanks still onboard. There were other tanks on the ramp, and a few lined up on the track ready to leave the sidings and head for the barracks, less than a quarter of a mile away. The hammering he had heard earlier was the Soviet tank crew releasing the chains so they could offload their main battle tanks.

Bradley grabbed the radio from his pocket. "Juliet, Bravo. Over."

In a matter of seconds, his radio crackled in response. He turned the volume down although he was sure he couldn't be heard.

"*Juliet.*"

"Jackpot, I'll be ten, over."

"*Roger, but signal three, three. Out.*"

The radio went back in Bradley's pocket. The embankment and large amount of metal in the area, from the railway lines, was clearly affecting the signal. There was no need for a long conversation. Jacko was an experienced operator and knew the score. Bradley trusted him. In fact, his life often depended on Jacko's skills and experience. It was only four weeks ago when they had come across a Soviet exercise, and the Soviet soldiers had swarmed around them like flies. They had raced through the wood close by, Jacko's arms a blur as he kept the Range Rover under control, the back wheels sliding in the mud, missing trees by mere millimetres. They had shot out of the wood, climbing up a verge onto a main road where a three-axle Zil 131, a Russian heavy goods vehicle weighing some six and a half tons, accelerated as the military driver caught sight of them. Jacko had pressed his foot to the metal. Sprays of earth and mud splattered the trees behind them as the Rover finally got a grip and careered onto the road, the Zil clipping the rear wing spinning them around, Jacko's arms twisting left and right as he fought to get control. He finally managed to straighten up and headed back into the woods they had just left. It was imperative they escaped as they knew the Soviets would be closing in.

They had finally managed to break out of the area and hide up to lick their wounds. Punctures in two tyres, the back end dented, but they had got away and then burst into nervous laughter. Ever since that day, when Jacko had earned his tour wings, Bradley had felt more confident when they were on operations. He too had been in a similar situation, driving the Range Rover when being chased, once with three flat tyres. It was a hair-raising experience.

Bradley moved around the trunk and crouched down behind the earthen mound. He pulled himself forward on his elbows and, once comfortable, scanned the area with his binos again. He could now see the spur line, the sidings the Soviets used to load and unload their tanks for shipping out of the city. The tanks were no more than a hundred metres away. He pulled out his pocket recorder, checked there was a fresh tape, and it was rewound to the start and switched it on, recording what he could see.

"Kilo Sierra, 0725. Ten T-64As unloading. New to the unit. One sentry, AK74, bayonet fixed, mag on. Patrolling the east side, looking pretty pissed off."

He zoomed in on the tanks and continued his commentary, his voice sounding more and more excited at having discovered new tanks for this unit.

"Turret numbers: 607, 608, 603, 602, shit!"

He dropped the recorder and clutched his binos with both hands, zooming in on one of the tanks furthest away. He picked up the recorder again.

"Mars-Bars. Three T-64s have Mars-Bars. 613, 615 and 616."

Binos went down as did the recorder and he pulled the camera off his shoulder. Zooming in with the 300mm lens, he clicked away at the tanks and their turret numbers, partly as a supplementary record but also as part of the intelligence build-up on the Soviet units in East Berlin. He snapped away, two or three shots of each tank, some close-ups of key parts of the main battle tanks, their optics, tracks, main gun and, of course, the Mars-Bars. Further analysis would be done when back at the operations room, and the boffins back at MOD, the Ministry of Defence, would also get copies to pore over. Satisfied he had taken enough pictures for now, at this range anyway, he replaced the lens cap and slung the Nikon back over his shoulder and grabbed the portable radio from his pocket.

"Juliet, Bravo, over."

The call signs for members of the section were the phonetic first letter of their respective first name.

"*Go ahead, over.*" Jacko's voice crackled in reply.

"We need to get closer, Jacko. Over."

"*North or south? Over.*"

"North, so find us a route. See you in ten, out."

Bradley secured the radio and picked up his pocket tape recorder again and started to recite. "Tanks being unloaded so probably bound for the local unit. Speed they're working at should take them a couple of hours. This is a new tank type for the unit, so they are probably unsure of them. Maybe more trains arriving, unless this is just a batch for them to train on. Need to keep a close watch to confirm if any T-54/55s or T-62s are sent out at a later date. Moving to get a closer look."

He placed the recorder back in his pocket and got back up to a crouching position and made his way into the trees again. The clang of hammers being used by the tank crew to strike the chains and release the tanks continued. He reached the edge of the embankment, checked his surroundings; then, at a running crouch, went up the side and over the top, stepping gingerly over the two sets of railway lines and down the other side. He made his way back to the Range Rover, the steady stream of gases coming from the exhaust indicating that Jacko was ready to move out. Opening the door, Bradley slotted into his seat, peeling the camera and binos off his shoulder and placing them back in the bag by his feet.

"T-64s, Jacko."

"T-64s?"

"Yes."

"That's a new bit of kit for this unit then, isn't it?"

"Yes, and with Mars-Bars," Bradley responded excitedly.

"What are those things again?" Jacko asked, remembering being briefed about them some time ago.

"I'll tell you on the way. We need to move."

"So, we're going north to get a closer look, yes?"

"The best place."

"I'll take us onto Zweiessler Strasse. Remember it?"

"Sure."

Chapter 3

East of the 'Ramp', Karlshorst, East Berlin. June 1983. The Red Effect –13 Months

Jacko shifted the vehicle into gear and slowly manoeuvred it through the trees until they were back on Bahn Weg, where he turned left, Bradley constantly checking, making a three-hundred-and-sixty-degree sweep ensuring they weren't being observed or followed. The engine growled as the Range Rover picked up speed, and Bradley, satisfied they were not being followed, pulled his kitbag up onto his knee. He pulled out the camera again and unlocked the large grey 300mm lens. It was the better lens to use in poor light, so he could keep the camera speed high, but it was bulky and awkward to use when trying to remain concealed. It was at least a foot long, shaped like a cone, the tip of the lens the size of a double fist.

He clipped on another lens, a 400mm one this time. This one was more compact, a mirror lens, black and tubular in shape. Its downside was it needed more light, so would have a negative impact on film speed. The light was getting better, so he would chance it.

"Well? Mars-Bars?" Jacko reminded him.

Bradley put the bag down into the footwell of the vehicle, close at hand and ready should he need it quickly. Checked the map and scanned the area yet again. They were now on Arnsberger Strasse, still amongst the holiday homes of the wealthier East Berliners. Probably party officials, surmised Bradley, or their families, or others connected to the Communist organisation that now ran the GDR. The select few.

"They were designed to defeat our HESH rounds."

"High Explosive Squash Head, right?"

"You do listen then." Bradley grinned.

"I live for your every word."

"Bollocks. Well, HESH rounds are thin metal shells filled with plastic explosive and have a delayed action fuse. The explosive is squashed against the side of the tank with the force of the strike and spreads out to form a disc."

"Like a small pizza?"

"Yes, Jacko, if you like." *Bloody truckies*, he mumbled jokingly. "Milliseconds later, this is detonated, and the shock wave is transmitted through the wall of the armour and, once it meets the crew compartment, the inner wall fragments at high speed, basically causing a mess inside."

"Now I know why I joined the RCT and not the Tank Corps."

"Me and you both. Well, these Mars-Bars are designed to defeat HESH rounds. They're made up of two steel plates," he held one flat hand above the other, "with a layer of explosives in between them, designed to explode when struck, preventing the explosive 'pat' from forming."

"What about Sabot rounds?"

"Not sure, but I think they reduce their effectiveness as well. Taking Dohlengrund?" Bradley asked, running his finger along his map.

"Yes, next left."

They turned left into Dohlengrund, very much back amongst the East Berlin version of suburbia. The Range Rover shot past Walslebener Platz on the left and a long right-hand bend took them into Beruner Strasse where they swung a left down Shackelster Strasse coming to a T-junction at the end. They found themselves up against a double railway line that ran north to south across the front of their vehicle, the one Bradley had walked across earlier. The embankment was well grassed but, apart from the odd tree, was fairly clear.

Jacko spun the steering wheel hard right and they turned down a hard-packed road, the railway line now on their left. He knew exactly where he was going. Fifty metres and they reached what they were looking for: a sharp bend taking them to an underpass that would get them to the other side of the railway line above them.

Jacko drove carefully through the tunnel, the square concrete walls barely two or three metres apart, his eyes flitting left and right, from wing mirror to wing mirror. Bradley also helped looking through his open passenger window, informing Jacko if he was getting too close. Jacko came to a halt, just before the black nose of the bonnet extended beyond the tunnel. He had deliberately stopped with the driver door as close up against the left wall as he possibly could, enabling Bradley to squeeze through his door and slip out.

Bradley squeezed between the wall and the vehicle. The underpass was damp with condensation and the walls cool to the touch. He made his way out into the open. Once out, his eyes expertly searched the area, stopping his scan at key points looking for tell-tale movement amongst the undergrowth and trees, his peripheral vision also sensitive to any sudden movement. He listened and could hear the roar of a tank; another was being moved off its rail transport and onto the sidings ready to be driven to the barracks of the local tank battalion, its likely final destination. He waited a few more moments, sniffing the air, smelling the diesel fumes, looking for signs of sentries, police, in particular the transport police and their dogs. He feared the dogs more than anything. They were vicious and he had witnessed that even the handlers were wary of them. He thought of the Mojos who guarded the British ammunition and nuclear weapons dumps back in Germany. The dogs were allowed to run loose in the compound during the night, and the next day the guards would go in with padded suits to retrieve them. The dogs were baited during the day. God help any Soviet spy who thought he would take a quick reconnaissance of those places. Bradley suspected the East German guard dogs were as equally aggressive.

To his immediate right, not much more than ten metres from where he stood, was a second double railway line, this one running east to west, in a dip that ran beneath the one they had just driven under. Ahead of him, some twenty metres, the track continued through a second tunnel under another railway line running across front of him, almost parallel with the one behind him. This was the one he was interested in: the spur line where they brought tanks and other equipment when going on or returning from an exercise; or, as now, bringing in new equipment for the first time. Looking left, he gazed over the undulating ground, scattered with trees and scrub, trapped between the two converging lines. Bradley and Jacko were hidden from the prying eyes of the tank crews, and anyone else for that matter.

But they wouldn't be taking the tunnel to get to the other side of the spur; they would be too exposed. He looked back at the patiently waiting Jacko and signalled the all-clear. Jacko had no issues with the wait; he knew the consequence of rushing ops like these.

Bradley waved Jacko forward and headed left, starting to walk south towards the Ramp and the sound of the tanks some one hundred and fifty metres away. Edging over to the right, he winced as he heard the growl of the Rover engine as Jacko pulled forward out of the tunnel and followed the tour commander's trail. The growl turned into a steady rumble as the black four-by-four crept after Bradley. Both were nervous. They were in enemy territory, hostile territory; the tank crew would be very protective of their charges. On paper, they were allies; in reality, they were bitter enemies. The basic Soviet soldier, particularly the newest recruits, would know very little about the terms of the joint occupation of Berlin.

Bradley continued to move forward, edging right, getting closer and closer to the spur line itself, knowing that up ahead the scattering of trees disappeared altogether on this side of the line and that they would then be completely exposed. His hand went up in the air and Jacko stopped moving forward, the sound of the engine gently ticking over along with the occasional clang from up ahead the only sounds. He moved towards the spur line and found the spot he was looking for. Here, the line split into two after this point: one continuing south to rejoin the main line, the one nearest them branching off and ending up at the Ramp where the tanks they were interested in were being unloaded.

16

Bradley peered back through the trees where Jacko was watching out for his signal, and he beckoned him forward. The engine growled and the Rover crawled towards the spur, the cab rocking as Jacko negotiated the rough ground. Bradley walked up onto the slightly raised embankment, checking left and right as he did so. The nearest flatcar was about a hundred metres away, and he couldn't see any activity at this end, so he continued over to the other side. Jacko followed in the vehicle, the chassis and body jolting violently as he surmounted the two sets of railway lines. Both were relieved once the vehicle was across the other side. Jacko steered the vehicle into the copse and turned left.

Bradley moved back to the tour car and looked through the open passenger door window. "Turn her around, Jacko. You'll have to reverse deeper into the copse from here."

"What's our exfil?"

"Back the way we came in. If that's blocked, then we'll go west. If it's really bad, then we'll just go across country until we can find a clear road."

Jacko laughed. "OK."

Bradley knew why he laughed. The last time they had gone across country at speed, they were chased by a BMP, an MICV (Mechanised Infantry Combat Vehicle). Thirteen tons of armour coming at you at a speed of thirty miles an hour had a huge impact on your bowels. It was definitely a tanner-a-bob, tanner-a-bob. They got away, but how the Range Rover, or its occupants for that matter, survived the battering they would never know.

"Zweiessler Strasse would be good though," responded Bradley, sharing in Jacko's humour.

"Let's get it done then."

Jacko turned the vehicle around and, with one arm across the back of the passenger seat, one hand on the steering wheel, he followed Bradley as he guided the reversing vehicle through the trees. Bradley guided him around any deep potholes that would not only jar the vehicle but could require additional power to get out, the noise potentially exposing their presence. Now they were in the middle of not a dense copse but with enough trees scattered about to give them some cover, maybe four or five hundred metres square.

Bradley held his hand up and drew the edge of his palm across his throat. Jacko brought the vehicle to a halt and switched off the engine. Bradley returned to the vehicle. Both men remained quiet, listening. Nothing; just the hammering up ahead.

"I'll do a quick recce first Jacko, then come back."

"Radio?"

17

"No. If I come running, you'll see me soon enough and I probably won't have chance to radio a warning. So, keep focused, mate. We're in the middle of a hornet's nest here."

"What do you need?"

"I'll take the camera with me now, but I'll need the monkey wrench when I return."

Jacko reached across the seat and pulled the camera out of Bradley's bag down in the footwell the passenger seat and handed it to him. It was a Nikon F3. Bradley checked the lens and film. He probably had at least fifty frames, more than enough left. Normally he would replace it with a full seventy-two, just in case, but he didn't want to hang around the area for too long. The drive motor was attached so there was no need to wind it forward manually after every shot.

"I'll be about ten minutes."

"Watch yourself out there."

He made his way south through the trees, feeling alone and isolated within seconds of being away from the Range Rover. After about fifty metres, he turned east, closing in on the spur line. The hammering continued in the distance to his right, and now he could hear the occasional shout in Russian from the tank crew beavering away at their tasks. He made his way towards the edge of the copse, the railway line suddenly appearing in front of him, no more than four strides away. Beyond it, a further three or four metres, the spur line. He was opposite the tail end of the line of flatcars and, on top of the last one, two T64s, one of them a T64BV1K, a command variant, and, more importantly, it was adorned with *kontakte* armour: ERA (Explosive Reactive Armour) bricks.

He knelt down, the excitement welling up inside, and looked along the length of the train. The next flatcar had two more tanks on it, as did the third. The fourth had only one on board; its companion had been driven onto the ramp. The remaining flatcars were empty, the tanks lined up ready to be driven to the barracks. It was now quiet. It looked as if the soldiers were taking a break.

Bradley scanned for sentries. None could be seen. He edged forward slightly. The tank crews seemed to be congregated around the single structure that constituted the Ramp's only building. On sneaking around there one dark night, searching for anything that had been dropped or left that may be of intelligence interest, Bradley had come across a senior sergeant educating one of the new recruits in another aspect of his training. The sergeant's trousers were bunched around his ankles, the recruit bent over a rickety table, with the sweaty NCO thrusting behind him. They were as startled to see Bradley as Bradley was to come across them.

Bradley pulled his camera off his shoulder, checked the settings, adjusted the 'f' stop until he was happy with the speed, and focused in on the tank closest to him, no more than ten metres away. He clicked away, constantly stopping to check he didn't have company, taking thirty to forty shots in total, covering the full tank then zooming in on specific aspects of interest. Once satisfied, he replaced the lens cap and made his way back to the Range Rover and Jacko. Time for the real work to begin.

"Everything still OK?" enquired Jacko.

"Yes, they're taking some sort of a break."

"You going for it then?"

"You bet. Pass me the monkey-wrench."

"I couldn't find it."

"It's in the black tool wrap in the back. I hid it so the bloody REME couldn't pinch it."

Leaving Bradley to pack the camera away safely, Jacko left the vehicle, checking the area about him as he did so. It had become second nature, and it was surprising how the slightest movement was picked up, often subconsciously. He went to the back of the vehicle and looked about him again. *You can get bloody paranoid doing this job*, he thought. Lifting up the rear window, he reached into the small compartment they used to keep stuff out of sight and pulled out the black tool wrap. He opened it up and took out the monkey wrench, an adjustable spanner, rewound the wrap and replaced it. Shutting the rear window quietly, he returned to his driver's position.

"Here you go."

"Thanks."

Bradley left the vehicle, handed Jacko the spanner before he shrugged off his parka and leaned in and threw it onto the back seat.

"Dressed for speed, eh?"

"Too bloody right. It's warming up now anyway." The stocky, five foot eleven, mousey-haired operator grinned back at Jacko. "Here we go again, eh, mate?"

Jacko, six foot one, but spindly and with a narrow face and dark hair, returned the smile. The adrenalin was pumping through both of them. Jacko knew what his commander was going to do. Equally, he knew the consequences if it didn't go to plan. It wouldn't be the first time they had been rumbled. They took some serious risks at times in order to gather important Intelligence. He handed Bradley the spanner again and wished him luck. Bradley eased the door shut with a satisfying click and Jacko gave him the thumbs up.

Chapter 4

West of the 'Ramp', Karlshorst, East Berlin. June 1983. The Red Effect – 13 Months

Bradley moved past the rear of the vehicle and stealthily made his way back through the trees. With his green barrack trousers, (they weren't allowed to wear combats as it might be interpreted as aggressive by their Russian allies,) and his light brown No 2 shirt beneath his woolly, green, army jumper, he blended into the background fairly well. He reached the edge of the copse again, where he was earlier, opposite the tail end flatcar. He again searched the area for any signs of a sentry, or indeed any of the crew.

The quiet was suddenly shattered by the roar of a UAZ 469, a small Soviet utility Jeep as it sped past on the other side of the tank-mounted flatcars, heading for the Ramp, leaving a trail of dust in its wake. The light breeze wafted exhaust fumes over to Bradley's position. It was now or never, he thought as he loped across the feeder line, a gap of four metres; then he was at the spur line and the last of the flatcars. He was panting as he ran up against the edge of the tank tracks that slightly overhung the platform, more from a sudden increase in his pulse rate than a lack of fitness. He was at the furthest corner. He made sure the spanner was secure and heaved himself up onto the left-hand edge of the wooden platform where he found himself up against the back of the T-64 command tank. The tank was facing left to right, in a position where it would be able to drive along the flatcars to then come off onto the Ramp. In front of it: another tank, facing the same way.

He decided to get to the other side where he would be less exposed to the tank crews further up the line. He shuffled along the end of the flatcar, gripping the back of the tank for extra support and lurched along, constantly checking about him for any indication of discovery. He clocked the characteristic exhaust vents at the rear for the 6TDF engine, capable of producing over one thousand-brake horsepower, and the ten-metre telescoping antenna lying along the top of the turret. When extended, it would provide a signal for the R-130 radio inside. He eased his way past the pair of supports for the optional fuel-drums that could be carried at the rear. None were present now. He needed to get to the front of this tank, positioning himself in between the two, to secure some of the ERA blocks. Being in between the two T-64s would make him harder to spot. He slipped around the side, placing the tips of his boots on the caterpillar track itself as the tank was so wide it extended beyond the platform. He tottered past the six stamped, small, evenly spaced, dual road wheels, his elbows resting on the tank sides. The height of the tank reached just below his shoulders. He paused. Moving on the balls of his feet was tiring, although he was conscious that time was passing. He continued again along the side. The T-64 had a drive sprocket at the rear, idler at the front and four return rollers. The first, second, fifth and sixth road wheels also had hydraulic shock absorbers.

He got to the point where the track guards started to curve down at the front and hoisted himself up with his elbows until he could squat down on the front of the glacis. He was relieved to finally be able to place his feet on a solid footing. He surveyed the sharply sloped upper glacis, its V-shaped water and debris deflector partly obscured by the ERA blocks that covered the front of the tank. The large infra-red searchlight on the left of the turret stared at him, and he reached up and touched the barrel of the 125mm main gun. He sensed the latent power and destruction that this smooth-bore gun could deliver. To his immediate right were four 81mm smoke-grenade launchers; a similar unit was positioned on the other side. The tank was also capable of generating smoke by injecting fuel onto the manifold, creating clouds of billowing smoke. This was a technique the tankies had used when Bradley and his team got too close during Soviet military exercises, engulfing them in choking, fume-laden smoke.

He looked around and, seeing it was all clear, wasted no time in getting the monkey wrench out and attacking the bolted down blocks. The blocks, or bricks as they were called, each about twenty-five and half centimetres by thirteen and a half centimetres, were slotted onto a pin, attached to the armour of the tank. At each end of its length, it was bolted down at each corner. He got to work with the wrench which was proving to be slightly too big for the job but holding it vertically he eventually managed to undo the first bolt. The first one took him almost two minutes, but the subsequent bolts were much faster to undo. He was conscious that the clock was ticking, and his good luck at being undisturbed could not last forever. Once the final bolt was removed, he was able to ease the ERA block off the pin. It was lighter than he had expected. He placed it and the bolts in the bag he had slung across his chest and shoulders, brought specifically to secure the items he had removed from the tank. He thought about getting a second one but didn't want to push his luck too far. Also, he had taken one from the edge, hoping it wouldn't be noticed for a while, or until at least well after he had gone.

He was about to clamber down from the tank glacis and drop off the front when his foot caught on the steel towing cable looped along the front, the spanner slipping from his fingers, bouncing off the end of the glacis, striking the rear of the tank in front with a clatter; then rebounding back onto the platform of the flatcar. He froze and cursed

21

under his breath at his stupidity. He quickly looked about him, fearful of discovery. *Clang!* The gunner's hatch on the top left of the turret was flung forward and a tank crewman thrust his head upwards. He was wearing a black, padded tank helmet, its iconic tubular-style padding traversing from front to rear, changed little from the World War Two era. The soldier rubbed the sleep from his eyes, stared at Bradley who was crouched on the edge of the tank's glacis and said something in Russian, completely unintelligible to the intelligence operator. They must have maintained eye contact for at least two seconds before Bradley broke the spell. He clambered down from the turret, awkwardly, onto the flatcar and, ducking under the barrel of the gun, made his way to the far side. He heard the Russian soldier scrambling to get through the turret hatch in order to pursue the trespasser, shouting a warning. Bradley got to the edge of the flatcar, dropped down onto his backside, his legs dangling over the side, and launched himself forward. He hit the ground hard but with both feet together, initiating a parachute landing roll, buckling his knees and rolling onto his hip, following through onto his shoulder, something he had done for real during his parachute training. Saying that, his first ever landing had resulted in him landing on his feet, arse and head. The pain he experienced landing that way ensured that he got it right the second time around. He groaned as the Mars-Bar in the bag dug into his side, metal against flesh and bone, not one he could win. He picked himself up and quickly checked on the progress of his, now, pursuer.

Standing on the turret, he was screaming his head off in Russian, jabbing his finger in Bradley's direction and calling to his comrades further along the sidings. The soldier, seeing Bradley looking up, made his way to the front edge of turret and dropped down onto the glacis. The chase was on.

Although Bradley's legs had been jarred by the jump and his side was throbbing from the impact of the ERA block, he set off at a sprint. One hundred metres to the Rover and potential safety. He heard the tank crewman's boots hit the ground and the grunt as he collapsed in a heap, obviously not parachute trained. Bradley smiled to himself. The Russians's curses got louder, along with shouts coming from the direction of the Ramp. Bradley looked over his shoulder on hearing more shouts and could see two or three soldiers pounding down the track towards him, yelling insanely, desperate to get to him. He was twelve seconds away from the vehicle and hopefully, although not always, safety. Ten seconds. He couldn't see the back of the Range Rover just yet, but he knew he was getting closer. He heard more yells behind but didn't look back. Nothing could be allowed to inhibit the speed he had built up.

Eight seconds and his breathing was starting to labour as he pumped his arms up and down, his boots pounding the ground beneath, his eyes searching for any ruts that could trip him up and effectively end his escape.

Seven seconds. He could just make out the back of the vehicle through the gaps in the trees.

Six seconds. Jacko's silhouette could be seen through the back window. Alerted by the shouts from the area of the Ramp, he was peering through binoculars, trying to seek out Bradley or any other disturbance he should be concerned about.

Five seconds. On seeing the speed his tour-commander was running at, Jacko knew there was a problem. He threw the binos onto the passenger seat, made sure all but one of the doors were locked, and started the engine.

Four seconds. The pounding grew louder behind Bradley as more Soviet soldiers joined in the chase. He swallowed hard and urged his legs to move faster. His thighs burned, his heart thumped, and his lungs felt like they would burst as he put one last effort into keeping a gap between him and his pursuers. His bag slapping against his side, reminding him of the contents and the consequence should he get caught.

Three seconds, he would make it. He heard another yell off to his right and could see what must have been the Soviet sentry on foot patrol responding to the calls from his comrades. The sentry dropped to his knee, pulled the AK-74 into his shoulder and took aim.

Two seconds. *Zip, crack*: the two sounds almost instantaneous. Bradley ducked automatically, losing his footing and stumbling forward, crashing to the ground, causing further yells as the pursuing enemy realised they had just been given an opportunity to capture the British upstart. He rolled forward, thumping up against the back wheel of the Range Rover, and quickly pulled himself up its side.

Jacko leant across the seat and pushed the passenger door open, revved the engine and screamed at Bradley, "Come on, for fuck's sake, come on! They're on you!"

Bradley threw himself bodily into the vehicle, his head practically landing on Jacko's lap. Jacko pressed the accelerator to the floor and the Rover pulled away, clouds of dust billowing behind them as it roared through the trees, branches slapping at the windscreen, before Bradley had even managed to drag his legs inside.

Zip, crack, zip, crack. A small branch dropped onto the bonnet, sliced off the tree by a 5.54mm round from an AK-74, fired too high. They roared away, almost comically, like something out of a Keystone Cops movie: door still open, Bradley's head in Jacko's lap and his legs still dangling outside, being flung from side to side as Jacko weaved through the trees.

Bradley finally managed to pull himself into the vehicle, straightened up and pulled the door shut just as it was about to be sheered off by a rapidly approaching tree. He looked back over his shoulder. The tank crew seemed as if they had given up the chase, although another weapon was aimed in their direction. He saw the muzzle flash and winced. They both heard the crack but didn't see or hear any evidence of a strike. Both knew from experience that trying to level an assault rifle, steady your breathing and hold the outward breath halfway out as you squeezed the trigger was not as simple as it sounded. After any major exertion, especially running flat out, it made it much harder, particularly trying to zero in on a moving target. It had been their lucky day.

Jacko spun the wheel to the right, the Rover tilting to the left as he took them straight over the double railway line of the spur where they had crossed earlier. He revved the engine as they bounced over the two sets of railway lines, the cab rocking violently as Jacko negotiated the steel tracks and the thick wooden sleepers. There was no time to slow down and take it easy on this return journey. Once across to the other side, Jacko careered left, this time the Rover's body lurching to the right, and headed for the underpass they had come through earlier. Bradley slipped his seat belt on over his shoulder and chest. He knew they were going to be in for a rough ride. He turned to look back over his left shoulder again, cracking the back of his head on the window as one of the front wheels struck a deep rut, the steering wheel torn from Jacko's hands.

"Fuck! Sorry about that," cursed Jacko, but quickly regaining control and getting them back on track.

"Shit! That bloody UAZ 469 is on our tail!" Bradley called out.

Behind them, a trail of dust streaming behind it, Bradley could see the Soviet Army Jeep tearing after them. It was probably more capable than the Range Rover across country, but on the roads, there would be no competition. That's where they needed to get to.

"How far?" yelled Jacko above the growling engine and rattling of the vehicle as they bounced and jolted ever closer to their escape route, not taking his eyes off the ground ahead even for a second.

"About fifty metres, but they're closing."

"We'll have to slow down for the tunnel; either one."

"Go right, right," instructed Bradley.

Jacko spotted the concrete opening up ahead and swung left, taking a wide sweep so he could come at the entrance straight on. This gave the

UAZ the opportunity to close the gap, just as Jacko nosed the bonnet into the opening.

"Hold on," he shouted.

Thwack. Screeeeeech.

The Range Rover ploughed through the narrow gap, the wing mirror on Bradley's side shattering as it struck the concrete wall. The front right wing caught the wall as well, scraping a layer of paint off down to the bare metal. They shot out the other side like a cannon ball out of a gun and Jacko turned hard right, the Rover feeling as if it would topple over at any moment but settling back down as he straightened her up.

The Soviet Jeep was not so lucky. In his desperation to close with the intruders, the driver failed to take a wide enough sweep and approach the entrance full on. His right wing struck the unforgiving concrete wall of the entrance, the forward momentum swinging the back end round, and the left rear struck the opposite wall. The Jeep ground to a halt. The Soviet NCO in the passenger seat cursed the driver for his stupidity.

Jacko turned left onto Shackelster Strasse and built-up speed until he was doing in excess of fifty miles an hour. "Clear?"

Bradley looked back again. "Yes, so far anyway."

Jacko drove down the street for about half a kilometer, still no sign of pursuit. He turned left to go under the continuation of the west-to-east railway line, bringing them onto Grabensprung.

"Where to?"

"Margate Bridge, Jacko."

"Why there?"

"We need to hide this stuff just in case we get bounced. We can come back for it later."

Margate Bridge was one of many bridges that crossed over the railway lines that circuited East Berlin. The city was a major rail junction. Beyond Margate, there was 'the-bridge' and, beyond that, 'a-bridge-too-far'; places they would hide up by to watch for troop trains either coming into East Berlin or transiting through to go on exercise – or the worst-case scenario: a troop build-up for the invasion of West Germany. It would allow them to keep a low profile for a while, well outside the confines of the city.

Jacko maintained a high speed, weaving in and out of the traffic. The word would be out by now, so the MFS and the VOPO – Volkspolitzei, East German Police, would be looking for them.

Bradley picked up the radio handset and puffed into it while he leafed through the code book on his lap. "Three-Zero-Alpha, this is Three-Zero-Bravo, over."

A pause.

"Hello, Three-Zero-Alpha, this is Three-Zero-Bravo, over."

25

Then, finally, a response. *"Three-Zero-Bravo, Three-Zero-Alpha, go ahead, over."*

"Three-Zero-Alpha, X-Ray, Alpha, Delta, Sierra, Golf, Alpha, Delta, over."

There was another delay as control checked the code.

"Three-Zero-Bravo, confirm X-Ray, Alpha, Delta, Sierra, Golf, Alpha, Delta, over."

"Confirmed. Will need Prep Three, over."

"The boss will be skipping around the office." Jacko laughed.

"Wilco, Three-Zero-Alpha, out."

"What now?"

"They will get EOD out. We'll need an explosives specialist to check out our package."

Jacko looked back into the rear of the vehicle where Bradley had placed his bag containing the ERA block. "It's not going to bloody go off, is it?"

"No, Jacko, you're safe. They'll also send out another unit to collect the bar, as the VOPOs may well be looking out for us. And they'll keep a watch on Checkpoint Charlie for any unusual activity."

"You mean prevent us from getting back in?"

"It's a possibility."

"So, what now?"

"I don't know about you, Jacko, but I need a drink. Something strong, but we'll have to settle for my flask of coffee."

Chapter 5

*KAL 150, John F Kennedy International Airport. 31 August 1983. The
Red Effect –11 Months*
"Air Traffic Control Tower, KAL 150. Is there an update on our
departure time, over?"
"KAL 150, wait, out."
The Boeing 747-230B, delivered to the Korean Airlines on 2 January
1973, was now sitting at Departure Gate 15, at the John F Kennedy
International Airport. It was 31 August 1983, and flight KAL 150 was
waiting to start its journey to Seoul. The passengers waited patiently.
Many were seasoned air travellers, perhaps businessmen or women
who took delays such as this in their stride. For the ones new to flying,
perhaps going on holiday or to visit family, the excitement of the trip
countered any feelings of disappointment at the delay. The flight was
scheduled to depart at 0350 UTC, Coordinated Universal Time, the old
GMT. It was now 0425 on 31 August.
"KAL 150, control tower. Good news, you are cleared for takeoff."
Captain Chen Khan, the pilot and first officer of the flight, responded,
"Thank you, tower."
"Have a good flight. Tower out."
He turned to his co-pilot, Pilot Officer Choi, and smiled. "At last, but at
least the delay means that the Seoul Airport services will be up and
running when we arrive. Take her out, will you?"
The co-pilot waited while the push-back vehicle moved the 350-ton
aircraft away from the gate. Once clear and disconnected, Choi
increased the thrust of the engines, and the airliner started to crawl
forward towards the runway. Arriving on runway 31L, Captain Khan
took over and the aircraft, bound for Seoul, finally took off, heading for
Anchorage and the Anchorage International Airport for refuelling, after
which it would continue its journey to its final destination: the capital of
South Korea. The flight deck crew and the cabin crew switched into
their usual routine of ensuring a safe flight and seeing to the needs of
their passengers. The time passed quickly, and they soon landed at
Anchorage to refuel.
Its fuel tanks now topped up, the Jumbo Jet KAL 150 lumbered down
the runway, steadily gathering speed until the pilot was able to rotate
the Boeing 747 and lift the laden aircraft off the ground, departing
Anchorage Airport at one in the afternoon, UTC time. The Jumbo Jet
steadily gained height as it climbed up into the early morning skies, the
pilot tilting the plane gently to the left before straightening up and

slotting into their assigned route: J501. Now, on the northernmost of the five passenger plane corridors available to them, the pilot and co-pilot confirmed with each other that they were safely in corridor Romeo 20, the North Pacific route that passed within eleven and a half kilometres of Soviet airspace to their north, along the Kamchatka Peninsula, a space fiercely guarded by the Soviet air force. The pilot and co-pilot settled down for the straightforward eight-hour flight, leaving the autopilot to do the bulk of the work and calling the cabin crew for a much needed cup of coffee. The cabin crew themselves were starting their job in earnest, going about their duties in the main body of the plane, ensuring the 269 passengers onboard, one of them being a Democratic congressman, were comfortable.

But, unbeknown to the pilot, passengers and crew, reasons that even to this day are not fully understood, they were slowly drifting off their assigned course. Although the Korean Airline had received its computerised flight plan, designating the various waypoints for KAL 150's route from Anchorage to Seoul, and the autopilot was making appropriate adjustments, taking account of wind speed and wind direction, and the plane's changing weight as fuel was burnt up, all was not well. After nearly half an hour in the air, a civilian radar at Kenai, on the eastern shore of Cook Inlet, tracked the passenger plane as being four kilometres north of where they should have been. The pilot, blissfully unaware of this deviation, continued with their flight towards Seoul.

For reasons unknown, Captain Chen Khan and his co-pilot failed to verify their position with Bethel, a small fishing village on the western tip of Alaska and were subsequently picked up by the King Salmon's military radar a full eight and a half kilometres north of their planned position. The pilot reported being on course, even though they had exceeded the safety margin for deviations such as these by a margin of up to six times. The permissible drift for a passenger airliner was two nautical miles per hour. The error continued.

By the second waypoint, KAL 150 was forty kilometres off course. By the third, an astounding one hundred kilometres off course.

Soviet Sokol Air Force Base, Sakhalin Island, 0500-0800 UTC. 1 September 1983. The Red Effect – 11 Months

"Comrade General, we have an unauthorised contact."

General Dimitriev, Commander of Sokol Air Force Base, on the base that day due to the impending test of a missile launch, strode over to the operator's screen. "What is it?"

"It's big, Comrade General, the size of a large bomber or perhaps a civilian airliner."

"Don't be ridiculous. They know this airspace is out of bounds. It has to be something else. A spy plane, perhaps?"

"I don't know, sir."

"Any of our own aircraft scheduled to fly in this area, for the missile test, maybe?"

"Nothing on record."

"Then check again," the commander snapped. He shouted across the control room to one of his junior officers, "Get me the operations duty officer, now!"

He marched across the room and snatched the handset from his subordinate. "Moskvin, we have an intruder in our airspace. I want an immediate launch."

"*What is it, sir? Is it an American spy plane?*"

"An intruder, as I have just told you. Now get a bloody fighter in the air." Dimitriev slammed the phone down before the officer could respond. "Get me General Kozerski, quickly."

There was a few moments' delay before the duty lieutenant passed the handset yet again to the commander of the Sokol Air Force Base.

"We have an unidentified intruder in our airspace, Comrade General."

"*Have you launched an intercept?*"

"We are about to, sir."

"*It should be in the air now, General Dimitriev. What if it is an American recce plane preceding a strike by American bombers?*"

"Yes, sir, but—"

"*Why haven't we seen it sooner?*"

"Since the arctic gales knocked out our radar, we have restricted capabilities, Comrade General."

"*I don't care. It shouldn't be there; now deal with it. Do you understand your orders, General?*"

"Yes, sir."

With that the line was disconnected and Dimitriev turned to one of the officers close by. "Have they launched yet?"

"Yes, sir, they're in the air."

"Patch the comms through to here. I want to hear this."

"Right away, Comrade General."

Within seconds, the speakers in the control room crackled to life, and the conversation between the interceptor and ground control could be heard throughout the control room.

"*Charkov, this is Tsaryov, over.*"

Charkov, the call sign for General Dimitriev, was called by the air combat controller, Tsaryov, from the Combat Control Centre of the Fighter Division.

Dimitriev grabbed the handset. "Tsaryov, this is General Dimitriev. Have they made contact, over?"

"Yes, sir," responded, Tsaryov, Captain Shabunin, the air combat controller. "Two pilots have been sent up, but we don't know what is happening yet."

"The target?"

"It's heading straight for our island, towards Terpenie Bay. It looks suspicious, sir, but it can't be the enemy. They wouldn't be this stupid, would they? Could it be one of ours?"

"Tsaryov, find that target."

"But it will be in neutral waters before we reach it."

"I don't care if it is over neutral waters. Find it!"

KAL 150, above Terpenie Bay, Sakhalin Island. 0500 hours, UTC

"KAL 017, from KAL 150, how is your flight?"

"KAL 150, flight OK. We're getting pretty strong tailwinds though. What's it like for you?"

"KAL 017, how strong and in what direction? How many knots?"

"KAL 150, fifteen knots, wind direction 360 degrees."

"KAL 017, are you sure? We have a fifteen-knot headwind, 215 degrees."

"KAL 150, that can't be right. We are on the same path."

Soviet Sokol Air Force Base, Sakhalin Island. 0500-0800, UTC, 1 September 1983

"Charkov, this is Tsaryov, over."

Tsaryov, air combat controller from the Fighter Division, Combat Control Centre, sounded tense as he called for General Dimitriev, the commander of the Sokol Air Force Base.

Dimitriev grabbed the handset. "Tsaryov, this is Charkov. Have they made contact yet?"

"Yes, sir. One pilot can see it on his screen. He can see it on his screen." The controller sounded excited.

"Has he locked on?"

"Yes, yes. He has locked on. He has locked on to the target."

"Wait, out."

The Sukhoi, 15TM Interceptor, call sign 602, piloted by Major Oborin, had slotted in behind the airliner, about six to ten kilometres back and slightly higher than the passenger plane, tracking it as it flew on its course. It was still too dark for the pilot to pick out the Jumbo Jet clearly. The Sukhoi, given the reporting name of Flagon by NATO, was a twin-engined, supersonic interceptor, built to tackle the ever more capable strategic bombers being introduced by Britain and the United

States. It was designed to target the American B-52 bombers and U-2s along with the British 'V' bombers. With its supersonic speed, look-down/shoot-down capability, the unarmed, poorly manoeuvrable Boeing was not in a position to outfly or defend itself from the Soviet combat aircraft. At the moment, the pilot, passengers and crew were oblivious to the drama being played out around them.

Dimitriev mulled over what he knew so far and what he needed to do next. "Get me Tsaryov again." Within seconds, he was again talking to call sign Tsaryov, Shabunin, the combat controller. "What is the update on call sign 602?"

"602 has the target in sight."

"He can see it?" How many jet trails are there?"

The speaker crackled.

"Say again, Charkov, you are breaking up."

"How many jet trails are there? If he can see four then it has to be an American Boeing RC-135."

"Wait, Charkov. 602, Tsaryov. Can you actually see the target?"

A major came alongside Dimitriev. "Do you think it is a spy plane, sir?"

"It has to be. They are full of all kinds of electronics and can identify signals through the full electromagnetic spectrum. They'll probably be listening to us right now," he said angrily.

"Then they'll pass it on to their base via secure comms?"

"That's right, Major, but we've caught them with their fat American pants down this time."

A second speaker crackled into life. *"Tsaryov, 602. I can see the target on the screen and visually. About eight kilometres away now."* The nasal-sounding voice of the pilot brought them back to the current situation.

"Roger, 602. Report missile lock-on."

Dimitriev interrupted. "Greckov, are you there?"

Lieutenant Colonel Greckov, call sign Moskvin, the Acting Commander of 41st Fighter Division, was in the combat control centre alongside Captain Shabunin and responded, his tinny voice coming over the speakers. *"Yes, Comrade General."*

"Well, what don't your officers understand, Colonel? The pilot has to be brought in closer, at least four kilometres, if he is to use his weapons. Get him in close and shoot it down!"

The speaker crackled; the conversation overridden by Major Oborin's voice. *"I see it. I am locked onto the target. It's on my radar screen. I'm locked on."*

"602, Tsaryov. Is the target responding to your calls?"

"No, the target is not responding to my calls."

"602, is the target still on a heading of 240?"

"Affirmative. The target is on a heading of 240 degrees."

"Roger, 602. Turn on your weapons."

"Tsaryov. Weapons on."

"Show me the route we think the intruder has taken, quickly," Dimitriev snapped at the Major next to him.

They made their way to a large table and the Major traced the wax pencil markings on the plastic overlay, which covered the map of their area of responsibility, with his finger. "It's definitely invaded our airspace over Kamchatka, sir."

"Get me General Kozerski now!" Dimitriev yelled to one of the junior officers.

Within a few moments, he was handed another handset: General Kozerski, Commander of the Far East Military District Air Force, had been waiting for this call.

"Morning again, Comrade General. I am calling in my update on the situation on the intruder in our airspace. The aircraft has definitely violated our airspace by flying over Kamchatka."

"Where did it enter?"

"Over Petropavlovsk, Comrade General. It is now crossing the sea of Okhotsk. It's about to enter Sakhalin airspace."

"Are your fighters tracking it?"

"Yes, Comrade General, a fighter from Sokol is about six to eight kilometres away and closing. He is tracking the target on a heading of 240 degrees. It is about thirty kilometres from our state border."

"Has it been challenged?"

"Yes, sir, but the target is not responding."

"Can the pilot identify it?"

"No, it is still too dark. He can see it and has a lock-on, but that is all."

"We must find out if it is a civilian aircraft, Comrade Dimitriev, before we take any action."

"A civilian aircraft? It has flown over Kamchatka already. It came from the direction of the ocean without giving any identification or informing us that it was there. It was in our airspace, Comrade General!" Dimitriev raised his voice, his patience being tested by his commander. "I am giving the order to attack as soon as it crosses the state border."

There was a pause; the heavy breathing of the Far East Military District Commander could clearly be heard as he held the handset close to his mouth. "Go ahead now. Don't wait for it to cross; destroy it now."

Dimitriev replaced the receiver and picked up the handset to call Tsaryov. "Tsaryov, Charkov. Get 602 to move in and destroy the target."

"Charkov, Tsaryov. Roger."

The speakers sputtered and the conversation between the combat controller and the duty operations duty officer could be heard.

"*Moskvin, Comrade Colonel, this is Tsaryov.*"

"*Yes?*"

"*The commander has given the go-ahead to destroy the target.*"

"*It might be a civilian aircraft. We must take all steps to identify it first.*"

"*Identification measures are being taken, but the pilot cannot see. It is still too dark.*"

"*OK then. If there are no lights, it can't be a passenger. The order is correct. Carry it out.*"

KAL 150, above Terpenie Bay, Sakhalin Island. 0500-0800 hours, UTC

"Tokyo Radio, this is Korean Air one, five, zero."

"*Korean Air one, five, zero. This is Tokyo.*"

"Korean Air one, five, zero, requesting permission to climb to flight level three, five, zero."

"*Requesting three, five, zero?*"

"That is affirmative. Now maintaining three, three, zero."

"*Roger, standby. Will call you back.*"

Captain Khan turned to his co-pilot. "This radio is bad. We need to get it checked out when we land."

"I'll make a note. At least if we can climb a bit higher out of these headwinds, it will improve our fuel economy so we can actually get there."

"*Korean Air one, five, zero. Clearance from Tokyo Air Traffic Control. One, five, zero climb and maintain a height of three, five, zero.*"

"Roger, Tokyo, one, five, zero, climb three, five, zero, and maintain. Leaving three, three, zero now."

"*Tokyo, Roger.*"

Sukhoi, 15TM Interceptor, call sign 602, above and behind KAL 150

"602, Tsaryov. Are you approaching target?"

"*Yes, I am approaching target. Moving in closer.*"

They all listened intently, only the hiss of the radio indicating they were still in touch with the interceptor.

"*Tsaryov, 602. The target's strobe light is blinking. I am within two kilometres. Target height 33,000. Instructions, over.*

"*Tsaryov, 602. Wait. Target is decreasing speed and climbing. It's going too slow. I'm going to pass it. I'll fly back around.*"

"602, Tsaryov. Increase speed."

"*I have increased speed.*"

"Has the target increased speed?"

"*Negative, its speed is decreasing.*"

"602, Tsaryov. Open fire, open fire on target."

33

"It's too late. I am alongside of it. It's going too slow, about 400 kilometres per hour. We have already flown beyond the island."

"602, Tsaryov. Roger. Take up a position for an attack."

"I will have to fall back if I am to hit the target."

"602, Tsaryov. Try and destroy it with cannons."

The comms hissed, blanked out as the 23mm gun pods on the fuselage pylons erupted, rounds firing in the direction of the passenger aircraft.

"I've tried. No success. Target now at 35,000."

Dimitriev, incensed, picked up a handset and broke into the conversation. "Greckov, cut out all of this crap. What the hell is going on? I repeat my command. Get your pilots to fire on the target, fire missiles, bring it down!"

The Commander of the 41st Fighter Regiment responded quickly, recognising his commander's impatience. "Task received. We will destroy the target with missile fire."

"Just carry out my orders and destroy it. Fuck, how long does it take to get into attack position? The target is already above neutral waters. Engage afterburners immediately. Tsaryov, bring in the Mig-23, call sign 502, as well. While we're wasting time, the intruder is getting away."

"Tsaryov, 602. Dropping back. Coming in above and behind. Will try missiles."

Oborin reduced the power of the fighter's turbojet engines, dropping right back, getting into a position where he could approach the unidentified aircraft from above and behind again.

"Tsaryov, 502. Ten kilometres to target. I see the target and 602 on screen."

"602, Tsaryov. Approach and destroy target now."

"Roger. I have lock-on again."

"Are you closing in on the target?"

"I am closing in on the target. I have lock-on. Distance to target eight kilometres."

"602, Tsaryov. Afterburner. Afterburner!"

"I have already switched it on."

"Launch!"

"Tsaryov. I have executed launch."

"Comrade General Dimitriev, 602 has launched."

"Greckov, I don't understand. What the hell is going on? Shoot it down. Now!" ordered Dimitriev.

"He has launched, sir," responded Greckov.

"Follow the target, follow the target. Get 602 out of there and bring in 502."

"Tsaryov, 602. Target destroyed. Low on fuel, returning to base."

"Colonel Greckov, this General Dimitriev. Why is the target still flying? Why did he not shoot it down?"

"602, Tsaryov. Break off attack, heading 360."

"Tsaryov, 602. Roger."

"Tsaryov, 502. What are my instructions? My wing tanks have lit up. Fuel low. I am turning left, heading of 180."

"Greckov, did Oborin see the missiles explode? Hello?" demanded Dimitriev.

"He fired two missiles, Comrade General."

"Ask him yourself. Get onto channel 2 and ask him yourself. Did he see the explosions?"

"602, Greckov. Did you launch one missile or both?"

"I launched both."

The Oval Office. 5 September, 1983. The Red Effect –11 Months

He sat down in front of the large Resolute desk, made from the timbers of HMS Resolute in 1879 and presented to President Rutherford B Hayes by Queen Victoria in 1880. A brass desk lamp sat on the highly polished surface at the far end. Behind him, the room featured three large, south-facing windows. In his charcoal-grey suit, crisp white shirt and navy and light blue striped tie, he looked every inch the President of the most powerful country in the world: The President of the United States. Behind him, the US flag and the President's flag stood proud either side of the centre window.

The cameraman gave the President the signal to start.

"I'm coming before you tonight about the Korean airline massacre, the attack by the Soviet Union against 277 innocent men, women and children aboard an unarmed Korean passenger plane. This crime against humanity must never be forgotten, here or throughout the world...

"...and make no mistake about it, this attack was not just against ourselves or the Republic of Korea. This was the Soviet Union against the world and the standards of decency which guide human relations among people everywhere. It was an act of barbarism, born of a society which wantonly disregards individual rights and the value of human life, and seeks constantly to expand and dominate other nations...

"...we have informed the Soviets that we're suspending negotiations on several bilateral arrangements we had under consideration...

"...I've told you of the negotiations we have suspended as a result of the Korean airline massacre, but we cannot, we must not give up our effort to reduce the arsenals of destructive weapons threatening the world...

"...we are more determined than ever to reduce and, if possible, eliminate the threat hanging over mankind..."

Chapter 6

*Control Centre of the Nuclear Ballistic Missile Warning Centre,
Serpukhov-15, Russia. October 1983. The Red Effect –9 Months*
The Soviet junior lieutenant placed the cup of coffee on the metal
desk in front of his duty commanding officer.

"I've just finished the duty roster for the next month, Comrade
Colonel. Would you like me to bring it in now, sir?"

The duty officer picked up the cup, sniffed the aroma, then put it back
down next to his peaked cap with its light blue band and piping, the
large saddle-shaped crown face down.

"Smells good, Azarov. No, I'll look at it later. Who is manning the
console?"

"Captain Bezrukov, sir."

Lieutenant Colonel Sergei Perov sat back, swinging his highly polished
booted feet up onto the desk in front of him, leaning his weight back,
precariously supported on the two thin legs of his uncomfortable metal
chair. He swung forward, grabbed his coffee again and then leant back,
rocking slightly the spindly chair. He took a sip from his favourite
porcelain cup, a gift from his wife on her return from a trip into East
Germany the previous year. It was Mycin, significantly superior to
anything that was made in Mother Russia, he thought. He felt guilty for
a fraction of a second about his disloyal thoughts, but then accepted
that his motherland couldn't expect to be perfect at everything.

"OK, I'll do a tour of the site once I've finished this." Perov held his cup
up towards his junior officer.

The lieutenant left to carry on with his duties, leaving Perov to his own
thoughts. The forty-four-year-old Soviet Air Defence Lieutenant Colonel
was the senior officer on duty at the command centre for the Oko
Nuclear Ballistic Missile Warning Centre, south of Moscow. The Oko
satellites, in Molniya, highly elliptical, and geosynchronous orbits were
used to identify the launches of ballistic missiles, primarily from the
continental United States. This command post at Serpukhov-15 was one
of two Oko control centres, the other one being at Pivan-1 in the
Russian far east. This western control centre, in the Moscow ablast,
communicated with four of the geosynchronous satellites on four of the
seven locations looking over the Atlantic. The other three, casting their
eye over the Pacific, were controlled by Pivan-1.

Perov finished his coffee with a sigh, lurched forwards so his chair was
on all four legs and placed his cup down on the desk, checking his

watch: still six hours of duty left. He didn't resent what he did; he was completing an important duty: protecting the motherland from a potential nuclear strike. Although he couldn't prevent it happening and many would be killed, at least he could contribute to the retaliatory strike on the NATO aggressor. He was about to pull himself up out of his seat when Azarov came charging into his room. At that very moment, an alarm started sounding in the control centre.

"Sir, sir, there's been a launch!"

Perov leapt up and strode briskly after his subordinate, straight into the operations centre that adjoined his office, his private space. He headed straight for the tracking monitor where Captain Bezrukov was hunched over, and quickly spotted the blip blinking back at him, indicating the launch of a US Minuteman Intercontinental Ballistic Missile. The bunker was alive with activity, alarms blaring, red lights flashing, and officers and NCOs manically tearing around the control centre.

"Quiet!" he yelled. "I can't bloody hear myself think."

The anxious staff got a grip of themselves and calmed down. A sense of order fell over the monitoring station.

"Another one, sir," Captain Bezrukov informed Perov, turning to his colonel who was looking over his right shoulder.

Perov looked on. Another blip appeared, captured by the satellite warning system, indicating a second launch. He rubbed his chin and mused, "Why only two? There should be more."

"Shall I sound the alert, Comrade Colonel?" Asked Azarov.

Perov turned to him and snapped, "No!"

"A third, sir," pointed Bezrukov, his voice strained. Trepidation was starting to set in.

All were starting to feel the cold fingers of fear as it slowly dawned on them that the United States had launched a nuclear attack on their country.

"Sir, we must inform the early-warning command centre," insisted the captain as he tracked a fourth launch. "We need to launch our own missiles before it is too late."

"It is our job to validate first, Captain."

"But—"

"No. Get me Pechora now."

"But sir—"

"Now, Captain."

Major Shvernick's boots crunched on the snow and he shivered as he walked towards the small building ahead of him. The Pechora early-warning radar station was draped in a white blanket, the cold of the northern Russian winter was biting hard. He made his way through the door and headed for the centre of the room where he lifted a wooden hatch, crafted into the wooden floorboards. Lifting it, he exposed a two-metre wide, circular steel hatch beneath it. He twisted the handle, lifted the hatch and dropped down inside, placing his feet carefully on the rungs of the steel ladder as he descended. He pulled the hatch down after him and twisted the handle again until it was secure. He slowly climbed down the ladder, facing the concrete-lined wall to which the ladder was secured, into the dimly lit gloom below. He passed the first two levels, each containing a bright yellow diesel-electric set, the upper one throbbing as it provided power and compressed air to the Unified Command Centre.

The thirty-metre-long, three and a half-metre-diameter, 12-stage metal container he was inside of, weighed twenty-five tons. The circular tube, mounted in a regular missile pit, supported by its own shock-absorbing framework, was part of the Russian missile launch system, and was designed to be used in an emergency under the threat of war. It contained the necessary communication and missile launch systems.

The major continued climbing down, cursing that they were testing the back-up communications for the radar site above, and that he was having to enter the dirt and smell of this dark and dank place rather than the relative comfort of the usual operations centre above. He climbed past the third, fourth, fifth, sixth and seventh levels, which housed the control systems, electric power supply and the missile launch apparatus, until he reached the penultimate level, number eleven, the final room being the operations room for the duty staff. He stopped outside a large, washed-out green door, with the number eleven stencilled on it in large black numerals and pulled the lever. He pushed the heavy, oblong steel door, its curved shoulders bedded into the circular steel tube, and stepped into the small control room, the captain on duty leaping to his feet.

"All quiet, Comrade Captain?"

"Yes, Comrade Major."

"Are the links set up? Is the feed coming through from the radar control room?"

"Yes, sir. Is the exercise going on for long?"

"As long as our General wishes it, Comrade Captain. We need to test our emergency procedures in case the unexpected happens. If there is a failure in the control centre above, then this is where we will need to operate from."

"Of course, sir. Sorry, sir."

"Anyway, a bit of discomfort won't do you any harm. Some of these men," he pointed to three others in the cramped control room, "have to spend hours at a time every day down here."

At that moment, the phone, attached to the communications desk, buzzed and the lieutenant who was sitting there unplugged one of the connectors and popped it into another directly below where a white light was flashing.

"Communications Officer, Pechora early-warning centre, Lieutenant Igoshin speaking."

The two other officers looked over, hearing the tinny voice reverberating in the earpiece of the handset. The lieutenant looked flustered.

"Yes, sir. No, sir. Yes, sir."

The officer held out the handset. "It's Comrade Colonel Perov for you, sir, from Serpukhov-15. He says it's urgent."

Major Shvernick made his way over to the wall-mounted communications block, the orange radar screen to the right flickering but showing no activity and grabbed the handset.

"Major Shvernick, sir."

"Are you getting any indications of a missile launch, Major?"

"No, sir, nothing."

"Are you certain?"

The major peered at the orange screen which received the input from the giant radar above. The 'Russian Woodpecker', as it was known, was notorious for the radio signal that could be sporadically heard on shortwave radio bands worldwide. It sounded like a sharp, repetitive tapping noise, hence the nickname. The high-powered, 10MW output, over-the-horizon radar system was another link in the anti-ballistic missile warning system chain.

"Nothing, sir, clear as a bell."

"Has it been tested recently?"

"Yes, sir, prior to our exercise starting. It is functioning perfectly. If there was a missile launch, we would have seen it by now. Is there a problem, sir?"

"No, Major, no problems. Thank you."

Shvernick replaced the handset into its wall-mounted cradle. "Strange." He shrugged his shoulders and ordered, "Right, Captain, I want to do a full tour of the facility and it had better be at 100 per cent. Lead the way."

Back at Serpukhov-15, Perov handed the receiver to the duty communications officer.

"Well, sir, anything?"

"No, they've picked up nothing. It's all clear at their end."

"Shall I call a general alert, sir?"

"No, stand down."

"But, sir, there are five missiles heading straight for the motherland. We have to retaliate," insisted Lieutenant Azarov, a slight panic in his voice.

"They've gone," jumped in Captain Bezrukov. "They've just disappeared off the screen."

Perov peered over his shoulder. The five blinking lights of potential intercontinental nuclear ballistic missiles heading towards the Soviet Union had gone. The screen was blank, with only a little atmospheric noise remaining.

Chapter 7

Chanticleer, UK Government Emergency War Headquarters, Corsham. 4 November 1983. The Red Effect –8 Months

The Prime Minister's chauffeured car, an armour-plated Jaguar, followed by a Range Rover containing her close protection team, drove at a fairly leisurely speed down the A4, Bath Road, in between the village of Corsham and Lower Rudloe. They passed a triangular- shaped copse on their right; hidden within it, one of the many concealed sections of the secret complex they were heading for.

A hundred or so yards further on, the driver turned left onto a leafy lane, making their way towards Westwells Road. They passed a large, grassed mound on their right; Personnel-Lift-1 concealed within, its two entrances disappearing inside; alongside it, the guardhouse controlling who could be admitted and who could leave by this route. Continuing east, and after only a short drive, the driver swung left into Old Shaft Road, being waved through at the checkpoint by a Ministry of Defence police officer as the Prime Minister's party was expected. Parking up next to the Personnel-Lift-2, the PM's close protection officer slid out of the passenger seat of the Jaguar, scanning the area quickly, even though they were in a secure area. The Range Rover pulled up a few yards away, disgorging the rest of the close protection team; the armed, plain-clothes policemen securing the area to ensure their charge, the Prime Minister of the United Kingdom Harriet Willis was protected.

A second Ministry of Defence policeman escorted them to the upper landing of Lift 2. Two lifts were available for them to use. Heaving back one of the blue-green, heavy concertina lift doors, followed by the inner secure cage door which rattled back until it was flush against the right-hand wall, the lift was now accessible. The policeman, the Prime Minister and a close protection officer entered the spacious, wood-panelled lift, a row of half a dozen wooden, collapsible chairs lined each side. The policeman slid the door shut with a clang as it locked into the latch, followed by the cage; then he manipulated the brass rotary controller and the lift car, installed in 1941, descended the one hundred feet to the lower level.

The Prime Minister made small talk with the security officer, a long-serving member of the MOD police force who had met the PM on a previous occasion. The lift lurched to a halt and the officer excused himself as he pulled back the internal lift gate on the opposite end, followed by the heavy concertina door. A slightly dank, musty smell filled the air and the PM's nose wrinkled slightly. The Prime Minister, met by an aide, exited the lift, followed by her tall, suited protection officer, and stepped out onto the lower lift landing. She was offered a ride on one of the battery-powered vehicles used to move around the underground site, but she refused, preferring to walk.

The PM, the aide and her CP officer, headed for their destination: the map room in Area 14. Their footsteps reverberated in the large concrete and sometimes brick-lined area of the bunker complex. The fluorescent lights cast an eery, unnatural glow over their route. Crossing the main road was a broad underground roadway, a kilometre long, that stretched from west to east, linking Personnel-Lift-1 to Personnel-Lift-2, the one they had just exited. Above them, some four metres in height, the concrete ceiling looked cold and damp, lined with pipes, ducting and cables, feeding the entire complex.

The Government Emergency War Headquarters, GEWHQ, was situated amongst a 260-acre network of government buildings below which lay, half a kilometre long and 600 metres wide, an underground blast and radiation-proof bunker. Construction of the bunker had begun in the late 1950s, requiring a fairly substantial upgrade at the onset of the intercontinental ballistic missile era. As well as blast-proofed, it was self-sufficient and could sustain the intended 4,000 occupants, in the event of a Cold War nuclear attack, in isolation from the rest of the country, for up to three months. It was, in effect, an underground city, equipped with a hospital, canteen, kitchen, laundry facilities, dormitories, storerooms and even an underground lake, along with a water treatment plant, that would provide them with all the water they would need.

The party entered a corridor between Area 12 on the left, the kitchens and dining area, and Area 13 on the right that housed the Ministry of Power and the Ministry of Agriculture. As the country was not at war, both areas were currently empty. They soon arrived at Area 14, the zone designated as the Prime Minister's Office, Cabinet Offices, Chiefs of Staff and the War Cabinet. Other areas within the labyrinth housed a general post office, a GPO telephone exchange, plant, such as generators, government communications centre, the War Office, Air Ministry, a BBC studio and more.

The map room in Area 14 was a bleak space in comparison with the cabinet rooms back at number 10 Downing Street, twenty metres by twenty metres, with concrete walls, floor and ceiling lit by fluorescent tubes. A group of tables had been pushed together to form one long conference table in the centre; a dozen wooden chairs, with red padded seats, were placed around it. To the left of the room, three large floor-to-ceiling windows overlooked the Cabinet Office conference room; to the right, a large three-metre by two-metre-wide map of the world was on display.

Chairs scraped back as six men stood up, two wearing suits, four in the military uniforms of their respective services. Lawrence Holmes, the Secretary of State for Defence, his thick shock of greying hair brushed back at the top and sides, strode forward to greet her. "Prime Minister, welcome to our salubrious map room." He smiled; his prominent eyebrows raised slightly as they shook hands. The Secretary of State for Defence and the Prime Minister were often at odds with each other, but today they were on neutral ground.

"Thank you, Lawrence." She walked to the end of the conference table. Jeremy Chapman, her Home Secretary, two small, dark curls prominent on his forehead, his hair starting to recede at the sides, also came forward to greet her. "Prime Minister."

The PM shook his hand then turned to the four men lined up on the other side of the table. "Thank you for attending today, gentlemen. We shall try not to keep you away from your duties for too long." She walked around and shook the hand of each one in turn: The First Sea Lord Alistair Palmer; Air Marshal Edward Walker; Thomas Fletcher, Chief of the Defence Staff; and Dominic Hamilton, resplendent in his full general's uniform, Chief of the General Staff.

"Well, gentlemen, let's get to it, shall we?" She walked back to the head of the table and sat down, an aide in the process of pouring her a glass of water. "It's not from the underground lake, I hope?"

The attendees of the meeting laughed and, with a scraping of chairs, sat down to make a start on the meeting. The PM was offered a cup of tea, which she refused. She placed her dark blue, patent leather handbag, on the table in front of her Its the colour matching her woollen dress and even darker blue, large buttons securing it along its length. With her bouffant hair and red lipstick, a circular brooch on the left of her outfit and a pearl necklace, she looked every bit the sophisticated, confident leader she was. An aide placed some papers in front of her, similar documents to those already set before the others.

"Will you start us off with an update, Lawrence?"

"Yes, Prime Minister." He shivered. "They could have warmed this place up a bit though."

"A hot cup of tea for the Secretary of State for Defence," she called to her aide. "That will warm you up from the inside, Lawrence. We are meant to be a war cabinet, don't forget." She smiled.

"Thank you, Prime Minister."

"Sucked into the Americans' games, more like," moaned the Home Secretary.

43

"Gentlemen," the PM said firmly. "The Soviet Union is a real threat. If the current tensions between the Soviets and ourselves, NATO that is, continue or escalate, we could very well be sat down here with the doors slammed shut waiting for the missiles to fall. So, let's get on with it, shall we? Lawrence."

The Defence Secretary picked up a sheet of paper from his folio and scanned it quickly. "The American command post exercise has been in progress for three days now. The Americans are pushing hard on their Psyops Programme, Prime Minister, although they are trying to keep that knowledge within a very small circle of people. Oh, and there is nothing in writing."

"I take it we are in that circle?"

"Yes, Prime Minister."

"The United States are giving the USSR a bit of a rough ride then?"

"Yes, they are definitely trying to spook the Soviets." He looked across at Edward Walker. "Isn't that the case, Air Marshal?"

Walker, who was sitting opposite between the First Sea Lord and the Chief of the Defence Staff, looked left towards the PM. "Yes, Prime Minister, they are certainly giving the Soviets the jitters."

Harriet Willis fixed him with one of her unwavering stares. "How?"

"By flying bombers directly at the Soviet Union," he responded. "They are sending bombers over the North Pole, flying them as close as possible to Russian territorial boundaries, and waiting to be lit up by the Soviet Air Force's radar."

"Then what?"

"Then, Prime Minister, they turn back. They're also using fighter bombers to probe along the Soviet's Asian and European borders."

Holmes interrupted. "It's a risky strategy, Prime Minister."

"Carry on, Air Marshal. How often are they doing this?"

"Yes, Prime Minister. At peak times? I'd say they're conducting up to three flights a week. At irregular intervals naturally, so the Soviet Air Force don't know when they're coming. They just spook them; wait till they've been lit up by Russian radar then head for home."

The First Sea Lord Alistair Palmer cleared his throat. "The US Navy has been doing much the same thing, Prime Minister. If the large naval exercise in 1981, involving over eighty warships where they got through the Greenland-Iceland-United Kingdom Gap undetected and carried out simulated attacks on Soviet targets, wasn't enough to frighten them then the fleet exercise in the Pacific, involving three US carrier battle groups, in May this year certainly was."

"But what about now?" interrupted the Home Secretary impatiently.

"Now, Home Secretary? US warships and submarines are operating in the Baltic and Black Seas and are routinely sailing into the Barents Sea."

"That's right in their backyard," added Holmes.

"They also have submarines simulating attacks against Soviet SSBNs beneath the polar ice cap," continued Palmer, unperturbed, used to interruptions from Members of the Cabinet at meetings like this.

The large, hollow-sounding room was suddenly silent as the Prime Minister reflected on what she had just heard. Before she could ask any further questions, an aide came into the room, excused himself and approached Lawrence Holmes. He whispered into the Defence Secretary's ear and handed him a piece of paper. The Defence Secretary quickly scanned it.

"Something urgent, Lawrence?"

"No, Prime Minister, just a routine signal about Grenada. Not like the flurry of activity we had toing and froing during October, prior to the American invasion," he said with a light laugh. He slid the message across the table towards Mrs Willis, who picked it up and swiftly scanned its content.

"Well, it was a Realm of the Commonwealth," she said as she read the message. She looked up again. "What is the current alert status?"

"Defcon 4, Prime Minister, but about to move up to Defcon 3," responded Dominic Hamilton, Chief of the General Staff.

"Remind me?"

"Defcon 3, Prime Minister, is called 'Roundhouse. It involves an increase in force readiness."

"Are we keeping pace with the American alert-states, Lawrence?"

"Yes, Prime Minister, we are moving our Bikini alert-state up to 'Black Special'. The French and the Germans are also following suit."

"Ah, the French. How are they taking all of this?" She said it with a smile.

"They are kicking up a bit of a fuss actually," answered the Home Secretary. "President Michaud is comparing the current situation to that of the Cuban missile crisis."

"Hmm," she murmured. "Détente does seem to be at a bit of a standstill at the present time."

"Aren't the Americans pushing things a bit too far, Prime Minister?" asked the Chief of the Defence Staff. "If they want to move the command post exercise up to Defcon 5, a planned nuclear attack, what's to stop the Soviets getting really spooked and launching a pre-emptive strike?"

"It's only an exercise," responded the Home Secretary with a slight smirk.

Harriet Willis jumped in. "The Soviets don't play games, Jeremy. There are still six days to go until the exercise is concluded." She turned to the Secretary of State for Defence. "I want a daily update, Lawrence. We

45

need to make sure we are in a position to support our American Allies at every turn regarding this exercise. And should it take a turn for the worse, we need to be in a position to react."

She pushed her chair back and stood up, the rest of the attendees following suit. The meeting was concluded. "I must get back to Chequers. Thank you, gentlemen."

Chapter 8

The Kremlin. 8 November 1983. The Red Effect –8 Months
"Come in, Yuri, come in." Baskov slowly stood up from his seat, the arthritis in his hips playing up. He moved from behind his desk, making his way around its large counter.

"Thank you, Comrade General Secretary."

They both air-kissed on their respective cheeks and then positioned themselves opposite each other on the long extension to the Russian leader's impressive desk.

"What have you got for me, Yuri?" Baskov leant forward, his thick eyebrows slightly arched as he asked his visitor. "Is it getting a bit fraught with the Americans? What are they up to? Are they going to attack? Why are they testing our defences so frequently, Yuri?"

The Chairman of the KGB, Yuri Aleksandrov, looked slightly startled by his leader's outburst. "We continue to monitor their activities, Comrade General Secretary."

"So, what have you discovered?"

"There is some concern amongst my department. The Americans are using unique message procedures of a type we've not seen before."

The Russian leader leant closer to his KGB chief. "In what way?"

"The message formats have changed; they are more sophisticated. The volume of traffic has also increased. In addition, Comrade General Secretary, during late October, there was a significant volume of communication between the United States and Great Britain."

Baskov laughed. "The actor and the Lady of Steel, Yuri. Maybe they share a bed together."

"Maybe they do," responded Aleksandrov, sharing his leader's humour.

"What about RYAN then? What about your foreign agents?"

"They are reporting that the Americans are at Defcon 3. That is war readiness."

"Get them working. We need to know what is going on over there, Yuri!"

"I have redirected existing agents to focus on RYAN; nothing else." Aleksandrov tapped some papers in front of him. "We have started recruiting new agents and will target a few honey traps. My directorate has already targeted hundreds of American servicemen, the German military, students and businessmen in West Germany and Berlin. We'll get to the bottom of it, Comrade Secretary."

"Who is driving them?"

"I have sent a Permanent Operative Assignment. That will ensure our agents over there will be methodical in their approach in uncovering what the Americans are up to."

"What about their allies, their British puppets and German lackeys? Are they on a high alert?"

"Yes, Comrade Secretary, both are at the same level. The French as well."

Baskov looked down at the meeting table, clearly sifting through his mind what he had just heard, along with previous conversations. He looked up again. "What about the military?"

"The *Glavnoye Razvedyvatel'noye Upravieniye* (GRU) are actively seeking information on NATO forces. They have a lot to do. The West are starting to build up their forces as well as introducing tactical nuclear weapons into Europe."

"We can only survive a nuclear strike, Yuri, if we pre-empt it. Their Pershing IIs have a flight time of only five or six minutes from Germany to our motherland. They have a real capability to hit us quickly, and it reduces our time to retaliate. I will call the council together today. This needs to be discussed further at the highest levels of the party. In the meantime, I want all of our nuclear capable aircraft in Poland and the German Democratic Republic to be brought to a high-alert status. I shall also order our ICBMs to be readied for launch."

"The Americans won't be able to detect our ICBMs state of readiness. Then, when the time comes to strike—"

"We need more intelligence, Yuri," interrupted Baskov, thumping the desk with his fist.

"Yes, Comrade General Secretary, I will send a Flash message to all of our residencies that the American bases are on a high alert and demand further information from them on the Americans' readiness for a first strike."

"What about the East Germans?"

"The *Hauptverwaltung Aufklärung* have been tasked to assist us."

"Good, Yuri, good. We are in a bad position. Is your foreign intelligence directorate computer programme still showing a negative trend for us?"

"Yes, Comrade Secretary, we are still currently losing the overall battle and the United States is steadily gaining ground.'

"This cannot continue, Yuri," responded Baskov, slapping the table again. "We are even buying grain from the West. Twice as much as our tenth-year plan and three times as much as our ninth-year plan; a quarter of it off the Americans." He thumped the table again.

"You are right, Comrade General Secretary, things are dire. Afghanistan is not going well for us, and Cuba is sucking in far too much money. We can't sustain that for much longer. The Angolan regime are struggling to hold back the American-backed insurgents and, to top it all, Nicaragua's Marxist government is being strongly challenged by their opposition forces, again supported by the interfering Americans."

"We are losing our way, Yuri. Our grand strategic assault on the West is fading. What about American public opinion?"

"They are not particularly supportive of us, General Secretary."

"They never have been, Yuri," responded Baskov with a laugh. "But neither have they been particularly supportive of their own country."

Aleksandrov leant forward. "But that is changing."

"In what way?"

"Since the Korean airline incident, and others, there is a steady groundswell of support forming. They're even starting to back the American defence build-up."

"Yes, but will they support their government when the money starts to run out for their Star Wars extravaganza?"

"This Strategic Defence Initiative will cost them billions, Comrade Secretary. Surely they can't maintain that level of expenditure and support their NATO conventional forces."

"But you said the American public were in support."

"They are. But their president has been telling his voters lies about our nuclear capabilities. Their technology is also improving every day, Comrade Secretary. Even children in America play with computers. Their weapons are becoming increasingly more sophisticated."

"We are ahead of them with our conventional forces currently, Yuri, but they are catching up with us. It has to stop; it has to stop now!" Baskov again thumped the table.

"But we are already spending twenty per cent of our gross national product on our military."

"I know. Our economy cannot afford sustain our current spend, let alone increase it."

"What's the answer then, Comrade General Secretary?"

"There is only one, Yuri. War! We must strike first and hard, while we can."

"Nuclear?"

"No, unless that is what the Americans want. We have a strong enough conventional army to take on and defeat NATO."

"What about a possible nuclear response? The American Pershing missiles are already on the European continent."

"We have our SS-20s. Anyway, when it gets to that, we sue for peace," Baskov responded with a sly smile. "The West German government aren't going to want a nuclear holocaust raining down on German cities, are they, Yuri?"

49

"But we keep our territorial gains achieved at that point?" Aleksandrov smiled. "Shrewd, Comrade Secretary."

"I will call the Politburo together. We need to meet."

"And meet with the military?"

"Yes, definitely."

"The Commander in Chief of the *Teatr Voyennykh Deystviy*, the Soviet Western TVD Command, Marshal Obraztsov, will have to take the brunt of any hostilities against the West. The main thrust of the attack will be under his responsibility."

"He has a large force under his command, Yuri, to fulfill that very role."

There was a knock at the door and Baskov called his assistant in. She was bearing a tray holding a pot of coffee, two cups and plate of Lepeshki biscuits. She pottered around the table serving the two senior Politburo members. As she was leaving the room, Baskov got up from his seat and walked to his desk, picking up a file that had been lying there. He returned to the table, dropping down into his chair, and slapped the file onto the table in front of Aleksandrov. "молот, Yuri, Exercise молот *84*."

"What about it, Comrade Secretary? Cancel it now and attack for real?"

Baskov picked up one of the biscuits and took a small bite, savouring the almonds and the extra special taste created by using sour cream rather than butter to make them. Through a mouth full of crumbs, some of them spraying the table, he whispered, "No, Yuri. We go ahead, but it will be an exercise with a difference."

He sat back, pushing the plate towards his KGB Chairman. Aleksandrov took one and dipped it into his coffee before taking a large bite, wet morsels decorating his tie. "Use the exercise as cover? But not all of our divisions, apart from those in East Germany, are at full strength."

"Yes. Use it to consolidate our forces ready to strike!" Baskov pounded the table again. "To build up our under-strength divisions, we can call up our reserve troops to complete their annual training, but not release them; keep them with their units."

"But the West will pick up on that, surely."

"Not if they are being called up for duties in Afghanistan. We can slowly wind down Afghanistan. It's not so important now. But NATO won't know that."

"It's war then, Comrade General Secretary, war."

Chapter 9

The Kremlin. 4 December 1983. The Red Effect –7 Months

The table was lined four on one side and five on the other, with the General Secretary of the Soviet Union choosing to sit behind his desk. On the right of the extended table, nearest to Baskov, sat Yuri Aleksandrov, Chairman of the dreaded KGB; next to Aleksandrov, Marshal Obraztsov, Commander of the Western Strategic Direction, Commander of the Western TVD, covering a front from southern Norway, Denmark, Belgium, Netherlands, Federal Republic of Germany, Northern France and, although not on the continent, Great Britain. To his right sat Army General Mantarov, Commander of the Southern TVD, responsible for southern Europe from the southern edge of the Western TVD boundary. Further right was Army General Golodayev, Commander of the South-West TVD. To Baskov's left, along the other side of the table, sat five other senior members of the Soviet Union's Defence Force. Nearest the General Secretary was Marshal Dolzhikov; next to him, a large man in resplendent uniform: Army General Zavarin, his uniform bedecked with medals, Commander of the Group of Soviet Forces Germany (GSFG), the most powerful conventional force in the Soviet Union's armoury. Then it was the Commander of the Central Group of Forces, Banin; Commander of the Northern Group of Forces, Colonel General Zhiglov; and Kaverin, Commander of the Southern Group of Forces. Although a large body of very senior officers, this was only a mini-STAVKA. The full Soviet *Stavka, Verkhovnogo Glavnokomaidovaiya-STAVKA*, commanding all of the Soviet forces involved in time of war, would be assembled at a later date.

Baskov banged his desk with the model artillery piece that often found its way into his hand and called the meeting to order. "Generals, please help yourself to a drink. Coffee and water only. We can have something stronger during dinner later," he said with a laugh. "We have an extremely important subject to get through today." He pointed to Marshal Obraztsov. "Comrade Marshal, please start off proceedings."

The marshal, responsible for the Western TVD, with the Polish, Czechoslovakian, Hungarian and the Groups of Soviet Forces under his command, opened the file in front of him and pulled out the operations order for мolot 84. The rest of the attendees went through the motions of studying a similar document and waited for the Commander-in-Chief to run through the briefing. Baskov left his personal copy in his folder, preferring to listen to its outline from the architect himself. He also used the time as an opportunity to study his generals, thinking through their respective strengths and weaknesses, and scanning their faces, registering the level of commitment they exuded, or any doubts they felt about the impending operation. There were no weaknesses, he thought, only strength. Their commitment was to the motherland. Nothing else was acceptable. If they were weak, they wouldn't be here.

"Operation молот 84, Comrade General Secretary, Comrade Aleksandrov, is the attack plan to liberate the Federal Republic of Germany, and force the North Atlantic Treaty Organisation, NATO, to concede defeat and leave Western Europe." Obraztsov looked around the room, looking for signs of disapproval, although he expected none. He continued. "The main effort will be from the Group of Soviet Forces Germany and General Zavarin." He looked at Zavarin who nodded. "His armies will be supported by our Northern and Central Groups of Forces." This time he looked at his other European group commanders who also nodded their acceptance of their role. They too sensed the Soviet leader looking at them.

Obraztsov continued. "The overriding first objective is to destroy the enemy's first line of defence, their first echelon. We then push through to the Rhine, Ruhr and North Denmark."

Baskov added his own thoughts, interspersed with thumps of his desk. "Momentum." *Thump*. "That's the key." *Thump*. "Destroy their first echelon quickly." *Thump*. "Then our second echelon of our first strategic echelon can smash right through them until their backs are to the Rhine."

The room was quiet. The Soviet leader nodded in Obraztsov's direction.

"Thank you, Comrade General Secretary. The Northern Group of Forces, led by Comrade General Zhiglov, along with the 5th German Army, 5th GE and the 1st Polish Army, 1st PVA, will thrust north through Hamburg and into Denmark. Now to GSFG's main task: Third Shock Army's first echelon will advance towards Hanover, their second echelon pushing on to Osnabruck. The second strategic echelon, 20 Guards Army, minus the elements we will use to take West Berlin, will come in behind 3SA and strike for Munster and Hamm, north of Essen, and eventually into the Netherlands and Belgium. North of them, 2 Guards Tank Army will advance through Bremen, Oldenburg and, finally, the Netherlands. There, the coast is a mere 400 kilometres from the GDR border. GSFG will push through to Cologne and Bonn via Bad Hersfield, using 8 Guards Army. The 3rd German Army will head for the Rhine at Duisburg and 1 Guards Tank Army, Wurzburg, Mannheim and Saarsbrucken. A mere 150 kilometres to the Rhine! 3 GE and 1 Guards Tank Army will be supported by 4 PVA."

"And the south, Marshal Obraztsov?" Baskov asked.

"The first and fourth Czechoslovakian armies will push into Austria. But that is just a sideshow, Comrade General Secretary. The main battles will be on the northern German plains, striking deep into West Germany through Braunschweig, Hanover and Osnabruck. The second thrust, using 1 GTA and 8 GA, will be straight for the Rhine, passing through the Fulda Gap."

"Should you need to concentrate on any one axis if necessary, which would that be?"

"The north, Comrade General Secretary. Our main effort will be focussed on their Northern Army Group. It is their weakest force."

"What about reinforcements?"

"The British are in Germany in force as is the Bundeswehr, naturally. But it will take time for the Dutch and Belgium armies to commit. British reinforcements will also have to be called up, and those reserves already available will have to cross the English Channel. And, as for the American reinforcements allocated for Northag, VII Army Corps, that will be delayed even further. It will be days before they will be in a position to make any difference."

"Isn't the Rhine the best option? It's a shorter distance. The Americans have stocks of equipment in Germany but, if we can interrupt their Reforger Operation and prevent their men getting into theatre, wouldn't the south be the best option?"

"Yes, Comrade General Secretary, if that is the case then we would switch our efforts. But we would be up against two German and two American Corps. If the French agree to support NATO, then we would have the French Army to fight as well. Also, the ground is better in the north: the northern plains are ideal for our superior massed tank attacks. Although the ever-growing German population has expanded the size and number of towns and villages in the area, providing them with some defensive positions, it is still the best option."

"I see. I trust the reorganisation of your force is progressing well, General Zavarin?" Baskov said, turning to the Commander of the Group of Soviet Forces Germany.

"It is, Comrade General Secretary. 2 Guards Tank Army now has three independent tank regiments. That's ninety tanks per regiment, and an additional tank battalion for each motor rifle division. That has increased the overall tank strength for that army from 700 to over 1,100 tanks."

Baskov nodded, clearly satisfied with figures being spouted. "And our elite Shock Army?"

"3rd Shock Army has been upgraded and now consists exclusively of four armoured divisions, giving them a force of over 1,200 tanks."

"3 SA will also fight on a narrower front, Comrade General Secretary, enabling them to slice through the Northern Army Group's meagre defences," interrupted Obraztsov.

Zavarin continued. "20 GA, currently surrounding Berlin, and 8 GA have been upgraded from three motor rifle divisions to two motor rifle divisions and two armoured divisions. This takes their tank force from just under 300 to over 700 tanks each."

Baskov thumped the desk. "NATO will not be able to stop us. Our forces will be far too strong. What about our Intermediate Strategic Reserves?"

Obraztsov responded. "The Baltic Military District has three tank, six motor rifle and two airborne divisions; Belorussian Military District, ten tank and four motor rifle divisions along with one airborne division; and the Carpathian Military District has four tank and eight motor rifle divisions."

"Excellent, excellent, Marshal Obraztsov." Baskov was clearly excited at the size of the forces available to him, knowing that, behind all of those forces, they still had the deep strategic reserve. "How will you be using our airborne and Spetsnaz?"

Obraztsov referred to his briefing notes. "Our GSFG Spetsnaz forces will, in the main, be used to support 3 SA operations. They will help to capture key bridges, attack and disrupt communications centres, and play havoc with NATO's supply and reinforcement routes. The Central Group of Force's Spetsnaz will be used to support 1 GTA." He shuffled his notes until he came across the one he needed next. "Our airborne forces have an equally important role to play. 7th Guards Airborne Division will land south of Hanover, securing bridges in that area of the River Leine and causing disruption amongst the enemy's rear. 76th Guards Airborne Division will later drop west of Hanover, supporting 3 SA's push west. 35th Air Assault Brigade will attack near Braunschweig; 83rd Air Assault Brigade at Peine; 104th Guards Airborne Division at Minden. It will create a major panic. 106th Guards Airborne Division will support 1 GTA in the south, attacking bridges in the area of Wurzburg, along with 31st Air Assault Brigade landing west of the Fulda Gap."

Baskov laughed. "Ah, they will have over forty thousand elite troops in their rear area. It will cause chaos, will it not?"

"Yes, Comrade General Secretary," the generals chorused as one, Zavarin adding, "There will be so many airborne divisions, helicopter assault troops and Spetsnaz behind their front line, they will never be able to consolidate a defensive position, Comrade General Secretary."

"An opportunity that our Operational Manoeuvre Groups can exploit," added Obraztsov.

"Yes," responded Baskov thoughtfully. "We will have an opportunity to see how much damage they can do."

"Is the date for the attack still 5 July, Comrade General Secretary?"

"Yes, Marshal Obraztsov, yes, it is. By tying it in with our annual exercise, we can have our troops in position for a quick strike."

"Won't the Americans and their NATO allies increase their preparedness, Comrade General Secretary?"

"No, Colonel General Zhiglov. We hold a large exercise in Europe every year and every year they have done nothing. This time it will be the same level of indifference."

"Will we be inviting observers as usual, Comrade General Secretary?"

"Yes, General It is part of the agreement we have with them. We are obliged to. But..." his bushy eyebrows scrunched together as he responded with a sly smile, "...it's what we let them see that counts." He slapped the desk, a deep laugh reverberating from deep down inside, his assembled officers joining in. Their confidence was absolute.

"What about our new tanks, Marshal?"

Marshal Dolzhikov pulled a sheet of paper from the portfolio in front of him, adjusted his glasses and responded. "*Obiekt 219*, the T-80. We now have over a thousand tanks in service, Comrade General Secretary. They have been introduced into our elite formations where they will be needed most."

"Thank you, Marshal Dolzhikov, but have the teething problems been resolved?" Asked Army General Zavarin.

Dolzhikov looked up at him sharply. "All new tanks have to go through a period of improvement and modification. The T-80Bs are performing admirably."

"Yes, yes, Marshal Dolzhikov," interrupted Baskov. "But will the new armour be fitted?"

"Yes, Comrade General Secretary. They will have Kontakte ERA-Explosive Reactive Armour for protection."

"All is well, General Zavarin," added Baskov, smoothing Zavarin's obviously ruffled feathers. "What about T-64s?"

"We now have over 9,000," continued Dolzhikov. "We also have 9,000 T-72s, and production has already been ramped up for both models. In total, the army has over 50,000 tanks at its disposal, more than enough for it to carry out its task."

Baskov nodded. "Continue with your brief, Marshal Obraztsov."

"To summarise, Comrade General Secretary, the Northern Group of Forces, with 1 PVA and the 5 GE will target Hamburg, Schleswigholstein and Denmark protecting the western TVD's right flank. 3 SA, 2 GTA and 20 GA will strike through Braunschweig, Hanover, Emden and Osnabruck, hooking left into the Netherlands and Belgium. In the centre, 3 GE, 8 GA and 1 GTA will push for Duisburg, Aachen, Bonn and Saarbruken, and will hook right, trapping the NATO forces in the north."

"Giving the Germans a taste of their own medicine, eh, Marshal?"

"Yes."

"And in the south?"

"That will be left to the 1 CSLA and 4 CSLA to occupy Baden and Wurtenburg."

Baskov sat back with a satisfied sigh and turned to his KGB Chairman. "Yuri, we need to know what the enemy is up to. Equally important is our own counter-intelligence."

"I agree, Comrade General Secretary. We will do our bit."

"Well then, gentlemen, we meet again tomorrow, this time with our Eastern European allies. We will all meet for dinner later tonight. Thank you."

Recognising they were dismissed, the generals pushed back their chairs, gathered their papers and left.

Chapter 10

1 British Corps Headquarters, Bielefeld. 18 January 1984. The Red Effect –6 Months

The Lieutenant Colonel sat down at the head of the table in the oblong-shaped conference room on the second floor of the brick barrack block. The furniture was sparse but serviceable and served the needs of the occupants of the room. The briefing was about to start.

"Well, Colin, slides ready?"

"Nearly, sir," responded the SO2 G2 Intelligence, Major Colin Archer as he picked up the slides one by one from the carousel confirming there were only two that had been put in upside down. He would remember to speak to the chief clerk once the briefing was over.

"Here's your copy of the intel report," informed Major Bill Castle, SO2 G3 Operations, as he handed out the top-secret document: one for Lieutenant Colonel Stevens SO1 G2 Intelligence, one for Colin Archer and one for himself.

All three were staff officers with 1 British Corps (1 Br Corps) based in Ripon Barracks, Bielefeld, part of BAOR, British Army of the Rhine.

"Thanks, Bill."

"Ready, Colonel," informed Major Archer as he made his way to the end of the table and sat down opposite Bill Castle, with the colonel to his right.

"Take us through your briefing, Colin. Then we can go through this op order," Colonel Steven said, tapping the top-secret document clipped inside a pink cover with a red diagonal stripe across it.

Archer pressed the button on the remote that was linked to the projector at the other end of the table, and the carousel noisily rotated one slot and a slide clattered down in front of the projector's lamp. The crest of the British Army of the Rhine, a heraldic shield with golden crossed swords on a red background and thick blue cross, flashed up on the whitewashed wall. He pressed the controller again. *Clack, click, clack,* the old slide was pushed up into the carousel which then moved forward one slot before dropping the next one down. This time it revealed a picture of the sleeve patch of a Russian motor rifle soldier: a shield-shaped, red patch of felt with a yellow border, yellow five-pointed star, and a yellow hammer and sickle in the centre.

"Operation *молот 84*, Hammer 84, sir. The Soviets are planning a big one this time." Archer leant forward and flicked the switch of the overhead projector, and the image from the vu-foil lying on top of the plate of glass suddenly appeared alongside the Soviet badge. Pushing

57

back his chair, he got up and walked to the end of the table, casting a shadow on the wall as his head occasionally interacted with the beams of light. He extended a stainless-steel pointer, a convenient ball point pen at one end, capped as it was currently not needed for writing with.

He pulled down two blinds at that end of the room and then tapped the wall. "Operation Hammer 84." *Tap, tap, tap.* "It's not just going to be big, sir. It's going to be bloody big. It's set to kick off on 26 June."

Clack, click, clack. The projector displayed a coloured map of East Germany, populated with irregular, dark patches of translucent orange, signifying the areas permanently restricted, PRAs, to British, French and American military missions patrolling East Germany: effectively no-go areas for the military missions, but frequently ignored by the intelligence gatherers as they searched for signs of Soviet military activity.

"As you can see, sir, we've been given the latest PRA map, with the additional temporary restricted areas. The TRAs are more numerous and bigger than usual."

"There's a copy in the intelligence briefing pack, sir," informed Bill Castle, sitting to the colonel's right.

Colonel Stevens turned to Bill, a tough, stocky soldier from the Gloucesters, the Gloucestershire Regiment. He was destined to become its commanding officer one day. "What's the increase, Bill?"

"Significant, sir, at least ten per cent. They've also added twelve new areas."

"But they've always added new restricted areas when they have major exercises."

"Yes, they do, sir, but this is twice the number, and the sheer size of some of them beggars' belief."

"Bill, will you switch vu-foils?" asked Archer.

Major Castle leant across the table and replaced the current vu-foil with a second one.

Archer tapped the wall again, the picture showing the order of battle of the Soviet forces involved in Hammer 84. "Just look at this, sir: five Armies from the Group of Soviet Forces Germany. That means that GSFG will effectively be mobilised in full. That's all nineteen divisions."

"Our potential adversary, 3 Shock Army, will be on the move then," mused Bill Castle.

"There's more, Bill," continued Archer. "Two Soviet armies of the Central Group of Soviet Forces, CGSF, based in Czechoslovakia, are part of it. That's six divisions; some 100,000 troops."

"They certainly mean business this year," responded the SO1 with a frown. "The entire bloody Russian Army will be on the move."

"I've not finished yet, sir." The SO2 G2 walked to the projector and pressed the button on top. *Clack, click, clack.* A map of Europe now shone on the wall next to the list of Soviet forces. He went back to the end of the table and tapped the wall showing one of the Eastern European countries. "Then there's the Northern Group of Soviet Forces, NGSF, based in western Poland. They will contribute three divisions, amounting to a further 45,000 troops." He tapped the wall again over another section of the map. "Hungary. The Southern Group of Soviet Forces, SGSF. Five divisions with around 50,000 troops." His pointer hovered over the Baltic. "11th Guards Tank Army, part of the Baltic Military District. That's six divisions, two artillery divisions, along with an airborne division. There will be four other divisions from the BMD. An additional 300,000 troops."

There was silence apart from the hum of the fans cooling the bulbs of the slide and overhead projector. The SO1 was stunned by what he had just heard; and not just with the scope and scale of the forthcoming Russian field exercise. He'd already had a brief preview, but hearing it out loud from one of his staff – the enormity of it was setting in. What shocked him most of all was the response from his masters and NATO in general when they had first been notified of this particularly large exercise. They seemed completely blasé, and Stevens, although mildly surprised, had accepted it at the time. Now though, reflecting on the flagrancy of the exercise, he was not so sure anymore.

"Can you slap on the next vu-foil, Bill?"

The major took off the vu-foil, his hands creating ghostly shadow puppets on the wall and he replaced it with a new one. He lined it up, so it was square onto the wall; then adjusted the projector head up and down with the wheel attached until it was in near perfect focus.

Major Archer tapped the wall again. A list stared back at them. "To summarise, we're looking at about 800,000 Soviet troops, that we know off, that are going to mobilise for this exercise. The Soviet Red Banner Fleet in the Baltic and their marines and the Soviet Groups of Forces in East Germany, Czechoslovakia and Poland. The most ominous force of all is based in Hungary. They will conduct a parallel manoeuvre called Danube 84." The tall, slim, dark-haired Intelligence Corps major frowned. "It's huge, sir. We've not seen anything this big before."

"Do you have the list of unit upgrades?" asked Colonel Stevens.

"Yes, sir. It's slide five, Bill."

Bill Castle did the honours again and a new list glowed on the wall.

"2 Guards Tank Army have received three independent tank regiments. Along with those, there is one tank battalion for each of its motor rifle divisions. That gives 2 Guards Tank Army some 1,200 tanks in total."

"And we expect them to target northern Germany, right?"

"Yes, sir," answered Bill Castle. "Hamburg, Bremen and Bremerhaven."

"That's right, sir," Archer concurred. He continued, "3 Shock Army, who undoubtedly will be targeting the area defended by 1 Br Corps, have now been converted to a full tank army, and consist exclusively of armoured divisions: four in total, giving them in the region of 1,300 tanks."

Castle turned towards the SO 1. "Makes our 800 tanks seem pretty paltry, sir."

"And not all of those are in theatre, Bill."

Archer continued, "20 Guards Army have increased in size from three motor rifle divisions to two tank and two motor rifle. That gives them over 700 tanks."

"Should it kick off for real, their airborne forces will also give us a headache," added Bill.

"Yes," Archer agreed, tapping the wall again, this time over the map of East Germany, west of Berlin. "One division in Rathenow and one in Cottbus, south-east Germany. In total, half a million spearhead troops in East Germany, plus the rest, along with Polish, East German, Hungarian and Czech Warsaw Pact forces. We need to monitor closely what's going on in the rest of the Warsaw Pact, sir. Don't want to be an advocate of despair, but this is not a time to be blasé."

"Have Brixmis and the Berlin section been tasked, Bill?"

"Yes, sir, along with the RAF. Corridor flights will continue naturally, and 92 Intelligence Company will be paying particular attention to troop movements."

"JARIC?"

The Joint Air Reconnaissance Intelligence Centre, based at RAF Brampton near Huntington in Cambridgeshire, was an imagery analysis intelligence centre. Manned by the Army Intelligence Corps, RAF Intelligence and Defence Intelligence personnel, they were there to exploit available imagery from the assets in the air and on the ground.

"Yes, sir, they've been tasked. Satellite photography and high-altitude flights are going to be a key means of intelligence gathering during this exercise."

"We need to see their analysis in a timely manner, Colin. I need to keep BAOR up to speed on what transpires."

"It'll be sorted, sir. Will you be briefing the NORTHAG as well?"

Stevens stood up and peered round one of the blinds and looked out onto the huge barracks area, reflecting on what he had just heard. "Yes, the Germans, Dutch and Belgians don't have the assets that we have. They'll need to be kept informed."

"A full NORTHAG meeting?" asked Colin.

"That is my intention, but they seem pretty laid-back about it all."

"Elections, budgets, unemployment; we can never compete, sir." Bill laughed.

"Next steps, sir?" asked Major Archer.

The SO 1 strode quickly from his position looking out of the window. "Colin, I want you to put together an intelligence group to track this exercise. I want to pool all the intelligence we can get and keep command updated. Clear?"

"Yes, sir. When?"

"Immediately. I have a bad feeling about this. Make sure you get input from 18 Int, JARIC, the military missions, Berlin Section, military attachés...the full works, Colin."

"Will do, sir. I'll get things moving as soon as possible."

"Now, Colin, today."

Chapter 11

14/20th Kings Hussars, Bergen-Hohne. 4 April 1984. The Red Effect –3 Months

"This is an alert; this is an alert. This is an Active Edge exercise alert. All military personnel report to their units immediately."

"Oh fuck." William patted the top of the standard square, yew-coloured, military-issue bedside table blindly, eventually finding his watch and pulling it close to his face, peering at it in the dark through one sleepy eye.

"This is an alert; this is an alert. This is an Active Edge exercise alert. All military personnel report to their units immediately."

The sound that came from outside the block of military flats grew louder as its messenger passed directly beneath the third-floor window of the block of flats.

"What's a matter, what are doing? I'm trying to sleep. Vicky will be awake any time soon," his wife muttered as she pulled the sheet and coarse blankets over her head to shut out the noise of her husband fumbling around.

"This is an alert; this is an alert. This is an Active Edge exercise alert. All military personnel report to their units immediately."

The disruptive-patterned, green, short-wheel-based Land Rover, a flashing blue light at the end of a metal stalk attached to the side of the Royal Military Police (RMP) vehicle, drove slowly through the married quarters on the outskirts of Bergen-Hohne, in the northern part of West Germany, the tinny sounding tannoy attached to the front of the Land Rover shouting out its message.

"It's a bloody alert!"

His wife wrapped her arm around his waist as he sat up. She hugged him and pulled herself in close. "Do you have to go?" she said sleepily.

"Of course I bloody do. I wish they'd waited until my hangover was clear."

Pulling himself free of his wife's grip, he placed both feet on the thin bedroom carpet and heaved his body out of the bed. He would have preferred to shower to help wake him up, clear his head, but there wasn't enough time. His squadron commander was probably already on his way. *Keen as mustard*, he muttered under his breath. He stumbled out of the bedroom, closing the door behind him, his wife already drifting back to sleep. He looked at his watch and hissed, "Oh...three...bloody ten in the morning. Wankers."

He headed for the spare room and flicked on the light, screwing up his eyes as he was immediately blinded by the sixty-watt bulb. He eased one eye open slowly then the other as his eyesight adjusted to the sharp pins being stuck into them. He pulled on a fresh pair of boxer shorts then a T-shirt, followed by a green woollen shirt, more like a rough blanket, freshly pressed and starched the previous day. He grabbed his combat trousers, a disruptive pattern of green, brown and black, from out of the wardrobe, pulled them on before collapsing on the single bed, and dragged on a pair of thick, green socks. He would rather have worn his coveralls, but the army were increasingly insistent that tankies wore full combats, particularly on exercise. Although he was meant to wear his black, 'combat high' boots, he chose to wear his NI patrol boots. They were designed for tours in Northern Ireland and he had worn them while patrolling in Belfast. They were much lighter, designed to make it easier for soldiers to 'hard target', sprint between points of cover, making themselves a much harder target around the streets of Andy Town and the Falls Road. His troop commander, Lieutenant Wesley-Jones, usually turned a blind eye. William always carried his heavy-duty boots with him though, just in case. Anyway, this might be for real, he thought, the mere flicker of a smile as he started to wake up, his senses and his sense of humour slowly coming to life. He tied off his boots and bloused the bottoms of his combats with green-coated elastic bands, an S-hook at each end.

He stood up, stamped his feet, then bent down and finally adjusted the bloused legs of his combat trousers until he was satisfied. He grabbed his combat jacket and pulled it on, buttoning it up before slinging his 58-pattern webbing over his shoulder, not wanting to wear it until the last minute. All he needed was his SMG (sub-machine gun) from the armoury and he would be ready.

He walked past the bedroom door and shouted *bye*, but his wife was already in a deep sleep, returning to her dream about Jason Donavan. He went through the main door of the flat, picking up his car keys from the small shelf just inside the door as he left, and headed down the stone steps, exiting two levels down. He shivered slightly. When it was summer in Germany, the weather could be extremely hot, often in excess of thirty degrees Celsius, but in the winter, it was just the opposite. He headed for his pride and joy: a brand-new Nissan Cherry estate car. Small, but it was his. A great tax-free perk. Now all he had to do was keep enough money in his Sparkasse bank account to stump up the monthly payments to pay for it. Four years to pay didn't seem long at the time; now though, it seemed endless.

He looked around, seeing other soldiers doing the same as him: heading for their cars. He unlocked the door, threw his kit over to the passenger seat, slipped into the driver's seat and quickly started the car. It started first time and he roared off leaving the block of flats. Close behind, other drivers and vehicles followed him, all heading to their respective barracks to report in for the Active Edge mobilisation.

On arrival at his destination, after a ten-minute drive, the barracks was a hive of activity. Royal Military Police, as well as the usual camp guard, were there to greet him. Showing his ID card, he was quickly waved through. He was soon at the entrance to the long line of vehicle sheds that housed the regiment's Chieftain tanks, troopers milling around getting their respective charges ready for action.

Corporal William Patterson, 'Patsy' to his friends, parked up and headed for the armoury to draw his personal weapon, the compact SMG, before reporting in. Weapon collected, he headed to his unit

"Morning, sir." Patsy saluted his troop commander.

"Morning, Corporal Patterson." The lieutenant returned the salute.

"The Sovs on their way then, sir?"

"If they waited for you, Corporal Patterson, they'd die of boredom. We're still waiting for Trooper Mackie, but Corporal Ellis is prepping so go and give him a hand."

"Sir. Sir, is it a command post exercise or are we going out into the field?"

"You'll be living it rough for forty-eight hours so make sure you've got all your kit."

"Sir." Patsy set off down the length of the tank sheds, one each side, most of the tanks still inside their dimly lit tank bays waiting to be warmed up and driven out. He headed for the furthest bay on the left, the one containing the tank belonging to Bravo-troop, Two-squadron, 14/20th Kings Hussars.

"Morning, Patsy, made it in, then?"

He looked up seeing his junior, and friend, looking down from the turret of the Chieftain tank that towered above him.

"Hi, Mark. They could've picked a better day for this shit."

"Or we could have drunk less last night, you mean." His friend laughed looking down.

Patsy climbed up onto the splashboard of the Chieftain Mark 5 tank and joined Mark Ellis on top of the turret.

"Is the BV on?"

"Of course. I need a brew before I can do anything. Need some pills too. Bloody head's pounding. Have you got any?"

Patsy went through his combat jacket's four pockets until he found what he was looking for. Extracting a packet of aspirin, he threw them over to his oppo. "Here, try these."

"Thanks, mate, I owe you."

The Chieftain Mark 5/3C, the 'C' denoting they were equipped with the new Clansmen radio system, had a crew of four. The tank commander, Lieutenant Wesley-Jones, a closet Welshman, or so the crew thought as he didn't have the usual plum accent and there was the occasional Cardiff twang, was also the troop commander, in charge of the troop's three Chieftains; the gunner, Patsy, the loader, Lance Corporal Mark Ellis; and the driver, Trooper 'Mackey', Mackinson.

Mark crunched on two of the tablets, pulling a face at their bitter taste.

"You're meant to swallow them with water, you prat."

"Now you tell me." He pulled out his water bottle and took a swig.

"Shall I make a brew then?"

"Might as well. It'll be at least a half-hour before we pull out."

They were soon joined by the fourth member of their crew: Mackey the driver. At five foot seven, he was just the right size for the cramped space allocated to the driver. They were also joined by their troop commander. "Glad you could join us, Trooper Mackinson."

"Sorry, sir."

"Well, let's get her wound up then. We're deploying, and our troop has the pleasure of leading the way."

"Yes, sir," responded Patsy, second-in-command of the tank. "There's a brew on, sir, if you want one before we move off?"

"Sounds just the job, Corporal." The lieutenant opened the top of his water bottle holder and took the three-quarter moon-shaped, black mug off the top, handing it to Patsy who in turn handed it to Mackey.

"So, that's two NATOs, Mackey."

"Yes, Corp," and he climbed onto then into the tank where the BV, Boiling Vessel, was positioned to carry out his order to make three teas, with milk and two sugars, picking up Ellis's mug on the way.

After a five-minute brew and a last-minute check of the tank, they were given the order to move out.

Mackey slid into his seat, situated centrally in the front of the hull, batteries and ammunition charge bins either side of him. He started the genny, the generating unit engine, needed to start the tank's main L60 engine, the two switchboards in front of him. He adjusted his seat position until he was comfortable, although he was reclined so much, he was practically lying down. He started the engine, the hacking cough turning into a throaty roar, plumes of white exhaust engulfing the rear of the tank, the noise of the multi-fuel, two-stroke engine, slowly accompanied by the rest of the thirteen tanks of the squadron, as they followed suit. Mackey pulled his headset on over the top of his beret and, above him, the tank commander pulled on his bone dome. They were now able to communicate. Mackey repositioned his seat, so he

65

was sitting up, the driver's hatch not yet closed down. He toed the gear shift of the armoured giant, ready now to drive out of the tank bay.

The tinny sound of Lieutenant Wesley-Jones sounded in his earpiece. *"Forward, slow."*

Mackey increased the revs, the engine roaring as it pulled the fifty-five-ton giant forward, clouds of white smoke spewing out behind it. There was enough light to enable him to see Patsy guiding him at the front, his view restricted at the best of times and, in the early hours of the morning and the tight space he had to manoeuvre out of, an additional pair of eyes was a necessity.

"Forward, forward," ordered his commander sitting in the turret above, the lieutenant's view improving with every foot of movement of the now squealing tank tracks. The tank slowly inched its way forward, easing its way out of the tank shed; the first one.

"Right stick."

In a low-ratio gear, Mackey pulled on the stick to his right, increased the pressure of his foot on the accelerator at the same time, and the heavy tank slewed around to the right until it pointed in the direction that would take them out of the barracks.

"Stop."

The tank commander looked about him. The way forward was clear, and the other two tanks in his troop were also manoeuvring ready to follow.

"Forward, slow."

Mackey depressed the accelerator again, grabbed the left and right stick, and the Chieftain lurched forwards, the rattling, squealing tracks propelling it between the tank bays either side, a hive of activity as the rest of the regiment prepared to move out. There was an ever-increasing cacophony of sound as more and more of the British battle tanks started up.

Mackey kept the Chieftain at a steady walking pace, making slight adjustments to keep the tank on target, the clatter of the tracks settling down to a steady rhythm as they headed for the main road.

The tank commander acknowledged Patsy as he climbed back up onto the tank, his task of guiding it out of the bay now finished, dropping into his position in the turret. If the commander looked down, he would see Patsy settling into the gunner's seat. Behind Patsy were charge bins and, beneath him in the floor, HESH (High Explosive Squash Head) rounds were stored. All the explosive ordnance, for greater survivability, was stowed below the turret ring. Looking down and forward, the commander would see Mackey his driver who also had charge bins either side of him. Below sat Patsy and, to the right, Mark Ellis settled into position as the loader for the 120mm rifled tank gun.

Wesley-Jones sat down on his two-piece seat, using the handle to his left to adjust its position, and twisted his bone dome until comfortable while he waited for the rest of the troop to catch up. A Land Rover, with a blue flashing light on a stalk at the side, pulled out in front of them, their escort to the exercise area. Wesley-Jones heaved himself up off his seat until his shoulders were above the turret and, looking back, he could see the other two tanks of his troop lined up behind him. He ordered the tank forward and Mackey steered the tank onto the road.

"One bravo, three bravo, on road over."

"Roger."

"All bravo call signs, we're heading for the range, but no deployment. Acknowledge, over."

"Two bravo, roger."

"Three bravo, roger."

"All bravo call signs, one bravo, out."

Wesley-Jones switched to the internal tannoy. *"No deployment, we're heading for the ranges. Back in by tonight."*

Ellis punched the air. "Fucking magic."

"Right, Mackey, let's go," called the commander.

Trooper Mackinson, his head just sticking above the driver's hatch, headphones over the top of his black beret, tinted goggles protecting his eyes, pushed down on the accelerator. The seven-hundred horsepower engine revved and the energy transmitted through to the drive sprocket powered the armoured giant forward. The engine screamed as it slowly gathered speed, only released as Mackey changed gear, only to build up the momentum again as the speed ramped up, the distinctive banshee-like sound of its multi-fuelled engine joined by the rest of the squadron as they too joined in the convoy. The tank lurched forward as the driver worked his way through some of the six forward gears until they hit a steady thirty kilometres an hour, all they were allowed to do on the range roads. The tank tracks had blocks of rubber arrayed along the treads, to protect the German roads and reduce the noise as they pounded along them, pacifying the complaints from the local population in some small measure during the large exercises the British Army and NATO conducted annually.

They headed for the lager where the squadron would congregate before spending their day honing their skills on the tank gunnery range. It was an opportunity to allow the L11A3 120mm tank gun to show its metal, as opposed to the 105mm of its contemporaries.

Wesley-Jones looked behind him through a cloud of white smoke, rocking against the Mark 2 cupola as Mackey changed down to negotiate a sharpish bend. He turned back round, facing forwards again, a spotlight on the front of the cupola, an L37A1 7.62mm machine gun to his left. Now they were on the move and not buttoned down, he was the eyes and ears for the driver. Although Mackey was sitting up straight, his view was very limited. But the tank commander felt fairly relaxed: they were just going to the ranges and Mackinson was familiar with the roads having driven this route many times before.

Down in the confines of the tank, the fighting compartment, Patsy and Ellis gave each other the thumbs up. They were just going to the ranges for the day and not a full deployment as they had feared. They could relax during the journey; their jobs as gunner and loader would start once they arrived at the ranges. For now, though, it was the tank commander and the driver's job. The fighting compartment extended the full width of the hull, with the turret suspended on a 'ball race' which gave it a 360-degree capability. The commander turned as Corporal Patterson popped his head up out of the turret's second hatch.

"Get your bone dome on, Corporal Patterson, you know the score."

"Sir."

Patsy reached down, grabbed the battered green bone dome, removed his beret and pulled on the helmet with its bulging ear covers, settling the earphones until they were comfortable.

"That's better. You know what the OC is like." He said it with a smile though. He had a good crew, the best in the squadron. In the last regimental-wide competition on driving, handling and shooting, his tank and his crew had won. Anyway, he was just as pleased they wouldn't be deploying today.

"Well, Patsy, just a short day. Your own bed tonight, eh?"

Chapter 12

East Berlin rail ring. 9 May 1984. The Red Effect −2 Months

Jacko handed his tour commander a mug of coffee and then he settled down on the carpet of grass that covered the edge of the railway embankment. It was Jacko's turn to sleep but he had experienced a painful bout of cramp while trying to catch some shut eye on the back seat of the Range Rover, hidden below them beneath the bridge. This was their second night out on Operation Bloodhound. They were due to be relieved by their second intelligence unit, Three Zero Alpha, later that morning at 0800. Their remaining unit, Three Zero Charlie, would also be out later that day. Intelligence headquarters were clearly worried about something.

They were covering the railway line that came into Berlin from the north-east. Any incoming traffic could either turn south and continue into the southern part of East Berlin, or head north and continue around the rail ring that would take them west, deeper into East Germany, bypassing the centre of the city. This was the likely route for military trains passing through, heading deep into Germany to transfer military equipment between barracks, or upgrade the equipment assigned to the many divisions of the Group of Soviet Forces Germany (GFSG). The worst-case scenario though was military trains passing through the outskirts of Berlin to reinforce the Russian Army already there, should there ever be a war between NATO and the Warsaw Pact. Coming from the east, the train's departure point could have been anywhere in Poland or Russia – the Belorussian Military District, for example.

This was their second night and, after shifts of four hours on, four hours off during the day, two hours on and two hours off during the night, waiting for that elusive military train, they were both tired, overtired. They had, so far, managed to stay out of the clutches of the VOPO (*Volkspolitzei*) and the *Ministerium für Staatssicherheit*, Ministry for State Security, MFS, nicknamed the Stasi. The Range Rover had been hidden amongst some trees down below and they hadn't used this site for some time. The occasional civilian snooped around, but the team had remained hidden until the locals went about their daily business.

They were now tired, but in good spirits. However, they were disappointed they had not seen anything yet and concerned that their sister unit would get all the glory of a sighting. They would see a train before they heard it. The steam locomotives had a single white headlight, and they would see it well before they heard the train approaching. Any military load requiring movement via the railway network would be moved by the *Deutches Reichsbahn* and pulled by one of their pre-war, refurbished steam trains. The *Deutches Reichsbahn*, formally *Deutches Reich* (German Empire), was founded when the Weimar Republic took national control of the German railways in 1920.

"Can't sleep, Jacko?"

Jacko turned on his side in the knee-high grass, sipping at his coffee, staring up at the expanse of stars twinkling above. "No, Sarge, too tired to sleep and too bloody uncomfortable on the back seat."

"Why don't you kip outside? It's warm enough."

"Bloody bugs all over the place. No sooner do I close my eyes, and I can feel them crawling all over me."

"Use a maggot and put your cam scarf over your face, you plonker," Bradley suggested, referring to their green army sleeping bags. He lifted his binoculars and peered into the darkness seeking out that telltale prick of light that meant a target was finally heading their way. Nothing.

They had been watching and waiting for over eighteen hours and, apart from the regular passage of high-speed passenger trains and a few civilian goods trains, they had seen nothing. Not a military train in sight. The Berlin rail ring was a major rail junction, and military traffic had to pass through the outskirts of East Berlin if it was to make a quick passage to the western part of East Germany. The two operators were at a location they called 'Newcastle Bridge', a rail bridge that crossed over a 'B' road near the district of Karow. The rail line ran in from the east, turning south-west into Berlin, passing their current location before heading north-west to track around the north of the city. Although trains could turn south, generally military trains wanting to head into the centre or to the south of the city would come in from the east further south of the city, running into Friedrichsfelde and Biesdorf; sometimes carrying cargoes of military equipment and troops to the various Soviet units in and around the eastern part of the city. Often, the troop trains would stop over at Pankow, Marzahn or Karlshorst sidings to let the priority passenger trains overtake. The section regularly did a tour of these railway sidings looking for a prize, a fully laden Russian military train.

Bradley suddenly stood up from his kneeling position, Jacko joining him, recognising the signs that something was about to happen. "Well?"

"A single light. It has to be one."

He handed Jacko the binos and he confirmed that he too could see the single white light indicating a potential troop train. "It has to be," he said handing back the binos, his voice excited, the need for sleep forgotten.

They both watched patiently as the light, growing stronger by the minute, crept slowly towards them as it approached the railway junction and the traffic signals. Eventually, they could hear the hiss of the steam engine, the puff of smoke ejected from the black smokestack, and the clanking of the coupling and connecting rods, driven by the steam-powered piston, as they rotated the four large driving wheels. Bradley's plan was to watch the train pass by, enabling him to check the cargo it was hauling. Then they would scramble down the gently sloping bank, climb back into the Range Rover and race to the next junction further along the line where they could confirm its final direction of travel. The silhouette of the black steam locomotive, the clanking of its rods and wheels, the rhythmic ejection of smoke and steam from its stack as it powered the train slowly towards them. The train started to lose way. As it got closer, they could pick out the two distinctive, familiar, bowed, black-plated shields that stood proud, curved around each side of the boiler near the front of the train. A sudden blast of steam and smoke burst from the stack as the engine slowed down to a walking pace, but still creeping towards their location. Towed behind the steam engine, of World War Two vintage, they could just make out a line of flatcars laden with tarpaulin-covered vehicles whose shape looked familiar, yet unfamiliar, to Bradley as he peered at them, in what little light the moon gave them.

"What are those?" whispered Jacko. "FROG-7s?"

Bradley remained silent, his eyes flickering over the steadily growing line of tarpaulin-sheeted vehicles whose shape grew ever more familiar. "No, they're not FROGs," he responded finally. "They're too big."

"But look at the spacing."

The large road wheels could just be seen below the tarpaulin cover.

"Look at the wheels, Jacko. They're evenly spaced apart. The FROG's two centremost wheels are closer together."

The sound from the locomotive steadily increased as it got closer, slowly crawling past them as they ducked down not wanting to be seen by the engine's driver or the fireman, the smell of smokey hot steam wafting over them. The rhythm slowed down further, becoming more erratic as it came close to stopping completely. Ten metres further on, with an explosion of smoke and steam, it came to a halt, clouds billowing into the early morning air, the clang of the flatcar buffers striking against each other concertinaed down the line as they too came to a complete stop. The noise settled down to a gentle hiss as the locomotive's crew stoked the fire, keeping the steam pressure up as they waited for the signals to change, giving them permission to continue their journey. Once stopped, likely as a consequence of priority traffic elsewhere on the circuit, they would wait before they either headed straight into the city, which was unlikely, went south, possibly, or turned north. This was the direction the section anticipated this train would go. Bradley scooted towards the flatcar opposite, Jacko remaining behind, keeping watch. Towering above Bradley was a SCUD-B, a ballistic missile and launch system. He looked along the line of flatcars but could see no further than the fourth one. He suspected there would probably be over twenty of them. Eighteen would be carrying the SCUD TELs (Trailer Erector Launcher vehicles); the rest would have either SCUD resupply or supporting vehicles. There was bound to be a goods wagon or two mixed in with the flatcars, carrying accompanying Soviet troops. They certainly didn't want to get mixed up with them. They would respond aggressively if they saw Bradley and Jacko examining their precious cargo. Looking back, Bradley held up his right hand and signalled, in a circular motion with his finger pointing upwards, indicating Jacko should move to their vehicle and get it ready for a quick getaway. He continued to move along the line, looking for the plate that would likely be attached to one of the flatcars and where, behind a perforated, sprung-metal grill, he would find the paperwork, the distinctive DR ticket indicating the destination of the load. Bradley smiled to himself: Soviet secrecy overcome by the Deutches Reichsbahn's efficiency.

Looking up, the foreboding missile launchers towering some five metres above him, the TEL itself over two metres, gave him a sense of awe. The launcher vehicle was nearly fifteen metres in length. Called a 9P117MV, it was based on an improved MAZ-S43 chassis, with an uprated 650hp D12AN-650 engine to power its thirty-five-ton weight. Bradley touched one of the eye-level rear road wheels, capable of taking its cargo on roads or across country at speeds of up to thirty miles per hour. He arrived at the middle of the vehicle where he could just make out the bottom of the door of the combat cabin that dipped down in between the two central road wheels. Behind that door, a crew of two or three would sit at the main console that would control the launch of the missile that was positioned above. Bradley knew there was a crew of seven but was unsure as to how many of them would actually be at the controls at the time of the launch; some would probably be situated in the shielded cabin upfront. The missile it carried was out of sight, beneath the tarpaulin, resting on its erector frame. The Scud missile, used in anger during the Gulf war, and hunted by the British Special Air Service, was just under forty feet in length, almost as long as the TEL itself. Powered by the Sayev 1KBkh M9D21, liquid-fuelled rocket engine, it had a range of up to 350 kilometres, a perfect delivery means for a tactical nuclear missile that could potentially be used on a European battlefield. Bradley continued to move forward, slightly nervous now, constantly looking about him for an unseen civilian, the Stasi, engine driver, or one of the escorting soldiers. He also felt a shiver when he contemplated the power of the weapons that were within an arm's reach of him. Never mind the power of the conventional chemical or nuclear warheads it could carry, he knew that the propellant, that would speed the missile to its target at over 1,600 kilometres an hour, consisted of nitric acid, nitrogen tetroxide and kerosene – an extremely volatile mixture in its own right. Should a war break out between the Warsaw Pact and NATO, and should it turn into a tactical nuclear exchange, these very missiles would most likely be aimed at NATO targets in West Germany.

Bradley jumped as the wagons jerked, the connecting chains between the flatcars rattling, the entire length of the train shuddered as the powerful locomotive at the front snatched them forwards.

"Shit," he hissed under his breath and immediately focused on the task in hand. The train could move off at any minute now. At the end of the flatcar, he could see the paler colour of the route ticket behind its protective cage and rushed towards it. He lifted the sprung-meshed grid that held the ticket in place and extracted it, stuffed it in his pocket and headed back towards the Range Rover on the other side of the embankment just as the train jerked again as if impatient to be on the move.

Another jerk. This time the wheels of the wagons started to turn as the train slowly gathered pace, moving faster and faster. Bradley got to the top of the bank and watched until he was sure he knew which direction it would take. It took the track that curved to the right, taking its load onto the rail ring, heading north. Now certain, Bradley scrambled down the side of the bank and could just make out the puffs of exhaust from the rear of the Range Rover and hear the engine gently ticking over. Jacko was ready. He made one last scan of the area and jumped into the front passenger seat.

"Let's go, Jacko. It's north."

"London?"

"Yes."

The Range Rover crept away from 'Newcastle', the code name for their present location, and headed for 'London', the code name for their next destination. The vehicle steadily gathered speed, no aggressive motoring or lights to advertise their presence. Once they were away from the habited area though, Jacko put his foot down and raced down Pankgrafen Strasse. He weaved the vehicle around the corners of the narrow road, occasionally tilting over if he took one too fast; doing over eighty kilometres an hour at times, and without lights, as he took them north-west, running parallel with the rail ring. Speed was of the essence if they were to meet up with the train again.

Bradley peered ahead through the windscreen looking for the turning on the left, the narrow, partially hidden lane that would take them south-west where the train might well stop again before continuing its journey north-west; then turning west to head deeper in country.

"There, Jacko!"

Bradley was thrown forwards as Jacko slammed on the brakes before turning violently left, the low-lying branches smacking the Range Rover's windows as they bounced down the narrow, weaving track. Bradley hit the button of the sunroof and the large hatch whined as it steadily slid back.

"Can't see a fucking thing," Jacko moaned.

Bradley climbed up onto his seat and hoisted his head and shoulders through the large cavity, gripping the front edge of the hatch as the vehicle ground and bounced its way along the track, heading towards the railway line that was now directly opposite them. He shouted down through the hatch, "I can hear it. Keep going."

Smack! A large branch struck Jacko's window. "Shit, shit, shit."

"Keep going!" Bradley ducked as a low-hanging branch nearly took his head off, some of the thicker twigs painfully scraping across the top of his head. He was suddenly thrown forwards as Jacko brought the tour car to a violent halt. "Fuck, Jacko!"

"Sorry, it was either that or we'd be sat on the rails in front of the bloody train. Can you hear it still?"

"I might if you'd turn the bloody engine off."

"Sorry." Jacko turned the key, and the Range Rover shuddered into silence.

"Nothing." Bradley slid down into his seat, opened the door and ran towards the railway line that crossed directly in front of them. He stepped onto the tracks and made his way into the centre, in between the two sets of lines. He peered south, looking for the solitary light that would indicate the steam engine was coming towards them. He cursed under his breath. They couldn't have missed it, surely. He crouched down then lay down next to one of the steel lines, placing his ear flat against its cold surface. He put the palm of his hand over the other ear and listened. At first, all he could hear was the muffled white noise inside his own head. But then, a deeper rumble was being transmitted down the line: faint at first, but growing steadily louder, the vibrations of the wheels turning on the track, the distinctive *click* as it passed over a joint. It had to be the one. Often it was touch and go. An impatient engine driver might anticipate the lights, keen to keep to his schedule and move slowly ahead, while another may be distracted, chatting to the fireman and not as fast off the mark. But tonight, they had struck lucky: it was on its way.

Bradley picked himself up off the rails, suddenly conscious of how vulnerable and exposed he was, concentrating on his target and not his environment. He laughed to himself; struck by a train would be his epitaph. He ran over to Jacko. "It's on its way. You do the count and I'll do the flash."

Then he ran to the Rover and hauled out a sports holdall, where the camera was, and placed it on the bonnet. Dipping in, he pulled out the Nikon F3, its chunky MD-4 motor drive attached, followed by the Metz flash attachment which he quickly connected. He plugged the lead of the oblong battery pack into the flash, switched it on then slung the battery pack, held by a leather strap, over his neck and shoulder. He was ready. The ASA rating was set for 6400. Although the pictures would be slightly grainy, it was good enough for what they needed tonight: evidence and clarification of their sighting. While Bradley moved up to the railway line to be in position and ready, Jacko turned the vehicle around so it was in the right location, should they need to make a quick getaway, before joining his tour commander.

"Can you see the light yet?"

"Yes. Seems to be nice and slow," responded Bradley, a tremor of excitement in his voice. "Get ready."

Bradley was on Jacko's left, angling himself so he faced the side of the oncoming train, and Jacko was on the right, his pocket memo recorder in his hand ready. Two minutes later, the train crept past them, steadily gathering speed. The flash lit up the area as Bradley took photographs of each piece of equipment as the wagons travelled past them. *Clack...clack. Clack...clack.* The tarpaulin-covered missile launchers looked menacing as they towered above the two intelligence operators. *Clack...clack. Clack...clack.* The high-pitched whine of the flash recharging could be heard in between the sound of the wheels on the rails, the occasional squeal of tortured metal against tortured metal.

Clack...clack. Clack...clack. "Launcher, launcher, launcher, launcher, resupply, resupply, goods wagon, Zil 131 box body, Gaz 66..." Jacko's voice could be heard amongst the mishmash of sound as he recorded on the hand-held tape recorder what he was seeing pass by in front of him.

Clack, clack, clack, clack. Phutt, whine, phutt, whine. Bradley took as many photographs as he was able, quickly making his way through the rest of the 72-frame film. Its purpose was not to provide detailed technical photography, but to provide a record and pick up on anything that the two operatives may have missed. All this information would be fed back to their sister intelligence unit in West Germany, a specialist

75

unit highly experienced in imagery analysis – not just ground photography but also images from the air and even satellites. The train sped past faster and faster until the brake car shot past them, and the train slowly dwindled into the distance, disappearing into the darkness.

"How many?"

"I reckon eighteen launchers and half a dozen resupply."

Bradley didn't respond.

"Did you get that? Eighteen?"

"Yes, thanks."

"What's up?"

"Doesn't make sense."

"What doesn't? Spit it out."

Bradley rubbed the side of his face. "They're headed for Magdeburg."

"How do you know that?"

"The rail ticket."

"So?"

"Three Shock Army already have a Scud-B Brigade. These belong to a different unit."

"Could they be for another GSFG unit?"

"I'm not aware of any Scud Brigade from GSFG being out of barracks. I'll check when we get back. Come on, let's get out of here."

They headed back to the vehicle, stowed their kit and made their way back to Newcastle where they would continue their watch; perhaps treat themselves to a lukewarm cup of coffee. After remaining alert for the sight of more military trains, at 0745, their stag finally over, they headed back towards Checkpoint Charlie. The replacement tour had contacted them to say they were infiltrating from the south, so they went west, leading any potential tail away from the location.

There comes a time when a simple, spontaneous decision can have significant, unforeseen consequences. Had Bradley known the outcome of his next decision, he would more than likely have headed back home without any detours. They were both weary, having had perhaps two or three hours' sleep between them, rubbing tired eyes as they sped along Alt-Biesdorf, looking forward to passing through Checkpoint Charlie, a quick debrief, then home for the three Ss: shit, shave and shower; a fourth S, if they had the energy for sex afterwards.

"Head for Karlshorst, Jacko."

"What?" Jacko turned to look at his commander in bewilderment. "Why?"

"Just a quick look."

"I knew something was bugging you. Ever since we saw that bloody train."

"Just do it, Jacko," Bradley responded sharply.

Jacko turned off the main route that would have eventually taken them to West Berlin and headed for the outskirts of the Soviet military camp in Karlshorst. They weaved through the various unnamed roads, lined either side by a patchwork of single- and double-roomed summer homes; somewhere for the wealthier population of this communist capital to escape from their pokey flat in the dull inner city.

"Towards the wall."

"What are you up to?"

"I want to look over the wall."

"What about the other side of the barracks? It's quieter."

"You can see bugger all from there."

A two to three-metre wall surrounded the entire Soviet camp; the camp shape an uneven rectangle with two of the sides being over a kilometre long. The patchwork wall was a strange sight. Made up of sections of wall taken from German homes after the end of World War Two, it was a mosaic. Some sections had a window frame or doorway bricked up, some were a mishmash of different brick types and colours, and some sections still had bathroom tiles adhered to their surface. On the opposite side of their current position, the wall was partially hidden by a thin screen of trees, but this side was fairly unprotected. There were many cracks in its poor structure, and it was Bradley's intention to walk along the wall peering through those cracks to look for...He didn't know what he was looking for; just something out of the ordinary, something that would satisfy the inkling he had that something wasn't quite right. He leaned down into the foot well and took a smaller auto-focus camera from a small pack he kept there and cracked the door open...

Everything happened in a flash, yet almost appeared to happen in slow motion.

As he pushed the door open, he heard Jacko shout, "Fuck, look out!"

At the same time that Jacko shouted, a white Lada cut across the front of the Range Rover and a second across the back. They were MFS (*Ministerium fur Staatssicherheit*), the East German Ministry for State Security. The door was wrenched back sharply on its hinges, pulling Bradley with it. He felt his arms being grabbed along with someone pulling at his jumper, dragging him down as another went to snatch his camera. As he lost his balance and slowly collapsed to the ground, he peered up into the faces of Soviet soldiers, the epaulettes of one identifying him as belonging to a tank unit.

Bradley was dragged along the ground as more and more Russian soldiers joined in the one-sided fray. He struggled frantically to break their grip, desperately trying to push himself back up off the ground. He was off the floor, in a crouch, when a boot swung towards him, striking him in the chest, the crack of his rib audible, a groan escaping his lips as he folded over. As he went down for a second time, wrenching his camera hand free, pulling it underneath him, he caught sight of a different sleeve patch, one that caused his stomach to knot even tighter. The shield-shaped badge didn't have the shape of a tank beneath a star but had the red Russian star, edged with gold, surrounded by a golden laurel wreath set on a black background with the Russian Cyrillic above it: *КГБСССР*: the military section of the KGB, the Third Directorate.

Bradley twisted his head so he could see in the direction of the Range Rover and shouted, "Red Rag! Red Rag!"

Jacko, the driver's door still locked, was about to leave the vehicle and come to his tour commander's aid when he heard the call. He hesitated for a moment, never thinking he would ever hear that call – but only for a second, knowing they were in serious trouble. He grabbed the Teleport 9, unlocked the door and pushed it open, now clear of Soviet soldiers after their failed attempt to get in. The soldiers had a better target, their main victim who they were swarming around. He ran – ran for his life. His boots thumped on the hard-packed road as he sped in between the summer houses. Looking back over his shoulder, he could see that two soldiers had seen him and were now running after him. He increased his speed and lengthened his stride, his lungs burning as he forced air in and out of his lungs. He looked again but they had given up the chase. He turned left, hurdling a low fence, and ran between two of the garden homes, ran round the back and stopped, bent double, his hands on his trembling knees, breath rasping. He held the radio close to his mouth. "This is Three-Zero-Bravo, any...shit!" He realised it was not turned on. He turned the switch and tried again.

"This is Three-Zero-Bravo, any Three-Zero call sign, over."

Silence...

"This is Three-Zero-Bravo, any Three-Zero call sign in the Karlshorst area, over."

He was still panting and bent over again, attempting to gain some control over his still laboured breathing. This short-range radio would not reach Section Intelligence Headquarters. His only hope was that the third unit was in the area.

"Any Three-Zero call sign, over."

Silence...

"Any fucking Three-Zero call sign in the area? We're in deep shit here, over."

His radio finally crackled a response. *"Three-Zero-Bravo, this is Three-Zero-Charlie. With you in figures five. Sitrep, over."*

The second boot struck Bradley in the stomach making him fold up, pulling his body into a foetal position, desperate to protect the vulnerable parts of his anatomy. He felt a boot striking the side of his head, just above his right eye, making him yelp involuntarily. He pulled his arms and legs in even more tightly, fear now making him retch as the Soviet soldiers continued with their punches and kicks desperately attempting to drag his arms out and get hold of the camera, he was protecting beneath him. His biggest fear was not the pummelling he was experiencing, although he was concerned about receiving a major injury, but a fear of being dragged into the Soviet camp, lost to political bargaining. While they fought over his release, he would be at the mercy of the Russian intelligence department. He wasn't sure why he was bothering. The film was blank, a fresh one he had put in earlier in the day. Routine, so they were ready for any troop movement they came across. Bradley always put the used film canisters in a small pull-string bag beneath his seat. It was safe for the moment. He had clocked at least three KGB uniformed troops amongst the throng of motor rifle and tank troops.

A boot struck his thigh, a numbing pain flowing down his leg before it froze, deadened. They clawed at his arms, desperate to pull them free of his body, releasing the camera he had been holding when they had dragged him from the vehicle. He pulled it in even tighter as another boot struck his chest, the pain unbearable as the boot rode up his broken rib, causing Bradley to move his free hand to the new source of pain. This was the opening the dozen or so attackers had been waiting for. Getting a better grip on his arms, they yanked them out, jolting his right shoulder painfully. They clawed at the camera, eventually pulling it free with a cry of victory, and the babble of guttural voices increased. Looking into their leering faces, the occasional gold-cap toothed smile, Bradley could see other military onlookers. He couldn't estimate the numbers at the time, but he would learn later that up to twenty Soviet soldiers, including a number of KGB, had been involved in the assault.

Suddenly, the surrounding troops moved apart. Jacko with his skinny frame found the strength to thrust them aside. A Soviet officer was seen sidling away, heading in the direction of the Soviet camp.

"Fuck. You OK?" Jacko reached down to help Bradley up.

"Yes, but they got the camera."

"I know. I saw them ripping the film out. No good to them though." Jacko smiled. "I saw you change the film." He steadied Bradley, pulling his arm over his shoulder as he could see he was unsteady on his feet.

"How about the Rover?"

"It's fine. The Sovs didn't bother with it. They were more interested in you. God, you'll have a nice shiner on your left eye tomorrow."

79

Bradley looked about him and could see a second Range Rover parked behind the white Lada and a Gaz-66 behind that. He suddenly crumpled and groaned.

"You OK? Stupid question, I know."

"Just hurts like hell."

As Jacko helped Bradley who was still unsteady on his feet, his body shaking, shock setting in, towards the second Range Rover, they saw the red beret of a Royal Military Police officer and an accompanying interpreter.

"Thank God," uttered Bradley. "Thank God."

Chapter 13

Inner German Border. 8 June 1984. The Red Effect – 4 Weeks
Keifer crouched down behind the sparse hedgerow, pulling his fiancée in close. He felt her shaking.

"I'm scared, Keifer, really scared."

He pulled her in even closer. "It's OK, I promise you. We'll make it."

"How far have we left to go?"

"About three kilometres, sweetheart. It's not far now."

"I'm tired, Keifer. I didn't get any sleep last night."

"Me neither," he said with a soft chuckle. "But once we're in the West, you can have all the sleep you want. I'll even bring you breakfast in bed: Westphalian ham, Gouda cheese, fresh bread rolls and some real coffee."

He saw the whiteness of her teeth as she smiled. One of his attributes was being able to make her feel good, no matter what the circumstances. She squeezed his arm. He had such confidence and instilled that confidence within her.

Keifer Freeh was twenty-two years old, an electronics student living in the German Democratic Republic, East Germany. His fiancée Adali Keller was more into literature and history, and longed for the day when she could have access to the books she had heard were freely available to everyone who lived in the West. They both lived in the small village of Lüttow, about fifty kilometres south-east of Lubeck and about seventy to eighty kilometres east of Hamburg in the Federal Republic of Germany. They were a mere two kilometres from their home now. Their village was just outside the five-kilometre wide *Sperrzone*, the restricted zone. But, at this moment in time, they were well and truly inside the highly protected area of the Inner German Border, the boundary between East and West Germany; patrolled by guards with dogs, mobile patrols, and, yesterday, they were overflown by a Hoplite, a small reconnaissance helicopter. Both had been in the *Sperrzone* all night, Keifer insisting that they become acclimatised to the area, familiarising themselves with the sounds and smells and raising their awareness of any activity that might occur around them. He was also concerned about trying to cover the full seven-kilometre trek to the border in just one night. It would push them too hard, particularly Adali, causing them to potentially make mistakes.

It was 8 June 1984. Keifer had led them both from the village into the zone the previous night where they had lain up in hiding during the latter part of the night. Then they spent the entire day hidden from the authorities. Keifer had done his eighteen-months conscription in the NVA, the *National Volks Armee*, and had hated every minute of it. But a switch had been flicked inside his head, and, one night, he and Adali decided that they'd had enough and wanted to escape to the West, to perceived freedom. So, he used his time in the army well: to hone his skills, learn the art of camouflage, deception and moving quietly, and, more importantly, how the NVA functioned. Using the premise that he was potentially interested in joining the *Grenztruppen der DDR*, the border guards, he learnt as much as he could about their organisation, how they operated, what border protection systems were in use. He proved to be such a competent soldier that the hierarchy tried to persuade him to make a career in the forces and were most put out when he declined. He was using some of the art of concealment he had learned during his training now. Both he and Adali wore home-made ghillie suits. Constructed by Adali, under the guidance of her fiancé, they consisted of dark green, thin cotton material, covered in netting of the same dimensions, with strips of light and dark cloth knotted to it. Although not perfect, when they lay on the ground close together next to some undergrowth or tall grasses, the edges of the ghillie spread out about them, they were well hidden. Keifer had even left both suits out in the rain for a month to weather and blend in even further with the countryside they would be hiding in. Applying a healthy dose of manure, much to Adali's distaste, completed the picture and ensured it smelled even less like a man-made outfit. The five-foot-four, slim, blonde East German National was into nail varnish, nice clothes and fluffy teddy bears. A rotten, stinking ghillie suit didn't quite go with that image, but she persevered, trusting Keifer's instinct that it would help them escape discovery.

Keifer shifted. "We need to move now, OK?"

He heard her sigh. "I can't do this, I just can't. I'm cold, tired, I want a pee and I stink."

He gripped her face gently between his two hands and pulled her in close to him. He could feel the wetness around her eyes where she had been crying and he kissed them, tasting the salty tears. "We...can...do...this. We can't turn back. If we go back now, there is a greater chance that we'll get caught than if we continue. If we turn around now, Adali, we will get caught."

He felt her head nod slightly.

"Right. I'll check the area; you take a pee. OK?"

She responded with a barely audible whisper. "Yes..."

Keifer moved away and did a complete 360-degree circuit of their position before returning. "All done?"

"Yes."

"OK. Move along the shrubs for about twenty metres and wait for me there. I will be right with you. Where did you pee?"

Had it been daylight, he would have seen her blush. "Over there, to your left."

"Start moving. I'll be right with you."

She moved off and he pulled the side of his ghillie suit up onto his shoulder, giving him access to the small rucksack on his back underneath. Reaching behind with his right arm, he awkwardly pulled a small plastic bottle, a spray bottle containing a mixture of water and ammonia, from the side pocket. He pumped the trigger until there was a steady spray of the repulsive- smelling liquid cascading over the area that Adali had just used for her toiletry needs and the area where they had spent the night. The pungent smell made him wince. The idea was that it would mask their trail from any dogs the guards might take on patrol with them. He moved backwards slowly, at a crouch, spraying the ground behind him until he bumped into his fiancée who was stationary, waiting for him.

He checked the immediate area and found a gap in the sparse shrubbery where they could easily pass through, pulling it apart as Adali pushed through it. He sprayed the side they had just left then moved about two metres to the right, north-west, until he came upon a stretch of patchy shrubbery that disappeared in the darkness towards the south-west, heading deeper into the *Sperrzone*.

The two men walked along the grassed area in between the signal fence to their right and the dog run on the left.

"Your dog really bad then, Gerhard?"

"Yes," responded the thirty-one year-old border guard, part of the infamous *Grenztruppen der DDR*. "He's being kept inside. The vet's concerned about him. I am as well."

"I can tell." His comrade Burlin Holzmann, also a border guard, laughed. He was much younger than his companion, only twenty-three years of age, and had been in the job for less than a year. "We see you walking him up and down rather than leaving him chained up on the dog run."

"It's cruel, Burlin, leaving them tied up like that." Gerhard's voice rose passionately. "Tied to a chain for twenty-four hours a day, seven days a week, in all weathers and only a box to sleep in."

"You've always been soft towards them. Someone told me you took one home rather than let it be put down."

Gerhard turned towards his companion and slapped him on the back. "He makes a great house dog, and God help anyone who tries to break in." He chuckled. "They have a shit life though." He patted the pockets of his splinter-pattern tunic top then rummaged through each one of the four pockets. He and his companion were dressed alike: splinter-pattern tunic top, with a black belt around the middle, over the top of matching combat trousers and black three-quarter-length black boots. They also wore soft forage caps, some basic skeleton webbing, and a knife and scabbard. Their uniform was very similar to that of soldiers in the National Volksarmee. The only thing that differentiated them from the East German Army were the green tabs on their shoulders marking them out as *Grenztruppen der DDR*. Each had an MPiK Kalashnikov automatic rifle slung over their shoulder.

"Can't you find your cigarettes, Gerhard? You know the leutnant doesn't like you smoking when on patrol."

"Bugger the leutnant, bugger them all. I need a smoke."

"Twenty minutes and we'll be at the bunker. You can sneak one there."

"Good idea, young Burlin, you're smarter than I thought. Anyway, they're all occupied down by the border crossing point."

"Probably. What's going on down there?"

Gerhard patted his pockets again, eventually finding the packet in his trouser pockets. "Here they bloody are. I'm not sure. But the Pionier Kompanie seem to be loosening some of the roadblocks and then placing them back."

"I saw that yesterday. They were digging up the Czech hedgehogs, freeing them from the concrete then putting them back."

"Crazy, the bloody lot of them. No point in having bloody great pieces of angle iron to stop vehicles if you can just lift them out of the way."

"Hmm, does seem a bit strange." Burlin took off his assault rifle and slung it over his other shoulder, quickly scanning the ground around him. Looking left, he could see the dog run and, beyond that, the patrol road; then the control strip: a freshly raked piece of ground that would easily show up footprints of anyone who tried to cross, even if they managed to miss the trip wire. The other side of the strip, two parallel fences, constructed from several overlapping, horizontal tiers of expanded steel mesh over twelve feet high, ran along the border. The inner fence was lined with SM-70s Splitter Mines, directional anti-personnel mines. Beyond those fences was the Federal Republic of Germany.

Ahead, about two hundred metres away, stood the *Beobachtungsturm* 11 (BT-11), a twelve-metre high, spindly tower made up of interlocking circles of three-centimetre-thick concrete laid on top of each other. On top, an octagonal observation building with glass windows giving a full 360-degree view of the surrounding area. Burlin shuddered at the thought of the times he had been up there on duty, knowing how unstable they were, a few having collapsed with borders guards still up top. To his right was the signal fence, *signalzaun*, a continuous expanded metal fence some several hundred kilometres long and two-metres high, lined with low-voltage electrified strands of wire. If an escapee touched or attempted to cut the strands of wire, an alarm would be activated, warning the border guards of their escape attempt.

Burlin nudged his comrade and indicated the tower up ahead. "I think the *Feldwebel* is up there tonight."

"He's in a bad mood again. Surprise, surprise."

They both unshouldered their weapons, put the slings around their necks, held their AKs in the ready position and pulled their uniforms into order. They became more alert the closer they got to the tower that dominated the immediate area and under the watchful eye of their senior NCO, who was no doubt watching them through his binoculars. Any minute now, they expected the one-thousand-watt searchlight to bathe them in a flood of light. They continued towards the tower where they would turn back and head south, and continue to patrol their sector of the *Schutzstreifen*, the heavily guarded protective strip that ran along the Inner German Border.

The two East German civilians crouched down at the edge of the border road that ran east to west where, north-west of their current position, it crossed the Inner German Border into West Germany, hopefully their final destination. The crossing point was lit up like a football stadium. This disturbed Keifer as the previous times he had reconnoitered the area the lighting had been fairly low-key. The crossing point was normally closed at night. He scanned the border crossing point with the binoculars he had purchased from a flea market. They were OK, apart from one of the lenses being slightly cloudy. Beneath the lights, he could pick out a number of vehicles: small utility vehicles, three trucks and some form of digger. The guards seemed to be furiously working on dismantling the border defences, but then putting them back into position. For one moment, he thought they may be dismantling the entire border, opening it up for free passage. They could then all pass freely into the West. He smiled to himself, knowing that premise was extremely unlikely.

They needed to move. They were well inside the *Sperrzone* now. Even though civilians were allowed in the area with a special permit, particularly those that lived within its confines, the couple would have great difficulty in explaining away their garb and being this close to the border. He whispered to his fiancée, "I've got my bearings, Addi. We need to head south a bit before we turn west again."

85

Adali shivered. Not from the cold. Although not warm, the cool air was not too harsh, but a thin layer of mist was forming around their feet. She shivered out of fear. They were in heavily guarded enemy territory now. That's how they saw the *Grenzer, Grenztruppen der DDR*: as the enemy.

"I'm so scared, Keifer." She gripped his arm tightly.

"It's OK, it's OK," he consoled her. "I know what I'm doing."

She peered into his blackened face; like hers, plastered in mud to cover the whiteness of their skin. The strength and confidence in her fiancé's features were obvious, the determination set. She relaxed slightly, intent on playing her part and not letting him down. Her Keifer would get them to the West and the freedom they sought. For the first time that night, she smiled. "I know. Let's go."

Keifer sprayed the area with his increasingly depleted bottle of ammonia spray and led them south. The area was quite damp, almost swamp-like in places, their footsteps sounding louder in their minds than they actually were in reality. There were numerous ditches, a metre deep in places, criss-crossing the area in lines east to west, a few running north to south. It was these that Keifer was using to aid their concealment as they moved closer and closer to the likely patrol areas. The ditches were too undulating and numerous to be patrolled easily, and probably too far away from the *Schutzstreifen* to receive constant attention.

They moved at a crouch along one of the ditches, their boots soaking wet, but their feet, although uncomfortable, were dry. Keifer's insistence that they wore a pair of thick socks, then a thin layer of waterproof plastic sheeting, followed by a second pair of thinner socks was paying off. Although in the long-term their feet would suffer badly, for now it was the best option. They came to a ditch that crossed in front of them, and he led them south before turning west again where they came to yet another junction.

He suddenly pulled her down next to him. He put his finger on her mouth. "Shush." He cocked his ears and listened; then strained to see through the darkness for any sign of movement. Nothing; it was a false alarm. They crept forward, Keifer keeping the pace slow the nearer they got to the death strip. They stopped again and Keifer checked his luminous watch. Two twenty. He was pleased with the progress they were making. He wanted them to get to the first of the fences by three, the time when most individuals would be at their lowest ebb. Having been up for most of the night, sleep would be slowly dragging at the guards' eyelids, and the temptation to close them for a few moments would be alluring, with the probability that sleep would overcome them completely. Or they would find somewhere to hide from their NCOs or officers and take a breather from the constant boredom of patrolling the seemingly never-ending border.

"Are you ready?" Keifer whispered to Adali.

She didn't verbally respond, but he sensed her head nodding in reply.

He put his mouth up against her ear. "We need to move really slowly now. The signal fence can't be far away."

She nodded again, and he helped her up. He felt his heart suddenly beat faster, panic welling up inside him, doubts flooding his mind, but he quickly quashed them. He had planned it meticulously, spending night after night in the *Sperrzone*, scrutinising every aspect of the border and its defences, making sketches of the main features of the daunting barrier ahead of them; a huge risk had he been caught with them in his possession. But, as a result of being able to study them in the relative safety of his home, he had a good perspective on what lay ahead of them both.

He tugged gently on Adali's arm and, after another twenty minutes making their way in the dark, they came to the edge of the final ditch. Once they left the safety of the channel, they would be extremely exposed: the ground fairly flat and free of undergrowth and shrubbery.

"You wait here, OK?"

"What happens now?" she whispered back.

"I'm going to move up to the signal fence, scout around and then come back for you."

"Don't be long. I'm really, really frightened."

"I won't, Addi." He put his arm around her shoulder and squeezed her gently. Letting go of her, he hoisted his rucksack higher up onto his shoulders and headed across the open ground, crouching as low as he possibly could. It wasn't long before he could see the dim shape of the fence ahead, the dark line of the mesh and the darker, evenly spaced, thicker vertical posts that held it up. He moved right up to it then lay down on the ground. He looked to his left and right. It was quiet apart from the occasional sound drifting across from the activity at the border crossing. The tower was on the other side of the fence, about a hundred and fifty metres off to the right. The one to the left was even further away. They wouldn't be able to see him though, unless they used the powerful one-thousand-watt searchlight that was available to the guards on the tower.

He examined the fence. He had been this close to it before, but on his own, on one of his reconnaissance trips. two-metre-high concrete posts supported a mesh fence with half a dozen barbed wire strands, attached to insulators, running along the top. Two pieces of angle iron, at a forty-five-degree angle, held them up and out, making it impossible to climb over without catching them. A further two lengths of wire ran along the mesh. All the wires were linked to an alarm system. If he caught, moved or tried to cut the wires, an alarm would be activated warning the border guards that the fence had been breached.

Keifer heaved his ghillie up, shrugged the bag off his shoulders, took out the wire-cutters from one of the pouches and started to cut the mesh just above the kickboard that ran along the bottom. He moved quickly; the clock was ticking. He stopped after every minute or so to listen and look about him. He knew the risk was great: a guard, or even one of the dogs, hearing the snip of the cutters. Keifer had selected a spot in between two of the dog runs which were fortunately a hundred metres apart. A westerly wind would help to keep his scent away from the dogs. He had two pairs of wire-cutters and had made sure they were powerful and very sharp. Wrapping a cloth around the blade each time, he made a cut, hoping it would deaden some of the sound. *Snip, snip, snip, snip.* Pause, look and listen. *Snip, snip, snip, snip.* Pause.

Once he had finished, the fence was cut along the bottom and along two vertical strips, just under a metre high and about two-thirds of a metre wide. When pulled up, the bend at the bottom was just below the first of the sensor wires. He took a quick look around then headed back to where Adali would be lying low. He was sure she would be worried.

Eventually he found the ditch and heard Adali's trembling voice call out to him. "Is that you, Keifer?"

He smiled at the naivety of the question. Had it not been him, she would now be a prisoner.

"Yes. Come on, we need to go."

Gripping her wrist, he helped her up and, keeping a hold of her hand, led her towards the signal fence. He soon found the place where he had prepared it. Gesturing for Adali to lie down, he proceeded to ease the section of wire upwards, pulling it towards him first so it bowed, as he had practised at home, then pulling up over the alarmed wire. Taking the thin strips of wire from between his teeth, he wrapped them around the recently cut edge, securing it to the main fence. He was ready.

Adali lay on her back and shuffled through the gap, Keifer placing one of his hands on her feet to give her some purchase, watching the alarmed wire at all times. Once she was through, he did the same. The wire was pulled back down and secured at the bottom and the sides with the twists of thin wire. Not perfect, but it was better than leaving a gaping hole. There was no time to waste. They were now in the *Schutzstreifen*, the heavily guarded protective strip, nearly a thousand metres wide. He rifled through his rucksack and took hold of a sealed plastic bag and pulled it out, half opening it to check on its contents:

heavily drugged pieces of lean meat. He had ground up over four dozen of his mother's sleeping pills and secreted the powder into sections of the steak. They walked slowly across the strip, not wanting any sudden movement to be noticed by a sleepy guard. Keifer steered them at an angle, heading for the dog run he thought would be somewhere to his right. He just hoped they could get close enough to throw the baited feast before the dog smelled or heard the two of them approach.

The darker shadow of the dog run slowly became apparent, the worn track where the dog had run up and down day after day standing out from the grassed area either side. Keifer could see the larger shape of the kennel; perhaps the dog was asleep in there. They crept closer, Keifer constantly scanning the area, looking for patrolling vehicles or guards, the searchlight from the tower, or the sound of shouts or sirens. Arriving at the kennel, there was no sight nor sound of the dog. Keifer was puzzled. Maybe luck was on their side. The collar, attached to a length of thin chain, which in turn was linked to the cable that ran the full length of the one-hundred-metre run, was lying on the ground next to the dog's home. He had a moment of panic. Perhaps the dog had been let loose and was running wild. He removed the meat from the packaging and tossed it into the kennel, just in case it returned. Checking his watch, three ten, he tugged at Adali's arm and they moved to the next barrier that awaited them. Arriving at the *kolonenweg*, two parallel lines of small, perforated blocks of concrete embedded into the earth, ensuring the patrol road was accessible all year round, they quickly crossed it. Looking about him, Keifer could see a faint glow of light to the north, where he saw the activity at the border earlier in the morning. Almost immediately the other side of the road was the control strip, a line of bare earth that ran in between the patrol road and the first of the main fences. It was raked regularly, ensuring anyone crossing it would leave a trail of footprints, clearly visible for the guards to see as they patrolled past.

Keifer knew that, once they stepped onto the strip, they were committed to seeing it through. There would be no turning back. He turned to Adali and whispered, "Keep directly behind me. We'll be moving slowly." He squeezed her hand in encouragement then pulled out a metre-long strip of flexible plastic that had been secured to the outside of his rucksack. At the end, the strip tapered into almost nothing and would bend at the slightest touch. He held it out in front of him at a narrow angle, almost vertical, and started off at a steady pace across the death strip, Adali close behind him, moving west towards the metal fence opposite, the penultimate barrier in their quest for freedom. The tip of the home-made detector was held so it was about a centimetre off the ground and about ten centimetres out in front of his feet. He moved forward slowly, holding the thicker end of the diviner loosely in his hand, waiting for the sudden twitch as it came up against a tripwire. If triggered, the tripwire would initiate a flare close by, illuminating the entire area, bathing it in a yellow light, indicating to the border guards that an escapee, or an animal, had crossed the control strip. The searchlight would be switched on instantly, seeking them out. Guards, and possibly a vehicle, would be dispatched to the source of the flare where only capture or death awaited the *Republikflüchtiger*, Republic deserter. In the last ten years, over two thousand had fled East Germany, escaping across the border, but hundreds had been killed in the attempt.

Keifer felt a sudden pressure on his fingers and immediately withdrew the probe, before moving it forward again with extreme care until it came up against the tripwire. He felt Adali close behind him and eased her back gently before crouching down to confirm that it was indeed a tripwire. He felt a chill as he disturbed the fine mist that blanketed the ground around his feet. He prayed for dense fog but knew that would be too much to ask for. He felt around with the tips of his fingers until they touched the thin, taut wire that was only a few centimetres off the ground. He whispered instructions into Adali's ear, rallying her at the same time. Both stepped over the tripwire carefully before making their way to the other side of the strip, Keifer checking for further traps, coming up against the most daunting barrier of all: the four-metre-high metal fence. It was formidable, constructed from several overlapping, horizontal tiers of expanded steel-mesh fencing.

Keifer was confident about scaling the fence, but less confident about Adali. He indicated for her to crouch down, the mist swirling about her as she disturbed it. They both removed their ghillie suits. They had served their purpose and would just hinder the rest of their progress. Speed and agility were of the essence now. Once they were discarded, he rummaged in his rucksack again and removed the contents he would need next. Not only was the fence forbidding but it had added danger. Mines! He undid the drawstring on the soft pouch and opened it up, removing the collection of wires and the device they were attached to, something he had built weeks earlier. Copper wire coiled around a magnet taped up and connected, by bell wire, to a home-made circuit board of transistors, capacitors and diodes powered by a nine-volt battery. A set of earphones, from his personal transistor radio and which would receive the feedback for him to listen to, completed the gadget.

He told Adali to wait where she was and plugged the earphones into his ears, turning on the detector. There was a satisfying hum transmitted through to his eardrums followed by a higher-pitched tone as he held the magnet closer to the fence. Holding the device about fifteen-centimetres away from the fence, he slowly waved it up and down as he moved along it until he found what he was looking for, the squealing in his ears signalling the discovery of a Splitter mine. He could just make out the darker shadow of the cone-shaped mine. The SM-70 was a directional anti-personnel mine. Activated by a tripwire connected to a firing mechanism, once detonated, the cone-shaped charge, filled with 110 grams of TNT, imbedded with eighty small, sharp-edged cubes of steel, would explode and spray its deadly load along the line of the fence with a lethal range of over thirty metres. Sixty thousand of these deadly Soviet-made mines had been laid along the Inner German Border. Other anti-personnel mines, over one million, had been laid along the border to deter escapers. Keifer couldn't dismantle it, he didn't know how, but at least he could ensure they were to the left and at the furthest distance from SM-70 further to the south.

He went back to get Adali and walked her to the point where they would climb over. Picking up the rucksack again, he removed the next, and last, of the items they would need to continue their journey.

"Here's your overshoes. Make sure your boots are laced up tight before you put them on. Once the overshoes are on, make sure they're tight as well. If they're loose, it will make it harder to climb."

"Check them for me when I'm done," she suggested, a tremble in her voice.

"We'll check each others, OK?" he said with a smile and a sound of confidence in his voice, although doubts were starting to cloud his thoughts.

Pushing the dark notions aside, he bent down to sort out his own boots. There were two straps: one went over the top of the front of his foot then under the sole, the other just in front of the ankle, wrapping around his foot beneath the arch. Both affixed on one side to a third strap that circuited the entire diameter of the edge of the boot's sole, supported behind the heel. A buckle on each strap connected them, securing them to his boot. At the toe, a hook jutted out. He tightened the buckle of the single strap that circuited his boot then the two buckles of the upper straps, tugging them hard to ensure they wouldn't slip when he put his full weight on the hooks. The holes in the fence were deliberately made too small to allow a foot or hand to get a grip and climb. The hooks were the only solution he could think of. It was too strong to cut through or pull the overlapping layers apart, and it was sunk into the ground preventing an escapee from easily tunnelling underneath it. He did the same with his second boot then made sure

Adali's were fitted correctly and were secure. They both faced the fence, ready for the climb, a small bale hook in each hand.

"You go first, Addi. Don't forget to keep your body away from the wires, OK? Keep that bum of yours stuck out. Don't catch it with your boots or hooks. I'll help you up."

She didn't respond. Had it been daylight, he would have seen her face frozen in fear. But, behind her dilated pupils, there was a determination to see it through; a resolution not to let her fiancé down, to start their new life in the West.

She went first, throwing her right arm up, followed by her left and hooking the fence with both. She gripped the wooden toggles tightly until her knuckles were white and lifted her right leg. Guided by Keifer, hooking the boot into the fence, she heaved herself up. With Keifer's hands either side of her slim hips, his shoulder providing additional leverage, she brought up her left boot. Clinging on and jutting outwards, avoiding the double strand of wire, supported by fifteen-centimetre prongs, in front of her. One at a time, she unhooked each hand and extended them further up the four-metre fence, straightening her knees, her fiancé ensuring they didn't touch the wires. Again, guided by Keifer, she lifted her feet over the wires, eventually above and free of them, her head less than two-metres from the top. He urged her on and started the climb himself, hanging outwards to avoid the tripwires that could easily set off the deadly mines. It took them twenty minutes to get over the top. Suddenly he heard her yelp. He jerked his head down and saw her left leg and arm flaying about, free of the fence, eventually swinging back crashing into it, the wires vibrating on the other side from the force of the strike. The silence was sudden, both breathing deeply, ears pricked for the sound of discovery.

"Quickly, we need to get down now!" hissed Keifer.

Adali climbed down, lowering her tired body the last metre, collapsing to the damp, grassy earth in exhaustion.

Keifer crouched down beside her. "Come on, Addi, we need to move. One fence left; then it's freedom."

The two border guards had reversed direction and were now patrolling south again, their ultimate destination a concrete bunker overlooking the control strip where Becker could finally partake in the smoke, he was so desperate for. They were so occupied in their heated debate about whether Magdeburg was worth a weekend away that they missed the darker patch of footprints that snaked across the raked control strip, partially hidden by the low-lying mist.

Keifer and Adali were now at the last obstacle: just one fence keeping them from escape. Once across, they would be able to sprint for the freedom they had talked about incessantly for months. There were no mines on this fence. It was just a case of clambering over it, using their special boots and hooks, and dropping down the other side. Keifer led the way this time and was quickly at the top, watching Adali as she soon joined him there. He climbed down and dropped the last metre, turning round ready to support his fiancée as she still had over two metres to go before she too could put her feet on solid ground. He felt good. All his meticulous planning and preparation had paid off. They were close to setting foot in the Federal Republic of Germany. She removed the left-hand bale hook from the fence, then her left boot hook and lowered both before again placing the two spikes into the small gaps lower down in the fence. Trusting in the security of her position, Adali then loosened and released her right hand and foot and repositioned them lower down. As she did so, the hook of her left boot, which had only just tagged the join of the overlapping fences, suddenly gave way unexpectedly. With most of her weight still on her left leg, it shot downwards. The sudden shock caused her to let go of the left bale hook as she swung outwards in a half-star shape, left arm and leg adrift. The force of the unexpected move twisted her right ankle and wrist, the bale hook was forced from her right hand, and her body arced downwards. Keifer rushed to help arrest her downward fall as her upper body slowly passed the one boot that was still attached. He grabbed for her outflung arm as it sped past, slowing her fall slightly, but not enough as, now upside down, he heard the sickening crack of her shattered ankle still trapped in the fence above her. A long, drawn-out scream of agony emanated from her pained mouth and, along with the rattle of the fence as she thudded against it, broke the silence.

Both Becker and Holzmann snapped their heads round at the sound of the blood-curdling scream, followed by the noise of the reverberating fence. With assault rifles unslung, they ran across the control strip, tripping a flare as they went, heading for the point where they thought the sound had come from. As a consequence of the dazzling light, they could see two shadowy figures on the other side of the outer fence. Fear suddenly welled up inside Becker, not because of the escapees but because the two figures had got that far without being discovered at the same time as he and his companion were patrolling the fence. There would be consequences when this was all over. Becker cocked his rifle, raised it at an angle and fired two shots into the air.

"*Halten sie, halten sie,*" he bellowed at the top of his voice.

"Shall we open fire on them?" asked a panicky Holzmann, fumbling with his AK, eventually managing to cock it and put a round up the spout.

"Don't be stupid, Burlin. There's two bloody fences in the way."

Crack. Crack. "*Halten sie, halten sie,*" he called again after firing two more shots into the air.

The lieutenant in command of this section of the wire was talking to his opposite number in command of the engineers, trying to ascertain what the point was of their current activity. Why were they effectively dismantling the border crossing, yet making it look fully functional? Although being evasive with his answers, the engineer actually had no idea himself. He had been given his orders and ordered not to discuss their activities with anyone. In fact, his engineers and the border guards in this vicinity had been confined to barracks, unless on duty.

Both started when they saw a flare burst into light, closely followed by the sound of two gunshots. The one-thousand-watt beam of the *suchscheinwerfer* (searchlight) stabbed the darkness and was immediately rotated around, by the tower guards, towards the sound of the gunfire. It immediately bathed the two escapees in its glow. One, a young man, suddenly blinded by the intense glare, shielded his eyes with his arm. The other, in front of him, was suspended from the fence, upside down, her twisted leg the only thing holding her up.

"Baer, the Jeep!" yelled the *Grenzer* leutnant. "*Schnell!*"

The Unterfeld junior sergeant ran for the Jeep, practically throwing himself into the driver's seat, and turned the ignition, the engine roaring into life as he gunned it. He called to two other border guards to join him. The leutnant dropped down into the passenger seat and slapped the dashboard. "Go, go!"

He undid his holster and pulled out his service pistol, cocking the weapon. The two *grenzer* in the back did the same with their AKs. They sped off, heading north along the patrol road then turned left onto the road that would take them across the border. A guard at the border crossing point lifted the barrier and the Jeep shot past, heading west towards the currently unmanned West German border control. The Jeep raced through the channel, smoke belching from its exhaust as it tore along the road, passing the death strip, the first fence and, finally, the last fence. The driver swerved left and bounced onto the verge that would take them around the unmanned West German barrier which, once passed, would allow the Jeep to swing right, back onto the road. The occupants searched ahead and to the left, looking for any signs of the escapees.

Crack. Crack.

"Foot down!"

"I'm going as fast as I can, sir."

"Left, left, down the track."

The Jeep turned south, leaving the road, and traversed left, heading for a rough track that ran alongside the outer East German border fence. The vehicle travelled down the bumpy track that was barely inside the East German border, running parallel with the fence line; to their right, another patrol road used by the West German border patrols: either the *Bundesgrenzschutz* (BGS), the Federal Border Protection, or even by military forces from the British Army of the Rhine or the British Frontier Service. The beam of the Jeep's headlights danced across the landscape, like theatre lights, picking out elements of the route and border barricade before being whipped elsewhere as the vehicle careered erratically down the track. The occupants were jolted from side to side as the *Grenzer* raced to head off the escapees.

Hubert Schiffer put the binoculars back into the car through the driver's open window and was about to open the door and climb back in when...*Crack. Crack.*

Mauer, who was sitting in the passenger seat, threw the door open. "Bloody hell, what was that?" He went to get out.

Schiffer pulled the driver's door open, moved the binoculars to the dashboard, and dropped into his seat. "Get back in, Nicklas!" he called urgently. "It's an escape. Sounds like it came from the south."

His colleague slammed his door shut and Schiffer revved the engine. The front wheels spun as he accelerated along the patrol road towards the sound of the gunfire. *Crack. Crack.*

"I think you could be right, Hubert." Mauer pulled out his service pistol, released the magazine, checked the rounds and slotted it back in with a click. Then, pulling back on the working parts, it loaded one of the eight 9mm rounds into the breech.

Schiffer looked across at his partner. "You won't need that. They don't come across the border."

"Even after an escapee?"

"No. I've seen a couple and the *Grenzer* always stay over on their side."

"But doesn't part of the land on this side of the fence belong to the DDR?"

"I know."

"What's that?" Mauer pointed at a pair of headlights running parallel to them, but slowly gaining ground.

Schiffer groaned. "Oh God, that doesn't look good."

Zip, zip. Two further bullets zipped above the heads of the young couple, followed by two cracks from the assault rifles behind them. Keifer supported Adali's body as best he could while he undid the straps of the overboot. The hook trapping her foot needed to be released. She shifted slightly and whimpered as the first buckle was released. As the last buckle was detached, her boot now free of its grip, she crashed to the ground in a heap, a long wail of pain escaping her lips. Keifer knew they had to move. Although they were on the far side of the fence, they still had at least forty or fifty metres to the actual FRG border.

"Come on, Addi, we have to move."

Her eyes were full of tears, the pain of her shattered ankle imprinted on her face. "I can't, it's so painful."

"Fifty metres, Addi, fifty metres. That's all."

"I can't..."

He pushed his hands beneath her armpits and heaved her up, turning her slightly so he could position his shoulder beneath her arm and pull it around his neck. She screamed again as her fractured ankle dragged along the ground. He hoisted her higher up onto his shoulder and placed his left hand around her waist, her right arm around his neck, supporting as much of her weight as he could. He shuffled them both forward and she hopped on one foot as best she could, although her ankle was swelling rapidly as she groaned with pain every time her ankle was jolted. They had gone no more than twenty metres when they were both suddenly dazzled by headlights.

"There they are!" called Baer. He slammed on the brakes and the Jeep slid to a halt on the stony ground. All four were out in seconds, rifles at the ready.

"*Halten sie, halten sie! Grenztruppen der DDR. Halten sie!*" the *Grenzer* leutnant bellowed.

Schiffer swerved the police car left. The binoculars slid along the dashboard, hit the other end and clattered to the floor, settling in the passenger footwell by Mauer's feet. "Get ready," he shouted, too loudly. The adrenalin was pumping. Their car headlights picked out the two East Germans. One seemed to be supporting the other as they stumbled south attempting to put some distance between themselves and the DDR Jeep. Both policemen got out of the car, engine still running, doors left ajar, headlights behind them projecting their shadows ahead as they strode forward, guns at the ready, to intercept the East German border guards who were now walking quickly towards the young couple.

Schiffer challenged the *Grenzer*, ordering them to halt. His pistol was drawn, held in both hands, pointing towards the uniformed men who were now no more than fifteen metres away. His knees slightly bent, arms held out in front of him, steadying his breathing, locking his body into position, he was ready to fire. Sensing his partner Mauer to his left, he challenged them again. He could see the escapees out of the corner of his right eye, lit up by the DDR Jeep. He challenged them yet again.

Crack, crack...Crack, crack.

Schiffer looked in the direction of the young couple and saw the taller of the two slump forward.

Crack...crack.

The one being supported jerked twice then fell forward. Two further shots and it was all over.

Schiffer screamed at them; fired two shots over the guards' heads. When he saw Mauer start to move forward shouting obscenities, waving his pistol about in front of him, he quickly moved in his direction to restrain him as the GDR Jeep pulled forward to recover the bodies.

He grabbed his partner, holding him back, knowing it was all too late for the young couple. "Bastards, bastards, bastards," screamed Mauer.

Chapter 14

There is an alarming curtain of silence from the Western European and American press as the biggest Soviet military exercise since World War Two is conducted close to the Inner German Border. Even the Federal Republic of Germany seems silent as these threatening Soviet military manoeuvres are carried out right on their doorstep. Exercise Hammer 84, a practice assault on NATO and the West, an attack that is considered as a defensive measure against a potential threat from the so-called belligerent West Germany.

Business as usual claim the Bonn defence ministry who clearly have no concerns over twenty Soviet divisions playing war games on their doorstep, stating that they are merely staff-based war games. Even senior NATO commanders are playing it down, see no Russians, hear no Russians. Just look at recent history. Fall Gelb, the Blitzkrieg attack on France and the low countries by over a million Wehrmacht troops in 1940, followed by Operation Barbarossa, the massive assault on the Soviet Union that took the entire world by surprise. Should we be worried?

Die Wahrheit, 25 June 1984

10ᵗʰ Guards Tank Division, Lindenwald, East Germany. 26 June 1984. The Red Effect −9 Days

Pushkin lifted the camouflage netting that had been spread over and around the T80BK, the command tank of the 2nd Battalion of the 62nd Guards Tank Regiment. Slender logs, usually carried on the back of the tank, had been used as props to keep the netting off the bulk of the tank, ensuring the crew had the freedom to move around and also disguising its shape. They were part of a much bigger force: 10 Guards Tank Division of 3 Shock Army. The regiment had moved into position the previous night and, after a few minor reshuffles to accommodate the full regiment of over ninety tanks, all they could do now was wait for further orders from regimental or divisional command. The unit had completed some minor manoeuvres as part of Exercise Hammer 84 but had now been designated as an army reserve and were to refit, refuel and arm; then await further orders. What surprised Colonel Oleg Pushkin, commander of the 62nd GTR, the most was the fact they were being fully armed and to a war-level status. He had received stocks of APFSDS (Armour-Piercing Fin-Stabilised Discarding Sabot), HE (High Explosive) fragmentation, HEAT (High-Explosive Anti-Tank), and even two of the new Kobra 9M112M tank-launched missiles for each of his

T80s. With thirty-eight main gun rounds, 300 rounds for the 12.7mm NSVT, anti-aircraft gun, and 1,250 rounds for the 7.62mm co-axial machine gun, they were in effect ready to go to battle. The dilemma that crossed Pushkin's mind was: with whom? There had been some unrest in Poland: labour strikes and union demonstrations. He hoped his unit wasn't going to be used to suppress the inhabitants of what was supposed to be an ally of the Soviet Union and a key member of the Warsaw Pact. More and more supplies had arrived for the regiment and the division under the cover of darkness. With plenty of fuel, ammunition and food for the men, they were capable of sustaining a number of days in battle, if required.

Pushkin clambered onto the glacis of the command tank, and a head immediately popped out of the tank commander's hatch to greet him.

"Sir. For what reason are we owed this honour of a visit?" asked Lieutenant Colonel Trusov.

"Making sure your bloody tankers have camouflaged their vehicles properly, Pavel."

"I suspected you'd be doing your rounds, sir, so I've already been around kicking arses." He laughed.

Pushkin clambered up the frontal armour, right of the barrel, and squatted down by the turret, in front of the smoke dischargers. "I knew you'd be on the ball."

"So, what the fuck's going on then, sir? The entire bloody division is crammed into this area. Why have we been pulled out of Exercise *молот 84*?"

During the last forty-eight hours, 10 Guards Tank Division (Uralsko-Lvovskaya Division), had moved in its entirety into the area of Lindenwald, East Germany, and were now spread out over an area of fifteen square kilometres. 62nd GTR was in the centre of the forest, 61st GTR to the north, and 63rd GTR somewhere to the north-west. Over 300 main battle tanks and their supporting units were cammed up waiting for further orders. The area occupied by the full division was situated thirty-kilometres north-west of the city of Magdeburg. Sometimes the crews could smell the smog on the breeze, coming from the direction of the industrialised city. With winter fires, the city was often covered in a blanket of thick, foul-smelling smog. To their south-east was Colbitz and Lindhurst, south-west Haldensleben, north-west Letjungen and, to the north-east, Ludentz. Directly north of them, south of Uchtspringe, a huge military training ground existed, the criss-cross tracks of heavy tank usage clearly visible from the air. A battered piece of ground, ten-kilometres long by five-kilometres wide, the division's units had often trained on there, the crews practising their skills at tank handling and the officers getting used to large-scale tank manoeuvres.

Pushkin held his hand up. "Hold up, hold up. The divisional commander will be briefing us later today or tomorrow. Perhaps we'll get more detail then. But in the meantime, for God's sake, be patient, Pavel."

"Poland?"

"I hope not. Unlikely." Pushkin shifted until he was more comfortable, sitting on the edge of the cold armour of the turret. "They would have chosen at least a motor rifle division for that. Our 248th MRR wouldn't be enough on its own."

"These monsters would soon put a stop to any of their tricks." Pavel laughed as he patted the solid steel of the turret.

"There wouldn't be any buildings left if these were let loose on the streets," responded Pushkin with a chuckle.

"Makes sense, I suppose. Infantry units would do better on the streets; the BMPs will give them plenty of support. Perhaps they just want our infantry to back up whoever gets the job."

"Maybe."

"Why have we got so much live ammo, though?" Pavel pointed through the turret hatch to the ammo bins below. "Christ, these bloody missiles cost a fortune."

"Reel it in, Pavel. You say too much sometimes. All will be revealed soon enough."

"I've only ever fired one of these missiles in the last twelve months."

"What's the status on your battalion?"

"Pretty good, sir. Thirty fully operational, one in maintenance."

"That's good."

"Most of the travel has been by road transport or rail. Plus, we've been taken out of the exercise early, so not surprising breakdowns are low." Trusov pulled a small flask from his pocket, unscrewed the top and offered it to his regimental commander. "It's good stuff, not that crap we're getting from supply."

"Don't let our beloved political officer hear you say that Pavel." Pushkin lowered his voice to a whisper.

"I know, I know, sir."

"Your mouth is going to be the death of you if you're not careful. And I mean that literally."

"I'll tone it down. Now, can I have my flask back, sir, before you drink it all?"

Pushkin took one last swig then passed it back. "You're right, it's pretty good stuff," he said, smacking his lips. "Talking of our beloved deputy divisional commander, I need to go and find him. He wants to go through the new announcements he's prepared for the troops."

"To our beloved Mother Russia," said Trusov, raising his flask.

"Make sure your men are up to speed, Pavel," Pushkin said sternly and slid down off the turret, bumped his way over the ERA (Explosive Reactive Armour) blocks and jumped off the front of the tank. He needed to seek out the deputy commander, the political officer, the deputy commander's responsible for 'technical' and 'rear', to get a quick update, and a fuller update from his divisional commander, Major General Abramov. Maybe they were finally going to find out what was in store for them.

12th Guards Tank Division, north-west of Gommern, East Germany. 25 June 1984. The Red Effect –9 Days

Fifty-kilometres away, another division belonging to 3 Shock Army, a key striking force of GSFG (the Group of Soviet Forces Germany), was settling down in an assembly area, their T64A tanks also cammed up amongst the forests chosen to hide them away from prying eyes. The forests were north-west of Gommern, about twenty-two kilometres east of the River Elbe. A group of Soviet officers were sitting around a mixture of temporary tables inside a large tent erected by the signals battalion headquarters. It had now been hijacked by the divisional commander of the 12th Guards Tank Division; a covered space where he could converse with his most senior combat officers. It was a select few. The commanders of his three tank regiments, the solitary motor rifle regiment and the 18th Independent Guards Reconnaissance Battalion. The other units had been excluded, along with the chief of staff, the political officer, who was also the deputy divisional commander, the other rear area commanders and the support arms. It wasn't a formal briefing; he just wanted to get some real feedback from his key unit commanders.

"I know you have lots of questions," stated the giant of a man who sat on a chair in front of them; a chair that creaked as a consequence of his weight every time he moved. The commander of the 12th Guards Tank Division, Major General Oleg Turbin, the 'Bear', was not overweight; far from it. He was just stocky, with a heavy, muscled, large frame. Many of his subordinates had felt the power of this man when they had failed to meet one of the tasks set by him. They did everything within their control to ensure there wasn't a second foul-up. "The truth is I don't know what's happening. For the moment, anyway. I have been ordered to secrete the division in the Lodderitzer Forest and await further orders. In the meantime, the division is to be made ready for full combat."

He lit another cigarette from the glowing stub in his hand before crushing the stub out on the table. Although not a chain-smoker, it was often difficult to identify a gap between each Belomorkanal brand, one of the strongest cigarettes in the eastern block, if not the world.

"Yuri, Rusian, Timur, have you started receiving fresh stocks of ammunition yet?"

Colonel Yuri Kharzin, Commander of the 48th Guards Tank Regiment, responded first. "Yes, Comrade General, we have a full load of main gun ammunition, along with rounds for the machine guns and our own personal sidearms."

"Fuel?"

"All tanked up, sir. I see there are POL bowsers in the vicinity as well, all with full loads."

"Yes, yes. Rusian, Timur, you as well?"

"Yes, Comrade General," they responded in unison; Commanders of the 332nd and 353rd Guards Tank Regiments respectively.

"Good, good. Akim, your foot sloggers ready?"

Akim Yermakion, Commander of the 200th Guards Motor Rifle Regiment laughed. As the only infantry unit alongside the three tank regiments, he was often at the butt end of their jokes; always being ribbed about his men being trench-diggers when in fact they had BMP2s, more than capable of keeping up with the tanks and could pack a punch themselves if needed. "Yes, Comrade General, but we are still short of spares for the BMPs."

"How many are operational?"

The young colonel, in his early thirties, referred to his notes. "All tanks are serviceable, and eighty-nine BMP are fully operational. Four BMP are operational, but in need minor repairs if we are to participate fully in whatever is expected of us, Comrade General. I can cannibalise a few to bring the rest up to scratch?"

"Definitely not!" Turbin thumped the table. "I want all vehicles in full-battle readiness, no exceptions. Make the lists available, and I will add my weight to your requests. We have orders from on high..."

"Absolutely, Comrade General."

A skinny figure in an ill-fitting officer's uniform, clearly tailored to fit his scrawny frame but failing badly, entered the tent. One of the junior officers gave up his seat for who was probably, next to their divisional commander, the most feared man in the unit: The Deputy Commander and Political Officer, Colonel Yolkin.

"Glad you could join us, Comrade Colonel. I was just getting an update from some of my officers."

"But is it not a full briefing, Comrade General? I was not informed."

"It is just an informal meeting, not a full briefing. Otherwise, the full divisional command would be here," Turbin responded gruffly. Although he had to step carefully with the political officer, he was far

102

from afraid of him. His skills as a divisional commander were widely respected, and many of the tactics used in Soviet Army tank units had been devised by him. He was destined for command of an army in the not-too-distant future.

"It's good that you keep your men informed, Comrade General. I heard you tell them that all their equipment needs to be fully functional for whatever task our masters have for us. Good, we must be ready."

None of them would challenge the political officer; make him aware that the lack of spares was a constant headache for the unit's officers.

"Have I missed anything?"

"No, Colonel Yolkin. There will be a full brief by the army commander tomorrow, I believe."

Yolkin wafted the smoke from in front of his face, a constant stream from the cigarette dangling in between Major General Turbin's nicotine-stained fingers drifting towards him. "That is my belief also."

"Right, dismissed," Turbin ordered. "I will be checking on your preparations every hour of the day. God help any of you that fail to meet my exacting standards." He stood up. "Get on with it then!"

Seats shot back as the assembled officers jumped up from their seats, saluted and quickly filed out through the tent flap, leaving the division's commander and deputy commander alone.

"Comrade General, you know that I should be in attendance for all briefings. It would be looked upon quite badly by higher command should they get to hear about it."

Major General Turbin took a deep drag of his half-smoked cigarette, expelling a stream of smoke high in the air before leaning forward until his face was less than a forearm's distance from Yolkin's.

"I am fully aware of my duties, Colonel Yolkin. If there is ever a command briefing, I will ensure that you are one of the first to be informed."

"But—"

"If you want to be in attendance every time I talk to or check on my men then you had better stick to me like glue. You can start by joining me at 0400 tomorrow morning when I start a complete tour of the division. We might have time for breakfast, but I doubt it. And if we do, it certainly won't be a leisurely one. I suggest we join the engineers and eat with them. Get some sleep, Arkaldy," he said, smiling. "It will be a long day."

The Bear stood up, stubbed out his cigarette on a plate he had been using as an ashtray, and walked towards the exit.

Yolkin jumped up, saluted and, in a shaky voice, said, "It is not my intention to doubt you, Comrade General, or interfere with the running of the division. As deputy commander, my role is to assist you. I would

103

like to join you tomorrow, but I already have tasks assigned. I must prepare my next political briefing for our loyal soldiers."

The Bear pulled the tent flap back and stormed outside, leaving the political officer to slump back into his chair, feeling slightly battered by the berating he had just received. Although he hated to admit it, even to himself, Turbin scared him.

7th Guards Airborne Division, Kaunas Airfield, Lithuania. 25 June 1984. The Red Effect –9 Days

"So, Stani, your boys ready?"

"Ready as they'll ever be, sir. Just don't know for what. They're pretty pissed off though. Geared up for a major drop during молот 84; then it's all called off!"

"Something's in the wind, Stani, I can feel it."

"Well, sir, we have the aircraft, we have the kit, and we now even have live ammunition. Supplies have been pouring in."

A loud reverberation emanated from behind them: the sound of aero engines growing steadily louder, joined by a steady *whop-whop* of rotor blades as a Hind D attack helicopter roared in behind them. The racket grew louder as it came in close, preventing all further conversation as it swooped in low over the airport, heading for the apron at the other end of the runway. The two airborne-officers quickly placed a hand on top of their pale blue headgear as the downdraft from the five rotor-blades made repeated attempts to blast them from their heads. Silence slowly returned as the helicopter did a circuit of the end of the runway before finally settling down. The two officers were dressed in camouflaged, one-piece coveralls, a blue and white horizontally striped shirt beneath. Although worn by airborne troops, the VDV (*Vozdushno -Desantyne Voyska*), the blue and white striped shirt was traditionally worn by the Soviet naval elite units. When Major General Mergelov, ex-naval infantry in World War Two, assumed command of the VDV in the 1950s, he adopted it for them, indicating that the airborne were an elite unit.

They were both perched on top of a BMD-1P, a mechanised infantry combat vehicle built especially for the airborne units. The *Ob'yekt 915* was basically a trimmed down version of a BMP-1: smaller, lighter aluminium armour, but keeping the 73mm, smooth-bore, semi-automatic gun. The two officers were part of the 108th Guards Airborne Regiment, their mother division being the 7th Guards Airborne based in Kaunas, Lithuania. The BMD was parked on the periphery of the airfield, on hardened ground, now slightly churned up by the movement of many of the airborne infantry combat vehicles. They were about half-a-kilometre from the airport's concrete apron, the assembled vehicles waiting for when they were called forward to be transported elsewhere. Many would be crated onto special pallets for an airdrop.

Suddenly, to their west, on the furthest point of the apron, an IL-76D, a four-engined, strategic-airlift aircraft was trundling towards the head of the runway, the whine and power of the engines moving it into a position ready for take-off. It swivelled round, its nose pointing east into a fairly gentle wind, the four engines building up power until all were screaming, the hefty wheel brakes barely able to hold it in check. Finally, the plane was given permission to take off, the brakes released, and the engines reaching an even higher pitch as they thrust backwards, pushing the aircraft and its maximum take-off weight of nearly 200 tons at a rapidly increasing speed down the runway. The airborne officers watched as it got closer, mesmerised by its power as it rushed down the runway that was laid out in front of them. It was a beast of a plane with its high-mounted, swept-back wings, tapering to blunt tips, four turbo-fan engines mounted on underwing pylons throbbing as they propelled the aircraft faster and faster down the runway. The sound ever louder from the engines as the high-mounted, T-shaped tail fin shot past them. With the pilot ordering rotate, the front four tyres slowly left the ground followed soon after by the remaining sixteen low-pressure tyres beneath the main body as it slowly took to the air, the sound diminishing as it flew east, eventually banking west, taking its cargo to a destination somewhere in East Germany.

"God, they're even more bloody noisy outside than they are when you're inside!" Lieutenant Colonel Stanislav Yezhov, battalion commander of one of the BMD assault battalions of the 108th Guards Airborne Regiment, laughed.

The BMD they were perched on was one of at least thirty lined up on the spare ground that ran along the far end of the runway to their south. The second battalion, which also had these specialist infantry combat vehicles, had theirs lined up at the opposite end of the runway, closer to the airport buildings. The apron was overcrowded with Mi-8 Hip, Mi-6 Hook and Mi-26 Halo helicopters and were now being joined by AN-12 Cubs and IL-76 Candid transport aircraft. The entire airport was overcrowded and buzzing with activity as the full regiment prepared to move to, as yet an unknown location.

"Still moving out at 0400 tomorrow, sir?" asked Yezhov.

Colonel Boykov thought for a moment, his mind suddenly occupied with the forthcoming plans to deploy his regiment. He just couldn't figure out what was going on. There was a large Soviet exercise, the largest ever, in progress and yet they were not involved. Live ammunition, along with other essential supplies, had been flooding into the camp at Kaunas for over a week now. A veteran of Afghanistan where he had commanded company and battalion-sized operations against Afghan resistance, everything he was observing now smacked of getting ready to go into battle. But with whom? It didn't make sense. The fifteen air assault brigades and numerous airborne divisions, his included, had been honed into effective, deep-penetrating, powerful shock-forces; something they had practised for real in Afghanistan. In a conventional war, they had specific tasks to fulfill: to destroy the enemy's nuclear capability, destroy or neutralise surface-to-air missile sites, disrupt logistics and lines of communication, and, more importantly, seize airfields, bridgeheads and key terrain. In effect, to maintain a clear passage for an operational manoeuvre group operating deep into an enemy's rear defences. They were good at it.

But at the forefront of Colonel Viktor Boykov's mind was where. And why? "Yes, Stani, 0400. Our vehicles will be airlifted to our destination, as will we. The main body of helicopter and airlift regiments will join us at Cochstedt. There will be a briefing the following day and all will be revealed."

"And the HQ elements?"

"I thought about assigning Hips, but the thought of being stuck in one of those things on a long trip..."

"Thank God, sir. We'd die of cramp and end up completely deaf."

"We'll fly with the Candids." Boykov said with a smile.

"If you'll excuse me then, sir, I would like to make some last-minute checks on my unit. I don't want you bollocking me for not being ready."

"Knowing you, Stani, your men will be poised and ready to move. But, you might want to give some of your comrades a nudge. I will be doing my rounds later and I expect them to be tight on this one."

Yezhov slid down the front of the BMD and onto the ground and turned and looked up at his regimental commander. "You look worried, sir."

"Not worried," Boykov said thoughtfully. "Just can't shake off the feeling that something big is coming our way."

"Your instincts have never let you down, sir, but on this occasion?" Yezhov laughed, saluted and strode across the hard ground to another section of BMDs to talk with his men. He could see them in the distance, tying down bits of kit on the rear decks and packing what personal kit they could in the small compartment in the back, leaving them relatively baggage-free for the flight tomorrow – apart from, of course, their personal weapons: the AK74 with its collapsible stock. Some crews would remain behind to drive the BMDs on and off the aircraft.

Viktor Boykov watched the officer walk away then looked west towards the airport, now bristling with activity. He too dropped down from the top of the BMD and walked towards the airport buildings, heading towards his other battalions to check on preparations being made. He stopped suddenly, reflecting on what Stanislav had said. *You're wrong, Stani,* he said to himself. *You're wrong.*

Chapter 15

Templin, Permanently Restricted Area, East Germany. 30 June 1984.
The Red Effect –6 Days

The green three-litre Senator moved steadily down the track, its strengthened suspension coping well with the ruts and grooves that had been carved into the ground by the passage of Soviet armoured and wheeled military vehicles. The driver steered the military-mission vehicle off the track and into the widely spaced trees of the forest, picking his way through until they reached the edge and overlooked the clearing that was their ultimate destination. They were in the permanently restricted area that encompassed Templin, a Soviet training area. Regularly used by Soviet armoured units for training of tank crews and small unit exercises, it was a stopping-off point for the military-mission officers in their quest to acquire photographs of the latest Soviet kit and, if possible, get inside one of their latest main battle tanks. As a consequence of Exercise Hammer 84, the Soviets had expanded the restricted area, enforcing a temporary restricted zone that made it even more difficult for the mission crews to get in close.

After the establishment of the four Allied zones-of-control following the fall of Germany at the end of World War Two, the exchange of military missions was introduced to effect liaison between the Western Allies and the Soviet Union. This agreement allowed members of a military mission to travel freely throughout the Soviet sector of Germany: the German Democratic Republic. Some areas were restricted on a permanent basis, with temporary restricted areas being added during large exercises or troop movements.

The British Military-Mission (Brixmis) crew were on the last stage of their tour. They had been out for two days and were returning to their headquarters in West Berlin once they had completed this recce. They had been here before and knew that, on the other side of the forest they were now driving through, there was a clearing often used by the Soviet Army. The tour commander, Staff Sergeant William Rawlings, a member of the British Army's Intelligence Corps, indicated for the driver to slow down as they approached the edge of the forest. It was just after four in the morning, just dark enough to make a covert entry into the restricted area, but light enough that they would be able to observe any activity underway.

The vehicle stopped, and the tour commander got out of the vehicle, taking his binoculars, camera and pocket tape recorder with him. Weaving around the tall, slender pine trees he made his way to the edge, leaning up against one of the trees at the outermost edge of the forest.

"Jackpot!" he said to himself.

He didn't need the binoculars to establish that a large unit was arrayed across the wide-open space in front of him. He positioned the binoculars in front of his face and scrutinised the vehicles. Something didn't seem right. It kept niggling at him, but he just couldn't put his finger on it. The sudden coughing sound of cold engines starting made him jump, clouds of blue smoke engulfing some of the tanks. After a few minutes, some of the armoured personnel carriers started to move, getting into a position of line-of-march. They were getting ready for a road march, thought Rawlings. He heard a rustle behind him and turned to see his colleague, Sergeant Ade Duffy, approaching.

"What have we got here then, Will?"

"Looks like elements of a motor rifle regiment."

"Getting ready to move out, I'd say."

"I think so too. Look! Look to the right. More poking out of the trees on the far side of the clearing."

"Got them. Look like command vehicles poking their noses out of the trees. Elements of a division?" Suggested Duffy as he lowered his binoculars, scratching his head, brushing bits of foliage caught in his hair from the branches he had walked under.

Rawlings zoomed in with the binos. "That's a BTR–60 PU moving out of the trees. So, what have we got? T-62s, BTR-60s..."

"It's getting lighter now. I'll nip and get the longer camera lens. Back in a tick." Duffy made his way back to the vehicle, picked out the 400mm mirror lens, another SLR camera body and returned to the treeline. "Any change?"

"Ade, that's a Polish unit, I'm sure of it."

"Don't be bloody daft. It's just part of this big exercise."

"Take a look for yourself. Check out the uniforms."

Duffy put the camera strap around his neck and scrutinised the unit again with his binos, focussing in on one of the tank crew. Although the light was still not perfect, he could make out the distinctive black coveralls and the floppy black beret he knew to be the uniform of Polish tank crew.

"Christ, you're right! What the hell are they doing here?"

"Look right: ammo carrier."

Duffy scanned right and could see an ammunition carrier alongside a T-62. "They're loading tank rounds."

"Take some photos, Ade. Then we need to get out of here. Something's not quite right about this."

"Aren't they just a part of Hammer?"

Rawlings turned to his colleague. "There are no Polish units involved in Hammer."

"Shit."

"Come on. Take some pictures and then let's get out of here."

Chapter 16

Chanticleer. United Kingdom Government Emergency War Headquarters, Corsham. 1 July 1984. The Red Effect –5 Days
The Prime Minister pushed back her chair and walked over to the large map of the world on the wall behind her. She swept her hand across the continent of Europe and paused for a moment as it hovered over Germany, before turning back to face the seven men sitting around the long meeting table opposite her. No longer the flimsy tables pushed together as a temporary measure, but a full-sized oak table brought onto the site at her request: a fitting piece of furniture for the reduced Cabinet that was now assembled there, again, meeting in the United Kingdom Government Emergency War Headquarters at Corsham. The 240-acre complex was built over thirty-metres underground, intended to be the hub of the UK's alternative seat of power in the event of a major worldwide conflict and, in the worst case, a nuclear exchange. Nicknamed 'Hawthorn' by some journalists, at a kilometre long, it was designed to accommodate the entire Cabinet Office and supporting civil servants: up to 4,000 people.

"It seems the Russian Bear is growling again," said Lawrence Holmes, the Swansea-born politician, as he brushed back his well-coiffured hair. "Things are taking a worrying turn, Prime Minister. The Russian Exercise Hammer 84 seems to be growing out of all proportion."

"More reports, Lawrence?"

"Yes," responded the Secretary of State for Defence. "One of our military liaison missions has reported Polish troops active in one of the restricted areas in East Germany."

"Polish troops in the GDR?!"

"Yes, Prime Minister."

"They are certain it was Polish troops they saw?"

"Yes. They are experienced operators."

"I assume they extracted themselves safely?"

"Yes, Prime Minister, but we have noted an upsurge in surveillance, and the authorities, both Russian and East German, are becoming more aggressive towards the missions we have over there."

Holmes looked across at Thomas Fletcher, the Chief of Defence Staff (the CDS). Fletcher was the professional head of the British armed forces and the most senior uniformed military adviser to the Government. "General Fletcher, you have some more intelligence for us?"

"Yes, Secretary, Prime Minister. First the shooting of the American military liaison mission officer."

"A Major Mortimer, wasn't it?"

"Yes, Prime Minister," responded the CDS, not surprised that Harriet Willis would know the man's name.

"We must send our condolences, Lawrence."

"I've seen to it, Prime Minister. Continue, General."

"We believe that he was attempting to photograph a tank storage shed and its contents near Ludwigslust."

"And where is that, General?" the PM queried.

"About one-hundred-and-twenty kilometres north-west of Berlin. He was shot by a Soviet sentry."

Holmes turned towards the PM. "The level of military activity being experienced by ours and the American missions in East Germany is exceptionally high. The CGS has further updates for us. General Hamilton, if you please."

The Chief of the General Staff pulled a sheet of paper closer to him, scanned it then looked back up. "The report from our liaison mission regarding the Polish unit is most disturbing. To see a Polish unit training in a Soviet exercise area is not unusual in itself. But for a full Polish division to be seen in East Germany at the same time as a large Soviet exercise is in full swing is unheard of. The unit in question, we believe to be the 12th Polish Motor Rifle Division, was observed in the Templin training area. It was seen loading live ammunition and preparing for a road march."

"And the significance of that, General?"

"Exercise Hammer 84 is primarily a Soviet exercise, Prime Minister, and we have not been advised, per protocol, that Warsaw Pact countries were involved."

"Could it just be a training exercise?" Asked Jeremy Chapman, the Home Secretary. "Are the Poles just taking the opportunity to use a vacated training site?"

"That is possible, Home Secretary, but I do have other sightings that make that option unlikely."

"Let him continue, Jeremy, and all will become clear."

The Home Secretary nodded, and the CGS continued. He picked up a report. "Brixmis have photographed TELs, Transporter, Erector, Launcher vehicles, travelling by rail in the vicinity of Finowurt. They're not certain of the type, but they could only be Scud, Scarab or Scaleboard."

"Nuclear capable?"

"Yes, Prime Minister," answered General Fletcher. "But can also carry high-explosive and chemical warheads."

The CDS continued again. "One of our human intelligence sources, codename Sparrow, has identified the movement of elements of a tank division in the area of Kuskin in Poland. The tanks seen were T-64As, and their turret numbers identified them as belonging to the Soviet 20th Tank Division. This division is part of the Northern Group of Soviet Forces. They were seen having their turret numbers painted out and were moving tactically and assembling along the Polish and East German Border. Another Humint source, Magpie, identified T-80 tanks, turret numbers again painted out, in the area of Kirchmoser, fifteen kilometres west of Brandenburg. The tanks were all laden down with additional material, indicative of an anticipated road march. Brixmis have seen a large number of tanks, probably belonging to 10th Guards Tank Division of 3 Shock Army. They were spotted close to Haldensleben, north-west of Magdeburg. The tour was detained for four hours and then escorted back to Potsdam. They eventually returned to their headquarters in Berlin, shaken, but unharmed. All their equipment was confiscated."

"Did we lose the photographs then?" asked the Foreign Secretary.

"Fortunately, no. They were able to replace the used film in the camera with a fresh one. Then the exposed roll was stuffed down one of the operator's underwear, and they managed to get it back to Berlin."

"What do they show?" asked Air Marshall Walker.

"The pictures confirm they were T-80s, the Soviet's most powerful main battle tank. They have also reported increased activity around the Letzlinger-Heide PRA. That's pretty close to the Inner German Border. The Berlin section is also reporting increased rail traffic, and a tank upgrade for the Soviet local units. What is becoming apparent though is that the Soviets and East Germans are becoming increasingly aggressive towards our and our allies' military missions operating in the East. An operator from the Berlin Section was attacked two months ago; three of our people have been detained and escorted out of East Germany; and the Americans have had one of their own killed. I have more reports if you want me to continue, Prime Minister, Secretary?"

Holmes waved his hand. "No, CDS, that gives us a pretty good picture of what is happening on the ground. Air Marshall, you have some additional information to back up these ground sightings, I believe."

"Yes, sir, I do."

"Excuse me a moment, Air Marshall. Have they recovered the body of the American intelligence officer, Lawrence?"

"No, Prime Minister." Christopher Chambers, the Foreign Secretary, answered instead. "The first reports coming back are pretty grim. It is being said that Major Mortimer was left to bleed to death. The Soviets supposedly just stood around and did nothing to address his wound."

"Are the rest of the crew safe?"

"Just the one, Prime Minister. He was very fortunate by all accounts; a bullet just missing him. He's on his way back to the States."

"Thank you. Sorry for the interruption, Air Marshall Walker. Do continue."

Walker stood up and flicked on an overhead projector that had been set up in the centre of the long table, his fellow officers shuffling their seats sideways leaving a clear passageway for the beam of light that now shone on the white painted wall behind them.

"The shots I will be showing you have been taken from the air by various platforms, including the SR-71, Berlin Corridor overflights and some satellite imagery. The initial analysis of the imagery by 18 Intelligence Company does not bode well."

He placed the first black and white slide on top of the glowing plate and an image of Soviet tanks seen from overhead were projected up onto the wall. "This was taken by an American SR-71 Blackbird. As you can see, these tanks are in a tactical formation in the area of the Lodderitzer Forest, a forest very close to the River Elbe west of Magdeburg. I would point out that this unit is not part of Exercise Hammer 84."

He paused, letting the information sink in. He replaced the slide with another. "This image is an overhead shot from an NRO KH-9, code name Hexagon, known as Big Bird. These images are extremely valuable as they are sent back to Earth in recoverable film-return capsules. Resolution from these is better than half a metre. All these shots are secret or NATO secret by the way."

The shot was at an angle, showing a large barracks area with lines of tank sheds, equipment lined up outside them.

"The tanks you are looking at have clearly been taken out of storage. The only reason for that would be for the exercise that is currently in progress, but it's a little late for that, or another purpose as yet unknown. The disturbing thing about the location of these tanks is that they belong to a tank division in the Baltic Military District."

The Air Marshall paused again but, before he could continue, Harriet Willis stepped in. "Thank you, Air Marshall. I don't think I need to hear or see any more. But what I do need to know from you all, gentlemen, is what is going on? What are you telling me?"

Lawrence Holmes leant forward. "The Soviet Army is mobilising, Prime Minister. We suspect that the exercise may well be there purely to provide cover for their troop movements."

She nodded. "Two hours ago, I was on the phone to the German Chancellor and the American and French Presidents. All three are on their way to London for a meeting to discuss NATO's defence posture going forward."

"Are the Alliance of a similar opinion that the Soviets may be up to no good? Surely the Soviet Union aren't going to want to start a war with the West? It would be madness, utter madness!" Blurted out the Home Secretary.

"Look at the evidence, Jeremy. Over a million Soviet troops are on the move, under the potential guise of an annual exercise. Along with that, we've seen Polish units on the march, and equipment in the Soviet military districts being taken out of mothballs. They have detained one of our liaison missions, confiscated their equipment and shot an American intelligence officer. What more do you want, Jeremy?" The Secretary of State for Defence responded angrily.

The Prime Minister patted the table gently. "And we have done nothing about it. We can't sit here and twiddle our thumbs anymore, gentlemen. It is time to act and act decisively." She pointed at the Home Secretary. "Jeremy, I want this place fully manned and operational within twenty-four to forty-eight hours."

"But, Prime Minister, that will disrupt our daily routine of running the Government and the country!"

"For God's sake, Jeremy, if the Soviet Army invades West Germany, routine will be well and truly lost. Why do you think that three of the most powerful Western leaders in the world are coming to London? Please, see to it, Jeremy. And promptly."

"Yes, Prime Minister."

"COBRA will be set up here, at this facility." (COBRA, an acronym for Cabinet Office Briefing Room A, where the crisis response committee would meet at times of a potential threat, from terrorism to foot and mouth.)

"We must keep it from the public for now, but what would you require to put the country on a war footing, General Hamilton?"

"I don't see how we can hide it from the public, Prime Minister. We will have to issue call-up papers to all of our Territorial Army units, reservists, and impound aircraft and ships to move men and supplies when ready; commandeer transport to start moving units across to West Germany within the next twenty-four to forty-eight hours."

"How soon could the Soviet Union strike – attack across the Inner German Border?"

The general rubbed his chin and looked left and right at his colleagues. They had obviously debated this very point prior to the meeting and had anticipated the question. "Based on all the intelligence we have to

115

date; they could strike within forty-eight hours. They would be without their full complement; some units are still playing at being on exercise and will need some time to rearm and for a minor refit. Three to five days."

"I don't need supposition, General, I need facts."

The Chief of the General Staff thought for a moment before he responded, choosing his words carefully; not in fear of the woman who was effectively his boss, but as a consequence of the black cloud descending on his mind at the thought that they might actually be going to war – a war he had trained for, but one he knew that, if it happened, would tear the world apart. "I'm sorry, Prime Minister, I can't...We can't." He indicated to the other military personnel present. "We can't be more certain than the earliest being within three days." He leant forward, the rest of the Cabinet following suit, drawn in to wanting to hear what he was going to say next. "But be in no doubt, Prime Minister, they could be in position to launch a full assault, with the majority of their Warsaw Pact Allies behind them: their first strategic echelon pretty much in place, their second strategic echelon not far behind, at the latest five days. Any later, particularly should NATO units start to deploy in earnest, they would have a much greater resistance to overcome."

"Should we not be mobilising fully now?" the PM asked the group at large.

"If we overreact on this, Prime Minister," the Home Secretary was the first to reply. "The consequences to our economy would be devastating. Impounding ships and planes, denying businesses of some of their staff by calling up reservists, not to mention the mayhem of securing all our key points."

"It will be an even bigger disaster to our economy if the Soviet Union cross into West Germany," she quickly responded. "We have to be prepared. If it means we get egg on our faces, then so be it. The responsibility is mine. Better than we have a hammer and sickle flying over Buckingham Palace. I want a full Cabinet meeting tomorrow morning then I will speak to Parliament. In the meantime, Jeremy and Lawrence, get the ball rolling. You too, Generals, Air Marshall." She looked at the Foreign Secretary. "Christopher, you need to pull in the Soviet Ambassador and find out what the hell is going on."

"Yes, Prime Minister. I will arrange it straight after the meeting has closed."

"Don't give him time to think or contact his masters, Christopher. Make him come to you immediately."

She looked through the glass partition at the opposite end of the room. Clerks were moving furniture about and unpacking papers that she had requested should be brought to the site. She sensed that she could well be spending a lot of time here.

Chapter 17

Bruggen, West Germany. 2 July 1984. The Red Effect –4 Days
The dark-green Volkswagen van made its way down Hoch Strasse, on the northern outskirts of Bruggen. The vehicle was in the process of doing a full circuit of the British Army base. This base was different from many of the others in West Germany; this base was special. 3rd Base Ammunition Depot was one of the largest depots in NATO and stored special munitions for use in the event of a war.

The two Spetsnaz operators were particularly interested in this site as it was purported to store nuclear weapons, something the Soviet Union would want neutralised in the event of a war, whether the Warsaw Pact attacked the West, or indeed if NATO decided to launch a strike with intention of returning East Germany to the fold. The Beetle van chugged along the road, keeping the perimeter of the base on their left in sight as much as possible, the idea being to do a full circuit. They kept their speed down to the local traffic limits so as not to attract the interest of the *Bundespolizei*. The German police were the last thing they needed breathing down their neck. They had been given some aerial and ground photography of the base, but they both knew from experience that there was no replacement for a CTR (Close Target Reconnaissance) eyes on. This area was awash with British units. The Royal Air Force Base, Bruggen was not far away. The British Army also had 3rd Base Ordnance depot's across the border in Belgium, at Broechem, Hier, Raust and Vremde. A petrol reserve depot in Grobbendonk, Base Supply Depot in Herentals, workshops in Emblems, Olen and Noorderwijk along with the 16th Base Vehicle Depot. These would be targets for other Spetsnaz agents; the 3rd Base Ammunition Depot, the target they were circuiting now, would be theirs. Two more agents had also been assigned to do a full reconnaissance of RAF Bruggen. RAF Bruggen was an equally important target. The HASs (Hardened Aircraft Shelters) each accommodated two Jaguar GR1s, air-to-ground strike aircraft. RAF Bruggen also operated Phantom FRG2s for air defence. The base was sometimes visited by the larger Vulcan bombers, capable of carrying and delivering nuclear bombs onto their target. All were protected by Bloodhound surface-to-air missiles and the more modern Rapier. Spetsnaz would focus on the air defence systems, leaving the aircraft and STARRNET communications tower and radar installations to the Soviet Air Force.

The Spetsnaz role was twofold. First, recce the site and, if possible, determine the actual location of the nuclear storage area within the base itself. Second, facilitate an attack to destroy the nuclear stocks and destroy as much of the base as possible. The passenger nodded to his comrade and the driver changed gear, swung the vehicle left down a link road, and headed for the town of Bruggen. They needed to plan their next steps, and, for that, they needed help. Both were experienced operators and knew the site would be well protected. High barbed wire fences posed no problem for the highly trained Spetsnaz soldiers; neither were they worried about the guards that patrolled the base. The guards were mainly from the Mixed Service Organisation, a civilian arm of the British Army of the Rhine, which employed mainly displaced persons. Many of them were former prisoners of war, concentration camp inmates who had survived the horror of such places as Auschwitz and who chose not to return to their native countries after the end of World War Two. They were affectionately known as MOJOs by the servicemen. It was the dogs that worried the Spetsnaz agents the most. Guards were generally predictable; dogs were another matter, particularly these. It was known that the dogs were tormented to make them aggressive and wild. Even the MOJO handlers were not safe and often had to wear protective clothing, padded suits, just to retrieve those dogs that had been allowed to roam free amongst certain key, fenced-in special weapons areas.

After completing their initial CTR, they made their way around the edge of Bruggen, skirting the town to the east, taking a turn off Boisheimer Strasse which took them into a small industrial estate. Pulling into a small yard, the gate left open for them as they were expected, they parked next to a set of large garage doors, the name above informing them that they were at the premises of 'Muller Courier Services'. They headed for the office, to the right of the industrial doors, the light still on, even at 6pm, and went inside.

"How did it go?" asked the fifty-five-year-old man in grey overalls, black patches on the knees and elbows, the owner of the courier business. He had a successful commercial enterprise operating in the Bruggen area and was extremely proud that he now owned six vans similar to the one that had just been parked up outside – although it was not without help, funded with money from the *Glavnoye Razvedyvatel'noye Upravieniye* (the GRU), the foreign military intelligence arm of the Soviet armed forces.

"Are we alone?" Enquired one of the Spetsnaz agents as he dragged a chair across the room and sat down on it in front of the desk.

The owner, a Spetsnaz sleeper and an ex-Special Forces operator himself, walked over to the window opposite, peered outside and proceeded to lower the venetian blinds, twisting them until they blocked all view into the office, but gave some visibility looking out.

"Yes, it's Sunday, so there was only a little overtime for one driver. How did the recce go?"

"It went well," the second Spetsnaz operator responded, a slim twenty-eight-year-old with thick black hair that covered his ears, whereas his comrade was shorter, stockier and chose to keep his brown hair close-cropped. "We got a good feel for the complex but need to go over the photographs again now we have a better perspective on the base's scale."

The owner left the window and walked over to a solid-looking, free-standing grey steel safe that was bolted to the floor. He bent down, inserted a key, tugged the heavy steel door open with a yank, pulled out an A4-sized envelope from the bottom shelf and chucked it on the desk. He stood up. "These are the latest. They came in the diplomatic bag this morning."

The one with the close-cropped hair sat on the edge of the desk and picked up the brown envelope, extracting the glossy prints, dropping them on the top of the desk next to the map his comrade had just placed there and was in the process of smoothing out flat. They shuffled through the pictures, matching them up to the relevant points on the map and laying them down on the outer edge.

The Sleeper placed a sheet of paper on top of the map. "These are the guards' schedules. Pretty regular; they've been doing the same routine for years."

"Accurate?" asked Cropped Hair.

"As best we can get. There is only me and one other, so we have to be careful. We can't hang around too long in case we get mistaken for the IRA." The Sleeper laughed. "They don't seem to be particularly suspicious about anything, and I haven't noticed anything to indicate they are on any alerts. That usually happens if there have been a few IRA bombs chucked at any of their camps. Searches of people and vehicles in and out of the camp are pretty thorough though."

"Not a problem for us. We certainly won't be going through the main gate," Cropped Hair joked. "Anything to drink?"

"Yes, in the cupboard next to the safe. There are some glasses too."

The dark-haired one got up out of his seat and in a couple of strides was at the other side of the desk, opening the cupboard door and removing the bottle in question along with three shot glasses. With vodka bottle in one hand and the three shot glasses gripped with his fingertips, he got up and placed them on the desk, shuffling some of the photographs aside. "You have a date and time yet?"

"No," responded the Sleeper.

The bottle glugged as Dark Hair filled the threes small glasses, each one to the brim.

"I am expecting the signal any day now, but I suspect it will be sooner rather than later."

Dark Hair handed a glass to each of them and knocked his shot straight back. "*Na zdorovje.*"

"*Spasibo*," his comrades responded as they too knocked their drinks back in one, banging the glasses down loudly then on the steel-topped desk.

Dark Hair quickly refilled the glasses. Sleeper waved his hand, but his newfound comrade thrust the glass at him.

"I'm driving."

"Aah, don't worry about it."

"You are in the West now, my friend. Not easy to get away with drinking and driving." He grabbed the glass out of Dark Hair's hand. "Just this last one, then. *Na zdorovje.*"

Sleeper had also been in the GRU's Spetsnaz as a full-time soldier. But now he had a different mission as a Spetsnaz agent: a sleeper. Infiltrated into West Germany in the mid-seventies and given the necessary funds, he had set up his courier business, providing courier services to local businesses, often travelling many kilometres across the country. This gave him an ideal cover for gathering intelligence on other parts of the country for the GRU: photographing bridges, ridges, potential river crossing points and, of course, military bases. He could familiarise himself with terrain that may potentially be of interest to the planners of a potential future invasion by the Warsaw Pact. He would feed back the intelligence he had gathered by leaving film and documents at pre-arranged 'dead letter boxes', where a member of the Russian Consulate would retrieve it and ship it back to the motherland via the diplomatic bag. His other role was in fact being enacted now: acting as a contact point and guide for a Spetsnaz unit that had been given instructions to plan for an offensive operation against a major British ammunition dump which was likely to also be a storage point for nuclear weapons. Like the two men that were with him now, Sleeper had also been trained in the art of killing, killing silently, along with sabotage and demolition; and, if called upon, to carry out the assassination of military commanders or senior public officials.

He looked at the two men. "This isn't just an exercise, is it?"

The two Spetsnaz agents, who had been infiltrated into the country the previous day posing as long-distance lorry drivers from East Germany, looked at each other. The dark-haired one, the leader, responded, "We have only been told that it is an exercise. But the situation between us and the West appears to be taking a turn for the worse. I think you could be correct: we may very well be doing this for real."

"I think I will have that other drink after all."

Dark Hair topped up their glasses for a third time. "Does that worry you?"

"No, it's what I was set up here for. *Na zdorovje.*"

"*Na zdorovje.*"

Glug, glug. The glasses were refilled.

"Anyway, the capitalists need teaching a lesson. *Na zdorovje.*" But his own secret thoughts were very different. He had come to like living in the West and had managed to carve himself if not a wealthy life, certainly a comfortable one. A war between the East and West could only be a bad thing.

"You OK?"

He looked up at the dark-haired soldier, conscious that he had been deep in thought. "Just reflecting on what needs to be done: accommodation, supplies, transport."

"The hotel we're in seems adequate."

"Yes, but only for another night. You are lorry drivers. I will need to move you somewhere else tomorrow morning. The German police will have a record of your passports by now. I have new ones for you."

"Where are our supplies?"

"There's a bunker about five kilometres south-west of here."

"How's it hidden?"

"It's a fairly dense forest. It's accessible, not easy, but then that suits our purpose. The bunker is in the centre."

"When did you last check it?" Cropped Hair asked.

"Day before yesterday."

"What's its condition?"

"Good, good. Its seals were intact. I opened some of the weapons packs and, apart from some needing a good clean, they were in good condition and operable."

"And the special weapon?"

"Intact. I hope to God we don't have to use it."

He was referring to a specially made suitcase which, with its contents, weighed close to fifty kilograms. It was a deadly weapon: a SADM (Special Atomic Demolition Munition) smuggled into West Germany three years ago. The Sleeper was responsible for placing it there and watching over its security. Assembled in the Soviet Union, they were made to facilitate the destruction of key NATO targets, such as nuclear weapons sites, communications sites and even power plants. This was what concerned the Sleeper agent the most: the thought of a dirty nuclear bomb being exploded in what had become his new home. Although less than half a kiloton, equivalent to approximately two hundred tons of TNT, it would still cause utter devastation, and the dirty radioactive fallout would contaminate a wide area. Then what? A full nuclear exchange?

"Fresh batteries?" asked Cropped Hair.

"Yes, I change them regularly. There's been no interruption to the power."

"Good." Dark Hair topped his glass up again and offered the bottle to the two others who declined. "I want to see it tomorrow."

"Of course. What will you need to take out?"

"Initially some explosives and enough weapons for the other six in our team that we are expecting, and of course ourselves. Can we store them here?"

"No, I have a shed on another site close by. We can use that."

"When are the rest of your team due?"

"We're expecting them by midnight tomorrow. Any unusual activity seen in the local area?"

"No, Comrade, nothing. No additional troop movements or enhanced security. It can't last though; the West must pick up the signals soon, providing something is going to happen on a much larger scale."

"They don't seem the slightest bit bothered by Hammer 84."

"Should they be?"

"Who knows, Comrade, who knows," Cropped Hair responded. "We'll certainly know when we get our next set of instructions tomorrow."

Chapter 18

Outskirts of East Berlin. 3 July 1984. The Red Effect –3 Days

Bradley hoisted his eighty-pound Bergen up higher, jumping it up so it would rest higher up onto his shoulders, pulling the straps tighter at the front, giving his hips a rest. Although he had added some additional sponge padding to the straps, secured with wide black tape, they still dug into his armpits, making them red raw.

It was two-thirty in the morning on the 3rd July. They had been in East Berlin since midday. He swallowed as he thought back to their fraught passage through Checkpoint Charlie. There had been a heated debate amongst the *Grenztruppen der DDR* officers on duty. They seemed reluctant to let the Section through, but eventually allowed them to pass.

Was he afraid? Yes, he was, as was Jacko tabbing behind him on the narrow track that was taking them through the forest. They both knew that potentially they wouldn't be going back. Should the situation between the Western governments and the Soviet Union deteriorate further and hostilities break out between the Warsaw Pact and NATO, he and Jacko had enough supplies to stay in the East for up to two weeks. Then their survival would be in their own hands; they would be dependent on their own skills to stay alive. Although trained in the use of covert OPs (observation posts) in Northern Ireland against the IRA during the height of the troubles over there, and in West Germany against KGB agents operating against the West, this was different. Recently, Bradley had been recalling the two-week survival course he had completed in the Bavarian mountains during a winter season two years ago. The instructors were from the British SAS, attached to the International Long Range Reconnaissance Patrol School based in Weingarten. He felt that all his training and operational experience would stand him in good stead. Unfortunately, Jacko was the weak link. There had not been enough time to get a partner for Bradley to Berlin in time, so the decision was to use Jacko, who had volunteered, because at least he was familiar with the East Berlin Sector.

Bradley lifted the image intensifier up to his eyes, the green shimmer helping him pick his way through the forest as they headed east. To his right, on the other side of the forest, a railway line ran parallel to them. Their destination was a copse on the other side of the autobahn that was just a few hundred metres ahead. It was at a point where the railway line crossed over the East German motorway. An OP there would give them a clear view of all rail traffic moving through the northern part of the city and vehicular traffic transiting the orbital motorway. The Range Rover had been well and truly hidden in a small forest that ran along the Hobrechtsfelder Chaussee. The hide had been recced earlier in the week. The vehicle had been driven into a dip, a gully, with thick foliage and trees lining either side. With a cam-net thrown over the top of it and some broken branches dragged from further afield, the vehicle would remain hidden, at least for a few days. Should the belligerent state of affairs between East and West diminish, they would be able to recover the vehicle and return to West Berlin and safety. If it all kicked off, they wouldn't need it again as they would be hundreds of kilometres behind enemy lines and would have a different task to perform. Once the MFS and Soviets started to search for them, knowing they hadn't passed back through Checkpoint Charlie, it wouldn't take them long to discover their transport.

Bradley heard a car passing up ahead, indicating they were getting close to the motorway. He stopped and turned towards Jacko, who nearly walked into the back of him, and whispered, "Ring up ahead. We'll get to the edge, check it out and then straight across. OK?"

Jacko acknowledged the order and Bradley moved off again, the forest providing them with good cover right up to the edge of the motorway. Ten minutes later, they arrived at the verge. It was quiet. At that time in the morning, it would be quiet, unlike some of the motorways in the West that seemed to be used constantly. Bradley spent a moment getting his bearings. To their north-west was Bucher Strasse; to their south-east Hubertusdamm and the railway line; and ahead, north-east, the Berliner ring road.

Jacko came alongside him, and Bradley whispered. "It's quiet now. Ready?"

"As I'll ever be."

They got up from their crouch, straining under the weight of their packs, and moved forward. Looking left and right for telltale vehicle lights, they stepped over the barrier, shuffled across the westbound carriageway, over the central reservation, across the eastbound carriageway and, within a matter of minutes, were out of sight, hidden in a small grove.

They followed the line of the autobahn south-east until they arrived at the site of the railway line where it crossed over the road, the Berlin ring road. Bradley knew exactly where he was going, having reconnoitered the location a week earlier, so they pressed on. A line of trees ran parallel to the railway line, on the north-west side of the embankment.

Bradley searched out the section he wanted: a mass of thick, three-metre-high undergrowth that had swamped the embankment and

125

grappled its way amongst the trees. "That's where we're headed for," he hissed.

They edged their way towards the thickest centre of mass, Bradley looking about him with the image intensifier, picking out landmarks, making sure this was the exact spot. Satisfied, he hissed to Jacko again as he dropped his Bergen to the ground, "Keep watch."

Bradley took a fairly hefty pack off the top of the Bergen, carrying it to the start of the undergrowth, and placed it on the ground. As he faced the mass in front of him, the railway line was directly behind and, below, the autobahn to his left. Picking up the pack again and crouching low, he pushed his way into the profusion of vegetation, quietly cursing as vicious barbs pierced and ripped into his exposed skin. Forcing his way in deeper and deeper, the pack held out in front, he finally got to where he needed to be. Lifting the pack upwards, he shoved it as high as possible into the thick carpet of stalks that crisscrossed overhead. Slowly unfolding, the pack opening inwards as he pushed higher, it unravelled into an igloo-like shape that gradually transformed the entangled undergrowth into a space that would be their home for the coming days. Bradley tweaked at the edges, bending the overhead shield, made up of a number of layers, into shape. The first was a thin layer of hessian, topped with a fine-mesh chicken wire; a waterproof layer on top of that; a further thin layer of hessian; and topped off with a cam-net. Now fully open, holding the foliage about them at bay, it would provide them with a dry and well-hidden home, and in relative comfort while they carried out the mission assigned to them. He called to Jacko, and they dragged their Bergens inside, pushing them to the back, using them as a further barrier against the advancing undergrowth. They now had a space of about two metres long by one and a half metres wide. All they needed now was to get organized and unpack their equipment that had been packed in reverse order: last in, first out. Just the key items to start with. Lying side by side on the waterproof ground sheet, no lights to help them, they had gone through the drill many times – so many times that they could do it blindfold. In fact, that is exactly how they did practice.

Jacko went back outside while Bradley hung strips of torn cam-scarf, a square of thin, green-mesh cotton, used to wrap around your neck and face, along the edges of the hide, with a double layer by the entrance. In the morning, he would need to check how covert their hide was, but he felt confident that if anyone stared into the blackness of the bush, blackness was all that they would see. He unravelled their sleeping bags and lay them down along the length of the hide. It was nearly complete. Two things remained to do: ready their weapons, two nine-millimetre Brownings, and the radio. They had considered bringing heavier weapons, but it had been decided that, if they got caught, an SMG wouldn't make a huge difference in the middle of hostile territory. Stealth was their best weapon. He checked both pistols were loaded, but not cocked. Once they were settled in their position then they would arm their personal weapons. Once he had sorted out the radio, they would be ready. They could then catch some sleep, two hours on, two hours off during the night, and four on, four off during the day. This would be their life for an indeterminate period of time, and it started now.

Chapter 19

What happens when an H-Bomb explodes?

An explosion from this type of bomb would devastate an area for many miles around. The bigger the bomb, the higher it exploded, would determine the amount of damage caused. But you can survive. The three dangers you will face outside of the immediate area, are HEAT, FALL-OUT and BLAST.

HEAT – the huge fireball it creates would be white-hot, lasting for up to twenty seconds, killing anyone in its immediate path and for many miles away.

FALL-OUT – the rising fireball would suck up huge amounts of dust from the ground and make it radioactive. As it rises higher and higher, carried downwind, it will be scattered over an area hundreds of miles long, forming a lethal corridor tens of miles wide.

BLAST – that would come after the intense heatwave would be at hurricane force levels, destroying all buildings in its path. Even those buildings further afield would have their windows shattered and may be unstable and unsafe.

Protect your Family – Handbook 1

Chanticleer. United Kingdom Government Emergency War Headquarters, Corsham. 3 July 1984. The Red Effect –3 Days

"Lawrence, the rest of the Cabinet can't get here for a couple of hours, so I wanted to talk through a few things with you and Jeremy before they arrive."

The Secretary of State for Defence was about to reply, but Jeremy Chapman, the Home Secretary, responded first. "The roads are incredibly busy, Prime Minister. It seems there is some mild panic buying occurring in parts of the country."

"My announcement later today will only make matters worse."

"I have instructed the police to cancel all leave, and officers will be expected to do extra shifts."

"Good. Troops on standby, Lawrence?"

"Yes, Prime Minister. They are also preparing to protect key points, such as power plants, bridges, communications buildings."

"I spoke to the Metropolitan Police Commissioner last night. He will be bringing some of his emergency plans into being," added the Home Secretary.

"This is going to turn this country and the world upside down." Harriet Willis sighed. "Do you have any better news for us, Lawrence?"

"I'm afraid the character of the news going forward is going to be very dependent on what happens over the coming days. As we established during the sitting at Westminster yesterday and the Cabinet meeting last night, we reaffirmed our commitment to NATO. At a meeting of the NATO Military Committee, I informed them of Britain's support and pledged our forces to fulfill their role in defending our ally, the Federal Republic of Germany. It was agreed without exception that NATO forces in West Germany should deploy. As approved, we will give our commanders the authority to deploy our forces when they see fit."

Prime Minister Harriet Willis leant forward. "They were all in agreement?"

"The Belgian Prime Minister was dragging his feet but came around in the end."

"We must let Christopher know. No doubt the Soviet Ambassador will be camping outside the Foreign Office once he hears about this." The PM looked through the line of large windows that separated this office from the lengthy Cabinet Office conference room that was also part of Section 14 of the Government War Headquarters at Corsham. Staff were in and out of the conference room, busying themselves with getting it ready for the forthcoming Cabinet, now referred to as COBRA, meeting.

"How is the preparedness of this facility progressing, Jeremy?"

"It's not fully staffed yet, Prime Minister, but will be by midday tomorrow. It is proving difficult for the Government to balance the everyday activities with moving to..." he hesitated, "...a state of war."

"Come on, Jeremy! We are at war, even if shots haven't been fired yet. Put some fire under them. I..want...this...ready...now." Her voice softened slightly. "We are going to have to run the country from here, whether we, or the rest of the country, like it or not."

"I will get on it immediately after the COBRA meeting."

"Good." She gave him the firm look that she was famous for. "We must be ready. What is ready?"

"The BBC studio is functional as is the Ministry of Information. The staff are testing the links as we speak."

The Defence Secretary changed the subject, taking some of the pressure off his fellow Cabinet colleague. "Have the Defence, Public Safety Regulations been put into effect yet?"

"Yes, along with the Public Safety and Order Regulations."

"That will help us to control the media at least," the PM mused. "We need foster as much calm across the country as possible."

"Complete control, Prime Minister. And with the BBC in block 16 next door to us, we can send out the right message."

"What about the Railways and Essential Services Act?"

"All done. Once Parliament agreed and signed it off yesterday, it was put into use almost immediately."

The PM stared through the floor-to-ceiling windows again. "I never thought we would be sitting here, putting this bunker to use for real."

The 'Chanticleer', the Government War Headquarters, was starting to come alive. The central stores were stocked with food and supplies to feed up to four thousand staff, although not all would be working in the main bunker complex. The bakery, with its automated breadmaker, a device that stood over two metres high, was gearing up to provide the bunker's occupants with fresh bread. The kitchen staff were in the process of giving the kitchen and its numerous ovens and stoves a deep clean. Although much of the kitchen equipment was from the mid-to-late sixties, it was still serviceable. Once fully up and running, the chefs and cooks would provide the occupants of the bunker with at least one hot meal a day. In the meantime, a tea bar had been set up.

Area 8, normally quiet and unused, clicked and chattered as exchange lights lit up on the GPO telephone exchange. A thirteen-metre long, fourteen-position unit, dedicated primarily to international communications, was ready for use. Just four operators were working there at this time. Close by was a smaller supervisors' and directory enquiries' desk, the four-metre shelf above it lined with the latest telephone directories.

"Yes, Lawrence, you can have your trains," informed the Home Secretary.

"For the movement of reinforcements, I take it?"

"Yes, Prime Minister. We have commandeered the majority of the channel ferries to transport the heavy equipment, and some troops naturally, but we will need the rail network to get them to the ports."

"Air?"

"Yes. All civilian aircraft are about to be grounded, and we will start to use them to get our troops into theatre."

"Numbers?" the PM asked.

"Providing they can fly to the Continent unhindered, initially five thousand a day, with most of their immediate personal equipment."

"That's good, isn't it?"

The Defence Secretary twisted in his chair before answering the question. "If we could move all our reinforcements by air, our full complement of initial reinforcements would be there in a matter of a few days. But they would be without some of their equipment. Without transport, supplies and ammunition, they would be more of a handicap than help. The priority has to be 24th Airmobile Brigade and the infantry brigades for the 2nd Infantry Division. They are the reserves. Also, they will guard 1 Br Corps rear area."

There was a rap on the door, and one of the PM's aides poked his head around the jamb of the door. "It's time, Prime Minister."

"Of course. Thank you. Lawrence, be so good as to turn the television on."

"It's time, then?"

"Yes, Jeremy. Once the American President has made his speech, the cat will be well and truly out of the bag."

The one-and-a-half metre TV screen came to life, and the camera in the airborne Oval Office zoomed in on the American President, sitting with his arms on a small desk, fingers interlocked, the US and President's flags behind him. He looked directly at the camera lens.

"My fellow Americans. Tonight, I am talking to you from Air-Force-One. It is with a heavy heart that I have to give you the following news. As I speak to you now, the forces of evil are lining up along the Inner German Border. They are intent on only one thing: to crush the country of free West Germany, to place it in manacles, to deny the German people their freedom. As a consequence, relations between the Soviet Union and the free West are deteriorating rapidly and, unless the Warsaw Pact take this opportunity to withdraw its forces that threaten a peaceful nation, a confrontation between NATO and the Warsaw PACT is inevitable.

"To quote the famous British Prime Minister, Sir Winston Churchill: 'I cannot forecast to you the action of Russia. It is a riddle, wrapped in mystery, inside an enigma; but perhaps there is a key. That key is Russian national interest.'

"I appeal to the Soviet Union and its people: do not put your national interest at the forefront of everything else. To enhance your position in the world should be by your own endeavours, not by trying to subjugate peaceful countries by force. Democracy will always prevail.

"I have spoken with the other leaders of the NATO forces whose troops are at this very moment lined up in defence along the borders of the Federal Republic of Germany. As one, we will not allow the Soviet Union to flex its military muscle and enslave us. We Americans would prefer death to having our liberty taken away from us.

My message to the leader of the Soviet Politburo is: we will not sit idle while you believe you can walk over us with military force. We will fight back with such ferocity that you will rue the day the idea ever crossed your mind.

I plead with you. Turn back from this dangerous path, withdraw your forces and NATO will withdraw theirs. Then, at a table of peace, we can air our differences.

To the American people, be strong. We will prevail."

The American national anthem started to play, and the Home Secretary got up and turned off the television. "Well, the cat is now out of the bag."

"Your speech complete, Prime Minister?"

Harriet Willis nodded her head slowly. "Yes. It will be the hardest speech I have ever had to make. So many people, so many soldiers, on both sides, are going to die if the Soviets complete what they have set out to do."

"If it goes nuclear then all will lose," added the Defence Secretary. "Everything is in place, Prime Minister. Our nuclear fleet are at sea, our V-Bombers are on standby. All we can do now is wait."

"When do the BBC start with their Civil Defence announcements?" asked the PM.

"As soon as your speech has gone out," responded the Home Secretary.

She turned to the Defence Secretary. "What indications are we getting of the Soviet movements so far?"

"The sensors, laid by Brixmis military liaison missions, are indicating heavy movement by Soviet forces, and the Berlin Section has reported heavy rail movement. The opinion of MOD is that troops and equipment from the Soviet Military Districts are being brought forward. The Baltic, Belorussian, Carpathian and Kiev MDs. But also, Polish and East German divisions are on the move. That has to mean they're serious and intend to go through with it."

"What about the border?"

"Our electronic warfare units are picking up nothing. The Soviets are maintaining strict radio silence. The western TVD have—"

"TVD?"

"The Soviet Western Theatre of Command, Prime Minister. There's been significant investment in their command-and-control structure. We believe there to be several hundred hardened bunkered command posts and communications centres. We also know they been practising crash-outs, similar to our Active Edge, with complete radio silence, and have proven quite successful at doing so."

There was a knock at the door and the same aide entered. "They're ready for you for a dry run, Prime Minister."

"I'll be right there," she answered. "Well, gentlemen, let me know when the rest of COBRA arrive. In the meantime, I shall go for a practice run of my speech."

Chapter 20

West of Aligse, West Germany. 3 July 1984. The Red Effect –3 Days

The four men patrolled through the small copse, west of the small village of Aligse, north-west of Lehrte and about eight-kilometres east of Hanover, the patrol leader knowing exactly where to take them. They had been here before, a number of times, on exercise, practising their craft, honing their skills in preparation for when the day came, and they would have to do it for real. It was two in the morning on 3 July. They had been on the move for the last two hours, having been dropped off covertly some eight-kilometres away to the north. The ground was quite dry and soft, even spongy, although very overgrown in places, that would make it difficult for vehicles to enter. *This will help reduce our signature*, thought the patrol leader.

The troop stepped carefully, placing their feet with as much precision as possible to keep any sound they made to a minimum. It was highly unlikely that anyone would be around at this time in the morning. Although tired after the four-hour flight from Britain to Hanover, waiting around at the airport prior to the flight, then trucked to Braunschweig where they had a chance to sort their kit out, they were still alert. They had been briefed that sleeper agents were believed to be operating in the area, watching for activity such as theirs. A civilian van then drove them to a position north of a copse where they were dropped off in the darkness to make the rest of the way under their own steam. Although the adrenalin was still ploughing through their veins, driven by the anticipation of their mission, finally doing for real what they had been training for the last five years, but not without a little sprinkling of fear, they would be ready for a breather on arrival at the patrol's destination.

Wilf stopped, checked his sat nav and looked about him. The trees, a mix of coniferous and deciduous, were plentiful, but not too close together for their needs. He scanned the area in front of him, a green shimmer from the image intensifier he was holding up to his eyes as it electronically amplified the ambient light available. He soon picked out the marker he was looking for: a particularly gnarled tree. He lowered the device, left it hanging on the strap around his neck, hoisted his weapon and moved forward again. Once he was alongside the tree, he marched fifty paces to the south until he found what he was looking for. Signalling the men behind him, they all came to a halt. Hacker, immediately behind him, stood watch while he checked out the mexe-hide. The other two, Tag and Badger, continued past them, their task to

133

conduct a full 360-degree circuit of the site, checking that they hadn't been followed. Unlikely as it was, they had to be sure.

Wilf undid his belt and shrugged off his heavy 100-pound Bergen and lowered it gently to the ground before opening up the entrance to the hide. Turning to Hacker, he indicated he was going inside. He placed his weapon on top of the Bergen and clambered down the aluminium ladder, entering through the less than a metre-wide prefabricated entrance, over two-metres below. He remembered digging it out last year as part of a three-week squadron exercise, practising then what they were about to do now for real. At that time though, they were aided by engineers under the guise of building temporary tank-berms, as a lot of spoil had to be removed from the site. He switched on his red-filtered torch and shone it around the interior, checking it for damage and to identify if someone had paid a visit. A dank and musty aroma wafted towards him, disturbed by the opening of the entrance. They had sweated for days, in secret, preparing the hide for operational use, living in it for a week during their squadron exercise, never imagining for one minute that a year later they would be back. This time for real.

Wilf shuffled forward. Although a substantial size as observation posts go, spending any length of time in this with three other men could become quite claustrophobic. It was T-shaped, the bar of the T measuring over five-metres long, by one-metre wide, with a missile trap and an Elsan chemical toilet at the far end. The offset stalk of the T-bar, three quarters of the way along was much bigger. Measuring two-metres wide by three-metres long, measured from the back of the T-bar, it would be their home until further notice. The key components of the mexe-hide were quite simple: pickets, spacers and arches to provide the frame and a flexible revetting material to cover the assembled framework. The revetting material was special: a layer of PVC coated in jute fabric, reinforced with half-millimetre thick galvanised wire, coated with a layer of soil up to metre thick on the roof. The frame had been sunk down two-and-a-half-metres into the ground. It would even provide some protection against a nuclear blast, providing the detonation was not in the immediate vicinity. The vast amount of thermal radiation would, should any of the material be exposed to it, simply destroy the layer of jute, leaving the wire that had been woven into the fabric to act as a mesh which would continue to support the hide. A direct hit would be another matter altogether.

At five-foot-nine, even wearing a helmet, Wilf could just about walk around the hide in an upright position. Badger, at six-one, would have to stoop slightly whenever he moved around inside. Wilf moved into the main compartment, seven by six, and checked it was serviceable.

Returning to the entrance at the western end, he clambered up and poked his head outside and hissed to Hacker, "pass the Bergens."

Hacker had been expecting the call and picked up Wilf's Bergen to lower it down into the entrance, followed shortly after by his own. As if on cue, Tag and Badger returned from their recce, giving the all-clear, their Bergens also swallowed up in the ever-shrinking space below. Eventually, all four were ensconced in the now cramped space, taking it in turns to empty their bags of those items that would be needed in the immediate future. They had two collapsible camp beds and two maggots (army sleeping bags). These would be positioned along the length of the T-bar. They only needed two, as two would always be on watch while the other two slept or carried out their ablutions or other duties necessary for their comfort and survival. During the day, they would operate a periscope in the roof of the hide, and, at night, they would need to use one of the two image intensifiers. At times, they would have to patrol outside, tracking down Soviet headquarters to report back on, or even sabotaging their communications equipment.

"Home from home already, eh, Wilfy?"

"Will be when you get a brew on, Tag," grumbled Badger. "You know you make the best."

"Yeah, yeah."

"Right," interrupted Wilf. "Tag, you make a brew. Badger, you and Hacker do one more circuit before we settle down for the rest of the night. I'll sort out the periscope and radio."

"Fuck, Wilfy, there's no one out there," exclaimed Badger.

"Get on with it, you moaning old sod. There'll be a brew waiting for you when you get back. Then we sort out weapons and kit. Now bugger off."

The two SAS troopers picked up their weapons: Badger his C7 carbine with its C79 optical sight and Hacker his favoured M-16 A2, with an underslung M203 grenade launcher. They headed out and would probably be gone for up to an hour. Badger complained about everything, that was his way, but he knew the importance of securing their position. In a matter of days, they could be surrounded by an entire Soviet Army. Ensuring they remained unseen was paramount.

"Whinging git," muttered Tag.

"I didn't hear you volunteering to go in his place..."

"Yeah, well I make the best tea, don't I?"

"I suppose."

"Wilfy, this is going to kick off, isn't it?"

Wilf joined his comrade, and friend, at the junction of the T-bar and crouched down, the blue light of the flame powered by the roaring gas from the camping gas canister they had brought with them, destroying

135

his night vision. It was Hexi-tablets when those ran out. He also recognised that they needed to be more disciplined going forward if they were to survive. Hot food and drink during daylight hours only, and quite possibly no hot meals or the luxury of tea if circumstances warranted it.

"It does sound like it's for real this time, Tag. The Prime Minister came out with some pretty frightening words on the BBC broadcast. Troops have started pouring across the Channel."

"Our briefing gave it less than forty-eight hours. I hope to Christ we get up to full strength by then or we are in some serious shit."

"There's not much a chance of that. There won't be enough ships or planes to get them over that quickly. It's not just Two Div, but all the supporting units for the RAF."

"Have we deployed yet?"

"Still in barracks, Tag, as far as I know. Don't want to go and upset the Soviets when we're supposed to be having peace talks with them."

"Load of bollocks. They could be preparing to attack while we're sat on our arses."

"Very succinctly put, Tag." Wilf chuckled. "Maybe the politicians can earn their pay for a change and come up with something. But, for now, I need to get the radio sorted so we can check in. I'll leave you to get that brew going."

Wilf felt his way back to the main section, the heat from the gas stove taking some of the chill off the man-made underground chamber. He pulled together everything he needed to set the radio up: their only contact with 1 British Corps, or even the outside world. Once surrounded by enemy forces, it would be the only lifeline with the rest of NATO who would more than likely be pulling slowly back against the sheer might of the Soviet armies up against them.

Wilf's team was what was known as a CPU (Corps Patrol Unit), reporting directly to the Commander of 1 Br Corps, one of the Corps of Northern Army Group that would defend the northern part of Germany. In addition, NORTHAG had a German, Dutch and Belgium Corps, along with an American Corps in reserve, once it arrived in theatre.

The four men of the patrol were from the 21st Special Air Service Regiment, based in England. The headquarters of the Territorial Army SAS unit was in Regent's Park, London. C-Squadron, to which Wilf and his men belonged, was quartered in Southampton. Wilf had spent eight years with the Regular SAS at Hereford before moving to 21 SAS as a permanent staff instructor, where so far, he had served for three years. Badger, Tag and Hacker were volunteers, with twenty years of service between them. They trained for one primary role: as stay-behind forces. They would hide until the main Soviet forces bypassed them; then they would come out and start feeding intelligence back to their headquarters: plotting the location of Soviet Divisional and Army Headquarters; movement of Soviet and Warsaw Pact formations; and, of particular interest, any nuclear capable artillery and missile launchers.

Once the radio was set up, the aerial pushed up alongside the periscope, Wilf called in. This was no ordinary radio. The PRC-319 was a fifty-watt microprocessor-based radio transceiver that could transmit in both the VHF and HF bands. He turned on his red torch, clipped it to his combat smock, sat down and pulled the electronic message unit onto his knees. The small alpha-numeric keyboard would allow him to type a message for his commander. As it was a burst transmitter, he could send the message data at high-speed giving them significant security over standard Clansman radios. With the short aerial, the radio had a range of about twenty kilometres; with the whip antenna they had brought with them, this could be increased to hundreds of kilometres, allowing them to stay in contact even though they may find themselves dropping further and further behind enemy lines.

Task complete, now he had informed HQ they were in situ, he moved to the periscope, a narrow green tube just over a metre long. As soon as he looked through the scope, he laughed.

"What is it, Wilf?"

"Bloody scope's filthy; forgot to clean it before we came down. Not that I'd be able to see much anyway at this time of night. I'll go and do it now before daylight."

"Brew's done, so don't be too long. Keep an eye out for the lads. The Hacker's out there and he'll shoot at anything."

Wilf made his way to the entrance, picking up his rifle on the way, shuffling down the T-bar, not much wider than his shoulders. He stopped by the entrance and looked back towards where Tag was also mixing some grub for them. *Living here for how long*, he thought. *A few days if the politicians sorted it out. A week? Or, if it all went to rat shit, weeks.*

Chapter 21

Bergen-Hohne. 4 July 1984. The Red Effect –26 Hours
"This is an alert; this is an alert. This is an Active Edge alert. All military personnel report to their units immediately. This is not an exercise. I repeat, this is not an exercise. All military personnel report to their units immediately."

William sat up slowly, grabbed his watch from the bedside table, and peered at the luminous figures and hands that told him it was one in the morning. He had been asleep for less than two hours. He felt movement alongside him as his wife also sat up, punching her pillows up so she was comfortable, and shuffled up close to her husband. Although William had slept fitfully for a couple of hours, his wife had lain awake thinking and worrying. Despite the fact that the soldiers' families had been excluded from the detail regarding the military's plans for evacuating the dependants living in West Germany, some information had filtered down. She was now starting to feel scared. Her husband would be leaving to deploy as ordered, and she had received instructions to be prepared should she and their daughter be required to move to the airport and be flown back to England.

"This is an alert; this is an alert. This is an Active Edge alert. All military personnel report to their units immediately. This is not an exercise. I repeat, this is not an exercise. All military personnel report to their units immediately."

"How long will you be gone?"

He put his arm around her shoulders and pulled her in close. "Just for a few days, sweetheart. We'll dig in somewhere, the politicians will do some more posturing, agree a compromise where they can all save face; then it will peter out and we can pack up and come back home."

"Just a few days then?"

"Yes, no more."

"Will me and Victoria have to leave tomorrow, do you think?"

"I don't know, I really don't know. They won't want to do anything too soon. It will cost a fortune flying everyone back. If they do, you can use it as a holiday and go and see your mum." He laughed. "Just be ready for when they call you, OK?"

"I will. We'll miss you."

He squeezed her tightly and kissed the top of her head. "I'll miss you both too. Give her a hug and a kiss for me tomorrow, right?"

"This is an alert; this is an alert. This is an Active Edge alert. All military personnel report to their units immediately. This is not an exercise. I

repeat, this is not an exercise. All military personnel report to their units immediately."

As he removed his arm from around her shoulders, she wrapped her arms around his waist and clung to him. "Don't go, William. Please stay with me and Vicky."

He felt her tears on his chest and he pulled away from her gently. "I have to, sweetheart. I have to go now." Throwing his legs over the edge of the bed, he stood up and made his way around the end of the bed. He left the bedroom without looking back, knowing that, if he did, he would see his wife sobbing. Seeing her shaking shoulders would make it so much harder for him to leave, and he knew he had to make the break now. He closed the bedroom door behind him and was about to turn left towards the spare room when he stopped. Decision made, he turned around and headed towards his daughter's bedroom. Easing the door open gently, he peered inside, his night vision still OK. He could make out his daughter's form under the Bambi cover, the steady rise and fall of her chest, the mop of thick black hair clearly inherited from her mother. Her face was just above the edge of her covers and he crept over, kneeling down by the side of the bed. He stroked her hair gently. She didn't stir; just the occasional twitch of her nose as she dreamt about her dolls or teddy, or the pet she kept asking for.

"You sleep well, angel. Daddy will be back to see you soon."

He heard Sam's nightdress rustle as she came through the doorway and he felt his wife's presence as she knelt down, sidling up beside him. Nothing was said, they spent a few quiet moments together as a family, both praying that it would not be their last. William had reassured his wife that the Warsaw Pact and NATO were just flexing their muscles and that his regiment, along with many others, would be out there to bare their teeth. But that was all.

His wife was not entirely convinced though. She could sense his unease and, in spite of the news on BFBS (British Forces Broadcasting Services) playing the situation down, there were constant announcements concerning civilians working abroad, and that soldiers' wives and families needed to fulfill their role in the evacuation programme for dependants that was being planned.

"She's beautiful, isn't she?"

"Just like her mother," responded William, kissing Samantha on the cheek. "I have to go."

"I'll stay here with Vicky for a while. I don't want to see you go. Be careful, William. Come back to us."

He kissed her again, then got up off his knees and headed out of Victoria's bedroom, hearing his wife's gentle sobs as he closed the door, and made his way to the spare room. Once in the spare room, he dressed quickly, knowing he was already running late. But he didn't care. They could throw the book at him if they wanted; he had needed to see his daughter one more time before he left to go into the unknown. He pulled on his combat trousers and the rest of his uniform then his boots. He didn't bother with his NI patrol boots this time but pulled on his combat highs. If it all kicked off, looking good would be the least of his problems, he thought. Survival would come to the fore. He hoisted his 58-pattern webbing onto his left shoulder and his kitbag on the other, crept out of the flat and bounced down the concrete steps to the ground floor.

Closing the main door behind him, he strode across to the car, threw his kit on the back seat, slumped into the driver's position and started the engine which turned over immediately. Other car engines were turning over as the married quarters' area came to life, with soldiers like himself answering the call to report for duty as ordered by the still roving RMPs with their Tannoy-mounted Land Rovers.

"This is an alert; this is an alert. This is an Active Edge alert. All military personnel report to their units immediately. This is not an exercise. I repeat, this is not an exercise. All military personnel report to their units immediately."

Another Land Rover drove past slowly, the blue, flashing light bathing the street in its eerie glow, the RMP Corporal nodding to William as they passed his car. They too were part of this call to arms, not mere spectators overseeing an exercise but fulfilling an operational role in support of the British military force that was waking up and slowly gathering pace.

William pulled out and headed towards the road that would take him to the barracks, a steady flow of cars joining the road ahead and also behind him. A queue had formed at the entrance to the camp as they were checked in. The seriousness of what was occurring was brought home to William when he saw soldiers digging in at the entrance to the camp, and an FV432 armoured personnel carrier had pulled across the road forcing cars to zigzag around it. He drove through and, moments later, was amongst the hive of activity by the tank sheds, the grumble of tank engines warming up, soldiers and tank crew rushing to and from different parts of the tank park fulfilling tasks given to them by their officers or NCOs. He parked up and dragged his kit from the car and was immediately accosted by one of his fellow crewmen, Lance Corporal Ellis.

"Give us your kit, Patsy. I'll stow it while you go to the armoury."

"Everyone else here?"

"Yep. Troop's pissed with you, so you'd better be quick."

"OK, mate. Grab this lot then." He handed his kitbag to Ellis and pulled his webbing on fully, recognising that everyone else was dressed ready to do battle. Mark Ellis headed back to the tank sheds where their Chieftain was parked up, and William tore off towards the armoury to collect his weapon. On arriving at the camp, he had seen the first indication that this was for real; on entering the armoury, he experienced his second wake up call. The staff-sergeant handed Patsy his sub-machine gun along with six empty 34-round magazines and 200 live rounds of 9mm ammunition which he had to sign for. He found a vacant space and loaded the six magazines, placing the curved magazines in his ammunition pouches when full, the remaining rounds in another pouch. Once complete, he left the armoury and made his way to the tank sheds, striding up the centre road that ran between the line of sheds either side. The pace around the sheds was almost manic; clouds of white smoke from the exhausts as the L60 engines coughed into life; others just ticking over to warm up ready for the order to move.

William waved to Mark who was sitting on the glacis of the tank, reaching out his arm so his fellow tankie could hoist him up. Now Patsy had joined the crew, call sign One Bravo was complete.

"Corporal Patterson, you honour us with your presence," announced Lieutenant Wesley-Jones as he climbed out of the turret.

"Sorry, sir, a bit of a queue in the armoury."

The Lieutenant scowled. "Go and find Sergeant Andrews. Tell him to round up the troop for a briefing."

"Sir." William winked at Mark Ellis then dropped down to the ground and went in search of the troop sergeant and to round the crews up for an update. Within a few minutes, they were all gathered around the troop commander's Chieftain tank.

The Chieftain tank was the backbone of 1 British Corps' armoured force and 1st Armoured, 3rd Armoured and 4th Armoured Divisions were the formations that would use them to stem the tide of any potential attack by the Warsaw Pact, standing up to the thousands of Russian tanks that would be thrown against them. The design of the Chieftain, the successor to the world-renowned Centurion, was essentially a trade-off between three divergent factors: on the one hand, firepower, provided by the 120mm tank gun, but in competition with mobility and protection. The primary role of the Chieftain was to defeat the enemy's main battle tanks, such as the T-64, T-72 and the latest model, the T-80, so heavy firepower was a necessity. But the enemy tanks could hit back, and hit back hard, so protection was equally essential. But both of these two factors had an impact on weight and size, so an appropriate power pack was required to drive it

141

into battle. This created a dilemma for the designers: to achieve the right balance between the three characteristics. The Chieftain tanks that the 14th/20th Hussars would go to war in were a culmination of those mutually conflicting factors.

Lieutenant Wesley-Jones called them in close. All were sipping mugs of tea that had miraculously arrived from somewhere. This could possibly be their last hot drink for some time. He shuffled his backside on one of the track guard stowage bins, his booted feet dangling over the edge. To his right was his crew: Mackey, the driver, Lance Corporal (L/CPL) Ellis, the loader, and Corporal 'Patsy' Patterson, his gunner. Sitting along the track guard of the tank opposite was Sergeant Andrews, tank commander of call sign Two-Bravo and the troop's second-in-command; sitting alongside him his crew: L/CPL Owen, his gunner, Trooper Wilson, his loader, and Trooper Lowe, his driver. To his left was Corporal Simpson, commander of call sign Three-Bravo, with his gunner L/CPL Moore, loader Trooper Robinson and driver Trooper Carter. These twelve men made up the crews for Bravo-Troop, Two-Squadron of the 14th/20th Hussars Regiment.

Wesley-Jones placed his cup down on the tank. "I've just been briefed by Major Cox. We will be moving to our wartime locations and deploying in a defensive posture around the town of Gronau. Although our deployment areas have never been revealed to us, we have conducted exercises in that area on a number of occasions. We are familiar with the lay of the land and the ground we will operate in. The difference is that we may well be establishing a defensive placement for real this time. All completed your checks?"

Sergeant Andrews responded first. "Yes, sir. This is for real, isn't it?"

"Yes, Sergeant. We have to assume that. The politicians are still talking, but there seems to be no sign of Soviet troops dispersing. Their claim is that they are on a planned, notified exercise and have no desire to finish it before it has run its course. Unfortunately for us, there are indications that the Soviet forces are massing close to the Inner German Border, and there have been reports of East German and Polish units also on the move."

"Why haven't we crashed out sooner then, sir?" asked Corporal Simpson.

"I don't think there's a straight answer to that, Corporal. The Soviets have been running these exercises for years. Nothing has happened as a consequence so far."

"We've become complacent is what you're saying then, sir," suggested Andrews.

"That may be the case, but we are where we are. There's no point in us bleating about it now. Our command on arrival at Gronau will be

Combat Team Bravo, our squadron headquarters; our battlegroup headquarters will be our own 14th/20th. We'll be leading the squadron and will be joined by a 438 detachment and an infantry platoon from the Royal Green Jackets. We move out in fifteen minutes, so wind up and let's get this show on the road."

Sergeant Andrews suddenly called out. "Shun."

They slipped off the side of their tanks, brought their arms to their sides and stood to attention as their officer commanding, Major Lewis, joined the group. As the commander of One-Squadron, he would be leading his fourteen Chieftain tanks and their respective crews into combat, should it come to that. But his responsibilities would be increased once his command became a combat team. In command of a combined arms unit, an armour-heavy subdivision of the 14th/20th battlegroup with infantry, and a guided weapons unit attached, his responsibility was considerable.

"At ease."

The major was short in stature, but his five-foot-seven height belied the seasoned soldier that had earned the respect of his men, particularly during their arduous tours of Northern Ireland. Like Lieutenant Wesley-Jones, he preferred to lead his unit from the front, getting to know the real men behind the faces, knowing their strengths and weaknesses: working on the weaknesses to make them better soldiers and men, and making use of their strengths to ensure his squadron was in the best in the regiment. You could only do that working alongside your men.

"Stand-easy, gentlemen."

The men relaxed, leaning against the cold slab sides of their tanks as they waited to hear what he had to say.

"As I have just heard your troop commander telling you, you will be moving out in under fifteen minutes, so I shall make this brief so you can get on the move. I'm sure you are all wondering what is going to emerge over these coming days, weeks. You are not on your own in that respect, I can assure you. I have been authorised to tell you that peace talks have taken a turn for the worse."

There was silence amongst the men as they looked at each other. Although there was an element of excitement at being crashed-out for real, with perhaps the opportunity to put into practice everything they had learnt and trained for over the last few years, fear was slowly starting to creep in.

"It is evident that Soviet and Warsaw Pact forces are gathering along the Inner German Border and deploying into assembly areas. Although talks continue, I have my own personal doubts that they will come to anything. The Warsaw Pact is mobilising, as are we. Although our

Government, along with the governments of our NATO Allies, has asked the Soviets to cease their manoeuvres until talks are concluded, the Kremlin have declined, declaring that we should withdraw our forces and return to barracks. Naturally we would be foolish to comply with that request. So, men, this is not an exercise; it is for real. Just apply the skills and expertise you have acquired during your training and practices, and we will come through this. There will be casualties. I can't promise survival. But, if we work as the close-knit unit we are, we will give a good account of ourselves and come through the other side."

He waited a moment and looked over the assembled men. Some he knew well, others not so well, but he was confident they wouldn't let him or the regiment down.

"Just carry out your duties as you have always done; then we will do our bit to ensure the security of this country and, as a consequence, the security of our own country. 4th Armoured Division is already moving into position, and by now reconnaissance units from 1 Br Corps will be in position watching likely border crossing points. 4th Armoured will take up a defensive position right across our front acting as a covering force giving us, and 3rd Armoured Division, the opportunity to deploy and dig in along our designated stop line. Our northern boundary will be south of Hanover and our southern boundary Einbeck, with 3rd Armoured Division to our south. The regiment will become a battlegroup headquarters, designated 14th/20th BG and will have mechanised infantry units from the Royal Green Jackets attached. Those RGJ units will come under our command. We have been designated Combat Team Bravo and will have a platoon of infantry and 438 swingfire assigned to us. As a consequence, we will lose delta troop who will be attached to the RGJ battlegroup. We will deploy along the western bank of the River Leine to the west of Gronau, although some elements will be across the river, dug in on the outskirts of the town itself. Your troop commander has the coordinates, and you are to start the move to your initial assembly area." He looked at his watch. "In the next ten minutes. A Land Rover from the admin troop will lead with an FV434 from the LAD at the rear of the packet. There will be no flashing lights or a blue-light escort. You are on your own. We are effectively operating under wartime conditions. Don't push the march too hard, but I want you off the road before first light. The rest of the squadron will be thirty minutes behind you, and the rest of the regiment fifteen minutes later. Any questions? Yes, Sergeant Andrews?"

"Sir. We have full ammo bins and our fuel tanks have been topped up, but will resupply be close by once we get to our destination?"

"Yes, they will. There will be two Foden fuel tankers to meet you there. Twenty-four thousand litres will be more than enough to top up your tanks along with the rest of your packet. They will also refuel the rest of the squadron on arrival."

"Who will be our RGJ contact on arrival, sir?" Asked Wesley-Jones. "And do we deploy immediately?"

"Lieutenant Stewart will meet you on your arrival. It is still to be confirmed, but he may be bringing one or two Milan firing posts with him. We will also be joined by some engineers, along with arty and air-observers at some stage, so keep your eyes peeled for them. The engineers will be laying bar mines on the approaches to Gronau, your final deployment area, so we will be expected to provide them with some cover."

"Understood. We'd better be going, sir, if we are to remain on schedule."

"Good point, Lieutenant. Get your troop moving."

"Shun," called Andrews again.

"Stand easy. And good luck. I'll see you down south in the morning."

The OC left and the troop dispersed to their respective armoured vehicles. Within minutes, the three drivers were revving the engines of their tanks, and they lumbered out of the sheds, one by one, and turned and moved down the central aisle to give the next one the room to swivel around on its tracks. Now lined up on the road leading out of the camp, a FV434, an armoured repair vehicle, last in line, a long wheel-based Land Rover upfront. In between, One-Bravo the lead tank, Two-Bravo the last Chieftain in the line-up, with Corporal Simpson and Three-Bravo in the middle.

Wesley-Jones gave Mackey the signal and the Chieftain started forward, the steady squeal of the tracks joined by noise from the remaining tanks as the packet started to move forward, rattling over the toughened concrete surface. The Land Rover drove down the centre corridor between the sheds, out through the barracks and onto the main road, the tanks pulling out onto the road behind it, the troop commander and Mackey peering ahead looking for the single convoy light reflecting off the white diff cover of the Land Rover as it led the way.

Wesley-Jones looked behind, checking the rest of his packet were keeping pace, as they slowly gathered speed, the lead vehicle taking them up to a steady thirty-kilometres an hour. This was going to be a tough journey for the tank commander and driver. It was hard enough concentrating on distance driving during daylight hours but, at night-time with only convoy lights to guide them and no escort, it was extremely stressful. Fortunately, German roads were generally pretty straight, with few climbs, as opposed to the winding country roads back in Britain. The packet made its way south, rattling along route three, passed the Naturpark Sudheide on their left, and through the village of Celle. Here, they were held up by RMPs for five minutes as priority traffic crossed their path. The entire British Army was on the move, heading to their wartime dispositions, ready to repel any potential invader. The military police controlling the flow of traffic released them and they continued their journey south, then south-west, then south again, moving onto an autobahn where they upped their speed to thirty-five kilometres per hour.

The Chieftain suddenly ground to a halt, its back end up in the air and the front dipping down. Wesley-Jones was flung forward, the air forced from his lungs as the rim of the hatch dug into his chest. He heard shouts and curses below as Ellis and Patsy were thrown about.

"What the fuck, Mackey?"

"Sorry, sir, didn't see the Land Rover had stopped."

He peered ahead and could see red-filtered torches moving around. Before he could react, the tank lurched forward again, and he could see darkened vehicles on the roadside – a random checkpoint, no doubt.

"OK, Mackey?"

"Yes, sir."

He suspected that Mackey had become mesmerised by the constant need to stare into the night, tracking the vehicle and the road ahead, and had lost concentration. He was as much to blame, if not more. He had an equal responsibility to keep watch on the road ahead. No, he thought, he had the greater responsibility. He was in command.

"You're doing a great job, Mackey. Thirty minutes and we'll take a ten-minute break."

"I'm fine, sir."

"I'd rather get there ten minutes late with an intact Chieftain than have it wrecked." Wesley-Jones laughed. They left the route 37 autobahn and turned onto route 7, through the small forest of Altener Wald. Their speed crept back up to a steady twenty-five. On the opposite carriageway heading north, he could hear, above the sound of his own small convoy, the rumble of tank tracks and the steady drone of high-powered engines as a squadron of Leopard I and IIs rattled by in the opposite direction, heading north. Probably a tank company from a unit belonging to 1 German Corps, heading north to their own wartime locations. They turned off the autobahn onto the B443 where their speed dropped back to twenty-five to thirty-kilometres an hour. Crossing over route 37 again, they headed south-west then south.

"You OK, Mackey?"

"Yes, sir. No need to stop. Wide awake now."

"Are you sure?"

"Yes, sir."

"OK. We could do with keeping on the move. You'll be excluded from the sentry rota, and you can catch up on some sleep when we get there."

"OK, sir."

"Corporal Patterson. Patsy!"

Patsy climbed up through his hatch. "Sorry, sir, nodded off."

"That's OK. Can you crack that flask and pass everyone a brew?"

"Sure, sir."

"Ellis awake?"

"No, sir. Can't you hear him snoring from here?"

The lieutenant laughed. "Leave him be then. He can take the first stag when we park up."

Patsy dropped back down into the fighting compartment to sort out drinks. They were well south of Hanover now and, apart from a few stops, had made good progress. They were roughly sixty miles from the barracks and, at 0530 in the morning, found themselves in the small village of Eime, three and a half kilometres west of Gronau and the River Leine. The River Leine, Blue Rabbit, was the stop line for the 1st and 3rd Armoured Divisions, 4th Armoured Division already moving into position further east, acting as the covering force to allow these two key forces to dig in. The troop had been allocated a lager at a farm on the outskirts of Eime, along Elzer Weg.

They backed the three tanks into large barns that had been made available by the farmer, the 434 under a cam-net outside and the Land Rover snug against one of the farm building walls. The German family were out almost immediately they had finished parking up, providing *bratwursts* and *brotchen*, with lots of *senf*, a favoured German mustard, for the weary troops and even a bottle of Alt beer each. Lieutenant Wesley-Jones immediately got to work preparing a message for his squadron commander who was probably not more than half an hour behind them. He had met with the RGJ Lieutenant. They were cammed up in a small copse close by. The rest of the troop, apart from those posted on sentry duty, were, once they had scoffed the food and drink provided by their hosts, destined to hit the sack and catch up on some sleep.

He pulled the A-5-sized pad out of its wallet, tore off one of the double-sided sheets and placed it in his BATCO wallet. The side he was going to use would be valid for the next eighteen hours. The BATCO (Battlefield Code) cipher sheet was composed of a plaintext character set consisting of twelve symbols, the digits 0 to 9, a decimal point and a change character denoted as 'CH'. The cipher table was a matrix of nineteen columns and twenty-six rows. The columns were divided into two groups. The seven columns on the left were numbered from 2 to 7.

The column under each of the digits had listed a randomly scrambled alphabet. The thirteen right-hand columns were numbered 0, 0, 1, 2, 3, 4, 5, 6, 7, 8, 9, CH and '.'. He wrote down the outline of the message in his notebook first. He selected one of the first seven columns using the key digit, searching for the row in which the key letter occurred. He continued tracing his finger over the pad until the message was complete. He read the message. *Two-Zero from One-Bravo. Infantry attached. In location Grid 494707. Await your arrival. Message ends.* Satisfied, he transmitted the encoded numbers, put the BATCO wallet away, grabbed his SMG and went in search of Sergeant Andrews to check on their security for what was left of the morning. He anticipated that they wouldn't be here for long as they needed to move into their main positions. The engineers would probably be in the process of digging their tank berms and preparing positions for infantry units. It was going to be a long twenty-four hours, he thought to himself as he clambered out of the turret.

Chapter 22

Lindenwald, East Germany. 10th Guards Tank Division/3 Shock Army. 4 July 1984. The Red Effect –23 Hours

The assembly area for the 62nd Tank Regiment, of the 10th Guards Tank Division, was a hive of activity. Colonel Oleg Pushkin, commander of the 62nd, and Lieutenant Colonel Trusov, commander of the 2nd Battalion, stood watching as a regiment of BM-27s growled past, each eight-wheel drive, Zil 135 chassis mounted with a multi-barrelled rocket launcher. They crawled past one by one, the large wheels grinding over the specially prepared route. Otherwise, by the time the eighteenth one had passed, the twenty-ton monsters would have made the track impassable for anything other than tracked vehicles. They were from the Group of Soviet Forces Germany's Missile Brigade, belonging to 34th Artillery Division. This was an indication of the importance of the role to be played by 3rd Shock Army, in particular 10th Guards Tank Division. Colonel Pushkin's 62nd Tank Regiment, along with 248th Guards Motor Rifle Regiment, were to be the spearhead in the attack on the NATO forces that would be stacked up against them on the other side of the Inner German Border, less than seventy kilometres away.

"I wouldn't like to be on the receiving end of that lot, sir." Trusov pulled out a packet of cigarettes from his tunic. It was light enough now that they could smoke, not that they had anticipated any NATO overflights. That would have been an act of war, and the Western governments hadn't got the guts to start anything, according to their divisional commander, General Kasapev. "Sir?"

Pushkin took a cigarette from the proffered pack of plain cigarettes. "Still smoking these foul things, Pavel?"

"You complain about them, but I've never seen you refuse one," Trusov shouted back above the noise of the engines as one of the BM-27 drivers put on the power to negotiate a particularly deep rut.

"It's not often you give anything away."

The last of the self-propelled multiple-rocket launcher systems, mounted on a chassis similar to that used to carry the FROG-7 missile, drove by. With two engines, one driving the right-hand set of wheels and one the left, they could power the vehicle to an impressive speed of sixty-kilometres per hour.

"Now, now, sir."

"But you're right."

"About what?"

"About being on the receiving end of that lot. It would certainly ruin your day."

"A step up from the BM-21s."

"Significantly." Pushkin held up his hand and ticked off his fingers. "Sixteen 220mm rocket launchers on each platform. What's that? Eighteen vehicles making it 288 rockets?"

"Sounds about right, Comrade Colonel. So, they'll be bombarding the NATO covering force ahead of us, or beyond?"

"Ahead of us. That's what has been agreed. We will have some major support."

Trusov pulled out a map and indicated that they should cross the track to where a small bivouac had been assembled and a table and a couple of chairs placed inside, for the use of the battalion commander.

"Can I go over a couple of things with you, sir?"

"Something bothering you, Pavel?"

"Just want to make sure my battalion doesn't let the regiment and division down."

"Head like a sieve, Pavel." The colonel laughed. "Come on then."

They made their way across the now deeply rutted track that ran through the trees and headed for 2nd Battalion's temporary HQ. Trusov held the camouflage netting up to allow his commander to duck underneath and enter the small two-by-two metre covered space. It was open at two sides, allowing enough light to enter and enabling them to see the detail on the map Trusov had laid out on the table. He withdrew his pistol and a spare magazine, using them as paperweights to keep the map flat.

Trusov leant over the table. "Right sir, Helmstedt. The division has a sector twenty kilometres wide. With Helmstedt north of the centre, that means a front from south of Grasleben in the north to south of Schoningen. We don't normally have such a narrow front."

Pushkin tapped the map. "As a result of us being able to bring our second strategic echelon up to strength, we are in a position to reduce our divisional fronts for the offensive. But our breakthrough sector has to be less than five if we are to concentrate our forces and punch through." He looked up at his battalion commander. "3rd Shock Army is the first and second echelon of the first strategic echelon. It is 3 Shock that is going punch through their lines. Our Northern Army boundary ties in with 2 Guards Tank Army and our southern boundary with 1 Guards Tank Army. The objective is to push two divisions of the first operational echelon forward, ours and the 7th. Our first echelon regiments, us and the 248th GMRR, will be the first to attack the NATO covering force." He pointed to the villages of Supplingenburg and Supplingen. "We have to try and bypass these, push north-west and strike north of Konigslutter. I intend to deploy the 1st Battalion from line of march and cover the flanks while you, Pavel," he patted his junior's shoulder, "have to punch right through the middle of the two villages. Don't stop. You have to smash through and secure the point north of Konigslutter. Keep going if you can but, if you get bogged down, I will release Aleksey's Motor Rifle Battalion. I shall keep the 3rd Tank Battalion in reserve."

"You make it sound easy, Comrade Colonel."

Pushkin slumped down in the canvas backed chair and pulled off his black beret and placed it on the collapsible square table. "Are you scared, Pavel?"

Trusov looked at his commander, black chest hair just poking above the front of his collar and tie, the same colour as his one-piece tank coverall. He responded. "I'd be a liar if I said I wasn't."

"Good." Pushkin pulled out a flask containing some vodka from his own personal stocks, took a pull on the drink and then passed it to his junior. "Not as good as yours, but it still has bite."

Trusov took the proffered container and pulled a face as he too partook of a drink. "So too has antifreeze."

"We shouldn't necessarily be scared, Pavel, but we should be very wary. We are up against the British, and they don't give in easily." The colonel swallowed another tipple and offered it to Trusov again who declined. "Ten years ago, or even five, I wouldn't have felt confident about going up against NATO." He leant forward. "But now, Pavel, we have the equipment that can finally match theirs, and in much bigger quantities. You saw those BM-27s. There's a lot more where they came from. They're going to be well and truly pounded before we even start to attack."

Trusov sat down on the seat opposite and swept his hand over the map. "With the 2nd Guards Army using the A2 autobahn as their southern boundary, and 1st Guards to our south, the enemy won't know which way to turn."

"Exactly. You concentrate on Konigslutter, leave the forest of Der Elm and north of Schoningen to the 248th. 1st Guards will be pushing from Schoningen up through Schoppenstedt to come in from behind."

"My battalion will do their bit, Comrade Colonel."

"I know, Pavel, that's why I've chosen you for the toughest job. Right, we move out in sixteen hours, so I want to do some last-minute checks with your fellow officers. Then I will get our final briefing from the general. Let them know that I will be holding a final briefing at 1800 before we move out."

"Understood, Comrade Colonel."

Pushkin stood up, as did Trusov, replaced his beret, returned his junior officer's salute and left the tent.

North-west of Gommern, East Germany. 12th Guards Tank Division/3 Shock Army. 4 July 1984. The Red Effect −23 Hours

The Divisional Commander of the 12th Guards Tank Division hit the wooden table three times with a half empty vodka bottle.

"We go to war soon," bellowed 'The Bear'. "To be selected as the army's *operacyjna grupa manewrowa* is a great honour placed on us by our commander and our motherland."

He looked around at his full headquarters: over twenty officers crammed into the smoke-filled marquee erected by his signals battalion headquarters. The fug increased as he lit up yet another of his foul-smelling Belomorkanal cigarettes. The full complement of the division's officers present were sitting around a mixture of temporary tables, communications equipment lined up on the one side, maps of the West pinned to some of the other sides. The commanders of the main teeth arms were present: the 48th, 332nd and 353rd Guards Tank Regiments, 200th Guards Motor Rifle Regiment, and the 18th Independent Guards Reconnaissance Battalion. There were men also from the signals battalion, self-propelled artillery regiment, surface-to-air missile battalion, guards engineer battalion, supply, repair, medical and the chemical defence company. The senior officers were also in attendance: The Chief of Staff, Pyotr Usatov, the two Deputy Commanders responsible for 'Technical' and the 'Rear', the Political Officer and Deputy Commander of the Division, Colonel Arkaldy Yolkin, and the Chief of Rocket Troops. The Commander of the Tank Division, Major General Oleg Turbin was a hard taskmaster, and he pushed his officers and men relentlessly to make his division one of the best in the Soviet Army.

The stocky general pointed at Colonel Yuri Kharzin, Commander of the 48th Guards Tank Regiment. "We march out to our new assembly area on the night of the fifth, tucking in behind the 7th and the 10th as they assault NATO's lines. I want your unit to move out first, Yuri. If we are to exploit any breakthroughs, we must be close enough to press forward. Your regiment will move out at dusk today, putting you in a position to take over an assembly area west of the Elbe. The rest of the division will follow you during the night of the fifth."

"Yes, Comrade General, we will be ready."

"Good. Make sure Colonel Kharzin has a supply unit to support him."

"Yes, Comrade General," responded the commander of the supply battalion.

The general turned to the Deputy Commander 'Rear', who was sitting to his right. "Our ammunition stocks complete, Borislav?"

"Yes, Comrade General."

"Good, good. Akim, your foot sloggers will be first in line of march when we move on the fifth. Your BMPs?"

Akim Yermakion, Commander of the 200th Guards Motor Rifle Regiment, grinned as he responded, used to the mickey-taking by a unit consisting largely of tank units. The only infantry unit alongside the three tank regiments, he was often at the centre of their jokes. "Yes, Comrade General, our spares situation has been resolved, thanks to Colonel Yolkin."

"Been throwing your political weight about, Comrade Colonel?" Turbin said to the skinny Political Officer with a chortle.

"It is always my intention to ensure that our division is ready to do whatever it is asked of it by our masters, Comrade General."

The reference to the army commanders and above, who directed their lives and actions, didn't go unnoticed by the Bear.

"So, all operational, then?"

The young colonel didn't need to refer to any notes as he responded proudly. "Ninety-three are fully operational, Comrade General."

The general moved on. "We know roughly where our area of operation will be, but we won't know for certain until our first operational echelon has beaten down the NATO covering force and started to eat into their main battle area. So, we will need to be flexible. We are a unique unit. An operational manoeuvre group is exactly that: manoeuvrable. We need to be able to weave our way through their defences, taking the line of least resistance, pushing west until we can move at will in their rear areas, tearing up their communications centres, logistics and supplies, and disrupting any reserves before they arrive in theatre."

"Comrade General, has it been agreed who our operationally subordinate reinforcements will be?" Asked the Chief of Rocket and Artillery Troops.

"Yes," responded General Turbin. "You will get a brigade of BM-27s from the TVD. They will be supporting the initial assault. Then they'll be assigned to your Divisional Artillery Group (DAG). Along with those, we'll have a regiment of 2S5s and most of the DAG from whichever division we pass through. Major Lagoshin."

"Sir."

"The front's air defence brigade will be providing us with a SAM regiment so we'll have additional overhead cover. You will need to set up comms with their command elements within the next eight hours."

"Sir."

"Major Zakrevsky."

"Yes, Comrade General."

"I need you to initiate communications with the fighter-bomber division. I will give you the details later. We've been promised at least 100 sorties during our initial commitment to battle. We shall be depending on those links to get the support in the right place at the right time."

"My men will be ready, sir."

"Good, good. One last thing then I want to speak to each of the commanders on their own. During our first day of battle, we will have the airborne prima donnas and a few other assets backing us up." The general laughed at his own joke and was joined by the rest of the officers. He lit another cigarette before stubbing out his current one in a blue china cup in front of him. He took a deep, satisfying draw and blew out a cloud of smoke.

"I have been promised a heliborne assault brigade, a river-crossing battalion, along with an engineer pontoon battalion to support our own engineer battalion. I also have a second commitment from the fighter-bomber boys, up to 200 sorties for the first day of battle."

He pushed the bottle of vodka across to Colonel Dorokhin, Commander of the 353rd Guards Tank Regiment. "Turin, top our glasses up."

The thirty-year-old colonel picked up one of the bottles on the table and, helped by Colonel Tsaryov of the 332nd Regiment, topped up the empty glasses all the officers were now holding. Once completed, the general pushed his chair back and stood up, his officers following suit. He raised his small, chipped glass in the air. "To our motherland, to our Uman Division. *Za Vas!*"

"*Za Vas!*" they all responded in unison.

"Our political officer has something to say. Then the briefing is over, and I will see you all individually. The floor is yours, Arkaldy."

Magdeburg-Cochstedt Airfield, East Germany. 108th Guards Airborne Regiment. 4 July 1984. The Red Effect −23 Hours

The two officers, dressed in camouflaged, one-piece coveralls, a blue and white horizontally striped shirt beneath, walked and talked near one of the aircraft aprons at Cochstedt Airport, situated thirty-kilometres south-west of the city of Magdeburg. The airport was built in 1957, as a Soviet Air Force Base, now one of the many forward bases being used for the impending attack on the West. The two men were airborne officers, the VDV (*Vozdushno -Desantyne Voyska*) blue and white striped shirt confirming their elite status. Their conversation was loud, as the activity in and around the airport was feverish.

There was the bassoon sound of the aero engines of the Illyushin II troop-carrying aircraft as they reached take-off speed. A steady stream of aircraft had been arriving and leaving the airfield ever since the 108th Guards Airborne Regiment had arrived: a mixture of AN-12 Cubs and AN-22 Cocks. There were even a couple of AN-124 Condors, barely in service with the Soviet Air Force. Although capable of carrying over 100 tons of cargo, it was not really suitable for carrying paratroopers due to pressurisation issues. Many of the aircraft had Aeroflot markings, commandeered for use by the military. The other side of the airport was swamped with a range of different helicopters, the *whop-whop* of rotor blades caused as a consequence of the manually induced noise from the main gearbox and transmission chains along with the main and tail rotors slicing through the air. There were Mi-2 Hoplites, small, lightly armed transport helicopters, capable of carrying eight passengers and used in close-air support. But, at the moment, they were being utilised as taxis, ferrying senior officers around as the tension and planning built up in readiness for the strike that they now knew was a matter of days away.

Bigger helicopters were also on the move, the Mi-8 Hips, able to carry twenty-four combat troops or play a significant role in close-air support, its two stub wings supporting four weapons pylons capable of carrying rocket pods, anti-tank missiles or machine guns. Heavyweight Hooks had also started to arrive but, as yet, none of the newer Mi-26 Halo.

The two airborne officers held a hand on top of their pale blue headgear as they moved closer to the activity. They were part of the 108th Guards Regiment, their mother division being the 7th Guards Airborne, based in Kaunas, Lithuania. They had been notified of the intended attack on the West and had received a warning order for the role they would have to play. Once the flow of the battle was apparent to the TVD command, their airborne unit, along with the rest of the division and many others, would be assigned targets well behind enemy lines. They didn't as yet know what theirs would be: Securing a bridge, high ground or blocking a supply route. Whatever it was, the Soviet Union had a significant airborne force at its disposal to make life very difficult for NATO.

"God, do you think we'll ever get used to this bloody racket?" Lieutenant Colonel Stanislav Yezhov, battalion commander of one of the BMD assault battalions of the 108th Airborne Regiment, laughed.

"You love it really," his regimental commander, Boykov, shouted back.

"This isn't going to be like Afghanistan, sir."

Boykov thought for a moment, thinking through what was likely to be expected from his unit. A veteran of Afghanistan, he was no stranger to battle and had certainly seen men mortally wounded or killed outright in some of the actions he had led. "It won't." He laughed. "Too bloody wet and cold for a start. Make sure you have your waterproofs."

They sat down on a battery-powered truck that was used to move small items of cargo about the airport.

"With fifteen air assault brigades and the other divisions vying for assets, it's going to put a bit of a strain on our air force."

"I've just been talking to an air force colonel. They are already commandeering aircraft," Colonel Viktor Boykov responded.

Yezhov stood up. "We don't want bloody civilians flying us into battle."

Boykov pulled him back down. "Sit down, Stani. They'll use the taxi drivers for routine stuff. We'll have military pilots for what we need to do."

"Thank God for that. If they had to help us to destroy the enemy's nuclear capability, destroy or neutralise their surface-to-air missile sites, disrupt logistics and lines of communication, they'd shit themselves."

Boykov burst into laughter, joined by his junior officer, a member of the ground staff looking at them strangely as he walked past.

"Have you any inkling, sir, any idea what target they have us lined up for?"

"Until it kicks off, they won't really know themselves. I wouldn't be surprised if we were used to support an OMG."

"Oh, a chancy one then." Yezhov smiled. "We take the ground and sit and wait for them to turn up."

"When you joined with me, Stani, you never said you wanted it easy."

"It certainly hasn't been that. So, what's next?"

"I want to run through some options with my senior officers. Go over some maps of our likely target areas and walk through a few scenarios."

"Makes sense, sir."

"Glad you think so!" Boykov shouted back as one of the large Mi-6 Hooks came in to land close by.

"Dry runs?"

"Yes, match units up to their aircraft, talk with the pilots, and agree a loading schedule for the BMDs."

"A pretty heavy workload."

"You're right again, Stani." The colonel smiled. "I think we should swap roles." He stood up. "Come on, let's get some breakfast then pull the lads together, and you can start to earn your high wages."

Chapter 23

North-west of Supplingen, West Germany. 0600 4 July1984. The Red Effect −22 Hours

The heavily camouflaged FV107 Scimitar eased forward gently, just poking its nose out of the treeline, the Jaguar J-60 engine, capable of taking the armoured reconnaissance vehicle to a top speed of eighty-kilometres per hour, purring gently. Its latent power obvious, impatient to do what it was best at, it was pushing the Scimitar along at speed.

The light tank was deliberately camouflaged, breaking up its telltale shape, helping it blend in with its surrounding environment. Scrim netting had been draped over its bulk, the crew making sure it didn't interfere with the movement of the turret or any of the other vital pieces of equipment that were required for the reconnaissance tank to operate effectively. Additional foliage, that matched their immediate surroundings, had been added, placed at strategic points, pushed into the netting or lashed to the sides, to break up the tank's obvious profile. The crew were satisfied that they merged well with their surroundings. It could give them the edge, delaying the time when the enemy could spot them, potentially saving their lives. Thermal imaging devices would be a different matter, but not all of the Soviet armour was fitted with it. If they were fitted with thermal imaging systems, they would soon pick out the heat of the engine at the front and the three crew members: the driver, gunner and commander in the turret.

It was 0600 and their orders were to sit there and watch and wait. Lieutenant Nicholas Campbell studied the 1:25,000 topographical map as best he could, checking the features marked on the map with those on the ground in front of him. They were sitting on a raised piece of ground on the south-eastern edge of a forest about half a kilometre north-west of the small village of Supplingenburg. Behind them, the forest stretched back for about five-kilometres. On their left arc, about a two kilometres away, was the village of Barmke. Three-kilometres to their east was Emmerstedt on the outskirts of Helmstedt, right on the Inner German Border. On their right arc was the village of Supplingenburg; in front of them a patchwork of cultivated fields, some sewn with potatoes and kelp, others with yellow corn. Much of it had been harvested as a consequence of the good weather that had just been experienced in West Germany. A second Scimitar of Lieutenant Campbell's troop was further north, providing an overwatch as their troop commander had moved into position. Two further Scimitars were about two hundred metres behind the forward two, ready to provide cover if the two tanks were bounced and had to withdraw quickly. His troop was a small element of 4 Armoured Division, on the leading edge of the covering force.

As the covering force for 1 British Corps, 4 Armoured Division had an important role to play. In fact, its role was crucial to the defence of 1 BR Corps' sector of responsibility. With three brigades, one armoured and two mechanised, it had been assigned an eighty-kilometre-wide front to defend: a massive task for such a small force. A division would normally only be expected to defend a front of thirty to fufty-kilometres but, for a covering force, this could be extended up to ninety. 4 Div had to cover an area that started just below Wolfsburg in the north to Bad Harzburg in the south, its task to delay any attack long enough to allow the bulk of 1 BR Corps to get into their wartime locations, dig in and prepare to hold off the potentially unstoppable force that would be rolling towards them. Lieutenant Campbell's troop was an inherent part of that covering force. 20th Armoured Brigade was moving into position between the south of Wolfsburg and north of Konigslutter, and 11th Mechanised Infantry Brigade had the province between Konigslutter and east of Wolfenbuttel. The third brigade in the division, 33rd Mechanised Infantry Brigade, covered the rest of the sector to the south. Two hundred and twenty-four tanks and less than 3,000 infantry were not a particularly powerful force to hold back the Soviet steamroller that could be heading their way. A couple of hundred Chieftain tanks against 3 Shock Army's 1,300 T-80s and T-64s seemed an unfair match. Following 3SA, there would be the Soviet's second strategic echelon, equally as powerful. 20th Armoured and 11th Mechanised Brigade had a key area to defend. Any advancing Soviet force would have to negotiate the large town of Braunschweig. Located in Lower Saxony, with a population of a quarter of a million people, it was a sizeable barrier to a straightforward advance. Their options were limited. Go straight through the town, clearly a poor option. Bogging down their infantry units in house-to-house fighting, restricting the movement of their main battle tanks, this route was patently not an option for a speedy advance. Bypassing the town to the north and south was the obvious route to take. To the north, they had relatively open ground and could take advantage of the Route-E3 autobahn that ran between Braunschweig to the south and Wolfsburg to the north. 20th Armoured Brigade had been given the mission to protect that route, its two armoured regiments, with their 114 tanks between them, more suited to the relatively open ground. They had the means to move around the battlefield quickly and block the path of the Soviet advance. Their task though was not to hold but to delay – but delay the enemy long enough to force their units to break out of their route of march and deploy. Long enough so they could inflict some major damage on the battalions or regiments they would come up against, blunt their attack, dent their confidence, test their command and control, and make them hesitant. Buy some time for the Corps. The more time available for the main body of the British forces in Germany to get in position, to dig in, build up their defenses; stockpile their ammunition, the better. And, just as important, buy time for reinforcements to arrive from Britain, particularly the 2nd Infantry Division.

Their allies would be doing the same. To the north of 1 BR Corps, 1st German Corps would also be deploying their covering force and primary forces into their wartime locations and, to the north of them, the 1st Dutch Corps would have some units moving forward, although the Dutch politicians had delayed making the decision to deploy and German forces were having to initially cover in their stead. To 1 BR Corps south, Northern Army Group were also waiting for 1 Belgium Corps to take up their positions.

Lieutenant Campbell's Scimitar was part of the reconnaissance platoon of the Second Battalion, Royal Green Jackets. 11th Brigade consisted of three battle groups: The Royal Green Jackets, the Royal Regiment of Fusiliers, and the Third Royal Tank Regiment. Each battle group was further subdivided into four combat teams. The Brigadier, in consultation with Major General Walsh, commander of 4th Armoured Division, had deployed a thin screen at the furthest most point of the FLOT (Forward Line of Own Troops) using the Royal Green Jacket's battle group. Further back, he had stationed the remaining two battle groups. One would cover a line from Braunschweig to Wolfenbuttel, with a combat team as far forward as Schandelah; one at Konigslutter; a third deployed in the town of Wolfenbuttel itself; and the fourth covering the south of Braunschweig. The 3rd Royal Tank Regiment battle group would be dug in further west. The Royal Green Jacket's battle group would eventually withdraw through these units once the pressure from the advancing Warsaw Pact forces became too great.

Combat Team Alpha, made up of an infantry company, supported by the mortar platoon and two Milan sections, each with five firing points, were disposed in and around the village of Supplingenburg, with Lieutenant Campbell's troop of Scimitars covering them to the north. Combat Team Bravo, two troops of tanks from the armoured regiment and a mechanised infantry platoon, covered the village of Supplingen further south. Combat Team Charlie was further south again. Two troops of tanks and a mechanised platoon had been allocated to defend the village of Frellstedt. The smallest of the combat teams, Combat Team Delta, with a single tank troop, mechanised platoon and the mobile Milan section, was arrayed along the wooded area, der Elm, that ran north-west to south-east behind the other three units. The majority of the battle group would withdraw through this woodland, Combat Team Delta covering the withdrawal as best they could. Ahead of the Green Jackets' battle group was a thin screen of Scimitars from the divisional reconnaissance regiment, 15th/19th Hussars.

Sergeant Ron Reid peered through his binos, covering the left arc, knowing his troop commander would be covering the right. His driver and gunner were below, asleep. There was no sleeping on the engine decks. This time it wasn't an exercise: they were out on watch for real. But it didn't seem real somehow, and he expected a call any minute now to tell him it was Endex and they could all go home. Saying that, back at the barracks there had been a sense of realism, although they still had a box of Herferder beer stowed onboard. There had been a greater focus on what they would really need: ammunition, rations and water. He pulled out a wax pencil to mark the plastic-coated map, identifying key points ahead, landmarks he could use when calling in fire for his gunner, or other units defending the line.

"Shit." The pencil slipped from his rubber glove-covered fingers and clattered down into the fighting compartment, disappearing into the turret monster. "I won't see that again till this is all over," he muttered under his breath. He rubbed his back against the hatch rim, the itch slowly making its way lower and lower down his back, irritated by the T-shirt and woollen shirt, topped with his combat jacket. It was too hot to wear a jumper and the Noddy suit provided a fourth layer that created too much warmth. The olive-green nuclear, biological and chemical Mark III suit was worn to protect the soldiers from a potential chemical or nuclear barrage by the Warsaw Pact. The double-layer smock and trousers, with an inner layer of charcoal-impregnated cloth and an outer layer of modacrylic and nylon, would protect the wearer for up to twenty-four hours. On his hands, Reid wore a pair of black rubber gloves with white cotton inners and rubber over boots covering his combat-highs. He adjusted the focus of the binoculars, the rubber gloves making it difficult for him to twist the dial. *Will they come today?* He thought.

Chapter 24

*South-east of Luneburg, West Germany. 0700 4 July1984. The Red
Effect –21 Hours*
The fifty-five-ton Leopard 2's liquid-cooled, 47.6 litre, V-12 engine
purred as the driver, located at the front of the main battle tank offset
to the right of its centreline, eased the tank forward into the berm
recently dug out by an engineer party. Once the driver had brought the
tank to a halt, the commander closed down in the turret, swinging it left
and right, checking that the barrel of the 120mm, smooth-bore main
gun was clear to move in a full arc. He also checked that, with the tank
hull down, in a closed-down situation, he would be able to see through
his six periscopes giving him all-round vision. As a third-batch, Leopard 2
A1, the commander's primary panoramic sight had been raised by
50mm, giving him an alternative view when closed down. The engine
continued to tick over as the tank commander rotated the turret one
last time before stopping it, so it pointed directly ahead. Satisfied that
he had a clear view of the terrain ahead, he pushed the circular hatch
up and back to the rear and climbed up until he was waist high above
the turret, the loader's hatch to his right with the MG-3 7.62mm air-
defence machine gun. He looked around at the copse they were hiding
in, the tank strewn with camouflage to help them blend in with their
surroundings, the trees behind reducing any sky lining. They were
positioned west of the Stecknitz Canal, south-east of the large town of
Luneburg, a pair of Leopard tanks dug into a small copse close to the
south-east edge of the village of Hagan. From here, they had a clear
field of view of the canal and, more importantly, a clear field of fire.
They were part of the 9th Panzer Brigade of the 1st Panzer Division, 1
German Corps' covering force, fulfilling a similar role to that of the
British 4th Armoured Division. Their respective aim was to hold back
any Soviet advance: keep their massive tank armies at bay until the
main battle area could be secured.

Using his binoculars, the tank commander, and also the commander of
the troop of Leopard 2s deployed close by, surveyed the ground ahead.
To his front, about 1,200 metres ahead, over open farmland, zigzagged
with a patchwork of cultivated fields, was the canal. To his immediate
left, no more than 1,000 metres distant, the 216 ran from west to east,
crossing the canal. To the west, it linked up with an autobahn behind
him, which ran north to south. To his immediate right, south-east, 1,500
metres away, just out of sight of his position, lay a minor road that
crossed the canal from west to east. This was being guarded by his

other two Leopards, their task to watch and wait. Engineers were preparing the bridges for demolition. His task was to provide them with cover, ready to dash forward and deal with any enemy armour that tried to get across. Part of the 33rd Panzer Battalion of the 9th Panzer Brigade, he was far from alone.

West of Rasdorf, near the Fulda Gap, West Germany. 0700 4 July 1984. The Red Effect −21 Hours

The M1-Abrams advanced down the narrow forest track, trees lining both sides of the route, an M3 Bradley Cavalry Fighting Vehicle, leading the way. Behind, another twelve main battle tanks of the cavalry unit followed in line of march. From the 1st Squadron of the 11th Cavalry, the 'Black Horse' Regiment, they were deploying as a screen, a covering force, for the US V Corps, one of four corps-size formations that made up the Central Army Group. The Cavalry Regiment would conduct a similar role to that orchestrated by 4th Armoured Division for 1 BR Corps and the 1st Panzer Division for 1 German Corps, both in the Northern Army Group.

As yet, NATO had no inkling where the Warsaw Pact main thrusts would be. But the menacing build-up of Soviet troops along the border was now becoming apparent, and the Soviet Politburo were still insisting that it was purely a defensive measure to counter the NATO Hawks accusation that the peaceful people of the Soviet Union of wanted a war; that they were only deploying their forces post Exercise Hammer 84 rather than returning them to barracks as a consequence of the sabre-rattling of the American President and British Prime Minister. Baskov had demanded that NATO desist from calling up their National Guard and reserves and return their divisions to their barracks before they would stand down.

One thing was certain: as far as the commander of CENTAG was concerned, the wasp-waist of Germany in the area of the Fulda Gap would be a tempting target. A powerful armoured thrust across 110 kilometres would find Warsaw Pact soldiers in the centre of the city of Frankfurt. A mere ninety kilometres further and the hammer and sickle flag would fly over the political capital of Bonn. Not only would they be close to the French border but also to the huge US Army supply depot at Kaiserslautern and numerous air bases close by. It would be disastrous for NATO, splitting the two army groups, NORTHAG and CENTAG, and effectively cutting West Germany in half.

As CENTAG's area had a largely mountainous and wooded border with the Inner German Border, the terrain was considered far more favourable to defend than the flatter, more open spaces of northern Germany. Although formidable terrain for a mass tank army to cross, the immediate area around Fulda was not as impassable as the NATO planners would wish for. The Fulda River, a mere twenty metres across and not much more than two metres deep, wouldn't even be considered a barrier by the Soviet Army. Their vast array of river-crossing equipment, from the PMP pontoon bridge, with its thirty-two river pontoons that, when deployed, had a span of nearly 400 metres, to the TMM vehicle-launched bridge system. During, or before, the period a bridge was being erected, or floated, the Soviets could use their GSP heavy amphibious ferry. A left and right unit, linked together, could ferry up to fifty tons across a river. Providing the circumstances were right, a main battle tank could even fire its main gun as it was ferried across. With the knowledge that a forward defence stance would not be effective, as the Warsaw Pact armies could concentrate their forces and choose which point, or points to punch through the thinly spread NATO forces, CENTAG had no option but to opt for a defence-in-depth strategy. Using anti-tank weapons on the forward slopes, where vegetation permitted, with main battle tanks hitting the advancing forces on the flanks, they could blunt an attack but pull back before they were overwhelmed, and then carry out the same manoeuvre all over again.

The Black Horse Regiment had been deployed to the Fulda Gap region of West Germany in May 1972. Its mission was twofold: conducting patrols of the Inner German Border, watching for any unwelcome Soviet or East German activity, and acting as the covering force for the US V Corps. Although the squadron manned an observation post in the area of Hunfeld, 1st Squadron had been ordered to move out and take up position's further east, as an attack by the Warsaw Pact was becoming more and more likely. Military commanders insisted that an attack was imminent, and likely to be within the next forty-eight hours. Although only a squadron, it punched well above its weight. It was a powerful force, with forty-one M1-Abrams, forty M3 Bradley CFVs, twelve M113 armoured personnel carriers, six M106 mortar carriers, four M577 command vehicles, and eight M109 self-propelled artillery.

As a replacement for the ageing M60A1, which was only protected by homogenous, rolled armour, the M1-Abrams was of an innovative design. The traditionally used homogenous armour had been replaced by laminate armour designed by the British Vehicle Research and Development Establishment at Chobham. Hence the nickname of Chobham armour. Its protection, against the weapon of choice for many systems, the shaped charge, was significantly improved.

Private First-Class Larry Poole gunned the multi-fuel gas turbine engine as they left a dip and started a gradual climb. Staff Sergeant Kyle Lewis, the tank commander and platoon sergeant, his head and shoulders above the turret hatch, rocked gently as he watched the Bradley ahead of them. The turret and its 105mm rifled tank gun were facing forwards, the track quite narrow. They were heading for their wartime deployment positions, crashed out as their senior officers were becoming more and more concerned by the hostility being shown by the Soviet Union. The commander of the Bradley bent his arm at the elbow, signalling to the right, the tank commander knowing it meant they were approaching the T-junction at the end of the track. He informed the driver, and, within a couple of minutes, they had moved onto route 84, the sixty-seven-ton tank swiveled around on its tracks, curving round to the right before continuing forward, sticking with the reconnaissance vehicle in front.

Tall trees lined the road either side of them, climbing away up the slope to their left, until they levelled off at 550 metres at the top of the Stalberg bei Hunfeld. The driver ramped up the tank's speed to a steady thirty-five kilometres an hour, leaving a trail of dust behind them. SSGT Lewis could hear his two other crew members laughing, knowing the lieutenant, their platoon commander, in the tank behind would be cursing PFC Poole. Kyle ordered him to take his foot off the gas and their speed dropped to fifteen. Four hundred metres further on, the density of the forest to their left thinned out slightly, the trees more scattered about a gentler slope. They had driven between two staggered knolls, the left called Marsberg, the unnamed one to the right they had nicknamed Clint, after the 'man with no name'. The platoon left the two knolls behind, driving into more open land, apart from a slightly raised piece of ground to their left, an extension of the Marsberg. A network of cultured fields filled the gap between the forest area and the village of Rasdorf, which had a population of less than a thousand.

The commander of the recce vehicle signalled again, this time with his left arm. Kyle gave the driver a warning that they would be turning left onto the low edge of the shallow reverse slope. The platoon of four M1-Abrams following behind would be tracking right. The Abrams roared as it swung left, churning up the ground as it made its way off the road and onto a track that ran along the lower slopes of the knoll extension. The engine whined as Poole pushed the armoured giant harder as they started to climb slightly, eventually stopping so the tank could be manoeuvred into a position where it could reverse up the gentle slope. From slightly higher up, but nowhere near the top, they could cover the open ground that was laid out in front of them. An enemy force, particularly a large armoured force, perhaps in battalion or regimental strength, would have to advance along route 84 if they wished to make any headway west. They would be forced to pass through the gap between the two knolls. It would make an ideal target for the eight Abrams, four each side, that could pick off the enemy armour as it approached across the fields or down route 84 itself. Three thousand metres to the rear, eight 155mm M-109 self-propelled artillery would be setting up to support the squadron, pounding the enemy whenever possible, adding to the devastation that would wreak havoc in the killing zone being created, making the Soviet advance west even more onerous.

SSGT Lewis guided the driver as he eased the tank gently into position. Situated on a small piece of ground where the slope levelled off for a short distance, but the undulating surface provided natural berms to hide behind. One such mound was in front where they could pull forward and be in a hull-down position. Lewis and his men had investigated this area and many like it. In fact, they knew this entire area like the back of their hands and had every intention of making the Soviet Army pay the price for even thinking of attacking their zone of control. Once they had destroyed a number of enemy tanks, they could reverse further up the gentle slope, the scattering of trees providing them with much needed cover from the enemy, turn around, and make their way west to the next deployment area. Other elements of the squadron would be waiting for them to pass, and the enemy would drive into yet another ambush.

Along the line of the forest edge, the four tanks, along with two M3 Bradleys, there to provide support in the likely event infantry would be used to winkle them out, adjusted their positions until the vehicle commanders were satisfied. Once happy, SSGT Lewis ordered the M1 to be pulled back, until it was in a turret-down position, then camouflaged. They would stay hidden until called forward to take on the enemy's armour.

The Bradleys would also keep watch, but slightly further up the slope. The M3 Bradley Cavalry Fighting Vehicle could certainly pack a punch. A heavyweight at twenty-five tons, with its Cummins VTA-903 engine, it could still travel at a top speed of sixty-kilometres an hour on roads. Its 25mm M242 chain gun would do serious damage to approaching mechanised infantry combat vehicles such as the BMP-1 and BMP-2. But with its dual TOW anti-tank launcher, it was equally as deadly for the Warsaw Pact's main battle tanks.

SSGT Lewis informed his crew that he was moving forward to complete a visual reconnaissance of the area out in front, instructing them to break out the cool box, packed with ice and bottles of Coke that were chilling inside. He climbed out of the turret, dropped down off the front glacis, and made his way to the natural berm ahead. Looking back, he shouted to the crew, reminding them to get the cam-net erected. Looking up, he could see the much higher hill behind him, covered in dense forest. Where they were now was decidedly sparser, but enough cover for them to hide in. His platoon commander would no doubt be along soon. He clambered up the shallow side and lay partly on top of the edge, his elbows supporting him as he moved his binoculars in a sweeping arc. Before he had chance to zoom in on some of the key areas, a body crashed down beside him.

"Well, Troop, are the Reds on their way?" The Lieutenant laughed, panting, wiping sweat from his brow after tabbing hard and fast. Even though he was twenty-five years old, he still retained some of his puppy fat and had the sort of soft-skinned face that belied his age, often being mistaken for an overgrown teen. Lewis liked him, even though he felt he could be a liability at times. But that wasn't a problem. Most of the time, the Lieutenant deferred to his Senior NCO, which suited Kyle Lewis who had been driving, commanding and competently firing a tank's main armament since he had first trained in an M-60.

"Hi, sir. We've got it pretty much covered here. With eight M1s and the Bradleys, we can certainly give them a bloody nose."

The officer punched his NCO's arm. "So, is the bet on then, Staff?"

Lewis laughed. "You know my tanks got the best gunner in the squadron, sir. It would be like taking candy from an infant."

"We'll see. So, what have we got?"

"They're going to send recce forward first, a mix of T-64s and BMPs probably. They can either use the L3170 and swing north-west or take the 84 and head west. Either way they will have to go across our arc of fire, and we should be able to hit them hard."

"It'll look like a tank graveyard by the time we're finished."

Lewis smiled, choosing to ignore his senior officer's display of naivety. "The likelihood, sir, is that they will hit the edges of the forests with arty fire first, so it will only be our surviving tanks that get to hit back. Once we've picked off their recce, the chances are we'll get hit again and again. Probably ground attack aircraft will have a poke at us."

"How long, then?"

"We hit as many as we can, move further up the slope and have another go; then we'll probably be pulled back."

"It's seems a waste of a good firing position."

Lewis looked at his baby-faced commander. "They will throw everything they've got at us to dislodge us from here. We couldn't hold back a tank regiment, or motor rifle regiment, if that's what they send. Eventually they'll push us off here, or outflank us..." He hesitated for a moment. "Or wipe us out."

Chapter 25

West of Magdeburg, East Germany. 12th Guards Tank Division/3 Shock Army. 1200, 4 July 1984. The Red Effect –16 Hours

Tank after tank sped along the E8 dual carriageway, a road regularly used by West German civilians going east to visit their families and friends in the western sector of Berlin. The British, and their allies, also used this, one of three corridors to transit through East Germany and join the rest of the troops guarding Berlin and the sovereign territory of the four occupying powers: Britain, United States of America, France and the Soviet Union.

The road now though was swamped with military vehicles – Soviet military vehicles. T-64As raced west, the 18th Independent Reconnaissance Battalion leading the way. There were two platoons of BMPs, mechanised infantry combat vehicles, a tank platoon, a BRDM-2 company, and a BRDM-2 Rkh, a chemical defence recce vehicle. The battalion rattled along the road, clearing a path for the rest of the division following on behind. One lane of the dual carriage on the opposite side was also being used for western flowing military traffic. Very little was moving east. The tail extended as far back as Magdeburg.

The entire division was on the move: three tank regiments, one motor rifle regiment and an air defence regiment thronged the roads. Behind them, engineers, signals, transport, maintenance and chemical defence units. The artillery regiment along with the SSM battalion, the self-propelled artillery and surface-to-surface missiles, had moved forward the previous day, to be in a position to support 10GTD in its assault. The roads were choked, making a perfect target for NATO had the two organisations been at war. But as yet they weren't.

Even further back, but equally as important to the division, there were over 100 POL trucks carrying fuel vital for supplying the armour and infantry in maintaining their advance. Sixty further trucks carried ammunition, equally as important. Across the entire division, over 500 trucks would provide support for the teeth arms, acting as the arteries to feed an ever-hungry giant. Two parallel routes had been chosen; more simply weren't available as the entire Warsaw Pact was starting to move its forces forward: one route crossing the River Elbe to the south of Magdeburg, and the second to the north. All would end up in the forests of Feichtinger Hohenzug and Bartenslebener Forst. Effectively, as 10GTD moved out, 12GTD would move in. They would then wait to be tasked. The division had already received a warning-order, directing the unit to prepare to act as an operational manoeuvre group (OMG) that would track 10GTD's progress and, when the opportunity presented itself, strike deep into NATO's rear.

General Turbin, 'The Bear', had been ruthless in his relentlessness to get the division in position as soon as possible so that, when his master called upon him and his men to do their duty, they would be ready. One battalion commander had already been sacked for failing to keep to his schedule, with a view to a court-martial at a later date. This spurred the others on, driving their men and vehicles hard. The general wanted his armour, infantry and logistics-tail off the roads before the battle started the following morning. The lead elements of his armoured division had to be in position, rested, armed and refueled. Ready. The soldier, a veteran of World War Two, recognised that it was tactically unsound consolidating his forces so close together. Should NATO resort to tactical nuclear weapons at the start of the war, his division would be decimated. It was an acceptable gamble. Dispersing his troops too far apart was not an option if he was to stick close to the retreating British Army and exploit any gaps made by the 10th, giving the 12th the opportunity to strike deep into the enemy's rear.

Chapter 26

Gronau, West Germany. Combat Team Bravo. 1200, 4 July 1984. The Red Effect −16 Hours

The engine of the FV4204, a Chieftain armoured recovery vehicle from the LAD section, hummed as the driver pushed it to full power, the dozer blade at the front gouging a three and a half metre furrow to a depth of roughly two metres – the perfect depth to allow a Chieftain to drive into the berm hull down, exposing as little of the tank as possible, in defilade. With the bulk of the hull behind the crest of ground raised as a consequence of the earth piled forward, the main volume of the tank would be behind hard cover, but its turret and main gun would be free to turn and pick out any advancing targets. A screen of trees behind the berm would provide a backdrop to blend in with. The dozer blades were far from perfect, the ARV having to take off a shallow layer at a time with the hydraulics occasionally failing. Lieutenant Wesley-Jones perched on the edge of the turret as he watched the ARV at work. It was actually an ARRV as it had an Atlas crane positioned along one side of the tank. He watched them scraping for a few minutes then picked up his binoculars to look further afield.

The small forest they were in was about five hundred metres by three hundred and was in a prominent position on the eastern edge of the Gronau. Barfelder Strasse ran east to west alongside, running through the centre of the village. As his tank was on the northern edge of the forest, he was able to look across the open fields as far as Betheln, about three kilometres away. Turning his gaze further east, he could see straight down the road, the one that linked this village to the next, almost as far as Barfelde, the outskirts less than two kilometres distant. There were four Scorpions from the regiment's reconnaissance troop in the vicinity of Barfelde, doing the same as they were: watching and waiting for the enemy to come. When those Scorpions, should they survive, came tearing down the road, he would know that the enemy wasn't far behind. The recce element might have delayed them for a few minutes, but not much more than that.

The ground to the left of the road was raised slightly, making a very shallow plateau. At the western edge of the plateau, he knew that two FV438s would be digging in, again ably assisted by a Chieftain with a dozer blade. Any enemy armour approaching from the east between Gronau and Betheln across open ground would make an ideal target for the two FV438s and their anti-tank missiles. Derived from a converted

FV432, the vehicle mounted a twin launcher for the Swingfire missiles. Twelve more were stowed inside.

Wesley-Jones swung the binos left again, zooming in on the movement around the two vehicles. A light-wheeled tractor, with a rear hydraulic bucket, was digging a foxhole for the crew. The crew of three were no doubt setting up the control unit fifty to a hundred metres away from the 438. This would enable them to completely hide the vehicle. The missiles could be aimed and fired from this remote location, the swingfire missile capable of making a ninety-degree turn once launched. With a range of up to 4,000 metres, the wire-guided missile, providing visibility was good, would be able to pick off the enemy tanks, or BMPs, as soon as they came into view. Their time there would be limited though as, once the firing point was identified, they would attract heavy fire from the advancing enemy and probably artillery. Their task wasn't to hold ground. They were there to take advantage of the open ground ahead of them to pick off the Soviet armour; to inflict casualties and force them to deploy, delaying their advance west. Then, they would scoot west, heading across the River Leine to set up again in pre-dug-out positions on the other side and start all over again, picking off the enemy as they got closer to the natural barrier that the river provided for the British units digging in on the western bank.

Wesley-Jones looked east again, picturing the advancing units that were likely to come towards them. Intelligence they had to date was telling them that they were up against the 10th Guards Tank Division. He knew their tank regiments had the latest T-80s. He was confident his Chieftains could play their part, but wished he had the more modern Challenger that had recently been issued to 7th Armoured Brigade.

He shifted on the edge of the turret, so he was able to face south-east, just as Patsy handed him a cup of coffee. He thanked him. It was welcome. Within an hour of the rest of the squadron arriving, followed by the regiment and attached units, his troop had been sent across the bridge to set up in defence of Gronau. Although managing to get a couple of hours' sleep, he and his crew, along with the rest of the troop, were starting to feel the strain from a lack of sleep and living rough. *Thank God for the BV*, he thought. At least with the boiling vessel, they could have hot drinks and food. But this position wasn't a permanent one either. Once they had ensured the enemy paid the price for advancing on Gronau, his troop would also withdraw across the river, the engineers eventually blowing the bridge, forcing the Soviet Army to find other means to cross to the other side. The bulk of Combat Team Bravo would remain on the western bank. Alpha and Charlie Troop, with their three Chieftains each and two sections of the Royal Green

Jacket's platoon that had been attached to the squadron, were digging in on the western bank. The third rifle section of eight men, the driver and a gunner staying with the battle taxi, with its peak engineering turret, positioned deeper into the village, were on the eastern edge of Gronau, on the edge of the village itself. The 432 would wait to be called forward and support with its L37A1 GPMG gun. Lieutenant Christian James, the platoon commander, had also allocated two 66mm LAW anti-tank rockets to the section, for close protection should they find themselves confronted by enemy armour right on top of them. Their primary role was to protect the two Milan firing posts that were covering the approaches to the village. They had been joined by a Sustained-Fire GPMG, along with the platoon HQ vehicle. Again, once they had blunted the enemy attack, if they were able to do so, they would scoot across the river to relative safety.

Wesley-Jones lowered his binoculars and took a long drink from his now cooling mug of coffee. The banshee sound of the ARV disappeared into the distance as it headed back across the river to support the rest of the combat team in preparing their positions. They wouldn't pull into their berms until the last minute, initially staying well into the tree line, knowing that any attack would be preceded by a heavy artillery bombardment or air strike. To his left was Two-Bravo, and to his right the other member of his troop. When the moment was right, they would shoot forward, settle into their defilade positions and take out any enemy tanks that presented them with a target. They were too small a unit to make a huge impact but would delay the enemy long enough to allow the units behind to dig in deep.

Spotting movement on the road ahead, he placed his black plastic, half-moon-shaped mug on the top of the turret and picked up his binos again. Roughly 500 metres out, he could see a 432 towing a trailer, followed by two engineers on foot. The engineers were manually placing eleven-kilogram barmines, anti-tank mines, on a conveyor belt that fed them to the trailer. On pallets of seventy-two mines each, the FV432 could carry 144 mines that were automatically armed as they passed along the conveyor. The minelayer was automatically digging a furrow, laying the mines into it at the correct depth and spacing, and filling in the furrow once laid. In just over an hour, a front of over 600 metres could be laid by just this one vehicle. Laying mines either side of the road would protect their flanks, forcing the enemy towards the centre where they could be hit from the flanks. The goal was to lay enough to enforce a killing zone. Main battle tanks, or mechanised infantry combat vehicles such as the BMP-1 or BMP-2, would hit the minefield and be brought to a halt. This would enable the defending forces to finish them off. The Soviet commander's only option then was to bring forward mine-clearing equipment, making another target for the NATO forces controlling the killing ground. Forward artillery and air observers would also be watching, ready to bring even more destruction down on top of the advancing enemy.

Patsy popped his head out of the turret and pulled himself up onto the edge, his feet dangling over the turret side, resting on the top of the smoke discharger unit.

"OK, Corporal Patterson?"

"Yes, sir. Just wondering what's happening to our families." The twenty-five-year-old corporal looked worried. His cam-blackened face revealed the odd white vertical streak, and Wesley-Jones wondered if his NCO had been crying. His heart went out to him. Although he wasn't married and had no children of his own, or none that he knew of, he had picked up an atmosphere of dread amongst some of the 'Pads'. He smiled inwardly. The nickname for married soldiers who had their own pad, was not meant to be derogatory; just a little jealousy from single soldiers at their comrades living in a flat or house of their own, free of the barrack-block mentality. "It's Victoria, isn't it? Your daughter?"

Patsy smiled, pleased his commander had remembered. "Yes. We call her Vicky. My mother-in-law hates us shortening her name. Game on." He chuckled. "This can't be for real, can it, sir?"

The lieutenant pondered for a moment, considering how to respond; torn between being a troop commander, yet wanting to share his doubts with a fellow human being. There might be a few military ranks between them, but these were his troop: men he had trained with for over a year now. He had come to know them well, understanding their quirks and sometimes helping with their problems.

"It seems to be the case, Corporal. There was a lot of expected activity as a consequence of the large Soviet roll out for Hammer 84, but the troop movements that are being picked up now contradict those perceived intentions of a peaceful training exercise."

"Do we know when they'll come, sir?"

"I don't honestly know. But, when they do cross, Four Division will hold them for as long as possible."

"That's a pretty big force, sir."

Wesley-Jones looked at his corporal, the number two of his tank. He didn't think it was right to be anything but honest with him.

"Twenty-four hours tops. They are spread across a front of nearly ninety-kilometres. All they can hope to do is delay them."

"Surely, they can do more than that?" responded Patsy, his voice with a hint of panic in it, realising that they could be possibly be engaging the Soviet tanks as soon as in twenty-four hours.

"They're not strong enough to hold them back. So, it's about hitting the enemy hard and then pulling back to fight another day. Then they can become the reserve and come to our rescue." Wesley-Jones laughed, trying to ease Patsy's concerns. "They asleep down there?"

"Yes, sir."

"Give Trooper Mackinson another hour; then he can take stag while you get some shut-eye."

"What about you, sir?"

"The OC will be around soon. Once he's paid us a visit, I'll grab some sleep."

Gronau, West Germany. Royal Green Jackets' section, Combat Team Bravo. 1200 4 July 1984. The Red Effect –16 Hours

The platoon sergeant, Bob Thomas, was talking to the section commander, Corporal David Carter, as they watched a light-wheeled tractor using its rear bucket to dig pits for defensive positions to protect the unit setting up. A JCB410, a rough-terrain forklift tractor, dropped a pallet of pre-shaped corrugated sheet metal panels close by. Half-moon-shaped, with interlocking edges, the panels would enable the soldiers of the Royal Green Jackets to quickly build good defensive positions, providing them with some cover from an enemy bombardment. The LWT finished its job and left, it too joining the force that was rapidly building up on the western bank.

"Let's get this lot organised then, eh, Dave."

"Yes, Sarg. The sooner I have some cover, the better I'll feel. And we can finally get a bloody brew going."

In consultation with the combat team and platoon commander, it had been agreed that they would not occupy the village. It was bound to be targeted by artillery or fighter bombers, and they could end up being at greater risk with buildings collapsing around them. So, they were digging in along the edge. Directly ahead and to the right, they had a clear field of view. Half right was the only problem. Less than five hundred metres away was a conurbation of half a dozen houses, Gut Dotzum. The sergeant was reluctant to put any men in there in case they became isolated and cut off during an attack. The solution had been simple. Two Scimitars would sit there to discourage any enemy forces using the buildings, and to provide early warning of any sneak attack, the enemy using the houses to block the defenders' view. Two Chieftains dug in on the edge of Wallenstedt, a kilometre to the south, could fire into their exposed flank. Pre-prepared artillery and mortar fire could be called in quickly to target any enemy concentrations on the other side of the small estate. The engineers had also been busy, laying off-route anti-tank mines along the side of the road. The French

173

mine was designed for vehicle ambush, placed at the side of the road with a thin electric 'breakwire' laid across the road. Once a vehicle broke the wire, they would be struck by a powerful shaped-charge.

Sergeant Thomas walked along the line of foxholes being padded out with corrugated prefabs. One of the Milan firing points was already part finished, the crew of two building overhead cover, camouflaging, so it would be difficult to spot them from the air. The Milan-2s, a second-generation anti-tank weapon, the firing post mounted on a tripod, was ready in place in the dugout. Mounted on the side of it was a Milan missile, a second encased missile lying alongside ready for immediate use. When a target came into view, all the operator had to do was keep the aiming mark on the target and the SACLOS guidance system would deliver it onto the target. Its maximum range of 2,000 metres would be more than adequate to deal with the enemy when they broke out into the open. Satisfied that the Gympy SF team, the second Milan firing point and the Mortar Fire Controller were getting on with their work, Thomas went into one of the houses in the village behind, climbed to the second storey and made his way into one of the side rooms where L/Cpl Graham was keeping watch over the ground ahead.

"Progressing well down there, Sarg?"

"Should be ready for nightfall. See anything?"

"Not a sausage. A few civvies have just left Goot Dotzy, or whatever it's called."

"Gut Dotzum. Your bloody German is lousy, Will."

"Yeah, I know, Sarg. But I get my food from the canteen, anything else from the Naafi, and I know how to order a beer."

Smiling at the L/CPL's simple outlook on life, Sergeant Thomas went to the window where the glass had been knocked and took in the view. Two huge features immediately stood out. Dominating the skyline was Hildesheimer Wald, south-west of Hildesheim. Thirty kilometres long, a forest running north-west to south-east, its maximum height nearly 300 metres, with numerous ridges and winding tracks, a watercourse running along its length, it wouldn't be an easy feature for the enemy to pass through. To the south-east was a second forest, Sieben Berge. The forest was even higher at over 400 metres and the ground undulated severely. What it did was to create a channel that led right up to Gronau. Although 4th Armoured Division would put up a simple defence using these barriers south of Hildesheim, it would be short-lived.

He had asked his company commander, Major Hunt, why they weren't digging in, in force, further forward.

"It's simple," the major had replied. "The enemy could be on us so fast and with such force that we just won't have time to consolidate our position. We need Four Div to slow them down, giving us a chance to identify their main axis of advance. We just don't have enough troops to cover the entire front in depth. So, we identify their axis of advance and reposition our battle groups as necessary. Don't forget, the Inner German Border reaches as far forward as Goslar to our south. That puts them past our front line."

It was the correct answer, but it didn't exactly fill the sergeant with confidence.

L/CPL Graham joined him at the windowsill. "Kind of wish this was just an exercise, Sarg."

"Me and you both. All the times we've moaned about being crashed out. We'll be OK though; we're far from being on our own. NATO's a pretty big army and the Soviets will bite off more than they can chew. Keep your eyes peeled. We should get a warning from HQ when they're on their way, but we don't want to be bounced."

"Sarg."

Thomas left Graham to continue with his vigilant overwatch and headed downstairs to talk to the section, keep them motivated, make sure they dug deep, and were well protected.

Chapter 27

Combat Team Alpha, north-west of Supplingenburg, West Germany. 1600, 4 July 1984. The Red Effect −12 Hours

The FV432, a British armoured personnel carrier, swung right off Am Kievergarten into Barmiker Strasse. The soldier stood up through the hatch, hanging on to the pintle-mounted 7.62mm GPMG (General Purpose Machine Gun), secured on top for additional defence, as the battle taxi turned sharply on its tracks. The 432 was carrying Major Andy Phillips, the commander of A Company, the 2nd Battalion the Royal Green Jackets, now designated Combat Team Alpha, and Company Sergeant Major, CSM Tobi Saunders. After a hundred metres, the 432 turned down a track that led across the end of two long farm buildings before coming to a halt behind a thick hedgeline interspersed with a number of trees. The 432-engine continued to tick over as the OC of Combat Team Alpha would be continuing his tour of his command once this visit was complete. The OC slid along the bench seats in the back, pulled on the lever and pushed the armoured door back on its hinges. It swung back to the left, and he jumped out, clutching his SLR rifle. If he was going to be in combat then he didn't want the small calibre SMG, or to rely on his 9mm Browning pistol, but something that packed a punch.

Apart from a few Scorpion and Scimitar reconnaissance vehicles out ahead somewhere, the defence line his combat team was on would be the first major contact any Soviet force would come up against in this sector. Any armoured or mechanised force coming from the direction of Helmstedt would likely split: one element going north using the A2 autobahn, passing north of the small Dorm Forest, another element approaching directly from the east. The high ground of der Elm Forest to the south-west of Supplingenburg and Supplingen would be a significant barrier, so any force coming from that direction would have the village of Supplingenburg to the north, Frellstedt to the south and Supplingen in the middle, directly in their path. Combat Team A had the task of covering Supplingenburg. The village, with a population of fewer than 500, had a minor road that ran through the centre, with another minor road that crossed the village to the east, running north to south. North, it joined up with the E8/A2; south it passed through Supplingen, two kilometres away. Some of the villagers had moved out during the last twenty-four hours, but many had stayed behind. Major Phillips was concerned for two reasons. If the Warsaw Pact attacked, and he was not yet sure that they would although the signs were slowly pointing in that direction, the civilians would come under fire from aircraft and artillery shelling as a minimum. The situation would get even worse when he and his men pulled out and the villagers were left to the mercy of Soviets who would move in. The German government hadn't made any effort so far to evacuate civilians close to the border. But when, or if, they did, a steady trail of refugees and their vehicles would cause mayhem for the retreating troops.

Alongside the CSM, they both ran at a crouch towards the tree and hedgeline. Not that they needed to keep out of sight: there was no enemy this side of the Inner German Border yet. But there was always a danger that they were being watched by GRU sleepers, or East German sympathisers, closet communists, but the deployment had to continue regardless. Phillips had warned his men to be on the alert for any strangers or anyone showing an unhealthy interest in their activities.

Behind him, the four 432s of the platoon he was checking were lined up, ten metres apart, along a second treeline, rear doors facing towards them so any troops pulling back could pile in quickly for a fast getaway. Cam-netting had been draped over all four, propped up with lengths of slim tree trunks that had been gathered for that purpose over the years.

Major Phillips threw himself down by the side of the lieutenant in command of the platoon, the lieutenant's face blackened with cam-cream, foliage protruding from his helmet and strategically tied on to his webbing, helping him blend in with his surroundings.

"Sitrep, Dean?"

"We're nearly done, sir."

"Run it by me then."

The young lieutenant had been commanding the platoon for less than a year, and had only been out of the officer academy, RMA Sandhurst, for fifteen months. But the OC had been pleased with his progress.

He pointed ahead and to the left. "Fifty metres east, left arc, sir, a group of four trees. I have two Milan firing posts covered by a half section."

"They're a bit exposed, aren't they?"

"A bit, sir. But it's in a slight dip and they have a full 180-degree target area. They can cover any armour coming up the road to pass through the centre of the village and the road that crosses our front. Also, there is a ditch that runs from the left of this treeline right up to their position. They can pull out under cover when necessary. Further out to their left are a couple of watercourses. Those will make it difficult for anyone coming at us from the north."

"Excellent. The rest?"

"The hedgeline to our north is covered by Two Section and two firing posts. Any armour that tries to flank us will get a nasty surprise. The rest of One Section is here with me. Three Section is covering the 51mm to the rear."

"Have you plenty of smoke rounds for the mortar?"

"Half a dozen, sir. That will give us enough cover if we need to bug out quickly."

"Sergeant Rose?"

"He's with the mortar team and Three Section. I'm keeping them in reserve until we know the enemy's line of attack."

"Make sure they're well dug in," advised the CSM. "We haven't got the luxury of the engineers this time. When the shit starts to hit, you'll need a decent hole to hide in."

"I tried to get a bucket loader," the OC informed his senior officer. "But the priority is to get the troops further back dug in."

A soldier ran behind them, running at a crouch, carrying more ammunition for the section's Gympy. The gas-operated, open-bolt machine gun had a rate of fire of up to 1,000 rounds a minute, although a rate of 700 was more likely. Belt-fed from the left, it gave an infantry section significant firepower, enabling them to put down heavy suppressive fire while the rest of the section or platoon carried out an assault, or it could cover a withdrawal.

The OC studied the lay of the land with the aid of binoculars, while the CSM chatted to the rest of the unit close by. The field of fire ahead was perfect. If the enemy came straight down the metalled road, they would be hit by Two-Platoon in the centre and this platoon and Three-Platoon from the flanks. If they chose to skirt the village, either side, they would expose their flanks to the British troops. The OC could then shift his combat team reserve where needed. The sun felt warm on his helmet, and the smell of grass and earth assailed his nostrils. If it wasn't for the circumstances they were in, it could even be considered a nice day.

The OC turned to Saunders who had just returned. "You ready, CSM?"

"Yes, sir. Two-Platoon next?"

"Yes. Dean make sure your platoon put their Noddy suits on. If we get an arty-strike or air-attack, there's no telling whether or not they're going to kick off with chemical weapons."

"I'll get on it now, sir."

"Good. We stand-to at 1830."

"Sir."

With that, the OC and CSM jumped up and ran back to the 432 which had turned around ready to take them to their next port of call: checking on the dispositions of the rest of Combat Team Alpha.

Chapter 28

Erxlebener Forst, east of Helmstedt, East Germany. 62nd Guards Tank Regiment/10 Guards Tank Division/3 Shock Army. 1800, 4 July 1984. The Red Effect –10 Hours

The forty-two-ton T-80 tanks tore up the ground as they weaved in and out amongst the trees of the Erxlebener Forest. They had travelled all the previous night, stopping further east during late morning and early afternoon, making the last dash to their final assembly area as dusk was setting in. The forest resounded with the whine of gas-turbine engines as the tanks jockeyed for position, ready to settle down for a few hours before they launched their attack on the West.

Lieutenant Colonel Pavel Trusov had left his crew to camouflage his battalion command tank so he could attend the divisional commander's final briefing. That was the last briefing they would get. Now it was just a waiting game. As ordered, he joined his regimental commander, Colonel Pushkin, for an informal chat – if there was such a thing with a superior officer.

A tent had been erected for the regimental commander and, when Trusov entered, the colonel's clerk who was fussing about with maps and papers was dismissed.

"Pavel, park yourself down and try this."

The colonel handed him a flask and Trusov took a drink, smacking his lips. "This isn't your usual rubbish, sir?"

"Your insubordination will get you into trouble one day, Pavel," Pushkin said, but with no seriousness in his tone of voice. "I take it your men are ready?"

"Of course, sir. Any changes?"

"None. Aleksey is moving his battalion right up to the border tonight, acting as security for you as you pass through the Lapp Wald Forest."

"Is it still going ahead?"

The colonel sighed. "Yes, Pavel." He leant forward conspiratorially. "I hope to God we haven't bitten off more than we can chew. The British aren't going to just sit on their arses, and the Germans are going to fight like demons."

"Are you against this, sir?"

"No!" Pushkin snapped. "Sorry, Pavel. Of course, it's the right thing to do. Just don't underestimate our enemy – any of them. The British like a good fight, the Germans are fighting for their country, their soil, and the Americans have equipment and resources coming out of their ears. We can get to grips with that; it's the bloody air force that worries me. They

179

have some exceptional aircraft and those A-10s scare the shit out of me. Move fast, Pavel, and keep moving. We have to break up their covering force. If we stall and get bogged down, we'll have the second echelon regiments up our arse."

"We'll not let you down, sir."

"You need to get some sleep if you can. The arty bombardment will be your alarm call."

Trusov got up out of his seat. "And you, sir?"

"I shall head back to RHQ. Division will no doubt be plaguing us for updates as soon as it starts. In the meantime, it's radio silence, thank God."

Trusov saluted and made his way out of the tent and headed into the darkness towards his command tank. He wanted a last-minute talk with his company commanders. He doubted any of them would get any sleep tonight. His stomach knotted; less than ten hours before they were committed. *Committed to what?* he thought. *Hell and damnation?*

Ten to fifty kilometres east of Helmstedt, East Germany. Front, Army and Divisional Artillery. 180,0 4 July 1984. The Red Effect –10 Hours

The major stormed from one BM-27 vehicle to the next, cursing his men to get their vehicles camouflaged as quickly as possible. He didn't expect NATO to do any overflights, but he was aware of their capabilities with respect to satellites and the latest inside-looking radar. A battery of six were lined up abreast. The 220mm high-explosive missiles had just been slotted into the sixteen tubes, and a resupply was already and waiting to rearm them the moment their bombardment was complete, and they had finished relocating. They would need to get out of the area quickly, to avoid a counterstrike by the enemy, and to move forward maintaining an appropriate distance between them and their advancing armies.

The launchers were in the upraised position, a forty-five-degree angle pointing over the cabs of the Zil-135 chassis. The major was eventually satisfied that the crews were finally draping their vehicles with camouflage netting, dragging it over the cab and launcher tubes. Dusk would do the rest.

Just west of Brandenburg, but east of the town of Genthin, on a flat piece of ground that up until now had been used for planting crops, 3rd Shock Army's twelve Scud-Bs, carried by the heavyweight MAZ-543 TELs and totalling over thirty tons, had destroyed any cultured crops that had been planted there. Dispersed in groups of four, then paired off, they had been aligned forty-five degrees to their direction of fire, the guidance system taking its cue from the number one fin. The launcher vehicles were currently at Readiness Level 2. The launch section commander, a lieutenant, was sitting in the combat cabin in the centre of the vehicle, in between the two large centre wheels. He was checking the weather data from brigade command. His Scud-B TEL was on one side of the battery command vehicle, and the second one, fifty metres the other side. The battery command vehicle was linked to the brigade's 9S436, another Zil-131 box body, by their R-142 radio. Closer to the time of the launch, they would receive additional information while they carried out the task of raising the missile ready to fire. For now, all he and his crew could do was wait.

The division's fifty-four 2S-3s, twenty-eight ton, armoured 152mm self-propelled artillery moved into position closer to the Inner German Border so that their eighteen-kilometre range could provide the necessary support for 10 GTD's assault in the morning. The crew of four had settled down for the night in the fighting compartment, within its rotary turret, hoping to catch a couple of hours' sleep before they started their preparations at two in the morning. Once the firing started, two additional gunners would join them, feeding rounds through the two hatches at the rear. 744th Guards Artillery Regiment was split up into three battalions of eighteen each: one north of Beendorf, one south of Waldeck, and the third had moved to the west of Marienborn. There was no British military train at Marienborn today, swapping an East German locomotive for a West German one, or vice versa, after their trip between West Berlin and Braunschweig. The trains had been suspended the day before, further increasing the tension between the Warsaw Pact and the West. The regiment's BM-21s were also deploying ready for the early start the next day. 12th Guards Tank Division, one of 3rd Shock Army's four divisions, had also sent their fifty-four 2S3s forward, ready to support the attack, along with eighteen BM-21 missile launchers, capable of firing a barrage of 720 122mm missiles, swamping its target over an area of one square kilometre.

Along with a battalion of 160mm mortars from the artillery reserve of the Western TVD, a fighter-bomber division and a ground-attack fighter division, it didn't bode well for the British 4th Armoured Division.

Chapter 29

East of Brandenburg, East Germany. 3rd Shock Army's SCUD-B Brigade. 0300, 5 July 1984. The Red Effect –1 Hour

The RKZ-1 radiosonde, attached to a balloon, was released by the Scud Brigade's meteorological section, an operator tracking its progress with the RPS-1 Bread Bin radar. The operator was sitting in the back of a 9S436 Zil-131 box-body truck, confirming the information was being transmitted. The system also carried out the requisite computations that would be necessary to programme the missiles with the appropriate guidance corrections. Wind could have a serious, detrimental effect on the missiles' trajectory. The operator was satisfied with the feed; the data would soon be ready to be transmitted to the SCUD TELs.

There was now a buzz of activity around the SCUD launchers as the missile erection process began. It was less than an hour before the missiles would be launched onto their targets in the West. But there were still checks that needed to be completed before they were ready to be fired off. The crew, now dressed in their NBC suits, looked like ghouls in the barely perceivable light of the early morning. The Soviet Army's nuclear, biological and chemical suit was a heavy, rubberised one-size-fits-all with elasticated sleeves and hood. It was hot, heavy and uncomfortable. The GP-5 mask, like a large swimming cap that extended over the face, with small, round glass eyepieces and a large canister-shaped filter at the end by the mouthpiece, was also worn. It wasn't because they suspected a chemical attack by NATO missiles or aircraft, or even because the warhead could have contained a chemical or biological compound, but because of the toxicity of the fuel used with the SCUD's R-17 missile.

The missile of Launcher-one slowly rose, lifted up on its cradle, projecting a look and feel of menace around it. It took three minutes before it was fully vertical, in its final launch configuration. There was a slight clunk as the missile cradle returned to its horizontal position, the tip connecting with the roof of the cab. The crew lowered the rear stabiliser jacks, large circular pads at the base ensuring the stability of the vehicle's launch platform. Other crew members, led by one of the two *Praporshchik*, a warrant officer rank, looked over the missiles' batteries and electrics, and pumped starter fuel to the engine turboprop. The *Praporshchik*, responsible for aiming the missile, adjusted the artillery panoramic sight fitted close to the access port, ensuring the missile was properly aligned. For the projectile to accurately hit its intended target, a precise survey and aiming was essential. Once the warrant officer was satisfied that his task was finished, he informed his commander, who in turn informed brigade command that all the checks were complete, and they were ready for the final launch preparations.

The lieutenant looked up at the missile that towered above him, the warhead over eleven metres high. It stood there, dominant, waiting for the ignition sequence that would set it off on its journey to cause mayhem and death. With a range of 300 kilometres, the warhead could be launched at numerous NATO targets, from communication centres and airfields to what the Soviets believed were storage sites for NATO nuclear warheads. As part of the 3rd Shock Army, the targets to strike would be specifically in support of the initial advance by the 10th and 7th Guards Tank Divisions. The lieutenant in command of the TEL checked in with brigade one more time, confirming that they were now at Readiness Level 1. The two *Praporshchiks* joined their commander in the combat cabin; the rest of the crew sat in the main vehicle cab. All they could do now was wait for the call that would spring them into action. Close by, three other SCUD-Bs sat, immobile, waiting for the command to launch. Half a kilometre away, four more SCUD-Bs sat lingering, and 400 metres in the opposite direction, four more. The Warsaw Pact had nearly 600 SCUD-B TELs. Nearly a quarter of those would be targeting the NATO forces opposite, across the Inner German Border, this morning. It was three thirty in the morning of 5 July 1984.

Lappwald, north-east of Helmstedt, East Germany. 62nd Guards Tank Regiment/10 Guards Tank Division/3 Shock Army. 0300 5 July 1984. The Red Effect –1 Hour

A BRDM-2 and BMP-1 negotiated the tracks through the Lappwald Forest. Further south and further north, moving parallel, a second and third group made their way east through the forest. Behind the central column, a BRM-1K reconnaissance vehicle followed close behind, with the motorcycles following up at the rear. Although the motorcycle platoon of the regiment's reconnaissance company would be better able to weave in and out of the forest, the noise they made was very distinctive, and stealth was important. Although thirty tanks were creeping through the forest, the trees were able to dampen much of the low growls of the engines as they moved through at a crawl.

The reconnaissance company of the 62nd Tank Regiment of 10th Guards Tank Division was leading the way. Five hundred metres behind the recce company, Lieutenant Colonel Trusov's tank battalion was following. Trusov's T-80BK command tank was leading one of the platoons of his first company. Although the battalion commander, he preferred to lead his men from the front, not only setting an example but also ensuring that his lead company of ten T-80s got to the right position for when they launched the attack. They were already across the Inner German Border, north-east of Helmstedt, probably no more than three kilometres from the town itself.

It was now three thirty on the morning of 5 July. Trusov's battalion had been ordered to push forward to their start line, as far forward as was safe before the barrage started, the barrage that would signal the beginning of the war. He was sitting in the turret, his shoulders above the turret-hatch as he peered into the gloom ahead. His unit was making good progress. The East German Border guards had cleared the border obstacles during the night, taking down the fences, removing any mines, moving any crocodile teeth aside that had been loosened days previous, giving the tank battalion a clear passage through.

He had ordered one of the soldiers from the recce unit scouting ahead to walk in front of them with a red-filtered torch to guide the armoured column along the track and through the thinly scattered trees. He could picture Chernokov, his driver, scrutinising the route, keeping one eye on the soldier upfront and another on the darker shadows of the trees that seemed so incredibly close. Not that a tree would bother the forty-five-ton giant, but the embarrassment of slowing the column by crashing the battalion commander's tank and throwing a track would be too much for Chernokov. Trusov trusted his driver to not make a mistake. They had been together as a crew for nineteen months and, during that time, he had proven his worth. Although he had anticipated being out of the army in five months, his two years' conscription over, his driver found himself driving the commander's tank into battle.

The soldier walking in front waved his torch frantically, glad when the crawling T-80 came to a halt; a slight panic that he would be the first casualty of war, trapped between a tank and the BMP-1 parked up ahead. A second soldier appeared out of the gloom, a major, his black, padded, ribbed tank-crew helmet causing his white face to stand out even more. The major climbed up onto the front of the battalion commander's tank, holding onto the barrel of the tank's main gun as he made his way to the turret and saluted his senior officer.

"Something ahead?" asked Trusov.

"No, sir. We're close to the edge of the forest. The motorway is about 200 metres away. There's not much traffic at this time of the morning."

"Are there clear sections to cross?"

"Yes, sir, there are sections that have no barriers or central reservation and can be crossed. Scouts have been forward, and I have allocated three BRDMs to position themselves at the three crossing points once we have your order to move."

"Have you recced the town?"

"A couple of scouts have been to the edge on foot, and there doesn't appear to be any military activity, but there is a heavy police presence."

Trusov thought for a moment. Checking his watch, he could see they had made better time than expected. It suited him, giving him plenty of time to deploy his battalion.

"Excellent. I will deploy the battalion in three company columns. I need you to allocate some of your men to guide them in. I will be the centre column; then one either side out to 100 metres. Got that?"

"Yes, sir, 100 metres either side your column."

The major clambered down and went to issue his orders to his recce company. Trusov looked right as an MTLB-RkhM-K pulled up alongside just the other side of a tree, the additional aerials that adorned it swaying as it came to a halt. The figure of his regimental commander bounded over to his T-80 and stepped up onto the front of the glacis, stepping over the ERA blocks until he was able to crouch down in front of the turret, his right hand, clutching an AK-74 he lay on the tank's gun-barrel.

"You didn't get lost then, Pavel."

"No, sir, I didn't." Trusov smiled at his commander's poor sense of humour.

"Battalion ready?"

"Yes, Comrade Colonel. Two and Three Company are deploying to my left and right and First Company is behind me."

"Good, once the shit hits the fan, you need to get out of here in a flash. Don't give them time to react." Colonel Pushkin leant in closer, tapping the edge of the turret with his fist to drive home what he was saying. "Don't worry about minor resistance, Pavel. Just punch through it. Division have agreed to releasing a company from the 248th, so they can watch your back. And if you get into real trouble, 1st Battalion is on your left and right flank. I've told Aleksey to hold a company back in reserve, so that's available to you should you need it. You've also got one of the AGS-17 BMPs along with a BMP from the AA platoon, and, supporting them, two ZSU-23/4s and one of the SA-9s. And, because Division think you are so special, they've assigned four Sa-4s."

"That's good to know. Their aircraft could cause havoc."

"Watch out for our aircraft as well. You'll have two Hind Ds from Division and eight from Army."

"More the better. What about Helmstedt? Who's taking care of that?"

"Don't worry about that. We have a battalion of border guards to secure the town. Let them earn their pay being real soldiers for a change."

Trusov looked at his watch. "Not long now."

"Just push, push, push. We'll be right behind you all the way."

"If I get stuck, you'll just overtake me, sir. No bloody chance of that."

"You'll do what you have to. They are expecting us, but deep down the soldiers on the ground don't think we'll come. They don't believe that this is going to happen."

"Do we know if NATO has been able to deploy and mobilise their reinforcements yet?"

Pushkin thought for a moment. "Command knows they have deployed, but they have left it late to dig in and prepare their defences in full. As for reserves, the Americans have got a lot of men to fly across the Atlantic. That's some distance. Then they have to get their equipment out of storage. As for the British, they have at least one of their forward divisions based in England. It will take them a few days to get here."

"That's going to cost them."

"It will."

"And the Dutch and the Belgians have been dragging their feet." Trusov laughed.

"They've come round, eventually. But that says it all, Pavel: they don't believe it's going to happen, they don't want to upset us, and they don't want to fight."

"1st Guards will have it easy in the north, then."

"Not with a German division acting as a covering force. You know those bastards like a good fight." Pushkin checked his watch. "Ten minutes, Pavel. I need to get back to HQ. I'd love to stay and join you in the fight, but Division will be screaming for me as soon as it all kicks off. Anyway, someone's got to win the war and watch your back for you." He patted the younger officer on the shoulder. "Don't stop, Pavel, don't stop. Cleave a way through their covering force so the regiment's second echelon can get to grips with their main force. 3rd Battalion and the foot sloggers will be right up your arse. I'm depending on you."

They both laughed, and Pushkin slipped down from the tank and ran across to the MTLB regimental command vehicle that would put him in touch with his three tank battalions, motor rifle battalion, artillery battalion, and the rest of his tank regiment assets.

Trusov dropped down inside his tank, into the cramped innards of the turret. Barsukov had his face up against the gunner's night-sight, checking his arc out front, making sure all the equipment was working correctly. Once they were in a fight, they would need everything to function if they were to make a good account of themselves, or just to survive. He pulled his face away from the scope and turned when he heard the boots of his commander clatter down behind him. Senior

Sergeant (*ста́рший сержа́нт*) Barsukov was an extremely competent gunner, and Trusov had complete trust in him.

"Just over five minutes, Sergeant. Everything OK?"

"Apart from being shit scared, sir."

"So, you should be with Kokorev driving this bloody thing."

"Thank you, sir," called a distant voice, a Junior Sergeant (*мла́дший сержа́нт*), tucked away upfront, in the centre forward of the turret, just beneath the tank's main gun.

"Sergeant Kokorev, we have every faith in you," called Trusov. Although both of his crew were very junior to him, and often in the Soviet Army were treated badly by senior officers, spending lots of time confined in a tank had the effect of lowering the hierarchical barriers. They had both been with him for over a year, so the Lieutenant Colonel knew their strengths and weaknesses, and they his foibles. He had faith in their skills and they in his as a tank and battalion commander; something they would all need to call on over the coming hours, days or even weeks.

"Five minutes and we'll pull forward about 100 metres; then stop and I'll signal One Company to pass us."

He looked at his Senior Sergeant in the dimly lit turret. "Ready?"

The gunner patted the chipped, yellow-painted autoloader to his right. "Me and my comrade here won't let you down, sir. He's been behaving of late."

Like the T-64 and the T-72, the T-80 had an autoloader. The *Korzhina* auto-loading system, fed vertically from an ammunition carousel, did away with the requirement for a fourth member of the crew. But it wasn't without its problems. Barsukov, however, seemed to have the knack of keeping the loader functional.

Trusov climbed back up into the top of the turret and checked the area around him. Apart from the engines that were still ticking over and the occasional sound of an accelerating gas-turbine engine as a T-80 manoeuvred left of the main column, all was quiet. His two companies, one each side, would be led to their locations by one of the recce soldiers, and, once in place, his battalion would be ready to advance. He checked his watch again: minutes to go.

Ten to fifty kilometres east of Helmstedt, East Germany. Front, Army and Divisional Artillery. 0355, 5 July 1984. The Red Effect −5 Minutes

The lieutenant received the signal from Headquarters and instructed his two *Proporshchiks* to carry out their respective tasks. The two warrant officers climbed down from the combat cabin. One went to turn on the missile batteries, the internal guidance system springing into life. The internal gyroscopes started to spin. It was 0355. Now the batteries had been initiated, the launch had to commence within the next fifteen minutes. They had plenty of time though: the launch was due in the next five minutes, giving them a buffer of ten. The other warrant officer checked over the physical state of the rocket. On completion, they returned to the combat cabin and waited, the lieutenant checking his watch frequently, his nerves starting to fray as a consequence of tiredness and the waiting.

The three men looked at each other but no one spoke. There was nothing to say that hadn't already been said over the past few days. The initial part of the deployment had been done with some excitement. They were getting the opportunity to do what they had been trained for, week after week: firing one of the rockets for real. The two *Proporshchiks* were fairly well educated, or at least above that of the normal Soviet conscript. They had to be to carry out the more technical role required of them. They had talked to each other about the battle that was to come, out of earshot of the lieutenant, and the initial euphoria of operating in a wartime scenario was rapidly dissipating as they began to think through the consequences of what their country was about initiate. For the lieutenant, educated at the 'Peter the Great Military Academy of the Strategic Missile Troops', the realisation of the consequences of his country's actions had sunk in much earlier: they were going to war with some of the most powerful nations in the world. Once their missile had been launched, they were committed. There would be no turning back.

A buzz from the consul in front of the lieutenant brought all of them back into focus. It was the signal to launch.

Twelve seconds: the launch sequence begins.

Ten seconds: the turbo pump begins to power up.

Eight seconds: the fuel is pumped into the rocket motor.

Six seconds: oxidiser is pumped into the rocket motor.

Four seconds: the rocket motor ignites.

Two seconds: at thirty per cent power, the rocket blasts into life.

Launch! The rocket engine switches to full power, like thunder, the TEL vibrating from the force of the thrust pressing down on the deflector plate, the stabiliser pads pressing into the earth, fighting back against the enormous 13,000 kilograms of thrust. A black, yellow and red cloud shoot out horizontally from the base of the rocket, a cloud engulfing the SCUD-B TEL as a fiery yellow flame blasts the rocket skyward.

The vehicle shook as it was buffeted by the power of the rocket's engines as the R-17 missile climbed faster and faster, gathering speed until it could reach its maximum of over 5,000 kilometres per hour. Gathering more and more speed, it climbed in an arc, heading for its unsuspecting target. Close by, three other SCUD-B TELs released their R-

17 missiles, four bright yellow streaks across a slowly lightening sky. Elsewhere, others were in flight, on a path to attack NATO targets in the West. Across the entire Soviet and NATO front, in the region of 200 R-17s were en route to cause mayhem and destruction.

The four graphite fins of the thrust nozzle adjusted themselves in minute movements as the inertial guidance system transmitted instructions to ensure it was on the right path and the rocket motor powered the missile to its intended target: the small village of Supplingenburg. Its sister missile was aimed at the same target. The other pair streaked towards Supplingen, further to the south. After a full minute, as the missile was not going the full extent of its full 300-kilometre range, explosive squibs shut off the flow of fuel and oxidiser, the engine losing power. At a height of close to sixty kilometres, the deadly missile and its warhead containing forty-two 122mm, high-explosive fragmentation submunitions fell silently, just the wind rushing past its sleek body and fins. Ready to deliver death and destruction on its target below.

Lappwald, north-east of Helmstedt, East Germany. 62nd Guards Tank Regiment/10 Guards Tank Division/3 Shock Army. 0400, 5 July 1984. The Red Effect

Trusov jumped as the artillery barrage erupted behind him. Looking back, he could see the glow in the sky, even through the foliage of the trees, almost like a false dawn, as hundreds of artillery tubes fired their deadly shells and missiles overhead, their target the NATO forces that were waiting for them. The rumble grew into a crescendo as first the 152mm 2S3s fired salvo after salvo, joined by the 160mm mortars, 122mm 2S1s, over 600 tubes in total allocated to 10th Guards Tank Division's breakthrough sector. Higher up, beneath a blanket of rapidly fading stars, Trusov could see streaks of light passing overhead, the image of the havoc and destruction they would cause making him shiver.

Barsukov popped his head out of the other turret hatch, unable to speak as his mouth gaped open as missile after missile and shell after shell streaked across the sky. The BM-27's 220mm rockets, one after another, screamed from the eighteen vehicles, one leaving a multiple-rocket launcher system nearly every second, delivering their lethal cargo on top of the NATO troops still in the process of digging in. Two hundred and eighty-eight, each with a ninety-kilogram warhead, would swamp an area with explosives a square kilometre wide. Trusov and his gunner looked on in awe. A blanket of death was about to descend on an enemy that was waiting patiently for an attack they thought would probably never happen.

Magdeburg-Cochstedt Airfield, East Germany. 7th Guards Airborne Division. 0400, 5 July 1984. The Red Effect

The airborne officers were crammed into one of the airfield buildings, commandeered by the divisional commander, at Cochstedt Airport, situated thirty-kilometres south-west of the city of Magdeburg. The officers, dressed in their distinctive coveralls and blue and white horizontally striped shirt, talked about the upcoming operation. From regimental commanders to battalion commanders, artillery and supporting units, over forty officers were in attendance. They knew something big was going on. Fighter bombers had left for targets unknown, and supersonic fighters circled the airport in pairs, a combat air patrol to protect the airfields and everything that was around it. Tracked SA-4 Ganefs, their two large missiles pointing skyward, covered the perimeter of the base, along with SA-6 Gainfuls, ZSU-23/4s and SA-9s, providing an umbrella that would allow the men below to prepare for the battle they were, at the moment, unaware of.

They were suddenly brought to attention as their commander entered the room. General Zimyatov, commander of 7th Guards Airborne Division, climbed up onto a platform that had been erected especially for the briefing so he could see all of his officer's present. He was immensely proud of his unit and his men. The unit had been awarded the 'Red Banner' of the airborne troops in 1971 and 1972, and later the 'Order of the Red Banner'. He cast his eyes over his officer's present. He had handpicked them all. A deep, badly repaired scar ran along the top of his right eye then up into his hairline, the consequence of a piece of jagged shrapnel scoring his face after being ambushed by the Mujahideen in Afghanistan. He made eye-contact with his two most senior officers, Colonel Vydina, commander of the 247th Caucasian Cossacks Air Assault Regiment and Colonel Viktor Boykov, commander of the 108th Guards Cossacks Air Assault Regiment, Kuban. The 108th had been awarded the 'Order of the Red Star'. The unit distinguished itself during Operation Danube to suppress the Prague Spring uprising. They conducted a number of dangerous and difficult missions, and many of the soldiers received awards: over 100 issued to the regiment. General Zimyatov was a young lieutenant at the time and was the recipient of one of those awards himself. Now, he commanded the entire division.

He quickly cast his eye over the rest of the assembled officers from the artillery regiment, independent guards' battalion, air defence battery, engineers and others. The room was silent, waiting expectantly to be told what was in store for them.

"Our brave forces have finally had to succumb to the threats to our motherland by the West and have made a pre-emptive strike against the enemy."

There was a sudden buzz amongst the assembled men. They had expected it and were now being told it was for real. The general held his hand up for silence. They quickly obeyed.

"10GTD is already pushing towards Hanover, with 7GTD to the north. We are advancing on all fronts, from the Baltic in the north and as far down south as Austria. You may be wondering why we have not been involved in the attack from the start. Yes, we have airborne and Spetsnaz units playing a role in helping the foot sloggers make headway." He got the laugh he expected he would. They were the elite, after all. "Their job is to smash the enemy's covering force and advance deep into the covering force area. Our task is to go beyond that. 12th Guards Tank Division has been assigned as an operational manoeuvre group. The minute 10GTD breaks the British line, opens a gap, the 12th will flood through it. That is where we come in. Once we know where that break is, we will strike – probably in an area south-west of Hanover, securing bridges and other important ground. Colonel Vydina and his men will be parachuted in. AN-12s, AN-22s and AN-124s have already been assigned to us. Colonel Boykov, yours will be a heliborne assault. All aircraft have been assigned. We have been given the highest priority. STAVKA see this as an opportunity to split the NATO forces, isolating the two army groups, giving us access to the coasts. There will be no questions at this stage, but I want all unit commanders to stay behind so we can run through our likely target areas. They will in turn brief the rest of you. Dismissed."

Chapter 30

Bruggen, West Germany. 0400, 5 July, 1984. The Red Effect
The men shuffled about in the back of the Volkswagen van as it drove down Hoch Strasse on the northern outskirts of Bruggen. The location they would attack had been agreed. It wasn't a suicide mission, but they knew they would be lucky to get away alive. They had already passed a number of *Bundespolizei*, the West German police, patrolling the area. Security had been stepped up during the last thirty-six hours, with extra police patrols. The West German Home Defence Brigades were also more active. Their target was special: 3rd Base Ammunition Depot, a large arsenal that stored special munitions, nuclear munitions, for use in the event of a war. That very war was about to start.

The eight Spetsnaz operators were fully armed with the latest weapons, supplied by the Soviet Union through the diplomatic mail, aided by one of the many 'sleepers' planted in the West. The additional six men had joined the group the previous night. The weapons had been stored in a secret bunker hidden in the West for years. The sleeper, funded with money from the *Glavnoye Razvedyvatel'noye Upravieniye* (GRU), the foreign military intelligence arm of the Soviet armed forces, would stay at home, ready to receive them once they had successfully completed their mission or, if they failed, to help hide them until they could mount a second attack.

Cropped Hair, who was driving the green van, turned to Dark Hair. "There's a van behind us."

"Been there long?"

"Don't think so."

Dark Hair leant forward and looked in the wing mirror to see a white van about fifty-metres back. "Keep an eye on it."

As the driver took another look, he exclaimed. "There's two now!"

Focusing on the vehicle behind, he didn't see the armoured car that pulled out in front of them. The front of the VW was immediately crushed as it ploughed into the steel sides, Cropped Hair's legs smashed and pinned by the bulkhead of the front of the vehicle. Dark Hair, who was leaning forward at the time, careered through the front windshield, his face torn to shreds as he past through, his skull crushed as it met with the now unmoving armoured vehicle they had collided with. Before the men in the back could untangle themselves, an explosive device, attached to the doors by the special squad that had been following behind, ripped off the double door, killing two of the operatives in the back. One of the others, firing at his unseen enemy, instigated a torrent of incoming fire. The van was bullet-riddled; the soldiers, Spetsnaz, in the back were killed almost instantly.

Two of the men who had been lying on the ground at the side of the white van stood up, as did the rest of the squad. They lowered their SMG machine guns but remained at the ready as the others moved forwards.

The Intelligence Corps captain turned to his sergeant. "Bugger, it would have been good to have got at least one of them."

"The Sleeper is still under surveillance, sir. He'll know something is up soon enough, so I suggest we pick him up now."

"You're right, Sergeant. See to it."

The sergeant left to make contact with others in the security unit, members of the Intelligence Corps Section, responsible for counterintelligence in this area. Other members of the team moved forward to confirm that the Spetsnaz cell had indeed been wiped out. One moved forward with a Geiger counter, checking if the vehicle contained one of the deadly SADMs (Special Atomic Demolition Munition), but they weren't to find one. That was to have been used by the Spetsnaz on their next operation, had they survived this one. A major threat to a British force's base in the rear had been eliminated. However, across the vast expanse of Western Europe, other Spetsnaz units were more successful.

Chapter 31

*Combat Team Alpha, north-west of Supplingenburg, West Germany.
0400, 5 July 1984. The Red Effect*

Lieutenant Dean Russell had called stand-to at just before four in the morning; his men, some rubbing the sleep from their eyes, propped their SLRs on top of the foxholes that had been dug out the previous day. It had been hard work as no bucket loaders had been available, the engineers being used to assist the units further back, helping them dig more permanent positions. Combat Team Alpha wouldn't be hanging around. All they had to do was blunt the attack, force the Soviet units to move from line of march and deploy. Report what they saw then pull back, leapfrogging their comrades behind before digging in for the next round. There had been groans from the men at having to dig so deep, but the platoon commander and platoon sergeant had been relentless in the pursuit of their soldiers, urging them on to dig deep, build solid berms in front, and camouflage their positions well. There was still radio silence, but runners had informed the lieutenant that all his men were in position. *Will it be today?* he thought.

His thoughts were interrupted by Sergeant Rose as he dropped down into the slit trench.

"Bloody hell, sir, if you'd dug any deeper, you'd have struck oil."

"Maybe I can sell it after this blows over." Russell laughed.

"Twenty minutes?"

"Yes, then release one in three to get some breakfast inside them."

"In the meantime, how about some of this?" The sergeant pulled out a flask of freshly brewed tea, hot and sweet.

"You're a lifesaver, Sergeant Rose." Russell unclipped the black mug from his water bottle and handed it to the sergeant, and the NCO topped up two cups until a cough either side prompted him to look over to the other slit trenches.

"Bring your bloody mugs over, one of you."

Corporal Martin Wood, the commander of One-Section sent one of his men to gather mugs. The contents of the flask would be stretched extremely thinly, but at least the boys would get a hot drink inside them. The ones close by, anyway. The corporal had three men forward on the left, about fifty metres away in a group of four trees. They would provide cover for two Milan firing posts. The rest of his section were in a line forward of the hedgeline. The gun group with the Gympy were in a slit trench on the far right, a gunner plus two, and, on the left, himself plus the driver he had called forward from the 432 and two others. One soldier was with the lieutenant; the tenth soldier would join them on his return from an errand. The lieutenant, in his trench, had his own runner and a signaler, plus one. The runner was also out, passing on some last-minute messages for his platoon commander. Two-Section covered a hedgeline to the north, perpendicular to One Section's main position, running west. Two Section covered a further two Milan firing posts. Armour that tried to flank Combat Team Alpha would have Milan missiles to contend with.

They shared their unexpected bounty, sipping on the hot sweet liquid as if it were a champagne cocktail, Lieutenant Russell scanning the horizon with his binoculars. He wasn't necessarily watching for the enemy, although that was always a consideration, but for the reconnaissance CVR(T)s out there. They were the furthest edge of the FLOT. The forward line of own troops, they would be watching and waiting for the enemy, should they come.

Russell still wasn't certain, but hoped it was just hot air on both sides of the fence, and eventually someone would back down. He couldn't see much; there still wasn't enough light. All he could hope for was to pick out movement: the dark shadows of small or large armoured vehicles racing towards them. Friend or enemy.

"Which way then, sir?"

"What?"

"Which way do you think they'll come?"

He looked at his sergeant's blackened face, barely able to pick out much more than a silhouette, an arm rising and falling as he sipped his drink. There was no chance of a second mug from the flask as a consequence of it being drained, filling all the other mugs that had suddenly presented themselves.

The lieutenant thought for a moment. He had tried to put his mind inside the head of an enemy commander. What would he do if he had a tank regiment at his disposal?

"Straight between here and Supplingen to the south."

"Suicide?"

The young officer gave a small chortle. "I can understand why you'd think that, Sergeant Rose. Come down the centre and they get hit from both flanks. Mines across their path, although we don't have that many. But what other options do they have?" He pointed his arm to his right and slightly back, in the direction of where Combat Team Delta were deployed. "There's the huge stretch of high ground of the der Elm Forest to the south-west of here. They would probably target that with motor rifle troops." He remained silent for a few moments before continuing. "To be honest, I haven't got a clue. Just know that when they hit us, it's going to be bloody hard."

A pair of boots dropped down into the trench, followed by the body of Infantryman Stewart Barker, the platoon runner, knocking Sergeant Rose aside as he stumbled in. Before the sergeant could chastise him for being so clumsy, they heard the Clansman radio crackle in the headphones of the signaller's radio set.

The signaller held one earpiece to his ear, leaving the other one exposed so his platoon commander and sergeant could hear it.

"All call signs, this is Zero-Alpha. We have movement on the Inner German Border. Contact likely. Acknowledge, over."

The signaller pressed the mike switch. "Zero-alpha, zero-one, roger, out."

They were listening in to the other platoons reporting in when Sergeant Rose screamed, "Gas, gas, gas. Gas, gas, gas." The call was taken up by the rest of the section

Lieutenant Russell held his breath; dropped his SLR rifle on the edge of the slit trench; ripped off his helmet; fumbled with the green respirator sack, the rubber NBC gloves making it awkward; yanked out his rubber S6 respirator; and, pulling the elasticated straps away from the back, tucked his chin into the mouthpiece area, pulling the top and sides up over his head. Checking the seal, tightening all six of the straps to the rear, he shouted, "Gas! Gas! Gas!" expelling the air to clear his mask of any contaminants that may have got inside. Tugging the green hood of his Noddy suit over his head and pulling the drawstring tight, replacing his helmet, his nuclear, biological and chemical immediate actions were complete.

He picked up his rifle and look ahead. With the picture that confronted him, he could see why his platoon sergeant had made the call. The horizon beyond the town of Helmstedt was lit up like a fiery dawn mixed in with a multi-coloured aurora borealis, the flashes constant. "Take cover!" He screamed. "Take cover!" The sound was muffled through the mouthpiece of the respirator.

One last quick look round; one last check on the soldiers of his platoon that he could see; then he scrunched down. Pulling his head low, he waited. Having no experience of what was to come, he assumed it would be worst-case. He'd read about it in books, listened to lectures at Sandhurst, but knew deep down that no amount of preparation could prepare him for what was to come.

The two R-17 missiles struck first. One dispersed its forty-two submunitions over an area half a kilometre square, along the edge of the village. Each 122mm submunition exploded violently, thousands of fragments from each one ripping into buildings, shattering windows and smashing down doors. The Company HQ Bedford lorry and one of the Land Rovers, cammed up against the side of one of the larger village buildings, were completely shredded. Little differentiation could be seen between the shredded cam-netting and the vehicles themselves, the destruction permanent. Three-Platoon took the brunt of the strike, the platoon lieutenant, his signaller and runner unrecognisable as three of the cluster munitions straddled the foxholes they were in, dug along the periphery to protect the southern end of the village and the right flank of Combat Team Alpha. The Milan firing post was completely destroyed along with its two crew and the two soldiers watching over them. Not only did they have to overcome the swathe of shrapnel, with a kill and injury radius of over twenty metres, but they also took a direct hit from the missile body itself. Others were crying out, screaming for a medic, the FV432 ambulance prevented from going to their aid, the Company Sergeant Major knowing it was far from over.

The second missile went off target, hitting somewhere between the two villages, peppering the open ground with numerous craters two to three-metres wide.

Combat Team Bravo, deployed in Supplingen to the south, was not so lucky. Both R-17 missiles struck, wiping out a third of the platoon guarding the northern flank of the village. These two strikes alone gave an indication of the proposed strategy of the first echelon of the Soviet attack: immobilise the two edges of the village and drive straight through the centre.

Lieutenant Russell compressed his body as far down into the slit trench as he possibly could and then some more as the first of the BM-27 rockets rained down across the front of their position. His ears rang as rocket after rocket exploded around them. He felt a weight crash down on the front edge of the trench, a lacerated arm, the sleeve of the shirt and combat jacket ripped off, the NBC suit covering the body was in tatters. Dean's helmet rattled as it was peppered with clods of earth and debris. He grabbed the arm and pulled the form down into the trench, covering the soldier as best he could with his own body. The hedgeline was torn apart behind them as three 122mm rockets shredded the shrubbery, splitting the trees and sending lethal splinters of wood whistling over the top of the cowering infantry.

Lieutenant Russell pressed his hands over his ears, his S6 respirator expanding and contracting as his rapid breathing sucked in air through the canister at the side. He was screaming inside his head, his eyes almost as wide as the oval lenses he was peering through, but seeing nothing. His ears hurt and he felt mucus oozing from his nose. Nausea plucked at his stomach, but he bit it back, the bitter taste of bile on his tongue burning his throat. The noise, the shock waves, battered his body and senses as another round of shells straddled the village, but further back.

Suddenly, it was as if the entire sector was engulfed in a huge suffocating weight, a tremendous pressure wave followed by an intense heat, with a constant stream of debris, branches of trees, pieces of brick, masonry and other items one could only guess at.

Lieutenant Russell sucked hard, fighting for air that was no longer there, panic setting in as he couldn't breathe no matter how hard he tried, resisting the drive to wrench his mask free and expose his lungs and skin to any nerve or blister agents that might be present. The pressure suddenly dissipating, he collapsed into the bottom of the trench, depleted. The level of noise rose higher and higher as more and more Soviet artillery joined in the bombardment of the NATO front line. The sounds of civilians screaming, wounded or dying in their beds, went unheard as the explosions reached a crescendo before stopping almost as quickly as they had started.

Thirty minutes of hell and the men of Combat Team Alpha felt that that was exactly where they were.

Chapter 32

South-east of Luneburg, West Germany. 0415, 5 July 1984. The Red Effect +15 Minutes

The fifty-five-ton Leopard 2's V-12 engine growled as the driver accelerated, the tank almost flying as it leapt over a brow of a hillock it had just crossed, the suspension squashed as it supported the machine's weight, pushing back upwards. The commander gripped onto the turret for his life, his body flung from side to side. The loader was also topside with his commander, gripping onto the MG-3 7.62mm air-defence machine gun, using it to keep himself from being tossed out. Speed was of the essence. A small heliborne landing was threatening an engineer unit desperately trying to blow a bridge as the Russian forces battered them from the east. Their task was still to protect the Stecknitz Canal, south-east of the large town of Luneburg, but a troop had been dispatched to reinforce their *kameraden* who were in dire straits. Part of the 9th Panzer Brigade of the 1st Panzer Division, 1 German Corps' covering force, their job had just started.

The lieutenant gritted his teeth, nearly biting his tongue as he was suddenly thrown violently sideways. But there would be no stopping, no slowing down. They had to get to grips with the enemy, slow them down, stop them, kill them before they could take an inch of German soil.

West of Rasdorf, near the Fulda Gap, West Germany. 0415, 5 July 1984. The Red Effect +15 Minutes

Private First-Class Larry Poole closed his eyes, tensed his body as the trees above and around them were torn apart. The shock waves from the shells that missed, rocked the tank from side to side, even the throbbing of the tank's gas turbine engine couldn't be felt or heard. Staff Sergeant Kyle Lewis, the tank commander, stared through the visors, but dust was all he could see. Buttoned down, all he and his crew could do was sit out the storm of the Russian artillery barrage and wait until it ceased.

"*Aaahh!*" Larry Poole screamed as the front of the thirty-five-ton tank was lifted off the ground, slamming back down as a 150-millimetre shell exploded directly in front of them.

Clang...clang.

Straddled by two more smaller-calibre rounds, shrapnel struck at the tank's armour, letting the crew know it wanted them and was going to do its level best to get them.

SSGT Lewis looked up at the inner top of the turret, praying that the armour would hold out. They had said it would; they had said it would be safe. His men were in their full NBC kit, in case the M-1 was punctured, and any gas found its way in, killing them all. It wasn't meant to be like this, he thought. They drive towards us and our superior tanks pick them off until they've had enough. It wasn't meant to be like this.

Chapter 33

Lappwald, north-east of Helmstedt, West Germany. 62nd Guards Tank Regiment/10 Guards Tank Division/3 Shock Army. 0410, 5 July 1984. The Red Effect +10 Minutes.

The thunderous roar built up behind them, streaks of light continued to pass overhead, hundreds of Soviet soldiers looking up into the sky, the view reminiscent of the Quadrantid meteor show in January and the Lyrid shower in April. Those were beautiful to watch, but caused no one any harm. The ones passing now were far more menacing. The repercussions from the artillery shells and rockets could be heard bracketing the British forces, less than six kilometres away to the west.

Crump, crump, crump, crump.

Shell after shell hit the front line of the NATO troops, pinning them down, numbing their senses, smashing their defences.

The Soviet radio nets were alive with chatter, units moving positions, preparations being made to advance and attack. Colonel Trusov received his orders to move out. He ordered Kokorev to move the T-80 forward slowly, the commander of the BMP-1 recce vehicle ahead acknowledging the order as well, leading the way. The colonel issued an order to his three companies, to take up their stage two positions, and the forest reverberated with the sound of slowly accelerating gas-turbine engines as the T-80 main battle tanks started their journey west. The battalion command vehicle's engine whined as Kokorev placed it into the first of its five gears and increased power. The tracks gripped the earth, laying a continuous metallic carpet for the six dual rubber-tyre road wheels to pass over.

Trusov ducked involuntarily as more flashes of light shot overhead, heading to batter the NATO defences even further as his battalion crept forward. He looked over the rear of the tank and could make out the dark shapes of the lead tanks of One Company who were following. After about 100 metres, he commanded Kokorev to pull off to the left and then stop. As agreed earlier, the lead tank of the company following, commanded by Major Mahayev, moved up, the officer acknowledging his battalion commander with a wave as he passed, the tank's engine growling as it picked up speed, the recognisable rattle of tracks added to as the rest of the company's ten tanks continued forward. Following behind was an MTLB-RkhM-K, one of his two battalion command vehicles that would assist him in keeping in touch with both the regiment and division. Following on, about 500 metres behind, would be his battalion transport and supply sections, carrying the fuel, ammunition and food supplies they would need to keep the battle momentum going. A maintenance section was available to help repair broken down tanks and recover those that had suffered serious damage. And, amongst all of those, UAZ-452 ambulances should the worst happen. Even though he felt supremely confident about his equipment and his men, Trusov knew that casualties were inevitable before the day was out.

Ahead of them, on the left and right, the second battalion would have started to move forward, getting into position, ready to break out into the open where they could protect Trusov's flanks as he thrust down the centre, pushing deep into the defences of the British Army's covering force – and, if needed, to come to his aid. Further to the south, two of the 248th Guards Motor Rifle Regiment's mechanised infantry battalions would be pressing forward.

Trusov ordered the driver forward, following on after the company ahead, the ground now rutted and churned by the heavy battle tanks as they worked their way through to the edge of the forest. The tank picked up speed and, within minutes, they were out of the confines of the forest, the slowly lightening sky revealing more and more of the terrain around them. At the hard shoulder of the autobahn, part of the recce company kept watch over the gap in the barriers that would be used to pass through. Soldiers from the regiment's engineer company had sneaked forwards earlier to deal with any barriers making sure the crossing was passable for the tanks.

They rattled over the tarmac road of the dual carriageway, the rear of a tank from the lead company just disappearing over the other side and back into the trees. Across the road, into the forest again for a few moments, then out into the open. Now, without any doubt, they were interlopers on West German territory. The plan was simple, or so Trusov and Pushkin hoped. One Company would head for the bare piece of high ground, Bruchteich, at 140 metres in height, and park up in line acting as a covering force to overwatch the rest of the battalion as it advanced. Two Company would track left through the trees and Three Company to the right.

They broke out into the open. Kokorev increased speed, the engine growling as they made the 600-metre dash, the heavy tank starting to dip and bounce as its torsion-bar suspension matched the undulating ground. The engine then screamed as Kokorev changed down, the tank rearing up and making easy meat of the slope ahead.

"Forward, forward, forward," guided Trusov, head still out of the turret. In front, two platoons of T-80s were lined up, in a hull-down position at the far side of the shallow hill, to the left and, behind them, the remaining troop of three in reserve. Kokorev slowed the tank to a crawl.

"Alongside, alongside," he called to Kokorev.

"Stop."

The tank rocked to a halt next to the command tank of the company commander, the major looking at the scene ahead through his binoculars. The rest of his forward unit had been ordered to button down. Hatches closed, ready to fight.

Trusov got his first glimpse of the ground they would have to cross: open fields. Ideal tank country, but also an ideal tank killing zone. Dawn was finally showing its face, its hue leeching into the countryside. Vivid flashes of red and yellow erupted along the line of British troops dug in to protect the two villages and the routes around them, adding to the colour.

Trusov checked his watch. Two and Three Company would be in position now, awaiting his order to move. He shifted higher in the turret to get a better view, bringing his binoculars up to his eyes to zoom in.

Crump, crump, crump, crump.

Clouds of white and grey smoke, like puffs of cotton wool, but yanked at the edges, spiking outwards, burst into life; some with yellow-orange hot cores at the centre, the expanding gases forcing lethal shrapnel in all directions. Suddenly the entire area flared up, swamped with a staccato of hundreds of small explosions, rippling across the entire front, enveloping the village on the right, Supplingenburg, in a blanket of death, blotting it completely from view. The BM-21s had struck, eighteen delivering over 700 122mm rockets onto the target.

Crump...crump, crump...crump.

More artillery bombarded the area, pounding the soldiers incessantly. No let up as the regiment's 2S1s joined in, followed by the 12th Guards Tank Division artillery group. The Division, as the second echelon of 3rd Shock Army, was patiently waiting for its turn to join in the battle but, in the meantime, its artillery assets didn't stand idle.

Crump...crump, crump, crump...crump.

Whoosh! Whoosh!

Two low-flying aircraft shot by above their heads, at treetop height, their engines spouting flames as the afterburners kicked in, the pilots banking left, then right, taking them around the higher ground of der Elm, their target NATO troops further to the rear; attacking the rear of the covering force or even the main force, hoping to disrupt defence preparations, or interdict reinforcements on the move.

Whoosh! Whoosh!

Another two Sukhoi Su-25 'Frogfoot' close-support aircraft shot past, their deadly loads carried on the five hard-points beneath each wing.

Crump, crump...crump...crump...crump, crump, crump.

The barrage continued without let-up, cleaving into the British defences, punching through the armour of some the 432s, shredding soft-skinned vehicles, destroying some of the well-placed minefields, killing civilians as well as soldiers.

Crump, crump.

Trusov was mesmerised, the crackling radio bringing him back to earth.

"*Two-zero, this is Two-three over.*"

"Two-three, go ahead, over."

"*TMMs and mine ploughs with us, over.*"

He looked at his watch, for probably the tenth time in the last twenty minutes. The barrage had been going for over ten minutes; it was time for them to pull out; to get close to the enemy before the barrage ceased.

"Understood. Two-three, Two-two, move in five minutes. Acknowledge, over."

"*Two-zero, Two-two, understood, over.*"

"*Two-zero, Two-three, ready, over.*"

"Two-three, keep the engineers back until called forward. Two-zero, out."

There was nothing else he could do now but check in with his commander.

"Six-two-zero, Two-zero over. Six-two-zero, Two-zero, over."

"*Two-zero, Six-two-zero. Go ahead, Pavel.*"

"Six-two-zero. In position. Confirm two-zero ready, over."

"*Two-zero. They're right behind you. Air defence has moved up with you. You know what you have to do.*"

"Understood. Two-zero, out."

There was nothing else he could do now but wait. Looking left, he could see the odd light in Emmerstedt, a small conurbation north-west of Helmstedt, the population waking up to the thunderous uproar that was coming from the west as the shells continued to strike the British lines. Supplingenburg was about four kilometres half right, Supplingen about five kilometres straight ahead. They would strike south-west first, before turning west, advancing at speed straight between the two villages, heading flat out for Konigslutter, pushing deep into the NATO-covering force area, keeping the momentum of the division on track.

Senior Sergeant Barsukov popped his head out of the turret hatchway, tapping his watch.

"Tell Sergeant Kokorev to wind her up."

"Two-two, Two-three, this is Two-zero. Move out, acknowledge the order, over."

"Two-two, advancing now."

"Two-three, moving now."

"Two-one, Two-zero. One minute. Standby."

"Two-one, acknowledged."

More shells pounded the enemy lines, the rate of fire slowing, the Soviet artillery crew starting to run out of steam.

Time seemed to grind to a halt as Trusov kept checking the large hand on his luminous watch. It edged ever closer.

"Two-one, go!"

The tanks ahead had been ready, and the engines roared, rearing up at the front as they were powered forward, down the other side of the slope as fast as they could safely go. Trusov's tank tore after them, keeping fifty metres behind the rearmost platoon. Although hedgerows often restricted their view, he occasionally picked out the two companies, one either side, slightly ahead. He rocked in the turret hatchway, bracing his waist against the edge, but flexing his body as the tank dipped on its suspension as it negotiated the dips, bumps and furrows of the farmer's fields, crashing through hedges without stopping; weaving around any object that was seen as too tough a barrier to cross. They were racing across the partially open ground at fifty-kilometres an hour, using speed as protection, but also racing to get close to the enemy before the barrage ended; the sound growing louder and louder above the tank's roaring engine, and the crunch as they yet again smashed through another hedgerow.

"Two-one, Two-zero. Stop, stop, stop."

Kokorev, expecting the command, slowed his commander's tank down, but lined them next to One Company's command tank.

"Two-three, Two-zero. Initiate 'springboard' now."

"Two-zero. On it."

The four TMMs and two mine plough tanks raced forward to their allotted positions, two SZU-23/4s sticking close, to provide air cover, their four 23mm guns facing skyward, ready to blast any low-flying aircraft out of the sky. Further back, behind them, two SA-9s, four 9M31 surface-to-air missiles each, capable of reaching up to 4,000 metres; even further back, the army level SA-4s would cover up to an altitude of over 20,000 metres.

Trusov tapped the turret impatiently, willing the TMMs to move quickly and lay their ten-metre folded scissor-bridge, to cross the narrow waterway that lay across their path, used by the farmers to irrigate their fields. Major Mahayev had repositioned his company, a platoon covering the right, their turrets swinging their main tank guns left and right as the gunners sniffed out potential targets, and three on the left. The third platoon held back in reserve. His company would be the last to cross.

Trusov checked his watch. Five minutes and the barrage would cease. *Come on, come on*, he whispered under his breath.

"Two-zero. Recce have found a fordable stretch. They're crossing now, over."

"Two-zero. Acknowledged."

"Two-zero, Six-two-zero."

"Six-two-zero, go ahead, over."

"One-zero will be up to your location soon, Pavel. You need to move out before they stick a barrel where it will hurt."

"Standby." He switched to the battalion net. "Two-three. Tell me you're moving, over."

"Two-zero. Engineers done, remaining recce crossing. We move in two minutes."

"Understood. Six-two-zero. We move in two."

"Good. Burn some fuel when you're across. Out."

Trusov couldn't help but smile. He imagined Division would be on Pushkin's back every five minutes. Three-Company confirmed they were crossing, as did Two further to the right. One-Company followed on behind them, clanking over the double-span TMM bridge, mine plough tanks following on behind, then the ZSUs followed by the SA-9s.

They were poised now, poised to attack and defeat the enemy. One-Battalion had split, one company moving south-east of the burning village of Supplingen, ready to keep the NATO forces occupied and pinned down; another company to the north-east of Supplingenburg, ready to carry out the same task. The third company, along with a mechanised infantry company from 248th GMRR, remained in reserve. They were also joined by BMPs carrying the man-portable surface-to-air missile SA-7 and the AGS-17, automatic grenade launcher.

Two battalions from the 248th were already attacking the high ground of der Elm, with elements pushing around the southern edge. The massive artillery strike that had bombarded the entire front allocated to 10th GTD had shattered NATO forces along it.

Trusov's battalion pushed forward, two companies up front, one in reserve.

"Two-zero, two-three. Contact, contact."

A T-80 from the left flank company had come across a fleeing Scimitar that was quickly dispatched by the gunner. Trusov dropped down into the tank. Time to batten down.

Chapter 34

North-west of Supplingenburg, West Germany. Combat Team Alpha.
0430, 5 July 1984. The Red Effect +30 Minutes

The silence was unnerving. Through the drumming in his ears and the material of his Noddy suit hood, all Lieutenant Russell could hear were the muffled groans of the wounded. He extracted himself from the dead soldier entangled beneath him and raised his head slowly above the parapet. Black face masks stared back at him as he scanned the line of One-Section's slit trenches. Behind them, buildings still burned, trails of smoke climbing upwards from numerous areas around their position. Craters pock-marked the landscape as far as the limit of his vision, restricted by the respirator and the explosive smog that hung in the air about them.

Suddenly, he switched into his platoon-leader mode, knowing what he needed to do if he and his men were to survive. He looked for the piece of standard issue 'No 2 detector paper' on the front of his NBC suit: it was clear. Had there been dark blue stains plastered all over it then the indication would have been that chemical agents were present. Pulling off his helmet, then his hood, he eased off the black rubber respirator and took a shallow breath. He didn't start twitching or feel lethal blisters on his skin or inside his lungs, and he could breathe normally, although he was sucking in a film of dust and cordite. His soldiers, seeing he was still alive, followed suit. His ears rang and a buzzing inside his head continued to interfere with his hearing.

Looking for his SLR rifle, Russell picked it up from the bottom of the trench and was trying to clamber out to check on his platoon. When his boots caught on something. His rubber NBC overboots made it difficult to move his feet in the confined space of the trench. He trod on something soft and recoiled in horror when he realised it was Private Brook's arm. The soldier's respirator was missing, torn from his face; his mouth gaping open, blood oozing from his ears, and staring eyes, his chest exposed to the air showing cavernous wounds, one of his legs at an impossible angle, shattered.

"Medic, medic," the lieutenant shouted at the top of his voice, the sound hollow inside his head. He heard other calls as Combat Team Alpha slowly came to life. He turned as something thumped on his shoulder, his signaller punching his arm to get his attention, pointing at the radio set. He grabbed the headset, putting one of the earphones against the side of his face and heard the call.

"Alpha-one, this is Alpha-zero. Sitrep. Alpha-one, sitrep, over."

207

He stuttered a reply, his body physically shaking as he tried to control it and form some words with his dry mouth. "Alpha-zero, Alpha-one. Going to check now, over."

"Fucking get on with it, Dean. I need to know your strength and casualties, soonest. They'll be on top of us any minute. We are already getting reports of Soviet recce. Over."

"Roger, sir, with you in figures two."

"One minute. Out."

Shit, the old man was in a foul mood.

"All Alpha-one call signs. Sitrep, over."

"One-one-bravo. Two minor injuries, patching them up. Equipment operable, over."

"Roger that." The two Milan firing posts had survived.

"One-two, two minor injuries, one killed. Equipment A-OK, over."

"Roger that."

"One-three, one killed, one seriously wounded, 432 KO'ed, over."

"Roger that. All call signs, enemy lookout. They are on way. Alpha-one, out."

The half-section with the Milan out in front of the forward line of the platoon had answered, but not One-one-alpha. Russell finally climbed out and ran across the edge of the trenches at a crouch, suspecting what he would find. One-Section's commander was dead, as were two soldiers with him; one of them had been flung into the platoon commander's trench. The 432 ambulance reversed at speed up to the trench, the two medics piling out to deal with any wounded, the CSM with them driving one of the surviving Land Rovers to take any of the lightly wounded to the collection point at the far end of the village.

"What's your status, sir?"

The CSM was covered in blood, not from any injuries, but from the men he had been helping to the company aid station.

"Three KIA, one serious, some minor wounds, and we've lost a 432, Sarn't Major. How have the other platoons come through it?"

"Three-Platoon have been hit hard, at least half a dozen killed, including Lieutenant Ward."

They didn't have time to finish their conversation as the signaller bellowed across, "One-one-bravo, sir. They have movement."

The CSM touched the young officer's shoulder. "I'll report to the OC. You see to your men. They're going to need you."

Russell nodded and ran to the radio set. "Alpha-one."

"Tanks, sir, bloody hundreds of them."

"Calm down, Corporal Reid, radio procedure. What can you see?"

"Tanks, sir, sorry. One-one-bravo. Tanks, left, right and centre."

"Alpha-one, with you shortly." Russell turned to the signaller and his runner, instructing both to follow him. They headed east, at a run, their 58-pattern webbing pouches bouncing as they ran. Keeping low, running along the bottom of the ditch, the shrubbery either side giving them cover, they quickly arrived at the position of the Milan firing point.

"Corporal Reid, I'm sorry, but Corporal Wood has been killed. I want you to go back and take command of the section."

"Martin...dead?"

"Yes. There's no time to talk about it now, Corporal. I need you to get back now and organise the section."

Lance-Corporal Reid nodded, looked at the two men of his half-section then headed back towards the village.

Lieutenant Russell threw himself down beside the corporal in command of the two Milans. "What can you see?"

The corporal was looking through the Milan optical sight. He answered without taking his eye off the targets. "There's a lot, sir. There's a company-size group coming left and maybe two or three approaching in between the two villages."

"Your target?"

"I can take out two, sir. One with each firing point; then we'll need to move. And bloody sharpish."

"Take them out. The minute you come under fire, or once you've fired your two shots, pull back. Understood?"

"Yes. sir," the junior NCO responded, relief in his voice.

"Straight to the 432. We'll probably be pulling out of here. This place is lost."

"We didn't hold it for very long, sir."

"No, we didn't. But the aim is to delay, and we did that. You two," he pointed to the two with minor injuries, "make your way back to the 432's. I'll leave my runner here. I need to check on the rest of the platoon."

"Got you, sir."

The lieutenant left and the corporal again focused on his target. The Milan wire-guided missile he controlled could travel over a kilometre and a half in twelve and a half seconds. He centred on the tank in his sights, the other post doing the same with another, and they launched their rockets. The cover on the missile housing popped off, and the missile flew from the tube mounted on the launcher system, a plume of orange and yellow flame shooting out of the back. The concept of Semi-Automatic Command-To-Line-Of-Sight (SACLOS) meant the operator had only to keep the target in his sights at all times. The missile, trailing a thin wire behind it that was linked to the launcher, homed in on the target, guided by the operator. The concentration was immense as the corporal focused on the centre circle on the moving tank. The missiles struck. There was an explosion, but the tank kept on moving.

His assistant took off the now empty tub and was ready to attach a second when the sound of helicopter rotor blades could be heard growing louder and louder as the Hind-D Gunship roared towards them, stopping suddenly at a height of 200 metres, its cockpit rearing up before returning to a level plane as the USPU-24 under-nose turret with its 12.7mm YakB 12.7 machine gun opened up. Firing at a rate of 4,000 rounds per minute, a short burst killed both Milan commanders and the other soldiers, their bodies ripped apart, the Milan posts smashed to pieces. They didn't see that their deaths would be avenged as a quick-thinking soldier fired a shoulder-launched blowpipe missile, which swept round as the operator, using the small thumb joystick, held it on target. The proximity fuse, sensing the double-stepped tandem cab of the Mi-24 Hind-D, exploded, shattering the cockpit and killing the pilot and weapons operator instantly. The out-of-control heli plummeted to the ground.

Lieutenant Russell, about to reposition the reserve section, bringing them forward for additional support for the Milan team, was handed the microphone and earphones of the radio by his signaller.

"*Alpha-one, this is alpha-zero.*"

"Alpha-zero, alpha one." He shouted his response, his hearing still impaired. "We're pulling out. Get your men in the 432s and head west. Don't use the roads; head north for cover. There are half a dozen Hinds buzzing around. Acknowledge, over."

"*Alpha-zero, alpha one. Wilco, out.*"

He handed the phones back to his signaller. "We're pulling back. Call all sections and get them back here."

Chapter 35

West of Burgdorf, West Germany. 0500, 5 July 1984. The Red Effect +1 Hour

Wilf was sitting at the RC-319 radio transceiver, the electronic message unit in his hands. They had just received a burst transmission: the news not good.

"Guys, they've gone and done it! The fuckers have come across the border!"

Tag and Badger, at a crouch, moved to the main body of the T-shaped mexe-hide, the stalk of the T.

"Hacker, Hacker, get over here," called Tag.

Hacker was off stag, getting some kip cocooned in his maggot, his long green sleeping bag.

"What is it, you wanker? It'd better be something good. Is she blonde?"

"The Russkies have attacked. They've crossed the border. They're on their way," Badger informed Hacker.

Hacker was out of his bag and joined his three comrades, all cramped at the one end of the shelter, within seconds. "Tell me they fucking haven't."

In the dim light of the shelter, he could see Wilf nodding his head. "I doubt we have twelve hours, twenty-four at the most. I want a full kit check; then I'll man the radio and Hacker, you cover the scope. It provides a good view now I've cleaned it. Tag, Badger, you get some kip, a full four hours. Then we'll do the same. I doubt we'll get much sleep for some time so let's rest now."

"I'll make us a brew first," offered Tag. "Not sure I can sleep just yet."

"I can't believe they've gone and done it," added Hacker.

"Well, they'll get what they deserve then, won't they," chuntered Badger. "They'll get a bloody good kicking. Then we'll come up behind them and meet them on the way back."

"Badger, the one-man army." Wilf laughed. "OK, brew, kip, then a briefing. Once we know the extent of their penetration, we can decide on our next set of actions. Make mine hot and sweet."

"Just like your women," offered Tag as he crawled back down the tunnel to make a brew.

Wilf's team was one of many corps patrol units scattered around West Germany. Armed to the teeth, a variety of explosives at their disposal and the knowledge of how to use them, they would be a headache for the occupying forces. They would also be the eyes and ears of 1 Br

Corps, amongst other assets, providing them with live, up-to-date intelligence that could be used to help Northern Army Group plan the defence of the northern part of Germany.

Outskirts of East Berlin. 0500 5 July, 1984. The Red Effect +1 Hour

Bradley peered through the image intensifier, the green shimmer showing him yet another military train passing through. Rail traffic had been intense during the past twenty-four hours, some trains stopping on the rail ring waiting for the junctions up ahead and the next train already coming to a halt a few hundred metres back. There was a real possibility of an accident, having so much heavy traffic on the rail network at the same time, ignoring all the usual safety guidelines.

The orbital ring road had also been busy. Columns of armoured vehicles, soft-skinned logistical units, created a constant drone as they headed to either encircle Berlin or move east to add to the ever-growing force building up against the NATO forces in West Germany. Bradley had reported Soviet, East German and Polish divisions heading east, a huge tidal wave that could only go in one direction when it burst.

Hearing another train approach, he recognised the shapes: T-62s. He counted a full battalion. T-62s meant these were tank units coming from deep in the Soviet Union, military districts sending their units to support the second strategic echelon or even a third. It slowed to a stop, the last wagon opposite and to his left, an opportune moment for Bradley.

He shook Jacko awake gently. "Going out, keep watch."

Jacko, lying alongside him in his sleeping bag, grunted a yes in response and Bradley left the hide. He clambered down the bank, checking carefully for soldiers or tank crew in the three goods wagons at the rear of the train. The large doors were shut, the tank crews probably asleep, taking an opportunity to rest up while out of sight of their officers. He crept down the side of the train, looking for clues as to the identity of the unit, something he could send back to HQ. He eventually came across a flatcar with two OT-64s, eight-wheeled armoured personnel carriers. The countries of origin for these were Poland and Czechoslovakia. Bradley suspected he was looking at a Polish unit – Czech forces would move through southern Germany – more evidence that the entire Warsaw Pact was on the move, and not just the Soviet Union.

The train jerked, indicating it would be moving again, and he made his way back to the hide to be met by Jacko handing him a hot, sweet tea. Even in the dim light, he could see Jacko was sprouting a dark beard and his face looked grubby, unwashed and had the look you acquire spending days and nights in a small, confined space with minimal sleep. "Thanks, Jacko. Anything?"

"A burst transmission came through about a minute ago, I'll leave you to decode. Anything?"

"Yep, Polish tank battalion."

"This is getting bad."

Bradley got to the radio set and checked the message.

"Well?"

Bradley's silence said it all. "They've closed off Berlin and launched an attack into West Germany."

"Oh God..."

"We just do our bit, Jacko. That's all we can do."

"We're in a safer place here than Berlin," Jacko surmised.

"Afraid not, Jacko. They know we're across here so they will come a hunting. There will be listening posts out trying to triangulate our position. We'll move tomorrow. One more transmission; then we'll move."

Chapter 36

Gronau, West Germany. Combat Team Bravo. 0500, 5 July 1984. The Red Effect +1 Hour

Lieutenant Wesley-Jones turned as he heard a Land Rover tearing through the copse behind him, coming to a halt behind his Chieftain tank. Major Lewis, the OC of Combat Team Bravo, leapt out of the passenger side and ran towards him, coming round the front of the tank and climbing up on top.

"They've done it, Alex. They've crossed the IGB."

"Oh God." Wesley-Jones groaned. "Are we holding them?"

The OC shook his head. "4 Div's forward units have taken a hammering. They're pulling back all along the front."

"What about the rest?"

"The Americans in the south and the Germans in the north are already under attack. We have to maintain radio silence. The EW units will be listening for us, no doubt. That's why I've come to tell you in person."

"Christ, sir, what's wrong with them? We don't want a bloody war."

"I know, I know. They're going to hit you hard, Alex. Hold as long as you can. I've given you full control over the forces this side of the river in our sector. Put up a fight, but don't lose men unnecessarily."

"How long have I got?"

"The thoughts are twenty-four hours, but I wouldn't bank on it. I have to go. Good luck."

They shook hands and the OC jumped back into his Land Rover and sped off to give other units under his command the good news.

Patsy popped his head out.

"Did you hear that, Corporal Patterson?"

"Yes, sir, we're fucked."

"Not yet, we aren't. You're in charge here. I need to pull the troop together. They need to be told."

Patsy dropped back down to share the news with his oppos Mark and Mackey.

Lieutenant Alex Wesley-Jones looked east. "Why? Why? Why?"

Printed in Great Britain
by Amazon